13 NEW STORIES
"ON THE CUTTING
—*Montreal*

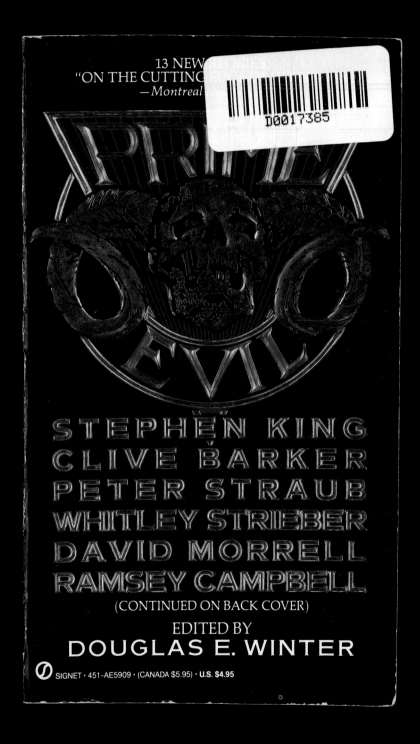

PRIME
EVIL

STEPHEN KING
CLIVE BARKER
PETER STRAUB
WHITLEY STRIEBER
DAVID MORRELL
RAMSEY CAMPBELL

(CONTINUED ON BACK COVER)

EDITED BY
DOUGLAS E. WINTER

SIGNET • 451-AE5909 • (CANADA $5.95) • **U.S. $4.95**

A TASTE OF TERROR FOR EVERY READER WHOSE NERVES ARE ACHING TO BE TWISTED TO THE SNAPPING POINT

STEPHEN KING, "The Night Flier"—from the undisputed master of modern horror, a fast-paced novella with a vampire theme that is at once chillingly familiar and shockingly different.

CLIVE BARKER, "Coming to Grief"—from the author of the *Books of Blood*, a moving novella about a woman tormented by her mother's death and her own childhood fears.

PETER STRAUB, "The Juniper Tree"—from the author of *Ghost Story*, a novella of a boy's innocent escape into the bright world of movie-house dreams that enfolds into a nightmare of sexual abuse and its lifelong consequences.

WHITLEY STRIEBER, "The Pool"—from the author of *Communion*, an unsettling tale of innocence and alien intelligence.

. . . And nine other mesmerizing tales of terror to hold you spellbound!

PRIME EVIL

"Far and away the hottest horror collection of the year!"
—*Macon Telegraph & News*

"A horror show carnival of the dark and the damned."
—*Tampa Tribune & Times*

DOUGLAS WINTER'S fiction, interviews, and criticism have appeared in national magazines. His books include the definitive biography and literary study *Stephen King: The Art of Darkness*, available in a Signet paperback edition.

PRIME Evil

New Stories by the Masters of Modern Horror

Edited by Douglas E. Winter

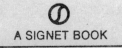

A SIGNET BOOK

NEW AMERICAN LIBRARY

A DIVISION OF PENGUIN BOOKS USA INC.

for Hilary Ross

PERMISSIONS AND ACKNOWLEDGMENTS

Introduction by Douglas E. Winter. Copyright © 1988 by Douglas E. Winter.

"The Night Flier" by Stephen King. Copyright © 1988 by Stephen King.

"Having a Woman at Lunch" by Paul Hazel. Copyright © 1988 by Paul Hazel.

"The Blood Kiss" by Dennis Etchison. Copyright © 1988 by Dennis Etchison.

"Coming to Grief" by Clive Barker. Copyright © 1988 by Clive Barker.

"Food" by Thomas Tessier. Copyright © 1988 by Thomas Tessier.

"The Great God Pan" by M. John Harrison. Copyright © 1988 by M. John Harrison.

"Orange Is for Anguish, Blue for Insanity" by David Morrell. Copyright © 1988 by David Morrell.

"The Juniper Tree" by Peter Straub. Copyright © 1988 by Seafront Corporation.

(The following page constitutes an extension of this copyright page.)

Prime Evil previously appeared in an NAL Books edition published by New American Library.

 SIGNET TRADEMARK REG. U.S. PAT. OFF. AND FOREIGN COUNTRIES
REGISTERED TRADEMARK—MARCA REGISTRADA
HECHO EN DRESDEN, TN

SIGNET, SIGNET CLASSIC, MENTOR, ONYX, PLUME, MERIDIAN and NAL BOOKS are published by NAL PENGUIN INC., 1633 Broadway, New York, New York 10019

First Printing, April, 1989

1 2 3 4 5 6 7 8 9

PRINTED IN THE UNITED STATES OF AMERICA

*. . . faranno dei cimiteri le loro cattedrali
e delle citta le vostre tombe.*

—DARIO ARGENTO

(. . . for the cemeteries shall be their cathedrals,
and the cities shall be your tombs.)

Contents

INTRODUCTION

What makes great horror fiction?

As a critic and reviewer, I have been called upon regularly to pass judgment on the writing of horror fiction's leading talents. I've probed the phenomenal success of Stephen King in a book-length study, and I've also published a history of contemporary horror, as told through the lives of its brightest and bestselling writers. As a compulsive reader and filmgoer, I've experienced nearly everything the field of horror has to offer. My own fiction returns with regularity to themes of violence and fear.

Nevertheless, I'm tempted to answer this question with the unblinking certainty of Supreme Court Justice Potter Stewart, who once offered as his definition of obscenity that he knew it when he saw it.

Many readers see the horror story as something that is packaged only in repetitive paperback editions, replete with potboiler prose, lurid covers, and corny titles that seem always to begin with the word "The." And most of the time, they are right. Today's tales of terror rarely offer anything new. Few plots bearing the "horror" label are fresh and exciting; indeed, most editors lament how easily these stories can be pigeonholed into recognizable types. (T.E.D. Klein, the original editor of *Twilight Zone Magazine*, once told me that he could fit over ninety percent of the submissions to his magazine into ten cliché categories). The writing itself is, on average, slick and superficial; at worst, the stuff of pulp adventure, written to the lowest common denominator.

For each original story or novel, there are hundreds that read like rote imitations of bestselling books or popular films, featuring the inevitable haunted houses, psychic children, small towns besieged by evil, or supernatural presences that presage an alien invasion. Judging from the bookracks, an audience exists for the fictional equivalent of hand-me-downs—writing intended to remind us of someone else's success.

To find great horror fiction, you must look beyond the garish packaging, the extravagant cover quotes, and indeed, the labels that publishers attach to their products. You must join me in an important bit of heresy:

Horror is not a genre, like the mystery or science fiction or the western. It is not a *kind* of fiction, meant to be confined to the ghetto of a special shelf in libraries or bookstores.

Horror is an emotion. It can be found in all literature. It is as at home in the pages of William Faulkner or Carlos Fuentes as in those of Stephen King. In recent years, it has appeared in the work of writers as diverse as J. G. Ballard, Robert Cormier, Jerzy Kosinski, and Jim Thompson. A glance back over the history of English and American literature shows that almost every writer of lasting importance—from Shakespeare to Joyce, from Hawthorne to Hemingway—has written at least one tale of the ghostly, of the uncanny, of a prime and overpowering evil.

"The oldest and strongest emotion of mankind is fear," wrote H. P. Lovecraft, and stories evoking fear have thus never lacked for tellers . . . or readers. That a stylized brand of "horror fiction" exists today is testament to our enduring—and apparently ever-growing—ability to find entertainment in the exercise of this emotion.

And there is no denying that we are entertained. In the words of Clive Barker, "There is no delight the equal of dread."

The Funhouse of Fear

Let's face it: fear is fun. A fundamental attraction of the horror story is that it sometimes offers the excuse to say, "Check your brains at the door, gang, and let's *boogie*." We don't really care if effects-oriented films like *Poltergeist* or *The Evil Dead* or *Aliens* have flimsy plots—after all, nightmares rarely follow a coherent storyline. The images alone work a special magic: the hideous faces popping into view, the suddenly grasping hands, the buckets of stage blood, are all props of a high-tech carnival. We love to see something so grotesque and so unexpected that it makes us scream or laugh (and sometimes we do both)—secure in the knowledge that here, in the funhouse of fear, this kind of behavior is not only accepted, but encouraged.

The operative word is escape. "Dreaming," reports Charles Fisher, clinical professor of psychiatry and director of the sleep laboratory at New York's Mount Sinai Hospital, "permits each and every one of us to be quietly and safely insane every night of our lives." His words apply as well to the waking dreams of horror fiction and film. We live in perilous times, and we need, on occasion, something more perilous than the gentler fantasies of romance or high adventure.

With each news report of Americans held hostage in foreign lands, of pain relievers laced with poison, of toxic waste dumps hidden beneath school playgrounds, the horror story seems more inviting—if only because it shows us that things could, after all, be worse. As Stephen King wrote in "The Mist":

> When the machines fail . . . , when the technologies fail, when the conventional religious systems fail, people have got to have something. Even a zombie lurching into the night can seem pretty cheerful compared to the existential comedy/horror of the ozone layer dissolving under the combined assault of a million fluorocarbon spray cans of deodorant.

That zombie seems cheerful because it is confined to the printed page or motion picture screen; in horror, we control our fears, put them into order, and, more often than not, defeat them. And no matter how desperate things seem, we are offered a simple escape from escapism: we can leave horror's funhouse at any time. Every horror story, like every nightmare, has a happy ending; we can wake up and say that it was all just a dream.

Or can we?

The Nightmare Becomes Reality

No funhouse would be complete without a hall of mirrors; we may discount the rubber masks and *papier-mâché* monsters as purest fantasy, but those warped mirrors reflect something undeniably real. We are drawn seductively to the chance to observe ourselves from odd angles, distorted perspectives—and, perhaps, to see things that we might not otherwise expect.

The horror story is not simply an escape; it also has a cognitive value, serving—consciously or not—as an imperfect mirror of the real fears of its times. The memorable horror films of the 1950s echo with the cold-war mentality, offering the "big bugs" of *Them* and *The Beginning of the End* in visceral response to nuclear threat, and *The Thing* and *The Invasion of the Body Snatchers* as indulgences in anti-communist hysteria, raging against "alien" lifeforms that threaten the American way.

A glance into the dark mirror of modern horror reveals no less reactionary trends. Conventional horror has always been rich with Puritan subtext: if there is a single certainty, it is that teenagers who have sex in cars or in the woods will die. Most books and films of the eighties offer a message as conservative as their morality: conform. The boogeymen of the *Halloween* and *Friday the 13th* films are the hitmen of homogeneity. Don't do it, they tell us, or you will pay an awful price. Don't talk to strangers. Don't party. Don't make love. Don't dare to be different.

Their victims, lost in the peccadilloes of the "Me" generation, waltz again and again into their waiting arms. Their sole nemesis is usually a monogamous (if not virginal) heroine—a middle-class madonna who has listened to her parents, and thus behaves. And it is proper behavior, not crucifixes or silver bullets, that tends to ward off the monsters of our times.

The Monsters of the Eighties

Those monsters have changed.

The vampire is an anachronism in the wake of the sexual revolution. The bite of Bram Stoker's *Dracula*, sharpened in the repression of Victorian times, has been blunted by the likes of Dr. Ruth Westheimer. The bloodthirsty count and his kin survive today because of sentiment rather than sensuality—as a fantasy of upper-class decadence, the commoner's forbidden dream of languorous *chic* (as in Whitley Strieber's *The Hunger*), or as a symbol of unmitigated corruption (as in Stephen King's entry here, "The Night Flier").

The werewolf, too, has grown long in the tooth; its archetypal story, Robert Louis Stevenson's *The Strange Case of Dr. Jekyll and Mr. Hyde*, also hinged on the Victorian mentality, with its marked duality of civilized gentleman and lowbrow brute. As class distinctions wane in our populist times, the duality blurs. The werewolf will live so long as we struggle with the beast within, but its modern incarnations—*The Wolfen, The Howling, An American Werewolf in London*—suggest that the savage has already won and is loose on the streets of the urban jungle.

The invader from outer space, that prominent bugaboo of the Eisenhower era, regained a brief vogue with the *Alien* films and John Carpenter's remake of *The Thing*, but has been transformed by the wishful fantasies of Steven Spielberg into a cuddly savior from the skies. The instant legacy of *Close Encounters of the Third Kind* and *E.T.* has been a series of lovable aliens, from the mermaid of *Splash* to the cozy extraterrestrials of *Starman, Cocoon*, and *ALF*.

Gone too are the survivals of past cultures—the mummies, the golems, the creatures from black lagoons; they cannot survive in a no-deposit, no-return society whose concept of ancient history is, more often than not, the 1950s.

The monsters of our time are less exotic and, discouragingly, more symptomatic than their predecessors. A soulless insanity sparks one of the finest horror novels of the eighties, Thomas Harris's *Red Dragon*. Child abuse is the relentless theme of the bestselling novels of V. C. Andrews, while the dissolution of family and marriage haunts the fiction of Charles L. Grant. The curses of socialization—notably, venereal disease—infect the films of David Cronenberg. Urban decay is the ubiquitous background of Ramsey Campbell's short stories. Stephen King glories in the malfunction of the mundane, giving life to the petty tyrannies of our consumer culture—our household goods, our cars and trucks, our neighbor's dog.

And the monster most symbolic of the eighties looks even more familiar. We may call them zombies, but as a character in George A. Romero's *Day of the Dead* pronounces, "They're us."

The Dead Next Door

Zombies have been part of the monster menagerie since the turn of the century, when West Indies voodoo lore gained a certain vogue; its stories of devil dolls, pagan sacrifice, and the walking dead were soon appropriated for such early classic films as *White Zombie*, with Bela Lugosi, and Val Lewton's *I Walked with a Zombie*.

But the modern zombie traces its heritage to 1968, when Pittsburgh filmmaker George A. Romero transcended the lowest of low budgets to produce *Night of the Living Dead*. In *Night* and its two sequels—*Dawn of the Dead* and *Day of the Dead*—Romero recast the zombie in a contemporary mold, abandoning the ritualistic trappings of voodoo to present a horrifically prosaic vision of the dead next door. Shambling, silent, eyes locked in thousand-yard stares, these are the people who work the late shift at the 7-Eleven, who take your change at highway tollbooths; in *Dawn of the Dead*, Romero likens them to mall shoppers, pale reflections of the mannequins poised next to them in storeroom windows.

As envisioned by Romero and the enthusiastic Italian pastiches of Lucio Fulci, zombies are the liberal nightmare: the huddled masses, yearning to breathe free, arriving on your doorstep with one thought in mind. "They want to eat you," reads one of the more charming film posters, for Fulci's *Zombie*; and their bite is infectious, bringing momentary death, then new life as part of a vacuous, drooling, cannibalistic whole.

Romero and Fulci—and writers like Stephen King (in *'Salem's Lot*), Peter Straub (in *Floating Dragon*), and Thomas Tessier (in his brilliant *Finishing Touches*)—subvert the conservative lesson of conformity that the traditional horror story seeks to teach. Zombies, they tell us, symbolize the state of conformity—mindlessness on a national scale—that has brought so much fear to our daily lives. Only through the intrusion of horror may we see our world clearly, know both its dangers and its possibilities. Otherwise, like the citizens of Clive Barker's most memorable story, "In the Hills, the Cities," who form into a giant and march off to battle, we are doomed:

> Popolac turned away into the hills, its legs taking strides half a mile long. Each man, woman and child in that seething tower was sightless. They saw only through the eyes of the city. They were thoughtless, but to think the city's thoughts. And they believed themselves deathless, in their lumbering relentless strength. Vast and mad and deathless.

In *Day of the Dead*, the last vestiges of rational order—soldiers and scientists—are trapped in an underground missile base with the detritus of civilization, from abandoned recreational vehicles to duplicate copies of income tax returns. The zombies wait aboveground, walking symbols of the ultimate mindlessness—nuclear overkill. In *Night* and *Dawn*, Romero proposed the standard solutions of Americana—religion, family, consumerism, superior firepower—but nothing has worked. As *Day* opens, the chief scientist is struggling to find something that will make the zombies *behave*; he is, of course, hopelessly insane. It is we who must learn *not* to behave like zombies. In the final trumps, the sole survivors are those who refuse to conform, rebelling against the sterile semblance of authority; they take an appropriately symbolic route of escape—ascending through an empty ICBM silo to find a paradise of peace.

To See the Dark

Great horror fiction has never really been about monsters, but about mankind. It shows us something important about ourselves, something dark, occasionally monstrous—and usually in bad taste. Its stories proceed from the archetype of Pandora's Box: the tense conflict between pleasure and fear that is latent when we face the forbidden and the unknown. In horror's pages, we open the Box, exposing what is taboo in our ordinary lives, and test the boundaries of acceptable behavior. Its writers literally drag our terrors from the shadows and force us to look upon them with despair—or relief.

And why not? Who doesn't want to see what lies behind the mask of the Phantom of the Opera? We *know* it won't be pretty. But still we say, like the best of Missourians: *Show me.*

That is not to say that great horror fiction is necessarily a realm of explicitness . . . or explanation. In the hands of a Clive Barker or a David Morrell—writers known for the extremity of their imagery—it is fiction that is graphic, often relentless, but never merely explicit.

How many times have you been disappointed by a motion picture adaptation of a favorite horror novel? The reason is usually simple: the pictures were those of the director's choosing, not those you had seen with your mind's eye while reading the book.

Reading is an intimate act, a sharing of imagination by writer and reader. Its power is no doubt heightened when the subject involves our deepest and darkest fears. When a writer chooses explicit images, spelling out his horrors, he (like a film director) provides the picture, depriving the reader of the opportunity to share in the act of creation.

But I question the recent trend toward explicitness in horror fiction for a more fundamental reason. Too many purveyors of the "gross-out" work from the proposition that the purpose of horror fiction is to shock the reader into submission. They indulge in cheap tactics like those motion picture directors call "pop-ups": the hand thrusting into view, the sudden close-up of a ravaged corpse. Yet shock is a visceral experience, a sensory overload from which most of us recover quickly.

Great horror fiction is not about shock, but emotion; it digs beneath our skin and stays with us. It is proof that an image is only as powerful as its context. Stylists like Dennis Etchison and M. John Harrison invoke more terror through a lingering shadow, a fugitive stain, than most "splatter" films can produce with gallons of spilled blood. That power—not merely to scare, but also to disturb a reader, to invoke a mystery that will linger long after the pages of the book are closed—is the hallmark of each and every writer represented here.

The ability of horror fiction to see the dark, to explore the void behind the face of order, is the key to its abiding lure. The field is responsible for countless films and paperback potboilers whose sole concern is the shock value of make-believe mayhem; but at its most penetrating moments—those of the immaculate clarity of insight which we call art—the horror story is not about make-believe at all.

At its heart is a single certainty: that, in Hamlet's words, "all that live must die." We're not looking for answers to that mystery; we know, if only instinctively, that these are matters of faith. What we are looking for is a way to confess our doubts, our disbeliefs, our fears; and the horror story offers the rare opportunity to laugh and to cry about the fact of our mortality.

When we enter the funhouse of fear, we descend into an ultimate abyss—we see the darkest night—and when we exit, moving out of the dark and into the light, we have faced our innermost fears and we have *survived*.

And then, don't you know, we are ready to try it again.

What makes great horror fiction?

Prime Evil is my answer: Thirteen stories created especially for this book by the most consistently original and haunting voices in contemporary fiction. Each writer was afforded the opportunity to work without any limitations as to style or subject matter or, indeed, length, and the offerings range from compact fables to short novels.

The result is a rare tapestry of fiction woven with strands of dark and decidedly idiosyncratic prose: from the manic enthusiasm of Stephen King and David Morrell to the mannered eroticism of Thomas Tessier and Whitley Strieber, the elegant wit of Paul Hazel and Thomas Ligotti to the enigmatic symbolism of M. John Harrison and Jack Cady, each voice is genuine and individual. There is an occasional element of *homage* (notably, to Henry James, Arthur Machen, Joseph Conrad); but the stories collected here are part of a dying breed—the kind of fiction that, in the words of wrestling's Captain Lou Albano, is "often imitated, but never duplicated."

My notebooks contain a saying, cribbed from a long-forgotten psychology text: "If you turn on the light quickly enough, you can see the dark." The writers of *Prime Evil* are that light, brilliant in their intensity. These are their stories: each a singular vision, in the waking world, of the darkest depths of our dreams.

Several people helped make this book possible, and to each of them, I owe a special word of thanks:

To my wife, Lynne, whose insights bettered this book at every stage; to Mike Dirda, Charlie Grant, and my agent, Howard Morhaim, for their friendship and good advice; to Gianni Scattolini, for knowing just the right words; and most of all, to my editor, Hilary Ross. After all, it was her idea.

—DOUGLAS E. WINTER
Alexandria, Virginia

IN THE COURT OF THE CRIMSON KING

> *The element of water moistens the earth,*
> *But blood flies upward and bedews the*
> *heavens.*
>
> —JOHN WEBSTER

STEPHEN KING, born 1947 in Portland, Maine, is the most popular writer of horror fiction in history. He is also one of the most prolific, with four original screenplays, ninety short stories, four fiction collections, and twenty novels (including, most recently, *Misery* and *The Tommy-knockers*) to his credit. Although each of his novels has its advocates, two of my personal favorites are *'Salem's Lot* and *The Dead Zone*. Those books intersect in "The Night Flier."

Stephen King

The Night Flier

Dees didn't really get interested—in spite of his private pilot's license—until the third and fourth murders. Then he smelled blood.

No pun intended, he told the editor of *Inside View*, who only looked blank. "Has anyone in the straight press picked up on it yet? The pattern, I mean?"

The editor, Morrison, bristled. He always bristled when Dees used the phrase, which was one of the reasons he used it. Well, if Morrison wanted to delude himself into believing a weekly rag that headlined stories like MY TWINS ARE ALIENS, RAPED WOMAN CRIES, and WOMAN EATS ABUSING HUBBY was part of the straight press, let him do it. Dees had seen editors come and editors go. He had worked for *Inside View* long enough to know what it really was: mind-meatloaf that overweight hausfraus bought at the checkout counter and ate in front of the soap operas along with their favorite ice cream.

But every now and then over his fourteen years at *View*, he had smelled blood. Real blood, not the fake stuff.

After the pair of murders in Maryland by the man he had begun to think of as the Night Flier, he thought he caught that unmistakable whiff.

"If you mean has anyone suggested these may be serial murders, the answer is no," Morrison said stiffly.

But it won't be long, Dees thought.

"But it won't be long," Morrison said. "If there's another one—"

25

"Gimme the files," Dees said.

He read them, this time closely, and what he read blew his mind.

I didn't see this before, he thought, and then: *Why didn't I see this before?* He thought Morrison was an asshole. Furthermore, he knew Morrison knew what he thought. Up until today, Dees hadn't cared. After fourteen years on the staff, he was the senior member, top hog in this particular sty, you might say, and he had been offered—and had turned down—the editorial job twice himself. Morrison was the ninth editor under whom he had served (and one of them, the delectable if inept Melanie Briggs, had often served under him—in a more informal capacity, of course).

But if Morrison was an asshole, how come it had been Morrison who'd spotted the Night Flier pattern first?

Briefly—just briefly—the idea that he might be burning out fluttered through his mind. The burnout rate was pretty high in this business, he knew. You could only spend so many years writing about flying saucers carrying off whole Brazilian villages (such stories illustrated, more often than not, by such things as out-of-focus light bulbs dangling from threads against black felt backgrounds) or out-of-work daddies chopping up their kids like kindling wood. It came down to shoveling shit with a typewriter. You got paid a lot, but shit was shit. There came a day when, he had been told, you woke up deciding it was time to look for new work.

He had heard of it but had never thought it could happen to him.

And it isn't, his mind insisted, but he was uneasy.

God, how could he have missed this?

He flew into Wilmington, North Carolina, a week later—pure hunch.

Well . . . instinct. Call it that, if you wanted.

Killer instinct.

It was summertime, and down South the living should have been easy and the cotton high—the song said so, anyway—but Dees was unable to get into the small Wilmington airport, which served only one major airline—Piedmont—a few commuter airlines, and a lot of private planes. There were heavy thunderstorms in the area, and Dees was ninety miles from the airfield, jouncing up and down in the unsteady air, looking at his watch and cursing. It was 8:45 P.M. by the time he was given landing clearance, and that was less than forty minutes before official sundown. He didn't know if the Night Flier stuck by the traditional rules, but the smell of blood was stronger than ever.

He had chosen the right place, found the right Cessna Skymaster.

He knew it.

The Night Flier might have picked Virginia Beach, or Charlotte, or Birmingham, or some point even farther south, but the last two murders had been at the mud-hole airport in Maryland, and Dees had called all the airports south of there that seemed right for the Flier's M.O., using his finger on the Touch Tone phone in his Days Inn motel room until it was sore.

Private planes had landed the night before at all of the most likely airfields, and Cessna Skymaster 337s at all of them. Not surprising, since they were the Toyotas of private aviation. But the Cessna 337 that had landed last night in Wilmington was the one he was looking for. He didn't know how he knew; he just *did*. That was good for the sake of the story (and he was more and more sure there *was* a story, maybe one big enough to make the *National Enquirer*'s Belushi–Smith scoop look like a pile of moldy hay), but it was maybe even a better thing to know just for the sake of knowing: there had been no burnout. A lapse, maybe, but that was all. He was still okay.

So far.

"N471B, vector ILS runway 34," the radio voice said laconically. "Fly heading 160. Descend and maintain 3000."

"Heading 160. Leaving 6 for 3000, roger."

"And be aware we still got some nasty weather down here."

"Roger," Dees said, thinking that ole Farmer John, down there in whatever beer barrel passed for air-traffic control in Wilmington, was sure one hell of a sport to tell him that. He *knew* there was still nasty weather in the area; he could see the thunderheads, some with lightning still going off inside them like giant fireworks, and he had spent the last forty minutes or so circling and feeling more like a man on a pogo stick than one in a twin-engine Beechcraft. Another eight or twelve minutes of that bullshit would have brought on a severe case of the fuel-tank shorts, necessitating a diversion to Charleston. Legit horror stories were hard to come by, but as some great sage or other had (or should have) said, no story, even a real gross-out like the Night Flier, was worth dying for.

He flicked off the autopilot, which had taken him around and around the same stupid patch of now-you-see-it, now-you-don't North Carolina farmland. No cotton down there, high or otherwise. Just a bunch of used-up tobacco patches now overgrown with kudzu. Dees was happy to point his plane's nose toward Wilmington and start into the steadily descending pattern, monitored by pilot, ATC, and tower, for the ILS approach.

He picked up the microphone, thought about giving ole Farmer John a yell, asking him if there just happened to be anybody dead down there, drained of his or her blood, then put the mike back instead. It was still at least half an hour until sunset—he had verified the official Wilmington time on his way down from Washington National. No, if no one had died there last night, they were safe . . . at least for a little while.

Dees believed the Night Flier was a real vampire about as much as he believed it really had been the Tooth Fairy who had put all those quarters under his pillow when he was a kid, but if the guy *thought* he was a vampire—and this guy, Dees was convinced, really did—that would probably be enough to make him conform to the rules.

Life, after all, imitates art.

Count Dracula with a private pilot's license.

You had to admit, Dees thought, it was elegant.

The Beech jounced as he passed through a thick membrane of cumulus on his steady downward course. Dees cursed and trimmed the plane, which seemed increasingly unhappy with the weather.

You and me both, baby, Dees thought.

When he came into the clear again, he could see the lights of Wilmington and Wrightsville Beach clearly.

Yes sir, the fatties are gonna love this one, he thought as thunder rumbled on the port side. *They're gonna pick up about seventy zillion copies of this baby when they go Krogering.*

But there was more, and he knew it.

This one could be . . . well . . . just so goddamn good.

This one could be *legitimate*.

There was a time when a word like that never would have crossed your mind, ole buddy, he thought. Maybe you *are* burning out.

INSIDE VIEW REPORTER APPREHENDS CRAZED NIGHT FLIER.

EXCLUSIVE STORY ON HOW BLOOD-DRINKING NIGHT FLIER WAS FINALLY CAUGHT.

"NEEDED TO HAVE IT," DEADLY DRACULA DECLARES.

It wasn't exactly grand opera—Dees had to admit that—but he thought it sang just the same. He thought it sang like a boid.

He picked up the mike after all and depressed the button. He knew the Flier was still there, just as he knew he wasn't going to be comfortable until he had made absolutely sure.

"Wilmington, this is N471B. You still got a Skymaster 337 from Duffrey, Maryland, down there on the ramp?"

Through static: "Looks like it, old hoss. Can't talk just now. I got air traffic."

"Has it got red piping?" Dees persisted.

For a moment he thought he would get no answer,

then: "Red piping, yeah. Kick it off, N471B, if you don't want me to see if I can slap an FCC fine on y'all. I got too many fish to fry tonight, and not enough skillets."

"Thanks, Wilmington," Dees said in his most courteous voice. He hung up the mike and then gave it the finger, but he was grinning, barely noticing the jolts as he passed through another membrane of cloud. Skymaster, red piping, and he was willing to bet next year's salary that if the doofus in the tower hadn't been so busy, he would have been able to confirm the tail number as well: N101BL.

He had found the Night Flier, by Christ. He had found him, it wasn't dark yet, and as impossible as it seemed, there were no police on the scene. If there had been cops, and if they had been there concerning the Cessna, Farmer John almost certainly would have said so, sky jam and bad weather or not. Some things were just too good not to gossip about.

I want your picture, you bastard, Dees thought. Now he could see the approach lights, flashing white in the dusk. I'll get your story in time, but first, the picture.

Just one.

He headed down more steeply, ignoring the descent beep. His face was pale and set. His lips were pulled back slightly, revealing small, gleaming white teeth.

In the combined light of dusk and the instrument panel, Richard Dees looked more than a bit like a vampire himself.

There were many things *Inside View* was not—literate, for one, overconcerned with the nuances of the stories it covered, for another—but one thing was undeniable: It was exquisitely attuned to horrors. Merton Morrison *was* a bit of an asshole (although not as much of one as Dees had originally thought), but Dees had to give him one thing—he had remembered the two things that had made *Inside View* a success. First, buckets of blood. Second, handfuls of guts.

Oh, there were still pictures of cute babies and

psychic predictions and diets that would supposedly work without the dieter having to give up anything (except the things he or she—she, most frequently—didn't like), but Morrison had recognized the change in the temper of the times when he came on board. Dees supposed that was why Morrison had lasted as long as he had (and, maybe, why he himself was a little jealous of the editor, with his dork's crew cut and teeny, mincing little feet and his cigarette holder). The flower children of '68 had grown into the cannibals of '88. The peace sign had gone the way of the Nehru jacket and the Beatle haircut. The country was into Rambo and Bernhard Goetz. The circulation of *Inside View*, which had taken a shallow dip in the late seventies and a steeper one in the early eighties, had begun to come up again under the dual administrations of those dual assholes, Ronald Reagan and Merton Morrison.

Dees had no doubt there was still an audience for *All Things Bright and Beautiful*, but the one for *All Shit Grim and Gory* had become a growth stock once again. Those in favor of the former had James Herriott. Those in favor of the latter had Stephen King and *Inside View*.

The difference, Dees thought, was King made *his* stuff up.

Their stringers had gotten the word six months after Morrison's name went up on the editor's door: By all means, stop and smell the roses on your way to work, but once you get there, spread these nostrils *wide* and start sniffing for blood.

And when it came to blood, no one smelled better than Richard Dees.

Which was why it was Dees, and no one *but* Dees, who was flying into Wilmington tonight while Gloria Swett went up to Nashville for what looked like the really big story . . . with Dee's complete blessing. Because the country and western singer with AIDS was going to look very small compared to this.

Instinct.

Instinct that had turned into knowing: knowing that

there was a human monster who apparently thought he was a vampire down there, a monster whose name Dees had already picked out but had not mentioned to anyone but Morrison. A name he would coin soon enough. And when he did, it would be plastered across the tabloid display racks of every supermarket checkout counter in America—screaming at the patrons in unignorable sixteen-point type.

Look out, ladies and sensation seekers, Dees thought. You don't know it, but a very bad man—possibly a woman but almost certainly a man—is coming your way. You'll read his real name and forget it, but that's okay. What you'll remember is *my* name for him, the name that's going to put him right up there with Jack the Ripper and the Cleveland Torso Murderer and the Black Dahlia.

THE NIGHT FLIER: COMING SOON TO A CHECKOUT COUNTER NEAR YOU.

Very soon.

The exclusive story, the exclusive interview . . . but what I want most of all is the exclusive *picture*.

He checked his watch again and allowed himself to relax the tiniest bit (which was, really, all Richard Dees *could* relax; he was one of those men who have only two speeds, totally off and overdrive). He still had almost half an hour till dark. He would be parking next to the white Skymaster with red piping (and N101BL on the tail in a similar red) in less than fifteen minutes.

Was the Flier sleeping in town or in some motel on the way into town?

Dees didn't think so. Dees doubted if all four murders would have taken place at the airfields themselves, had that been the case.

One of the reasons for the Skymaster 337's popularity, besides its relatively low price, was that it was the only plane its size with a belly hold. True, it wasn't much bigger than the trunk of an old VW beetle, but it was roomy enough for three big suitcases or five small ones . . . and almost certainly could fit a sleeping or hiding man, provided he wasn't the size of a pro basketball player. The Night Flier could be in the Cessna's belly hold, provided he was (a) sleeping in the fetal position with his knees drawn up to his chin; or (b) crazy enough to think he was a real vampire; or (c) both of the above.

Dees had his money on (c).

Did I find anything underneath where that plane was parked? the not exactly sober mechanic at the little airport in Maine had asked, repeating one of Dees's inspired, instinctive questions. He thought it over. Dees didn't press. He knew when to press and when to wait. Instinct again.

The mechanic had been an old geezer wearing a coverall so stained you could barely read the name *Ezra* picked out in gold thread on the right breast. The coverall—where it wasn't black with oil—was blue. The cap sitting askew on his head was a fluorescent orange where it wasn't marked with oily prints so clear a New York cop would have admired them. He was stroking a chin that hadn't felt a razor blade in three days, maybe four. His eyes were bloodshot. The only smell stronger than oil or sweat on him when you got up close was sharp and pungent. The geezer either had been rolling in a juniper patch recently or putting away a considerable amount of gin. All in all, Dees had been glad his own plane didn't need any servicing that day.

Still, he waited, hands stuffed in the pockets of his expensive slacks.

Now, it's damn funny you should ask that, the mechanic said at last, *because I did find sutthin'.*

That was how he said it: *sutthin'.*

Big pile of dirt.

He looked at Dees, who had asked the proper question: *That right?*

Oh, ayuh. Kicked it with m'boot.

Pause.

Nasty stuff.

Another pause.

Goddamn stuff was squirmin' with worms.

Yet another pause.

And maggots, the mechanic finished.

Now, with his altimeter winding down from four to three thousand feet, Dees thought: No hotel or motel for you, my friend, am I right? When you play vampire, you're like Frank Sinatra—you do it your way. Know what I think? I think when the belly hold of that plane opens, the first thing I'm gonna see is a shower of graveyard earth (and even if it isn't, you can bet your upper incisors it *will* be when the story comes out), and then I'm gonna see first one leg in a pair of tuxedo pants, and then the other, because you are gonna be *dressed*, ain't you? Oh, dear man, I think you are gonna be dressed to the *nines*, dressed to *kill*, you might say, and the auto-winder is already on my camera, and when I see that cloak—

But that was where his thoughts stopped; that was where they broke off as cleanly as a broken branch.

Because that was when the flashing white lights on both runways went out.

The gin-head mechanic had been one of the employees at the Cumberland County Airport, a dignified-sounding name for a pocket airfield that consisted of two Quonset huts and two crisscrossing runways. One of the runways was actually tarred. Because Dees had never landed on a dirt runway, he requested the tarred one. The bouncing his Beech 55 (for which he was in hock up to his eyebrows and beyond) took when he landed convinced him to try the dirt when he took off again, and he had been amazed and delighted to find it as smooth as a coed's breast.

Oh, and the field also had a wind sock. Patched like a pair of old dad's underdrawers, but it was there. Technology comes to the boondocks, Dees had thought. Will wonders never cease.

Cumberland County was itself the most populous in Maine, but the town for which it was named was the apotheosis of Hicksville, U.S.A. It sat between an even smaller (and mostly deserted) town with the un-

likely name of Jerusalem's Lot, and the much larger—
and plusher—town of Falmouth. A visit to the Falmouth
police station to pick up what particulars the local fuzz
would part with convinced Dees of two things. The
first was that Falmouth cops didn't consider themselves hicks. The second was that they were.

The Cumberland field existed mostly on the landing
fees paid by rich summer residents who found it easier
and quicker to get in there than at the Portland Jetport, where the air traffic grew more congested each
year. Falmouth, hick town or not, had some nice
stretches of beach . . . and a great golf course.

Also, the landing fees at Cumberland County Airport were roughly twenty-five percent of those at the
Portland Jetport.

When Dees arrived, it was high summer and the
place was as busy as it ever got—which meant it had
awakened from deep hibernation to a light doze. At
this, the bustling height of its season, it employed a
mind-dazzling array of four employees: two mechanics
and two ground controllers (the ground controllers
also sold chips, cigarettes, and sodas; further, the gin-
head told Dees, the murdered night controller, Claire
Bowie, had made a damn decent cheeseburger). Mechanics and controllers also served as pump jockeys
and janitors. It wasn't unusual for the controller to
have to rush back from the bathroom, where he was
swabbing out the john with Janitor-In-A-Drum, to
give landing clearance and assign a runway from the
maze of two at his disposal.

All this was so challenging that the night controller
at CCA sometimes only got six hours' sleep a night.

Shortly before dawn on the morning of July 9, a
Cessna 337, tail number N101BL, had radioed Claire
Bowie for landing clearance. Bowie was a bachelor
who had been working the night shift at the airfield
since 1954, when pilots sometimes had to abort their
approaches (which, in those days, was known simply
as "pulling up") because of the cows that sometimes
wandered onto what was then the single runway.

Bowie got the radio call from the Skymaster at 4:32

A.M. and gave the requested clearance at 4:36. The time of landing he noted as 4:49 A.M.; he further recorded the pilot's name as Dwight Renfield, and the point of N101BL's origination as Bangor, Maine. The times were undoubtedly correct. The rest was bullshit.

Bowie had no flight plan filed for a Cessna N101BL departing Bangor or anyplace else, but he simply assumed it had been misfiled by the day controller (or maybe used to wipe up a spilled cup of coffee), and he made no effort to check with Bangor.

At CCA, the atmosphere was loose, and a landing fee was a landing fee.

Dees had checked Bangor, and as far as they were concerned, N101BL had flown out of nowhere.

As for the pilot's name, it was a bizarre joke. Dwight just happened to be the first name of an actor named Dwight Frye, and Dwight Frye had just happened to play, among a plethora of other parts, the role of Renfield, a slavering lunatic whose idol had been the most famous vampire of all time.

But, Dees supposed, radioing UNICOM and asking for landing clearance in the name of Count Dracula might have raised suspicion even in a sleepy little place like this.

Might.

He wasn't really sure.

After all, as the ginny had said, a landing fee was a landing fee.

Landing fees or no landing fees (and "Dwight Renfield" had paid his promptly, in cash, as he had also paid to top off his tanks, and judging from the amount of money found in Claire Bowie's wallet, he also must have tipped in currency of the realm . . . and lavishly), Dees was astonished by the casual treatment N101BL had received. This was, after all, the era of drug paranoia, and most of the shit came into small harbors in small boats, or into small airports in small planes . . . planes like ole Dwight Renfield's Cessna Skymaster, for instance. Bowie should have been suspicious and followed up on the missing flight plan, if only to keep his own skirts clean.

That was what he *should* have done, but he hadn't. Had Bowie been bribed as well as tipped? If so, it hadn't been in his pockets. The police report specified a total cash amount of ninety dollars. You didn't bribe anyone—not even a hick—to cover for a plane whose belly hold just might be full of toot for the old snoot, with ninety bucks.

Try this, though: "Renfield" bribes Claire Bowie. Bowie takes his windfall home to his bachelor pad and sticks it under his underwear or something. The next night, "Renfield," maybe coked to the gills and so paranoid that he's got a permanent charley horse in his neck from looking behind him, decides to kill Bowie. Then the cops come along, and in the course of the investigation one of them finds the cash in one of Bowie's bureau drawers. The cop sticks the wad in his own pocket. Deppity Dawg's ship just came in. Pennies from heaven.

But it didn't hold water and Dees knew it. Bowie had a reputation for honesty. Dees had never met an honest man in his life, except maybe for a psychic—maybe the only *real* psychic Dees had ever tried to recruit for *Inside View*—named Johnny Smith, who had kicked Dees off his porch and threatened to shotgun him. And since Smith had later tried to assassinate a member of the House of Representatives—not the president or even a fa-chrissakes senator but a fucking *representative* from *New Hampshire*—Dees felt that Smith's uncharacteristic honesty could be chalked up to insanity and safely forgiven. But Claire Bowie seemed to have no vices demanding enough to justify the risk a bribe would have entailed.

But even if he *had* taken one, which had later disappeared into some cop's pocket, what about the rest of the Cumberland County Airport staff? There weren't many of them, but enough so that maybe all four had spent the day walking around the white Skymaster with the red piping. If "Renfield" needed to bribe one, he needed to bribe all . . . and Dees *knew* he hadn't, because he had asked point-blank and had accepted the denials (heated denials, by and large) calmly and at face value.

This bunch of Yankee clodhoppers was too dumb to lie. Simple as that.

Dees supposed he could understand the ginny's lack of interest in the plane easily enough. The ginny, who had provided most of his information, looked like he might be able to find his way from the airport's one hangar to the gas pumps without a map, but probably not much farther.

Also, he was the only one of the bunch to answer Dee's question about the bribe with regret rather than anger.

But what about the others?

Christ only knew. Some of it was doubtlessly the fault of the mass deregulation that had come into vogue with the Carter administration, overpopulating the skies and understaffing the smaller fields, when the commuter carriers suddenly discovered there was no FAA strong enough to keep them out of the bigger ones (like the Portland Jetport) anymore. In lieu of anything better, he supposed he had to chalk the rest up to that unspoken small-town credo of you-mind-your-business-and-I'll-mind-mine.

But it wasn't like a Lucky Strike. It didn't satisfy. It didn't quite ring true.

Also, let's face it, gang: The possible negligence of a bunch of small-town air mechanics and controllers wasn't the sort of stuff *Inside View* readers really went boolsheet for, anyway. *The New Republic* or *Atlantic Monthly* could have that one, if they wanted; Dees wanted the Night Flier.

The gin-soaked mechanic looked surprised when Dees asked how he thought "Renfield" had left the airport.

"Musta taken a cab, I guess," he said.

"Did Claire Bowie say anything about a cab the next day?"

The ginny scratched his whiskery chin. "Nope. Not that I recollect."

Dees made a mental note to call the cab companies

in the area first thing. At that time he was going on what seemed like the perfectly reasonable assumption that the guy slept in a bed like everyone else. But Dees wasn't going to trust this mechanic, who appeared to have come to a stage in his life where the things he didn't recollect outnumbered the ones he did roughly three to one.

"What about a limo?"

"Nope," the ginny said more positively. "Claire didn't say nothing about no limbo, and he woulda mentioned that."

Dees nodded and made a mental note to call the limo company, or companies, in Falmouth, if there were any, second thing. He would also question the rest of the staff, but he expected no light to dawn there; the ginny said that he had had a cup of coffee with Claire before Claire left, and another with Claire when Claire came back on duty, and he, the ginny, was going off (except, Dees guessed, I bet your cup of coffee looked quite a bit like a glass of gin, didn't it, old-timer?), but that he was pretty sure none of the day people had talked to Claire.

There was a night mechanic, but he had called in sick earlier that day, and his story checked out. Bowie had been alone when he was killed. Except for the Night Flier, of course.

It all looked like a dead end.

He was about to thank the ginny and walk away when he said: "He did say one funny thing, ole Claire did." He scratched open the left pocket of his coverall, removed a pack of Chesterfields, offered it to Dees for nearly half a second, and then took one himself. While he lit up, he looked at Dees from beneath the wrinkled and folded lids of his bloodshot eyes with an expression of half-baked craftiness. "Might not mean nothing, but it sure musta struck Claire perculyer, I guess, because ole Claire, you know, most times ole Clair wouldn't say shit if he had a mouthful."

"What was that?"

"Don't quite remember," the ginny said. "Sometimes, you know, when I forget things, a picture of Andrew Jackson sorta refreshes my memory."

"How about one of Alexander Hamilton?" Dees asked dryly.

After a moment's consideration (a *short* moment), the ginny agreed that sometimes Hamilton did the trick, and a ten changed hands. Dees thought that a portrait of Ben Franklin—hell, maybe even one of George Washington—might have done it, but he was only an impatient man, not a totally mean one.

"Claire said the guy looked like he must be goin' to one hell of a fancy party," the ginny said.

"Oh?" Dees said, thinking that if this was all there was, maybe it should have been Lincoln, after all. "Did he say why he thought that?"

"Said the guy was dressed to the nines. Tuxedo, silk tie, all that stuff." The ginny paused. "Claire said the guy was even wearin' a big cloak. Red as a fire engine inside, black as a woodchuck's asshole outside.

"Said when it spread out behind him, it looked like a goddamn bat's wing, it did."

It was not just the throat-ripping that had intrigued Morrison; in a society where large doses of cocaine had given subnormal clods the ability to imagine (and the insanity to carry out) what amounted to ritual acts of vengeance, throat-rippings were just not unique enough to titillate *Inside View* readers. The fact that almost every drop of Claire Bowie's blood had been gone was, however.

Maybe Morrison was an asshole when it came to his illusions that there was any real dignity or importance about the job he was doing, but he was no dummy. He knew a good VAMPIRE STALKS SMALL MAINE TOWN story when he saw it as quickly as he knew a good "BIGFOOT STOLE MY BABY!" ANGUISHED MOTHER CRIES story, or Morrison's own personal favorite: OVER HALF OF RUSSIAN POLITBURO INFECTED WITH AIDS, DEFECTOR CONFIDES IN TOP-SECRET CIA MEMO.

On a slow week he would have used it as the "second shouter" below the main head, but Bowie had not been killed during a slow week, and this had pleased Morrison. He had his good instincts, all right, better than Dees had at first thought, and now they were telling him they had a potential top headline-in-the-making here.

His instincts told him the guy might do it again.

Sure enough, three weeks later the guy did. In Alderton, New York.

One of the things that surprised Dees about the case of the Night Flier (and considering what he had seen of human nature and human behavior, it might really have been the only thing) was that Alderton had been the Flier's only one-night stand . . . and he still hadn't been caught.

The Alderton airport was even smaller than the one in Cumberland—one single dirt runway and a combined Ops/UNICOM that was no more than a shed with a fresh coat of paint. There was no instrument approach; there was, however, a large satellite dish so none of the flying farmers who worked here would have to miss *Dallas* or *Wheel of Fortune* or anything really important like that.

One thing: The dirt was just as silky-smooth as the runway in Maine had been. Dees thought: I could get used to this. No big thuds over asphalt patches, no potholes that want to ground-loop you after you come in . . . yeah, I could get used to this real easy.

At Alderton, nobody had asked for pictures of Hamilton, Jackson, or anyone else. At Alderton, the whole town—a community of just under a thousand souls—was in shock, not merely the few part-timers who had run the tiny airport almost as a charity (and certainly in the red), along with the late Buck Kendall. There was no one to do any talking to, anyway, be it for pay or for free. No one had been there that night but Buck Kendall, no one had *seen* anything but Buck Kendall . . . and Buck Kendall was dead.

"Must have been one mighty man," one of the part-timers told Dees. "Ole Buck, he went two-twenty, and he was easy most of the time, but if you got him riled, he made you sorry. Seen him box down a fella in a carny show that came through P'keepsie two years ago. That kind of fightin' ain't legal, of course, but Buck was short a payment on that little Piper Cub of his, so he boxed down that carny fighter. Collected two hunded dollars and got it to the loan comp'ny about two days before they was gonna send out some-one to repo it, I guess." The part-timer paused. This guy knew a hell of a lot less than the gin-head, but Dees liked him better. He looked genuinely concerned, genuinely sorry. "Guy musta tooken him from be-hind," he said. "That's the only way I can figger it."

Dees didn't know from which direction Gerard "Buck" Kendall had been taken, but he knew that this time the victim's throat had not been ripped out. This time there were holes, holes from which "Dwight Renfield" had presumably sucked his victim's blood. Except, according to the coroner's report, the holes were on opposite sides of the neck, one in the jugular vein and the other in the carotid artery. Neither were they the discreet little bite marks of the Bela Lugosi era or the slightly gorier ones of the Christopher Lee flicks. The coroner's report spoke in dry centimeters, but Dees and Morrison both could translate well enough; from the size of the wounds, the killer either had teeth the size of one of *View*'s beloved Bigfeet, or he had made them in a much more prosaic fashion: with a spike.

Spiked him and drank his blood.

The Night Flier had requested permission to land at Alderton Field shortly after 10:30 P.M. Kendall had granted permission and he had noted the number, which Morrison had at that time almost memorized: N101BL. He had noted "name of pilot" as "Dwite Renfeild" and the "make and model of aircraft" as "Cessna Skymaster 337." No mention of the red pip-ing, no mention of the sweeping bat-wing cloak that was as red as a fire engine on the inside and as black as a woodchuck's asshole on the outside, but Morrison felt they had enough.

The Night Flier—who had flown into Alderton shortly

after 10:30 on the night of July 19, killed that strapping fellow Buck Kendall, drank his blood, and flown out again in his little Cessna 337 sometime before Jenna Kendall came by at 5:00 A.M. to give her husband a fresh-made waffle and discovered his exsanguinated corpse instead—had, in Morrison's mind, just gone to the head of the class.

In other words, he was ready to make the Flier a first shouter.

At the time Dees remembered thinking that if you *gave* blood, all you got was a cup of orange juice. If you took it, however—*sucked* it, to be perfectly specific—you got headlines.

There had been occasions when it had occurred to Dees—just in passing, mind you—that God's hand might have shook just a tiny bit when He was finishing off the supposed masterwork of His new creative empire.

The Night Flier would have been the shouter with Dees's passive approval (and without Dees's inventive moniker; Morrison was a good editor but a creative slouch, and he would have been perfectly happy to stick with the adequate, but humdrum, modern-day Dracula, as if there hadn't been thirty of those and forty modern-day Jack the Rippers in the last century or so) and without his byline, because Morrison hadn't been able to interest him. Dees flipped through the reports, saw the connection, figured the guy for a nut with a fetish that had been worked to death (at least in the tabs) already, and who would be caught the next time out. As far as Dees had been concerned then, the only thing about the case that was even halfway interesting was the fact that this might be the first homicidal maniac in history who flew to his victims.

Morrison asked him why he thought Drac, which was what Morrison was then calling him, would be caught the next time.

"Because he's a doofus, like all of them," Dees had said, and tapped the Skymaster's tail number. "If you were going to rob banks, would you do it in the same car with the same license number every time?"

"Oh!" Morrison said, looking surprised. "But . . . that makes it even a little weirder, doesn't it, Rick?"

Dees didn't show it, but inside he bristled. There was a disc jockey named Rick Dees. The man was an idiot. If there was anything he hated more than being called Rick, it was a girl or a story that wouldn't put out.

Although he didn't know it, any chance Morrison had of interesting Dees (who was the closest thing to a star reporter *Inside View* could boast) in the Night Flier, at least then, disappeared. Dees's mind closed with a snap.

"I don't think so," he said.

"Oh." Morrison looked disappointed. "Well, I'm gonna run it as a shouter, anyhow."

"Fine," he said, and walked out of the office.

Rick, he thought. *Rick, for chrissake. The man really was an asshole. Let him have his week. Two weeks from now he'll get himself a picture of some walleyed kid and he'll have to crop the picture because the kid will have wet his pants, and that'll be the end of his modern-day Dracula.*

Later that day, one of the country's biggest country and western stars tearfully announced that she had contracted AIDS from her equally famous country and western star husband. Hubby had supposedly died of cancer late the year before, and the folks at *View*, including Morrison and Dees, had had their doubts about *that* little story ("I got four guys in Nashville," Dees told Morrison, "willing to sign affidavits that swear old Mr. Down Home America was twangin' one whole hell of a lot more than his guitar"), but they'd had to back off. After examining the affidavits Dees had collected, the lawyers representing the company that provided *Inside View*'s libel insurance—a company that could have given Morrison's vampire all sorts of lessons about even more efficient ways of putting the bite on people, at least in the humble opinion of Richard Dees—had decided they didn't have quite enough hard evidence, and so they'd had to back off. Not this time.

The Night Flier ended up as a two-column item near the back of the following week's paper. Morrison spent most of his time in his office with the door closed, talking and smoking himself hoarse, finally emerging with a smile like that of a new father. He announced to Dees and everyone else within earshot that he had just made a deal for the dying nightingale's memoirs, as told to an *Inside View* reporter (Dees himself, they had all thought then), for three million dollars.

"Poor bitch said he'd whored away most of the dough, what he hadn't spent on cars"—Morrison chortled—"and she had to have something to leave her kids. They had eight."

"Jesus Christ, that guy really *must* have been AC/DC," Dees marveled, and then they both exploded into laughter.

But that was the night Morrison's Dracula and Dees's Night Flier struck again, this time killing two. He had flown into Duffrey Airport in Maryland, same Cessna 337, same number . . . but he had flown in *the night before*. As in the first slaying, the plane had spent a whole day sitting undisturbed and unreported on the ramp before dark fell and the killing—not to mention the blood drinking—began.

When Dees asked Morrison if he could look over the files again, and when he later asked Morrison if Morrison could send Gloria Swett (a two-hundred-pounder referred to by many staffers, male and female alike, as Gloria Suet) to Nashville instead, Morrison had at first looked dumbfounded . . . then gratified.

"Why? What was it that finally got to you?"

Dees considered and rejected half a dozen answers. Instinct. That was all. It always came down to that. Just instinct that this was going to end up being the bigger story.

But because he supposed Morrison needed *something*, he said, "I guess it's just barely possible a guy could rob three banks in the same car with the same license number. But are you going to tell me he could park all day in front of the third bank in that car before pulling the job? There's something very screwy here. I want to find out what it is."

And now, four miles west of Wilmington Airport and three thousand feet above the ground, things had just gotten a lot screwier.

It wasn't just the runway lights that had gone out; half of the fucking *town* had gone black.

The ILS was still there, but when Dees snatched the mike and screamed, "What the fuck's going on down there?" he got nothing back but a screech of static in which a few voices babbled like distant ghosts.

He jammed the mike back, missing the prong. It thudded to the cockpit floor at the end of its curled wire, and Dees forgot it. The grab and the yell had been pure pilot's instinct and no more. He knew what had happened as surely as he knew the sun set in the west . . . and it would do that soon now. Very soon. A stroke of lightning must have scored a direct hit on a power substation near the airport. The question was whether or not to go in, anyway.

"You had clearance," one voice said. Another immediately (and correctly) replied that that was so much bullshit rationalization. You learned what you were supposed to do in a situation like this when you were still the equivalent of a student driver. Logic and the book tell you to head for your alternate and try to contact ATC.

Landing now could cost him a violation and a hefty fine.

On the other hand, *not* landing now—*right* now— could lose him the Night Flier. It might also cost someone (or several someones, considering the murders of Ray and Ellen Sarch in Duffrey) his life; but Dees considered this of almost no importance at all . . . until an idea went off like a flashbulb in his mind, an inspiration that occurred, as most of his inspirations did, in huge type:

HEROIC REPORTER SAVES (fill in a number, as large as possible, which was pretty large, given the amazingly generous borders that mark the range of human credulity) FROM CRAZED NIGHT FLIER.

Eat *that*, guys, Dees thought, and continued his descent toward Runway 34.

The runway lights down there suddenly pulsed alight again, as if approving his decision, then went out again, leaving blue afterimages on his eyes that turned the sick green of spoiled avocados a moment later. At the same moment the weird static coming from the radio cleared and Farmer John's voice screamed: *"Haul port, N471B: Piedmont, haul starboard: Jesus, oh, Jesus, midair, I think we got a midair—"*

Dees's self-preservation instincts were every bit as well honed as those which smelled blood in the bush. He never even saw the Piedmont Airlines 727's strobe lights. He was too busy banking as tightly to port as the Beech could bank—which was as tight as a virgin's cooze, and Dees would be happy to testify to that fact if he got out of this shitstorm alive—as soon as the second word was out of Farmer John's mouth. He had a momentary sight/sense of something that seemed only inches above him, something as big as the wing of a prehistoric bird, and then the Beech 55 was taking a beating that made the previous rough air seem like glass. His cigarettes flew out of his breast pocket and streamed everywhere. The half-dark Wilmington skyline was crazily tilted. It felt as if his stomach were trying to squeeze his heart out of existence. Spit ran up one cheek like a kid whizzing along a greased slide. Maps flew like birds. The air outside now raved with jet thunder as well as the kind nature made. One of the windows in the four-seat passenger compartment imploded, and an asthmatic wind whooped in, skirling everything not tied down back there into a tornado.

"Resume your previous altitude assignment, N471B!" Farmer John was screaming. Dees was coldly aware that he'd just ruined a two-hunded-dollar pair of pants by spraying about a pint of hot piss into them, but he was partially soothed by a strong feeling that old Farmer John had just loaded his Jockey shorts with a truck-

load or so of fresh Mars Bars. Sounded that way, anyhow.

Dees carried a Swiss Army knife. He took it from his right pants pocket and, holding the wheel with his left hand, cut through his shirt just above the left elbow, bringing blood. Then with no pause

(*instinct*)

he made another cut, shallow, just below his left eye. He folded the knife shut and stuffed it into the elasticized map pocket in the pilot's door. Gotta clean it later, he thought. Do it or you could be in deep shit. But considering the things the Night Flier had gotten away with, he thought he'd be okay.

The runway lights came on again, this time for good, he hoped, although their pulsing quality told him they were being powered by a generator. He homed the Beech in again on Runway 34. Blood ran down his left cheek to the corner of his mouth. He sucked some in and then spat a pink mixture of blood and spit onto his IVSI. Never miss a trick. Instinct.

He looked at his watch. Sunset—only fourteen minutes away now. This was cutting it much too close to the bone.

"*Pull up, Beech!*" Farmer John yelled. "*Are you deaf or on something?*"

Dees groped for the mike's kinked wire without ever taking his eyes from the runway lights. He pulled the wire through his fingers until he got to the mike itself. He palmed it and depressed the send button.

"Listen to me, you chicken-fried son of a bitch," he said, and now his lips were pulled all the way back to the gum line. "I missed getting turned into strawberry jam by that 727 because your shit genny didn't kick in when it was supposed to; as a result I had no ATC comm. I don't know how many people on the *airliner* just missed getting turned into strawberry jam, but I bet *you* do, and I know the cockpit crew does. The only reason those guys are still alive is because the captain of that boat was bright enough to allemande right, and I was bright enough to do-si-do, but I have sustained both structural and physical damage. If you don't give me a landing clearance right now, I'm going to land, anyway. The only difference is that if I have to land without clearance, I'm going to have you up in front of an FAA hearing. But first I will personally see to it that your head and your asshole change places. Have you got that, *hoss*?"

A long, static-filled silence. Then a very small voice, utterly unlike Farmer John's previous hearty "Hey bo'!" delivery, said, "You're cleared to land Runway 34, N471B."

Dees smiled and homed in on the runway.

He depressed the mike button and said, "I got mean and yelling. I'm sorry. It only happens when I almost die."

No response from the ground.

Dees headed in, resisting the impulse to look at his watch again.

Duffrey was what had convinced him, although even before then, Dees had begun to wonder if he hadn't made a serious mistake.

In Duffrey, the Night Flier's Cessna had spent another entire day on the ramp. It was the blood the readers would care about, of course, and that was how it should be (world without end, amen, amen); it was the elderly married couple who should have died in each other's arms but had not, and who should have been found in pools of blood but had not, because there was no blood left in their bodies; it was for them that the readers should and would care (the following month would have seen their golden wedding anniversary, sob-sob, choke-choke), but it was that failure to report an aircraft already involved in two previous murders that convinced Dees there was a real story here, and maybe a very big one.

He had landed at Washington National and rented a car to take him the sixty miles to Duffrey, because without Ray Sarch and his wife, Ellen, there *was* no Sarch/Duffrey Airfield. Aside from Ellen's sister, Raylene, who was a pretty fair mechanic, the two of them had been the whole shebang. There was a single oiled dirt runway (oiled both to lay the dust and to discourage the growth of weeds) and a control booth not much bigger than a closet attached to the Jet-Aire trailer where the Sarch couple lived. They were both retired, both reputedly as tough as nails, both fliers, each devoted to the other.

Further, Dees learned in those few harum-scarum days before his flight into Wilmington that the Sarches put drug dealers and child abusers in about the same category. Their only son had died in the Florida Everglades, trying to land in what looked like a clear stretch of water with better than a ton of Acapulco Gold packed into a stolen Beech 18. The water *had* been clear . . . except for a single stump, that was. The Beech 18 had exploded. Douglas Sarch had been thrown clear, his body smoking and singed but probably still alive, as little as his grieving parents would want to believe such a thing. Doug Sarch had been eaten by gators deep in the 'Glades, and all that remained of him when the DEA guys finally found him a week later was a dismembered skeleton whose few remaining shreds of flesh seethed with maggots; a charred pair of Calvin Klein jeans; a white silk shirt; and a sport coat from Bijan New York, which contained the son's wallet . . . and two ounces of nearly pure cocaine.

"It was drugs and the motherfuckers who run 'em killed my boy," Ray Sarch had said on several occasions, and Ellen Sarch was willing to double and redouble on that one. Her hatred of drugs and drug dealers, Dees was told again and again (he was amused by the nearly unanimous feeling in Duffrey that the murder of the elderly Sarches had been a "gangland hit"), was only exceeded by her grief and bewilderment over the seduction of her son by those very people.

Dees could, and would, use all of this stuff, of course—although not right away. A story like this was like Maxwell House Coffee: good to the last drop. But you started with the equivalent of a violent shriek of brass. Later on, after the initial slavering interest had been sated—How did he kill them? Did he really drink their blood? Was he able to keep it down after he drank it or did he puke? Did he torture them? Did they scream?—there would be a caesura. Then, after two weeks or so, the brass would be replaced by the sobbing violins.

Following the death of their son, the Sarches had kept their eyes peeled for anything or anyone who looked even remotely like a drug transporter. They had brought the Maryland State Police out to the field four times on false alarms, but the state Bears hadn't minded because the Sarches had also blown the whistle on three small transporters and two very big ones. The last had been carrying twenty-seven pounds of pure Bolivian cocaine. That was the kind of bust that made you forget a few false alarms, the sort of bust that made promotions.

So on July 27, in had come this Cessna Skymaster with a number and description that had gone out to every airfield and airport in America, including the one in Duffrey; a Cessna whose pilot had identified himself as Dwight Renfield, point of origination, Wilmington, Delaware, an airfield that had never heard of "Renfield" or a Skymaster with tail number N101BL; the plane of a man who was almost surely a murderer.

"If he'd flown in here, he'd be in the stir now," one of the Delaware controllers had told Dees over the phone, but Dees wondered.

The Night Flier had landed in Duffrey just before midnight on the twenty-seventh, and "Dwight Renfield" had not only signed the Sarches' logbook but also had accepted Ray Sarch's invitation to come into the trailer, have a beer, and watch a rerun of *Gunsmoke* on the CBN cable network. Ellen Sarch had told all of this to a friend at the Duffrey Beauty Shoppe the following day. The friend was a woman named Selida McCammon, and when Dees asked how Ellen Sarch had seemed, Selida had paused and then said, "Dreamy, somehow. Like a high-school girl with a crush, almost seventy years old or not. Her color was so high, I thought it was makeup, until I started in on her perm. Then I saw that she was just ... you know ..." Selida McCammon shrugged. She knew what she meant but not how to say it.

"Het up," Dees suggested, and that made Selida McCammon laugh and clap her hands.

"Het up! That's it! You're a writer, all right!"

"Oh, I write like a boid," Dees said, and offered a smile he hoped looked good-humored and warm. This was an expression he had once practiced almost constantly and continued to practice with fair regularity in the bedroom mirror of the New York apartment he called his home, and in the mirrors of the hotels and motels that were *really* his home (for he spent much more time in places where the drinking glasses came sealed in plastic containers than he did in the place to which his bills and bank statements came—Dees was not the sort of man who got much personal mail, and that was the way he liked it, oh-ho, uh-huh). It seemed to work, for the woman's own smile broadened, but the truth was that Richard Dees had never felt good-humored and warm in his life. He had, as a kid and as a teenager, believed that these emotions did not exist at all; it was simply a masquerade, a social convention like the one that made girls say, "Oh, please, don't touch me there," when what they really wanted was for you not only to touch them there but fill "there" with about eight inches of blue steel. Later he had decided such feelings—and, perhaps, even love (although on that subject he continued to be an agnostic) —were real. He simply couldn't feel them. Well, maybe that wasn't so bad. There were quadriplegics out there. People with cancer out there. People with memory spans of twenty minutes or so out there.

The loss of a few emotions wasn't much beside stuff like that, was it? Dees thought not.

As long as you could stretch the muscles in your face the right way, you were all right.

It was no easier or harder than learning to wiggle your ears. And it didn't hurt. Once in a while there was a voice inside that asked him what he wanted, what his *own* inside view was, but Dees didn't *want* an inside view. Dees didn't *want* to be good-humored and warm, let alone love or to *be* in love. He wanted only four things:

1. To not want wanting.
2. Photographs.

He was better at writing, he knew that, but he liked the photographs better just the same. He liked to touch them. Two dimensions.

3. Dirt. Filth. Horror.
4. To uncover them before anyone else.

Richard Dees was a humble man with humble wants.

So the Night Flier had come into the little mom-and-pop operation that was the Duffrey Airfield. On one wall of the little office in which the Sarches had worked together, there had been a red-bordered FAA notice suggesting there was a fellow driving a Cessna Skymaster 337, tail number N101BL, who might have murdered two men. This man, the notice said, might or might not be an individual who called himself Dwight Renfield. The plane had landed. "Dwight Renfield" had almost surely spent much of that night and all the following day in the belly hold of his plane: a sitting duck who had not been potted.

The Sarches, so vigilant that they were willing to hit the fire alarm if they even smelled smoke, let alone saw fire, had done nothing. Ray, in fact, had invited the guy in for a beer and a touch of the tube. Had treated him like an old friend instead of a suspicious character. His wife had made an appointment at the Duffrey Beauty Shoppe, which Selida McCammon had found surprising; the Sarch woman's visits were usually as regular as clockwork, and this one was at least two weeks before she should have been in. Her instructions had been unusually explicit; she had not wanted just the usual perm but also a cut . . . and a little coloring as well.

"She wanted to look younger," Selida McCammon had said, more bemused than amused, which wasn't unusual, Dees supposed, in light of the result.

Ray Sarch?

He had called the FAA at Washington National to tell them to issue a NOTAM to remove Duffrey as an active airfield, barring a major incident—he was, in other words, closing shop.

He said he thought he was coming down with the flu.

That night, the two vigilant fire wardens had, in effect, burned to death. Ray Sarch was found in the little control room, his head torn off and cast into the far corner, where it sat on a ragged stump of neck in a pool of congealed blood, staring into the corner with wide, glazed eyes, as if there were actually something there to see.

His wife had been found in the bedroom of the Sarch trailer. She was in bed. She was dressed in a peignoir so new, it might never have been worn before that night. She was old, a deputy had told Dees (at twenty-five dollars he was a more expensive fuck than the Maine gin-head, but still worth it), but when you saw them that way, the look was unmistakable: She had been dressed for a lover, not a killer. Those huge, spike-sized holes were driven into her neck, one in the carotid, the other in the jugular. Her face was composed, her eyes closed, her hands on her bosom.

Although she had lost almost every drop of blood in her body, there were only spots on the pillows beneath her, and a few more spots on the book, which lay open on her stomach: *The Vampire Lestat* by Anne Rice.

The Night Flier?

Sometime before midnight on the twenty-eighth, during the early hours of the twenty-ninth, he had simply flown away.

Just like a boid.

Or a bat.

Richard Dees touched down in Wilmington seven minutes before official sunset. While he was throttling back, still spitting blood out of his mouth from the cut below his eye, he saw lightning strike down with blue-white fire so intense that it imprinted itself on his retinas for nearly a minute, revolving through half a rainbow of sickish, fading colors. On the heels of the bolt came the most deafening thunderclap he had ever heard; his subjective opinion of the blast's sonic power was confirmed when one of the windows in the passenger compartment, which had been stellated by the near miss with the Piedmont 727, coughed inward in a spray of junk-shop diamonds.

In the brilliant glare he saw a squat, cubelike building on the port side of Runway 34 impaled by the bolt. It exploded, exclaiming fire into the sky in a pyre that, although brilliant, did not even come close to the power of the bolt that had ignited it.

Like lighting a stick of dynamite with a baby nuke, Dees thought confusedly, and then: The genny. That was the genny.

The lights—all of them, the white lights that marked the edges of the runway and the bright red bulbs that marked its end—were suddenly gone, as if they had been no more than candles puffed out by a strong gust of wind. All at once, Dees was suddenly rushing at better than eighty miles an hour from dark into dark.

The blast of the explosion struck the Beech like a fist—did more than strike it, hammered it like a looping haymaker. The Beech, still hardly knowing it had become a ground-bound creature again, skittered affrightedly to starboard, rose, and came down with the right wheel pogoing up and down over something—some*things*—that Dees vaguely realized were landing lights.

Go port! his mind screamed. Go port, you asshole!

He almost did before his colder mind asserted itself. If he hauled the wheel to port at this speed, he would ground-loop. Probably wouldn't explode, considering how little fuel was left in the tanks, but it was possible. Or the Beech might simply twist apart, leaving Richard Dees from the gut on down twitching in his seat, while Richard Dees from the gut on up went in a different direction, trailing severed intestines like wire and dropping his kidneys like a couple of oversize chunks of birdshit.

Ride it out! he screamed at himself. Ride it out, you son of a bitch, ride it out!

Something—the genny's secondary LP tanks, he guessed when he had time for guessing—exploded then, buffeting the Beech even farther to starboard; but that was okay, it got him off the dead landing lights, and all at once he was running with relative smoothness again, port wheel on the edge of Runway 34, starboard wheel on the spooky verge between the lights and the ditch he had observed on the right of the runway. The Beech was still shuddering, but not badly, and he understood that he was running on one flat, the starboard tire shredded by the landing lights it had crushed.

But he was slowing, slowing; the Beech was understanding that it had become a different thing, a thing that belonged to the land once again. It was seventy . . . it was sixty . . . and Dees was relaxing when he saw the big Learjet looming ahead of him, parked insanely across the runway where the pilot had stopped on his taxi out to Runway 5.

He bore down on it, saw lighted windows, saw faces staring out at him with the gape of idiots in an asylum watching a magic trick, and then, without thinking, he pushed full right rudder, bouncing the Beech off the runway, into the ditch, missing the tail of what looked like a Lear 25 by approximately an inch and a half. He was aware he was screaming, whizzing more hot water gaily into his pants, but really aware of nothing but the *now* exploding in front of him as the Beech tried to become a thing of the air again, helpless to do so with the flaps down and the engines dropping revs but trying, anyway; there was a leap like a giant burp in the dying light of the secondary explosion, and then he was skidding across a taxiway, seeing the General Aviation Terminal for a moment with its corners lit by emergency lights that ran on storage batteries, seeing the parked planes—one of them almost surely the Night Flier's Skymaster—as dark crepe-paper silhouettes against a baleful orange light that was the sunset, now revealed by the parting thunderheads.

I'm going over! he screamed to himself, and the Beech *did* try to roll; the port wing struck a fountain of sparks from the taxiway nearest the terminal, and its tip broke free, wheeling off into the scrub where friction-heat awoke as a dim fire in the wet weeds.

Then the Beech was still, and the only sounds were the snowy roar of static from the radio, the sound of broken bottles dripping and fizzing their contents onto the carpet of the passenger compartment, and the frenzied hammering of Dees's own heart.

He had slammed the pop release on his harness and was on his feet, headed for the pressurized hatch even before he was totally sure he was alive.

What happened later he remembered with eidetic clarity. But from the moment the Beech skidded to a stop on the taxiway, ass-end to the Lear and tilted to one side, to the moment he heard the first screams from the terminal, all he remembered was having to get his camera, needing his camera. It was a Nikon. He'd bought it in a Toledo hockshop when he was seventeen and he'd kept it with him ever since. He had added lenses, but the basic box, scratched and dented in a couple of places, was exactly the same. The Nikon was the closest thing Dees had to a wife. It was in the elasticized pocket behind his seat. He remembered pulling it out and seeing that it was intact: he remembered that. It had survived the landing safe and unbroken, so maybe there was a God, after all.

Dees threw the hatch lever, jumped down, almost fell, and caught his camera before it could strike the concrete of the taxiway and shatter.

He looped the narrow leather strap twice around his neck like a noose and began sprinting for the terminal. Hearing a thunder-grumble. There was a breeze. It was on his face, but he felt it more clearly around his groin, because his pants were wet.

Then a thin, drilling shriek came from the General Aviation Terminal—a scream of mingled agony and horror. It was as if someone had slapped Dees across

the face. He came back to himself. He centered on his
goal again. He looked at his watch. It wasn't working.
Either the concussion had broken it or it had stopped.
It was one of those amusing antiques you had to wind
up, and he couldn't remember when he had last done it.

Was it sunset? *Was* it?

Another scream came—no, not a scream, a screech—
and the sound of breaking glass.

Sunset didn't matter. He ran.

More screams.

More breaking glass.

Dees ran faster, vaguely aware that the genny's
auxiliary tanks were still burning. He could smell gas
in the air. He was keenly aware of wet cloth clinging
to his privates. He seemed to be running in cement.
The terminal was getting closer, but not very fast. Not
fast enough.

*"Please, no! Please no! PLEASE NO PLEASE NO
PLEASEPLEASE NO NO NONO—"*

This scream, spiraling up and up, and suddenly he
heard a howl that was either laughter or contempt, a
sound an animal would make, a sound that was almost
human all the same.

He saw something dark and flailing shatter more
glass in the wall of the terminal that faced the parking
area—that wall was almost entirely glass—and saw the
bright blinks of glass in the emergency lights on the
corners of the building. The dark shape stopped flailing. It landed on the ramp with a soggy thud, rolled,
and Dees saw it was a man.

The storm was moving away, but heat lightning
flickered, and as Dees ran into the parking area, panting now, he saw it, finally saw it: the Night Flier's
plane, N101BL painted boldly on the tail. The letters
and numbers looked black in this light, but he knew
they were red and it didn't matter, anyway. The camera was loaded with black-and-white. It was armed
with fast film and a smart flash, which would fire only
when the light was too low for the film's speed.

The Skymaster's belly hold hung open like the mouth

of a corpse. Below it was a clot of earth in which things squirmed and moved.

Dees skidded to a stop. Tried to bring the camera up. Almost strangled himself. Cursed. Unwound the strap. Aimed.

From the terminal came a long, high, drilling shriek—that of a woman or a child. Dees barely noticed. The thought that there was a slaughter going on in there was followed by the thought that slaughter would only fatten the story, and then both thoughts were gone as he snapped three quick shots of the Cessna, making sure to get the gaping belly hold and the number on the tail. The auto-winder hummed.

Dees ran on. More glass smashed. There was another thud as another body was thrown out onto the cement like a human rag doll. Dees looked, saw confused movement, the billowing of something that *might* have been a cape . . . but he was too far to tell. He turned. Snapped two more of the plane, these shots dead-on. The gaping belly hold and the pile of earth would be stark and undeniable in the print.

Then he whirled and ran for the terminal.

The fact that he was armed with only an old Nikon never crossed his mind.

Dees stopped ten yards away. Three bodies out here, two clearly adults, one of each sex, one that might have been either a small woman or a girl of thirteen or so. It was hard to tell, because her head was gone.

Dees aimed the camera and fired off six quick shots, the flash flickering its own white lightning, the auto-winder making its contented little whizzing sound.

His mind never lost count. He was loaded with thirty-six shots. He had taken eleven. That left twenty-five. There was more film stuffed into the deep pockets of his slacks, and that was great . . . if he got a chance to reload.

Dees reached the terminal and yanked open the door.

*   *   *

He thought he had seen everything there was to see, but he had *never* seen anything like this. *Never*.

How many? his mind yammered. How many? Six? Eight?

The place was a butcher shop.

Bodies and parts of bodies lay everywhere. He saw a leg; shot it. A ragged torso; shot it. Here was a man who was still alive, a man in a mechanic's coverall, and for a weird moment he thought it was the gin-head from Maine, but this guy was bald. His face appeared to be split open from forehead to chin. His nose lay in open halves.

Dees shot it.

His gut was heaving up and down, high waves in a gale.

How many? How many shots? he screamed at himself.

For the first time in seventeen years he had lost count.

Blood was splashed up the walls. Blood lay in pools on the worn linoleum. The bulletin board—where, undoubtedly, an FAA warning about N101BL was tacked up—was splattered and dripping like a shower someone hadn't quite turned off.

There was a desk, and beside it was a snack rack.

Stuck to a bag of Cheez-Doodles was a staring blue eyeball.

Dees shot it.

And that was all.

All he could take.

He saw the sign: REST ROOMS. An arrow below. He ran for it, the camera flapping.

The first one was marked with a human shape, and since it didn't have a triangle superimposed on its torso, that made it the men's room. Dees didn't care if it was the aliens' room. He was weeping, weeping in great, harsh, hoarse sobs. He didn't know they were coming from him. It had been years since he had wept. He hadn't wept since he was a kid.

He slammed through the door, skidded like a skier

almost out of control, and grabbed the edge of the second basin in line.

He leaned over it, and everything came out in a rich and stinking flood, some of it splattering back onto his face, some landing in brownish clots on the mirror. He smelled the chicken Creole he'd eaten for lunch and threw up again, making a huge grating sound like overstressed machinery about to strip its gears.

Jesus, he thought, oh, my Jesus, he isn't a man, can't be a man—

That was when he heard the sound.

It was a sound he had heard a thousand times before, or maybe ten thousand, a sound that was commonplace in any American man's life . . . but now it filled him with a dread and a creeping terror beyond all his experience or belief.

It was the sound of a man voiding into a urinal.

There were three urinals. He could see them in the vomit-splattered mirror.

There was no one at any of the urinals.

Dees thought: Vampires. They. Don't. Cast. Reflec—

Then he saw reddish liquid striking the porcelain of the center urinal, saw it running down that porcelain, saw it swirling into the geometric arrangement of holes.

There was no stream in the air.

He saw it only when it struck the dead porcelain.

That was when it became visible.

When it struck the lifeless porcelain.

He was frozen. He stood, hands on the edge of the basin, his mouth and throat and nose and sinuses thick with the taste and smell of chicken Creole, and watched some invisible creature void its invisible and inhuman bladder.

I am, he thought dimly, watching a vampire take a piss.

Somewhere sirens were warbling, coming closer.

It seemed that the bloody urine went on striking the porcelain, becoming visible, and swirling down the curved surface of the urinal to the holes forever.

Dees didn't move.

I'm dead, he thought.

In the mirror he saw the chromed handle go down by itself.

Water roared.

Dees heard a rustle and flap and knew it was a cape, just as he knew that if he turned around, his life would end.

He remained frozen where he was, his hands biting the edge of the basin.

A low, ageless voice said, "Don't come after me. I know you. I know all about you."

Dees moaned. More water ran into his pants.

"Open your camera," the ageless voice said.

My film! part of Dees cried. My film! All I've got! All I've got! My pictures! My—

Another dry, batlike flap of the cape. Although Dees could see nothing he sensed the Night Flier was closer.

"Now."

His film *wasn't* all he had.

There was his life.

Such as it was.

Or might be.

He saw himself whirling, seeing the Night Flier, a creature that was more bat that human, a grotesque Thing splattered with blood and torn hair; saw himself snapping shot after shot while the auto-winder hummed . . . but there would be nothing.

Nothing at all.

Because you couldn't take their pictures, either.

"You're real," he croaked, never moving, his hands on the edge of the basin, blood now beginning to run from the palms.

"So are you," the ageless voice rasped, and now Dees felt the breath of the Night Flier stir the hackles on the back of his neck, smelled the crypts that were the Night Flier's breath. "For now . . .

"Last chance. Open your camera."

With hands that seemed totally numb, Dees opened his Nikon.

Air slashed past his face; it felt like moving razor blades. For a moment he saw a long white hand, streaked with blood; saw long, ragged nails silted with filth.

Then his film parted and spooled spinelessly out of his camera.

There was another dry flap. Another stinking breath. For a moment he thought the Night Flier would kill him, anyway. Then he saw the door of the men's room open by itself.

He must have eaten very well tonight, Dees thought, and immediately threw up again, this time directly onto the reflection of his own staring face.

The door wheezed shut.

Dees stayed right where he was for perhaps three minutes after the door had wheezed shut.

He stayed there until the sirens were almost on top of the terminal.

He stayed there until he heard the cough and roar of airplane engines.

A Cessna Skymaster 337.

Then he walked out of the bathroom on legs like stilts, struck the far wall, rebounded, and walked back into the terminal. He slid in a pool of blood and almost fell.

"*Hold it, mister!*" a cop screamed behind him. "*Hold it right there! One move and you're dead!*"

Dees didn't even turn around.

"Press, dickface," Dees said, and went to one of the shattered windows. With exposed film still straggling from his camera like long strips of brown confetti, he stood there and watched the Cessna accelerate down Runway 5. For a moment it was a black shape against the bellowing fire of the genny and the auxiliary tanks, a shape like a bat, and then it was up, it was gone, and the cop was slamming Dees up against the wall hard enough to make his nose bleed and he didn't care, he didn't care about anything, and when the sobs began to tear their way out of his chest again, he closed his eyes, and still he saw the Night Flier's bloody urine striking the curved procelain, becoming visible, and swirling down the drain.

He thought he would see it forever.

PAUL HAZEL, born 1947 in Bridgeport, Connecticut, is one of America's leading fantasists, known for his elegant, mannered prose and a penchant for wordplay. His *Finnbranch* trilogy—*Yearwood, Undersea,* and *Winterking*—is a complex and brooding jeremiad filled with dark mystery, magic, and transformation. "Having a Woman at Lunch" is Hazel's first horror story.

Paul Hazel

Having a Woman at Lunch

I am engaged, as are Mr. Waymarsh and Messrs. Pendennis and Malesherbes, in the manufacture of a certain small article of domestic utility. We lunch together every day at a nearby establishment where JoAnne attends to our wants. Mr. Pendennis is the financial officer. Malesherbes sets the price and writes up orders. His lunch, these last twenty years, is grilled beef on a bed of crisp lettuce, two pieces of buttered toast, and, when JoAnne clears the table, a single cup of English Breakfast tea. Pendennis, whose taste is more catholic, prefers stews or fish. Waymarsh, the assistant director, will, of course, eat anything; but, the menu being limited, six days out of seven, after a considerable furrowing of his brow, he settles on mackerel. Myself, whenever the weather is balmy and the clerks give me no trouble, I prefer tripe.

It had seemed, always, so perfect, so exactly the right thing . . . until Cecily.

Cecily was twenty-six, or perhaps twenty-seven. Her hair, which was worn in masses of lazy tangles down to her shoulders, was the color of corn silk. Like corn silk, it tended to darken. Over the space of weeks it would turn a sort of a drab yellow-brown until, through the agency of feminine science, it was magically restored. To our credit, we were never scandalized. Her ankles, as Pendennis was quick to notice, were as slender as a schoolgirl's. "Half the thickness," Pendennis reported to us on the day he first saw her emerging from the director's office, "as those of the cows in accounting."

We smiled knowingly. They were his cows, after all, Betsy Teeling and the two Monicas, the greater Miss McGuffin and the lesser (although equally ruminant) Miss Halliday: accounts receivable, accounts payable, and payroll.

"The director's to have a new secretary, then?" I surmised.

Pendennis let his spoon sink among the parsnips and gravy and grinned. A superior grin, I thought, full of secret reconnaissance.

"Purchasing," he said. He gave a poke to something on his plate, then met our eyes squarely. "Head of purchasing."

"You m-must be m-mistaken," Malesherbes sputtered.

"Not at all," said Waymarsh, who, being the director's right hand, was in on everything. He speared the last morsel of fish, depositing the fragment daintily under his mustache. Untroubled, he then sipped at his coffee. "Do you suppose," he asked, "we could have some nice apple crumble?"

"W-what do you mean?" Malesherbes protested, so agitated that he tore the napkin away from his chin.

"Or a tart," Waymarsh continued.

"That . . ." Malesherbes began, overwhelmed. His ample face reddened. "That woman!"

"Miss Cecily Hart," Waymarsh said evenly. "Five years with Bernham and Maggotty. And a degree."

"Impossible," Malesherbes said.

But it was true. That same afternoon, the director summoned us into the great turret office from which, his suspenders stretched over his abdomen, he could observe the efforts of his foremen and, as important, could be seen by them.

"The modern age," the director announced, glowing with well-being and confidence, "demands, I think, now and then, some small concessions."

Malesherbes looked apprehensive.

Waymarsh, allowed to sit in the director's presence, smiled at us benevolently. He was a placid, otherwordly

man. His buttocks planted comfortably in the director's furniture, he accepted his place without question.

"Women," the director said, "or so I've been told,
purchase ninety-seven percent of all household articles. Their economic power, not to put too fine a point
on it, gentlemen, is extraordinary. And yet, all these
years, we have never . . ." He turned abruptly and,
gazing out over the working floor, saw, I had no
doubt, the conspicuous absence of women. He looked
back. "Even *here*," he said significantly. "Especially
here, in our own inner sanctum . . ."

"I quite agree," Waymarsh joined in, because the
decision had already been made.

"Long overdue," said Pendennis.

Malesherbes tried not to look miserable.

The director placed his arm round Malesherbes's
shoulder. "I knew I could count on you," he said,
pleased. He pushed a button on the intercom. Very
quickly, the outer door opened. Ushered in by the
director's large-bottomed secretary, the young woman
glided toward us.

"Miss Hart," the director said.

One by one we shook hands with her. Her grip was
firm. Her breasts, secured carefully, never moved.
Under one slender arm she carried a clipboard.

"Charmed," said Waymarsh.

"Likewise," said Malesherbes, trying not to seem
disappointed.

It was Pendennis, however, who invited her to lunch.

"On Wednesday," he told us, when it was already
too late.

"Just what do you think we will talk about?"
Malesherbes fumed. He stared into the cup containing
the sodden bag of English Breakfast tea and, as if
already under the influence of her alien presence,
pulled at the short hairs of his nostrils.

"We will speak as we always speak," I suggested,
"and offer her a cigar."

"But we don't smoke," complained Malesherbes.

"It's a joke, John," Pendennis told him.

"Not to me," Malesherbes answered sullenly.

* * *

On Wednesday I had to park in the lot behind St. Stephen's and walk over. Nevertheless, it was still ten till noon when JoAnne took my coat and hung it neatly next to the others.

"Don't we look dapper." JoAnne smiled.

"Only thing I had clean," I protested, not certain why I was apologizing.

Pendennis, who was watching the door, wore a tie I'd never seen. What little hair he had was lacquered and parted. Waymarsh was fitted out in a black pinstripe. Malesherbes, on the other hand, had left his wretched sailor's cap clamped over his forehead. He merely stared when Pendennis suggested it was common courtesy to remove it.

"You're being ironic, of course," said Waymarsh.

"I'm being myself," Malesherbes grumbled.

"You've never worn your hat inside," I corrected him.

Malesherbes laughed inexplicably. "But I've meant to. Surely intention counts for something."

We might have left him alone after that. Yet when JoAnne came around the counter with his plate of grilled beef and her notepad, Pendennis waved her away.

"Just a few minutes," he said. "We're expecting one more."

Horrified, Malesherbes watched his lunch retreating toward the kitchen. "You've no cause," he whispered.

"Cause enough," said Pendennis.

"Twenty years of grilled beef," Waymarsh reminded him. "Which is more than ample cause, I should think."

Malesherbes stared at the bare table. "It's what I like."

"That's what worries me," said Waymarsh.

"I'm going to order a chop," Pendennis interjected.

Each of us looked at him in wonder.

"Because of the occasion," he said brightly.

"Nonsense," said Malesherbes. But by then the rest of us were already standing.

* * *

In our hearts, I am certain, we never truly believed she would come. By nature and habit we were unprepared for the company of young women. Pendennis and I were bachelors. Waymarsh was a widower. In the evening he read books on horticulture or went to lectures at the university. Faced with the willowy presence in the doorway, he trembled. Pendennis, whose fault this was, suddenly examined his shirtfront and prayed, I imagine, for death.

Cecily crossed in front of the counter and, watched by the barman, turned immediately in our direction.

"Am I late?" she inquired. "Have you already ordered?"

Her hair was unkempt and windblown and easily the most startling shade of refurbished yellow I had ever seen.

Choosing blindness, Waymarsh took off his spectacles. "No, not at all, Miss Hart," he said softly.

"Cecily," she insisted.

Waymarsh offered his large damp hand in her general direction. "Harold," he whispered.

"Patrick," said Pendennis bravely.

"Desmond," I told her.

Malesherbes, however, was silent. Unnoticing, Cecily sat down beside him.

"What are you going to have?" she asked.

Malesherbes looked to see if she was making fun of him.

"Pendennis is having a chop," I said. "And I shall have tripe."

Waymarsh's brow furrowed as he considered the list on the chalkboard. "I was thinking of mackerel," he said tentatively.

"How wonderfully different you all are." She laughed, smiling because Pendennis and I had smiled. She turned again to Malesherbes. "Really, you must tell me as well," she said, "for I intend to be guided by experience."

For a moment I thought I detected a conciliatory movement in Malesherbes's left eye; but he would not be goaded. When the returning JoAnne began writing up orders, he fussed with the silverware. Little droplets of moisture glistened on his broad upper lip.

"Are you ready, John?" JoAnne finally asked him.

"Nothing," he said.

JoAnne looked at him suspiciously.

"There is nothing here," he said loudly. At intervals he dragged the prongs of his fork on the tablecloth. "Just stones," he muttered, making a face. "And stinking black weed." The ranging fork came precariously near Cecily's elbow. All at once he looked up.

Across the table from him were men he knew. Perhaps seeing Pendennis, Waymarsh, and myself helped to settle him. "It has been my experience, Miss Hart," he said almost calmly, "that the blackest weed is the most inedible."

Cecily turned away nervously.

"It is useful to understand," I explained, "that he was once stranded."

"On a rock," Pendennis added.

"East of Newfoundland," said Waymarsh. "In the Atlantic."

"Without—" I continued.

"Are you ready?" interrupted JoAnne, who over the years had heard all she wanted to hear about the ship's foundering. (Thirteen days, we had told her, and just one tin of biscuits.)

"John!" JoAnne cried.

Malesherbes shook his head dully. His fatted jowls wobbled.

Exasperated, JoAnne moved behind Cecily's chair. "And you, miss?"

"Trout," Cecily whispered: a single trembling syllable, leaping and, as if distrustful of light and air, vanishing.

There could not have been a worse beginning. When the trout was presented, Cecily took several bites to be sociable, then, pressed quietly to the back of her chair, sipped a glass of cold water and waited. Pendennis coughed. From his face I could tell that the chop was tough. The tripe was delightful, but with Malesherbes staring emptily at the tablecloth, I hadn't the stomach for it.

"Were the rest of you sailors?" Cecily asked at last.

"We were army," we told her.

"North Africa," said Waymarsh, poking mechanically at his mackerel.

"Burma," said Pendennis. He pulled at the chop. "The Philippines."

"Before you were born. Likely before your parents were," I said.

With that Cecily laughed again, a little less uncertainly, revealing a diminutive pink tongue. "Surely not as old as that." She smiled.

It was at that moment, deflected from the chop, that Pendennis's knife jumped at her finger.

Pendennis fought to regain his balance, lost it, and fell, adding the weight of his chest and arm to the knife's unexpected acceleration. An instant later he lurched upward. But by then the tip of Cecily's finger, severed at the joint, had rolled to a stop in front of Malesherbes.

After that everything seemed to happen at once. Cecily moaned. Pendennis, ashen, was blubbering. He kept asking himself how on earth had it happened and telling Waymarsh and the waitresses who had come running that it was an accident. To keep the blood from dripping, I had lifted Cecily's arm over her head while Waymarsh swaddled her finger in napkins. In the confusion it was only myself, I thought, who had seen what Malesherbes had done with the small lump of flesh.

Nevertheless, I was relieved when, early the next morning, Pendennis stopped at my desk.

"It was clearly an act of folly," he said. "All the same, I must admit some admiration."

I did my best to look puzzled, but he grinned.

"Still, you seemed shocked," I reminded him.

"I've invited her again," he said slyly. His grin widened. "As an act of contrition."

*　　*　　*

Cecily was wearing a bandage. Because of it, she needed a hand with her coat from JoAnne and assistance from Waymarsh with her chair.

"It must be painful," I said.

"It is," she acknowledged.

Her cheeks were pale. When she smiled, which she managed halfheartedly, I could see that her eyes were darkened, less able to focus. Nonetheless, suddenly she looked up.

"This is an important job for me," she said earnestly. "It is necessary, therefore, that I have sound relations with you all." Her lips turned up determinedly at the corners, without revealing her teeth. "Sound business relations."

"You're right, of course," said Waymarsh.

"I can't imagine it could be otherwise," Pendennis told her.

Soon JoAnne brought our coffee. She leaned down to Waymarsh and, while he wrinkled his brow, dutifully wrote "mackerel" on her notepad although the kitchen had set the fish out for him the moment he had come through the door. Nor was it likely that either Pendennis or myself surprised her. Yet she seemed uneasy.

"And you, John?" she asked.

But, although Malesherbes shook his head, he was smiling.

This time, I am saddened to say, it was my knife that slipped.

At the start of the next week, JoAnne needlessly set the chalkboard on a chair across from us.

"Whatever happened to that unfortunate young woman?" she asked.

"Vanished," said Pendennis.

"Walked out without notice," Waymarsh corrected him.

"Without so much as a word," I said evenly, meaning to bring the conversation to a close.

"Pretty thing, though," JoAnne persisted. "Poor child. So susceptible to accidents."

With a sigh, she brought her pencil to her notepad. "Well, what will it be today, gentlemen?"

"Just coffee," said Waymarsh.

"The same," replied Pendennis, his head low, so that the twinkle in his eye remained hidden.

JoAnne watched him uncertainly.

"Coffee," I echoed.

Malesherbes drew a sandwich wrapped in waxed paper from his pocket. "Tea," he said firmly. "A nice hot cup of English Breakfast tea."

One by one, when JoAnne turned her back, we brought out our sandwiches.

"We might try a dollop of mustard," Pendennis suggested.

"And pepper," Waymarsh said thoughtfully. "I have in mind to try pepper."

"I believe you will find it excellent as it is," Malesherbes reassured them.

Carefully we unfolded the paper.

Between the slices of bread I could see the layers of pale pink meat. There would be no fat, I was certain. The pieces had been trimmed expertly by Malesherbes himself, late last evening, while we watched. Nevertheless, just for a moment I reconsidered the possibility of tripe. Odd, I thought, how tastes change. It had seemed, always, so perfect, so exactly the right thing . . . until Cecily.

DENNIS ETCHISON, born 1943 in Stockton, California, is known for his masterful short fiction, the best of which has been collected in *The Dark Country* and *Red Dreams*. His other books include the novel *Darkside* and the anthologies *Masters of Darkness* and *Cutting Edge*. Also a talented screenwriter, his work in Hollywood may have inspired the story that follows.

Dennis Etchison

The Blood Kiss

She had told herself that it might never get this far, all
the while hoping against hope that it would. Now she
could no longer be sure which was the delusion and
which the reality. It was out of her control.

"*Chris*? You still here?" It was Rip, the messenger
boy who had hung around long enough to become
Executive in Charge of Special Projects. Whatever,
exactly, that denoted. He caught the door as he passed
her office, pivoting on one foot and swinging the other
up to cross his knee with his ankle, the graceful pose
of a dancer at rest or the arch maneuver of a runner
pretending that he was so far ahead he no longer had
to hurry. She couldn't decide. She studied him ab-
stractedly and feigned amusement as he asked, "Aren't
you going to the party tonight?"

"Do you care whether I go to the party tonight?"

"Sure." He grinned boyishly, as though forgetting
for the moment that he was thirty-five years old. "The
network's going to be there, you know." He glanced
up and down the hall, ducked inside and lowered his
voice to make a joke of his naked ambition. "You
hear what we're getting for Milo?"

"Let me guess," she said. "A belly dancer? No, that
was for his birthday. A go-go boy from Chippendale's?"

Rip imploded a laugh. "You've got to be kidding.
He can't come out of the closet till the third season."

"You never know." You wish, she thought. Closet,
my ass. I could tell you some things about Milo, if you
really want to know. But you probably wouldn't be-

lieve me; it wouldn't fit your game plan, would it? Milo the Trouser Pilot. Dream on. "I give up," she said, "what?"

Rip closed the door behind him. "We hired this bimbo from Central Casting. She's going to come in—rush in at five minutes of twelve, all crying that she just totaled Milo's car out front. You know, the white 450SL? She's so sorry, she's going to pay for everything, *if her insurance hasn't expired*. Milo's freaking, right? So she gets him up to the bedroom where the phone is, she's looking for the number, she starts to break down, she whips off her dress and offers herself—when all of a sudden, surprise! It's a strip-o-gram! Happy Valentine's Day! We're all coming. You got a camera, Chrissie?"

"I'll bring my 3-D."

"What?"

"See you there, R. Right now I've got to retype my outline." What time's it getting to be? she wondered.

"You mean 'Zombies'? I thought it was all set."

"It is. But Milo had some last-minute suggestions. Nothing major. He wants it on his desk tomorrow morning."

"Great," said Rip, no longer listening. "Well, don't work too hard."

If I don't, she thought, who will?

"And Chrissie?"

"Yeah?"

"Have yourself a fabulous evening, stag or drag. Remember, *Don't Open the Door*'s headed straight for Number One—we've got it made! Uh, thanks to your episode, of course. 'Queen of the Zombies' is going to put us over the top!"

"Thanks for telling me that, R."

And don't call me Chrissie, she thought as he let himself out.

I have it made, you have it made, they have it made, we have it made. . . . I'd like to see them, Milo or anybody else in this production company, do the real work for once: interviewing writers, extracting stories, rewriting all night so there's something more than high concept to give the network. . . . I should have stayed a secretary. At least I'd sleep better.

But then where would they be? And where would *I* be? Back in Fresno, she thought. At my parents'. Instead of here, scuttling around behind the scenes to hold this surrogate family together. If I had a dollar for every time I've saved Milo's tight little ass the night before a pitch . . .

With stories like this one, she thought, shuffling papers.

I finally found the right one. Oh, didn't I. This time, miraculously, it was all there when it came in over the transom; the only real work I had to do was to punch it up a bit and hand it to M for the presentation. The perfect episode to launch the second season. That's what they called it. I wanted them to think it was mine, let's be honest. And it worked. Am I really supposed to give back this office for the sake of an abstraction? Who is Roger Ryman? With the specifics changed it will be all but unrecognizable by the time it shoots—I'll see to that; they'll let me do the script. Who else? And with it will come a full credit at last, Guild membership. . . . Who will be the wiser? Ryman is probably earning an honest living somewhere, and better off in the long run. He'll never see it. I'll bet he doesn't even have cable.

But what if one of his friends sees it?

Forget it, Chrissie. *Chris.* You're psyching yourself out.

You wanted it this way, admit it. You did.

She removed the last sheet of her latest revision from the typewriter, the one incorporating the changes from today's meeting with Milo, and began proofreading from page one:

QUEEN OF THE ZOMBIES

by

Christine Cross

1. 24-HOUR SUPERMARKET—NIGHT

Three o'clock in the morning. The market is under siege—by the walking dead.

Zombie shoppers converge on the <u>produce de-partment</u>, where the NIGHT MANAGER and a CHECKER, his girlfriend, are hiding behind the lettuce. He's got to get her out of there before they spot her. They want something more than fruit and vegetables.

He makes it to the p.a. system, grabs the mi-crophone, announces a special on liver as a di-version. The zombies shamble off to the <u>meat department.</u>

He sends the CHECKER crawling to the front door—but now zombie reinforcements are pour-ing in from outside. She changes course, sidles between the aisles, is pressed back to the <u>meat department,</u> where the zombies are busy feasting on liver.

One lone zombie arrives at the end of the cold case. All the meat is gone. Rings the bell with thick, jerky movements. No answer. So he climbs up over the counter, grabs the BUTCHER hid-ing there, lifts him, sticks a hand into the BUTCH-ER's abdomen and takes his liver.

As the feeding frenzy continues, the CHECKER is splattered with blood and guts. She screams.

"CUT!"

We see that a movie is being shot in the market. But the GIRL who plays the CHECKER won't stop screaming. As the zombies take off their masks she runs from the set, hysterical.

"Great!" the DIRECTOR says to his FX MAN. "Only next time more blood, okay, Marty?"

He goes off to find the GIRL.

*   *   *

2. OUTSIDE

In the parking lot, the DIRECTOR comforts
her. She wants to please, knows she's not giving
him what he needs, but it's too much for her.
She's cracking. She's about ready to get on the bus
back to Indiana.

The DIRECTOR needs her. She's going to be
the Queen of the Zombies. He sends her back to
the Holiday Inn. A hot bath, rest—what else can
he do for her? He'll even rehearse her later, in
private, if that's what it takes.

She put down the pages. Perfect, and so was the rest
of it. Now it really moved. Screw the outline, she
thought; I could go to script right now, while I've got
the momentum, if Milo didn't need to send this version to the network for approval first. A formality. I
could keep working—I didn't want to go to that
godawful party, anyway. I can have it done ahead of
schedule. . . . They'll finally realize how important I
am to this operation. It might even occur to Milo that
he needs an Associate Producer. Why not?

Was he still in his office? She could pay her respects
now, beg off for the evening, explain that she's going
home to work. That would impress the hell out of
him. Wouldn't it?

She clipped her pages together and reached for her
purse.

The hallway smelled faintly of disinfectant, and in
the distance she heard the bump and rattle of waste
baskets as the cleaning woman moved from room to
room in the building, wiping up other people's messes
for them and making things right again. As Chris
passed the reception area she saw the cart of brooms
and cleansers behind a half-closed door, and beyond,
through the window in Rip's office, the skyline darkening under a band of air made filthy by another day
in the city. It was later than she had thought.

"Good night," she called out.

The cleaning woman straightened and wiped her
heavy hands on her uniform, then let her arms hang

limp with palms open, as if afraid to be accused of stealing. Her face was flat and expressionless.

"Have a nice—nice holiday," Chris added. Well, it wasn't really a holiday. Did the woman even understand English?

Before she went on they exchanged a last glance. The other's gaze was steady and all-accepting, beyond hope and yet strangely at peace. There was a hint of disapproval in the deadpan face; it left Chris vaguely uneasy, as if she were a teenager spotted sneaking in or out of her bedroom. In fact the look was almost pitying. Why? She lowered her eyes and moved away.

She rapped on Milo's door, then entered without waiting for permission.

The room was empty. Of course he hadn't bothered to say good night. Why should he? He never had before. That would change, of course. She had had her office for three days, but it would take a while for that to sink in for all of them. Things would be different around here soon enough.

She saw the usual signs of a hasty departure. A row of empty Coke cans, a drawer still pulled out for Milo's feet, a flurry of message slips like unfilled prescriptions curling next to the phone, a rat's nest of papers teetering at the edge of the desk.

In spite of herself she found the sight more touching than appalling. He needed someone to bring order to his life, to tidy up after hours each night. He couldn't do it alone. It wasn't his fault, she reasoned; it was his nature. . . . She felt like the sister who corrected his homework for him while he slept, the girlfriend who slipped him answers to the big test, the mother who saw to it that his hair was combed before he left for school. She was none of these things, she knew, but soon he would recognize her worth. The days of being taken for granted were over.

She smiled as she crossed the office and set her corrected outline triumphantly on the glass desktop, where it would be waiting for him in the morning. He couldn't miss it.

She stacked the message slips, centering her pages

between the overflowing ashtray and the rings left by his coffee cup. She positioned his paperweight to hold the pages in place, aligned a pencil on either side to frame them, and started to leave.

The cart was clattering out of Rip's office, heading this way.

What if the cleaning woman rearranged things further, slid the pages to the bottom of the wrong pile?

Chris would have to tell her not to touch the desk.

But what if she could not make the woman understand?

She sighed and emptied the ashtray herself, dumped the cans into the waste basket, wiped the glass top and lined up the rest of his artifacts so that nothing on the desk would have to be touched. As she pushed his notepad under the phone and made ready to leave before being caught in the act, the bell within the phone mechanism tolled once, disturbed by the impact. She blinked.

And saw what was written on the top page of the pad.

She blinked again, reread it, her mind racing to understand.

It was in Milo's familiar scrawl, his last memo of the day. She had no trouble making it out. It read:

BILL S. TO WRITE QUEEN OF THE Z'S. WHO'S HIS AGENT?

She stared at it.

She put her hands on her hips, shifted her weight to one foot, then the other, looked out the window and saw nothing but blackness, and read it one more time before her eyes began to sting. The meaning was unmistakable.

Milo had already assigned someone else to do the full script.

She was not even in the running.

She never had been.

She would be lucky to receive a split credit. No, probably not even that much.

Suddenly the scales lifted from her eyes.

She could already envision another writer's name on

the screen. Perhaps Milo's alone. It had happened before.

It follows, she thought. God, does it ever.

And I didn't even see it coming.

Of course she wouldn't be able to file a protest, because that could lead to an arbitration that might reveal the true author whose work she herself had appropriated.

I have, she thought, been had. Again.

But this time I'm not going to settle for the bone they've tossed me. Not now.

This time it stops here.

She picked up the ashtray and hurled it across the room. It smashed into the framed LeRoy Neiman print hanging on the wall. Then she took back the pages and walked out of the office, bits of broken glass sticking to the soles of her shoes and grinding underfoot.

Startled, the cleaning woman stepped aside.

"Not this time," Chris told her through tears of rage. "*Comprende*? I—I'm sorry. Excuse me. . . ."

I've made a mistake. A terrible, terrible mistake.

Or someone has.

* * *

In her office, she riffled through the file until she found the original draft synopsis, submitted without an agent by an unknown whom she had never met, Roger R. Ryman. He had included both his home and work phone numbers on the title page.

She throttled the receiver, breaking a fingernail as she dialed.

At first he didn't recognize her name. But when she said the magic words, *Don't Open the Door,* he remembered the series and his submission and almost squeezed through the phone to lick her face.

Yes, he would meet her anywhere, anytime.

She gave him Milo's address.

He didn't think it at all odd that she asked him to meet her at a Valentine's party.

3. AT THE HOLIDAY INN

She calls home tearfully. She's getting ready for that bath when the DIRECTOR walks in.

Everything's going to be all right. You can do it, he tells her. He'll work with her personally. He takes the part of a zombie during their run-through, touches her, grabs her, enfolding her. She responds desperately, forgetting the script. She needs him. And she thinks he needs her.

* * *

4. LATER

She calls home again—but with a different story this time. Yes, she's doing okay. She's going to make it out here, after all.

"And Mama? I met a man. Not just any man. He's wonderful, so kind. He really cares what happens to me...."

Great, she thought. Now the only question is, Which one is he?

Bodies of all sizes and shapes streamed past her, arrayed in costumes of one sort or another—heart-shaped hats, dresses with arrows, shoes with cuddly designs, kitschy T-shirts, enameled pins, patterned head-bands, pastel jogging suits from the Beverly Center, ersatz camp from Melrose Avenue. Teddy bears lurked in corners with *billets-doux* pinned to their bibs; Mylar balloons drubbed at the ceiling like air bubbles at the surface of an aquarium. She gasped for breath as unidentifiable people bobbed around her, all luminous collars and teeth under the ultraviolet lights, and searched for an opening before the pressure of the music closed in on her again. As she swam against the flow for the nearest door, something like a pincer tried to grasp her thigh, while in the shadows the bears with their shiny black sharks' eyes seemed to move their heads, following her progress.

* * *

Another record began to pound, "Waiting Out the Eighties" by the Coupe de Villes, as long-necked men with trimmed mustaches collected around a garish buffet in the kitchen. She had almost passed through when she noticed a huge, dyed pâté, its top cleaved to resemble the wings of a gull in flight. The center collapsed to reveal a dull, livery interior as the men dipped *hors d'oeuvres* into the mold and made jokes, a thin film of workout sweat glazing their receding hairlines. She recognized the most animated of the conversationalists.

"Rip . . ."

He grasped her shoulder and drew her to arm's length, holding her until he finished his joke, as though she had intruded on an audition. When he finished he threw back his head and laughed too loudly, his Adam's apple bouncing up and down in a vigorous swallowing motion. Finally he turned to her.

"Chrissie, love!" He pulled her closer. "Mark, I'd like you to meet our new Story Editor."

"Rip, have you seen . . .?"

"No, I don't know where Milo's scampered off to. But I'll bet he's up to no good." He hooked a thumb at the ceiling. "Try topside."

"Rip, if anyone asks for me . . ."

"If I were you, love—" Rip winked. "I wouldn't disturb him just yet."

I'm on my own, she thought. I always have been. The rest was an illusion.

"Never mind." She hoisted a fresh champagne glass, emptied it. "See you at midnight," she said, slipping through to the stairs.

There were a lot of voices up there. Perhaps that was where she would find what she was looking for. It was getting late, and she had to have everything in place before the fireworks started.

5. MAKEUP AREA—THE NEXT DAY

She's in the chair, getting the coddling she needs from her new family. The MAKEUP MAN is kind, sensitive. She may have left her real family back home, but at last she feels that she belongs somewhere.

When she leaves the chair, the MAKEUP MAN and CREW change their tune. The poor kid's getting to be a pain. She's too nervous, high-strung, dangerously unstable. But it's too late to replace her. Time is running out.

* * *

6. ON THE SET

She breaks down again. The DIRECTOR tries to coach her but it's still not enough. She's too insecure. After take twelve, she pleads with him for the chance to do it again.

"Tell me the way you told me last night. I only want it to be good."

"That's all I want, too," he tells her.

The dim stairway was tricky. A blur of zippy, ironic faces as she ascended: young men without sideburns and casually elegant young women dragged along like camp followers, their made-up smiles fixed and grimly determined. Her wrist brushed something cold and slick. It was a heart-shaped satin pillow, carried as an offering by someone of indeterminate gender. She drew away and hugged the wall as she stepped over sodden paper plates; she made out an imprint of two lovebirds billing and cooing beneath half-eaten potato salad and drooping chicken wings.

"Excuse me," she said.

"Excuse *me*," said the person with the pillow. "Are you the one?"

"I hope so," she said, averting her eyes and hurrying on. Then the words and the masculine timbre of the voice registered. She stopped, looking back.

"I beg your pardon," she said, "but . . ."

Below, a nostalgic sixties strobe light flickered over dancing heads, rendering them all as anonymous as extras.

She felt as if she were still trapped in a pattern that

had been set decades ago. It would never change unless she did something about it. This was no time to falter. She remembered something her father had said to her before he went away. *When you sit, sit. When you stand, stand. But don't wobble.* The last few hours had brought his words home to her; now she understood.

Where was he? Time was running out.

She scanned the tops of the heads below, but the man with the heart was gone.

She stared back down the stairs, panicking. He must not get away.

From the other side of the stairwell, something shiny thrust out to touch her.

"You are," said the man with the satin pillow. "I can tell."

* * *

"Thank God."

She pressed him up the stairs to the second landing. A dimmer hallway stretched ahead, cut across by shafts of subdued light from the several bedrooms. She did not remember which was Milo's but knew she must find it before the appointed hour. From below she heard a rush of excitement. Was the girl Rip hired here already?

"Come with me," she said. "We have to talk."

7. HOTEL DINING ROOM

The DIRECTOR is having dinner with his PRO-DUCER. The pressure is on to finish in time. But the DIRECTOR can do it. He's done it before. The last scene is going to be a killer.

In the scene the GIRL's boyfriend, the NIGHT MANAGER from the supermarket, will lead sol-diers to a graveyard to rescue her. There will be lots of pyrotechnics.

Now the GIRL appears in the dining room. She sits down without being invited, expecting to be warmly received. She assumes that she is part of the DIRECTOR's life now. She waits for his greeting. But he only looks at her. He takes her aside and tells her impatiently to grow up. This is real life.

* * *

8. FX TRAILER

The DIRECTOR goes to his FX MAN for help. The GIRL is hanging everybody up. He can't let it go on this way. Nothing is more important than the picture.

What scenes does she have left? They go over the storyboards: only the Burning of the Zombies. The NIGHT MANAGER will lead the attack on the grave-yard, shotgunning dummies of zombies behind the gravestones. Then the National Guard lobs grenades in—the boyfriend will have to run a careful path around the explosive charges. Once the dummies are blown, he'll torch them with a flamethrower.

All they need from the GIRL is a close-up of her as she receives a blood squib from the shotgun, her shocked expression as she comes to her senses and recognizes her lover at the instant he kills her. Then cut to an exploding dummy.

Is there a way to shoot around her? Long shots, a better dummy, more blood and effects to cover? The other zombies will be blown away using dummy substitutes, but they need her for the reaction shots—she's the Queen of the Zombies.

MARTY is always one step ahead. He's saved the DIRECTOR's ass time and again. This time he's already made an alginate cast of the GIRL. He's got a full latex body mold of her ready as a backup. It is lifelike to the tiniest detail. It's more than a dummy—it can be worn by a double, if necessary. Now they can finish with or without the GIRL.

You're a genius, the DIRECTOR tells him. This is going to be a bloody masterpiece regardless of actors. They're nothing but trouble, anyway.

She led him on down the hall. There was a lilting peal of laughter from the first bedroom; from the second she heard boisterous chatter and through the unlatched door glimpsed a pale hand with razor blade describing furiously in the air above a horizontal mirror. The third was closed, with a crude sign attached to the doorknob: PRIVATE—OFF LIMITS. That, she guessed, was Rip's doing.

She pulled the man with the heart into the adjoining bathroom. The connecting door was ajar; in the bedroom, the soft, filtered glow of a small lamp. It was enough. "Here, we can be alone. . . ."

He stood uncertainly in the middle of the bathroom floor. "I've been waiting for you," he said.

"I know. I've been waiting for you, too," she told him, and heard giggles and footsteps approaching in the hall.

*　　*　　*

"Busted," he said.

"No." She backed up to secure the door. "Not us."

Leaning against it, she allowed her eyes to flutter shut. She waited for the room to stop spinning so that she could make the speech she had rehearsed. When she opened her eyes, he had moved closer.

He stood before her and tilted his head quizzically.

"But you don't know what I've got planned, do you?" she said. "I should explain."

"You don't have to," he said. "I think I understand."

"How could you?"

"I told you. I've been waiting a long time."

"Forgive me. I'm being rude. I don't mean to be. It's just that it's all happened so fast . . ."

"Take it easy," he said. He withdrew to give her breathing space and sat on the edge of the tub. "I don't mind waiting a little longer." A reflection from the tiles glinted playfully in his eyes.

Good, she thought. He's game.

"As long as it's not too long," he said.

In the hall, the footsteps and the giggling drew nearer.

9. ON THE SET

The GIRL arrives with notes in hand, more eager than ever to please her director.

But he's not in his chair. Somebody else is—a woman.

The DIRECTOR's WIFE. The crew is gathered around, laughing and reminiscing. The WIFE is now the center of attention. The GIRL is displaced.

She finds the DIRECTOR and tells him off. He uses people. He doesn't care about anything but blood, blood and more blood. Why did he lead her on? She'll tell the world, starting with his WIFE.

He tells her the facts of life. "She already knows." He doesn't need the GIRL anymore. The relationship is a wrap.

As she runs from the set, the WIFE observes. How sweet and innocent the GIRL looks. "I hope she doesn't take it too seriously. I used to—but now we lead separate lives. I learned a long time ago that this is his only real world—making movies. It's all he lives for. Real flesh and blood can't compete. The only thing he's truly married to is his capacity for illusion. . . ."

*   *   *

10. GRAVEYARD—THE LAST NIGHT

The crew is working feverishly to rig everything for the climax.

The DIRECTOR lingers after the rest of the crew have gone home. At 4 A.M. he finishes checking every detail. The zombie dummies are propped up on armatures behind the tombstones, the oil-smoke pots are ready, the crosses are tilted just so. Nothing left but to call "action" at dawn. For now, he'll catch an hour's shut-eye in his trailer.

"It won't be long," she said when the footsteps passed.

He shook his head sadly. "It's been such a long, long time," he said at last. "I'd almost given up hope. But you are the one, aren't you? Yes. You are."

"I'm the one," she said. "Now listen . . ."

He waved the stuffed heart. "I've been carrying this around, trying to find the right person to give it to." He made a sound that was halfway between a laugh and a shudder. "But no one would take it."

"You didn't need to do that," she said. Something to recognize him by? She could not remember any mention of it on the phone. It was a good idea, of course; it would have made him easier to spot. Or was it a gift? "What is it?"

He stood and came closer, holding it out. "What does it look like? I wanted to give it away, but there were never any takers. I wonder why that is? But now you're—"

"Yes, of course. There isn't much time. I don't know where to begin. You must be wondering why I brought you here."

"It doesn't matter."

"It does! That's what I'm trying to tell you. I see a lot of people . . ."

"So do I," he said. "Or I did. That's all over now."

Somehow he had gotten across the floor and was now only inches from her. She couldn't see his face; in the shadows he could have been anyone. She recalled a brief flash on the stairs: kind features, pained eyes, a hangdog expression. That only made her feel worse. She forced herself to go on. She could make things right. It was not too late.

Before she could speak, he braced his hands on either side of her head and leaned in to kiss her.

At first she was too dumbfounded to resist. Then she thought, Oh Christ, not at a time like this. Then she thought, What did he imagine when I called him, led him here . . . ?

My God.

"Wait," she said, breaking and turning aside.

But he pressed her and enfolded her mouth again.

At that moment someone pushed on the other side

of the door at her back, trying to gain entry. Her front teeth struck his with a grinding like fingernails on a blackboard.

"Sorry," mumbled a voice from the hall.

She spread her hands against his chest. "No," she said, "please, you don't understand. That's not what this is about."

"What *is* this about, then?"

"Will you hurry up in there?" said the voice from the hall.

She was shaken, confused. But there was no time for that. The clock was ticking.

Now there was a pounding on the door.

"This way," she said, and dragged him through the connecting door to the bedroom.

"I wish you'd make up your mind."

"Listen," she said, "my name's—"

"I don't care."

"You sent me a story, right? I showed it to my producer. He liked it. So much that he wants it for next season. *But not to buy it.* Oh, I'm sorry, I'm not making myself clear. It's my fault, too. I'll tell you about that later. But you'd better get down to WGA Manuscript Registry first thing in the morning. File whatever you've got—preliminary drafts, notes, anything."

"Why should I do that?"

"I'm trying to help you! They're going to steal your story. When Milo comes up here, I want you to tell him who you are."

She took the pages of the original version from her purse.

"I had to warn you. Whatever he says, don't back down. We're in this together. Now any minute all hell's going to break loose. Regardless of anything, know that I'll stand up for you. I want to make it up somehow. Maybe you'll end up hating me, I don't know. But I've got to try. I'm truly sorry. Believe that."

She inhaled, exhaled, wishing her heart would slow

down. In the bathroom a few feet away, someone locked the doors.

The bedroom was quiet, the lighting cool. On the nightstand the contents of a lava lamp flowed together, heated up and broke apart again into separate bodies, endlessly. Her mouth hurt; it was warm and wet. There was a sound of water running.

"What, may I ask," said the man, "are you talking about?"

"I'm trying to tell you that I'm all for you," she said, "no matter what."

Impatience flared in his eyes.

"Make up your mind," he said.

* * *

11. AT HIS TRAILER

The graveyard is spooky—he almost feels that he's being followed. He's about to enter the trailer when a ghoul appears. It's the GIRL, in full ghastly makeup.

He tries to get rid of her, knowing she's not really needed. But this time she's coming on differently. Not whining and needful, but happy as a puppy dog and all set to please. See? She's ready, and she's going to be perfect. She's even worked out a little something extra for her moment of death. It's her own idea and she's sure he's going to like it. If she can just try it out on him first.

She seems to have accepted reality. She really wants more than anything else for the picture to be good, after all. The same thing he wants. It's all that matters. She realizes that now.

"You've taught me a lot. More than you know. Now let me give you something back—what you really want. I want it now, too."

12. IN THE TRAILER

She runs through her expressions as he stands in for her lover. She screams on cue. Almost perfect. She needs to try it with the shotgun. She's brought it with her, already loaded with wax blood bullets. She's thought of everything.

"You want it to be real, don't you?" She presses him to take the prop gun. "We have to do it right. I want you to see how much I'm willing to give you. Let's do it all the way. And this time you're going to get everything you want. I promise."

He's reluctant, but he plays it out. When she starts screaming, he fires the shotgun. The look in her eyes is one of peace at last, as blood explodes and she sinks down the wall to the floor.

"Jesus, that was great! What a take! If we'd had a camera..." He leans down, shakes her. "Cut. That's it. You've finally got it. Hey, what's the...?"

He touches the wound. <u>It's real.</u> When she handed him the gun, it had a live round in the chamber. She had planned it that way.

He cleans up frantically to get rid of the evidence —no one will believe what really happened.

<u>What</u> <u>about</u> <u>the</u> <u>body?</u>

A desperate plan. He'll replace her dummy on the set with the real thing, propping her up, behind the tombstone like all the other dummies. The evidence will be blown to hell, then burned to a cinder. When the flamethrower hits her, the rubber makeup will burn like napalm. There won't be anything left.

He'll put her into position himself. No one will notice.

*   *   *

"I'm doing you a favor," she told him. "At least that's what I'm trying to do. If you'll let me."

"Are you the one?" he repeated more forcefully.

"Yes. I mean no." She evaded his grasp once again. "I mean . . ."

"But you said you're the one." He waved the heart-shaped pillow.

"Not like that," she said. "This is about something more important. Don't you see?"

"I should have known. You're not who I thought you were."

"Yes!"

"Which is it?" he said, angry now.

"Just—not the way you mean it!"

He was about to leave.

"This is very important to me," she said.

"To you," he said. "It always gets down to that."

"And to you! What's the matter with you? Haven't you heard a word I've been saying? Can't you . . .?"

He glared down at her. He tapped the pillow into her chest. "It never changes. You're just like all the rest." He tapped her again more aggressively. "It's always me, isn't it? *Isn't it.*"

"What do you mean?"

"What do *you* mean?" he said fiercely, directly into her face.

Her scalp began to tingle. Who is this man? she thought. I've made another mistake, the biggest one of all.

"Wh-who are you?" she said.

"Who are *you*," he said, "to ask that? Who the fuck do you think you are?"

She tried to dodge him as he lunged for her, a lifetime of disappointment igniting his rage. He grabbed her and flung her against the hall door before she could get it open, pushed himself in front of her. The pillow thrust up under her chin, forcing her head back. It wasn't soft, after all. It had something dangerously hard inside it. In fact it wasn't a pillow. It was an elaborate, padded Valentine gift box.

He raised it high. She saw the red heart poised to strike her, the satin covering worn, tattered, stained but still a deep crimson, like his face and the roadmap of years there, like the blood that ran from his cut lip. She didn't know who he was. He could have been anyone.

He was a madman.

Suddenly the door rattled. It rammed into her spine as someone tried to open it. She was driven into his arms.

"Huh? Oh. Sorry." Milo's voice through the crack, and behind him the sound of hysterical, theatrical weeping. "Come on. There's another phone down the hall."

"Wait!"

"Have fun . . ."

The man in front of her hesitated. In that moment she made her move and sprang for the doorknob. But he was on her. She twisted around and snatched the heart, heavier than she had imagined, and hit him with it. When he would not let go of her she swung it at his face again and again. She heard a dull breaking sound as she struck bone. The box broke and lumps of candy went flying, shriveled and hard as rocks. He dropped to his knees, a mystified look in his eyes, and toppled forward.

Then other people were in the room, Rip leading the way. Cheerful whispers turned to gasps.

"What have you done?" someone said.

"I didn't do anything! He—he was—"

"He was what? What did he do?" A tall woman moved to comfort her. She smoothed Chris's hair, saw the bruised lips, the torn buttons, the wild look. "It's all right now. He tried to assault you, didn't he? I've seen his kind before. The bastard."

"Who is that guy?" someone else said. "Who invited him?"

"I'll call a doctor."

"It was self-defense," said the woman, holding Chris too tightly. "Don't say a word to anybody. Do you understand? You had no choice. Who knows what he would have done to you if he'd had the chance? Something much worse. You know that, don't you?"

Chris had never seen her before. Now she could not remember any of the other faces, either.

She tore free and rushed to the stairs.

Below, in the empty living room, the music had

stopped. One solitary young man remained. He stood up self-consciously.

"Excuse me," he said, "but do you know a Christine Cross?"

She stared at him dumbly. She could not think of an answer.

"Well, if you see her, would you mind telling her that I've been looking for her? My name's Roger. I'm supposed to meet her here. Hey, is something wrong? Is that blood on your . . .?"

Without breaking stride she ran outside, the taste of blood, her own or someone else's, drying to salt on her lips.

13. DAWN

All is ready: backlight through fog, tilted crosses. Zombies propped up like shooting-gallery targets.

The DIRECTOR tells MARTY to use extra-strength charges. He doesn't want to see anything left when the smoke clears, not even the animal blood and guts inside the dummies.

"Action!"

The boyfriend, the NIGHT MANAGER, runs like a soldier through a mine field. Dummies are shotgunned one by one, then blown up, then torched. All except the GIRL. She will be the last shot. Where is she for her close-up?

We don't need her, says the DIRECTOR, winking at MARTY. She's not on the set? Who knows where she is—probably on the bus back to Indiana. Who cares? This is my picture and I say we don't need her. We've got a perfect dummy. Just blow it up—now.

"Action!"

The NIGHT MANAGER advances on her, shotgun ready. But before he can fire, her head lolls to one side.

"Wait," calls a SCRIPT GIRL. "Her head's out of position—it won't match."

"I'll fix it," says MARTY.

"No!" The DIRECTOR can't let anyone handle her—they'll discover it's a real body. He'll have to do it himself.

"Watch your step!" yells MARTY.

The DIRECTOR threads a careful path to her tombstone. Tries not to look at her face as he adjusts the head. There. He stands back.

Ready?

"Hold it," says MARTY. Now there's blood running out of her mouth. The shot still won't match.

"Just get it, will you?" says the DIRECTOR. He grabs the shotgun and prepares to fire the blood pellet into her himself. But before he can pull the trigger, her head lolls again as she starts to come to. She's not dead!

He pumps a shot into her, another. But the bullets aren't real this time. Her eyes open and look at him, seeing him there in her moment of triumph. She smiles.

"Die," he mutters, "die . . .!"

She raises her arms, zombielike, as if to embrace him.

He lunges at her, his hands going for her throat to make it right for the last time. Her arms go around him, pressing him to her in a final paroxysm—and the wires attached to her body make contact, setting off the charge. They are blown up together, married in blood for all eternity.

It's the last shot, the best effect of the film.

END

[Dennis Etchison wishes to acknowledge the contributions of Richard Rothstein, Gail Glaze, Bruce Jones, and April Campbell to "Queen of the Zombies," an outline for a script that was never written, and to thank them for their assistance in developing earlier versions of what now constitues a part of the short story "The Blood Kiss."]

TURN TO EARTH

All the flowers of the spring
Meet to perfume our burying:
These have but their growing prime,
And man does flourish but his time.
Survey our progress from our birth:
We are set, we grow, we turn to earth.
—JOHN WEBSTER

CLIVE BARKER, born 1952 in Liverpool, England, began his career as a playwright and illustrator but took the field of horror by storm with his six intensely graphic *Books of Blood* (whose final three volumes were published here as *The Inhuman Condition, In the Flesh,* and *Cabal*). His most recent work includes the novels *The Damnation Game* and *Weaveworld,* and the motion picture *Hellraiser.* The sentimental, quiet horrors of "Coming to Grief" confirm the range of Barker's substantial talents.

Clive Barker

Coming to Grief

Miriam had not taken the shortcut along the rim of the quarry for almost eighteen years. Eighteen years of another life, quite unlike the life she'd lived in this all but forgotten city. She'd left Liverpool to taste the world: to grow; to prosper; to learn to live; and, by God, hadn't she done just that? From the naïve and frightened nineteen-year-old she had been when she had last set foot on the quarry path, she had blossomed into a wholly sophisticated woman of the world. Her husband idolized her; her daughter grew more like her with every year; she was universally adored.

Yet now, as she stepped onto the ill-bred gravel path that skirted the chasm of the quarry, she felt as though a wound had opened in her heel and that hard-won poise and self-reliance were draining out of her and running away into the dark; as though she'd never left her native city, never grown wiser with experience. She felt no more prepared to face this hundred-yard stretch of walled walkway than she had been at nineteen. The same doubts, the same imagined horrors that had always haunted her on this spot, clung now to the inside of her brainpan and whispered about the certainty of secrets. They still lay in wait here, idiot fears concocted of street-corner gossip and childish superstition. Even now the old myths came running back to embrace her. Tales of hook-handed men, and secret lovers slaughtered in the act of love; a dozen rumored atrocities that, to her burgeoning and overheated imagination, had always had their source, their epicenter, here: on the Bogey-Walk.

That's what they'd called it; and that was what it would always be to her: the Bogey-Walk. Instead of losing its potency with the passage of the years, it had grown gross. It had prospered as she had prospered; it had found its vocation as she had done. Of course, she had grown into contentment, and perhaps that weakened her. But it, oh, *it* had merely fed on its own frustration and become encrusted with desire to take her for itself. Maybe, as time had passed, it had fed a little to keep its strength up: but it needed, in its immutable heart, only the certainty of its final victory to stay alive. Of this she was suddenly and incontestably certain: that the battles she had fought with her own weakness were not over. They had scarcely begun.

She attempted to advance a few yards along the Walk but faltered and stopped, the so-familiar panic turning her feet to lead weights. The night was not soundless. A jet droned over, a longing roar in the darkness; a mother called her child in from the street. But here, on the Walk itself, signs of life were a world away and could not comfort her. Cursing her own vulnerability, she turned back the way she'd come and traipsed home through the warm drizzle by a more roundabout route.

Grief, she half reasoned, had battened upon her and sapped her will to fight. In two days' time perhaps, when her mother's funeral was over and the sudden loss was more manageable, then she would see the future plainly and that pathway would fall into its proper perspective. She'd recognize the Bogey-Walk as the excrement-ridden, weed-lined gravel path that it was. Meanwhile she'd get wetter than she needed taking the safe road home.

The quarry was not in itself such a terrifying spot; nor, to any but her, was the path along its rim. There'd been no murders there that she knew of, no rapes or muggings committed along that sordid little track. It was a public footpath, no less and no more: a poorly kept, poorly illuminated walkway around the edge of what had once been a productive quarry and was now the communal rubbish-tip. The wall that kept the walkers from falling a hundred feet to their deaths below was built of plain red brick. It was eight feet high, so that nobody could even see the depth on the other side, and was lined with pieces of broken milk bottles set in concrete, to dissuade anyone from scrambling up onto it. The path itself had once been tarmac, but subsidence had opened cracks in it, and the Council, instead of resurfacing, had seen fit simply to dust it with loose gravel. It was seldom, if ever, weeded. Stinging nettles grew to child height in the meager dirt at the bottom of the wall, as did a sickly scented flower whose name she did not know but which, at the height of summer, was a Mecca to wasps. And that—wall, gravel, and weeds—was the sum of the place.

In dreams, however, she'd scaled that wall—her palms magically immune to the pricking glass—and in those vertiginous adventures she'd peer down and down the black, sheer cliff of the quarry into its dark heart. It was impenetrable, the gloom at the bottom, but she knew that there was a lake of green and brackish water somewhere below. It could be seen, that choked pool of filth, from the other side of the quarry; from the safe side. That's how she knew it was there, in her dreams. And she knew, too, walking on the unpiercing glass, tempting gravity and providence alike, that the prodigy of malice that lived on the cliff face would have seen her and would be climbing, even now, hand over clawed hand, up the steep side toward her. But in those dreams she always woke up before the nameless beast caught hold of her dancing feet, and the exhilaration of her escape would heal the fear; at least until the next time she dreamed.

The opposite end of the quarry, far from the sheer wall and the pool, had always been safe. Abandoned diggings and blastings had left a litter of boulders of Piranesian magnitude, in whose crevices she had often played as a child. There was no danger here: just a playground of tunnels. It seemed miles and miles (at

least to her child's eye) across the wasteland to the
rainwater lake and the tiny line of red brick wall that
beetled along the top of the cliff. Though there had
been days, she remembered, even in the safety of the
sun, when she would catch sight of something the
color of the rock itself stretching its back on the warm
face of the quarry, clinging to the cliff in a tireless and
predatory pose not a dozen yards beneath the wall.
Then, as her child's eyes narrowed to try to make
sense of its anatomy, it would sense her gaze and
freeze itself into a perfect copy of the stone.

Stone. Cold stone. Thinking about absence, about
the disguise required by a thing that wished not to be
seen, she turned into her mother's road. As she selected the house key, it occurred to her, absurdly, that
perhaps Veronica was not dead: simply perfectly camouflaged in the house somewhere, pressed against the
wall or at the mantelpiece; unseen but seeing. Perhaps
then visible ghosts were simply inept chameleons: the
rest had the trick of concealment down pat. It was a
foolish, fruitless train of thought, and she chided herself for entertaining it. Tomorrow, or the day after,
such thoughts would again seem as alien as the lost
world in which she was presently stranded. So thinking, she stepped indoors.

The house did not distress her; it simply reawakened
a sense of tedium her busy, clever life had put aside.
The task of dividing, discarding, and packing the remnants of her mother's life was slow and repetitive. The
rest—the loss, the remorse, the bitterness—were so
many thoughts for another day. There was sufficient
to do as it was, without mourning. Certainly the empty
rooms held memories; but they were all pleasant enough
to be happily recalled, yet not so exquisite as to be
wished into being again. Her feelings, moving around
the deserted house, could only be defined by what she
no longer saw or felt: *not* her mother's face; *not* the
chiding voice, the preventing hand; just an unknow-
able nothing that was the space where life used to be.

In Hong Kong, she thought, Boyd would be on
duty, and the sun would be blazing hot, the streets

thronged with people. Though she hated to go out at midday, when the city was so crowded, today she would have welcomed the discomfort. It was tiresome sitting in the dusty bedroom, carefully sorting and folding the scented linen from the chest of drawers. She wanted life, even if it was insistent and oppressive. She longed for the smell of the streets to be piercing her nostrils, and the heat to be beating on her head. No matter, she thought, soon done.

Soon done. Ah, there was a guilt there: the ticking off of the days until the funeral, the pacing out of her mother's ritual removal from the world. Another seventy-two hours and the whole business would be done with, and she would be flying back to life.

As she went about her daughterly duties, she left every light burning in the house. It was more convenient to do so, she told herself, with all the to-ing and fro-ing the job required. Besides, the late November days were short and dismal, and the work was dispiriting enough without having to labor in a perpetual dusk.

Organizing the disposal of personal items was taking the longest time. Her mother had acquired a sizable wardrobe, all of which had to be sorted through: the pockets emptied, the jewelry removed from the collars. She sealed up the bulk of the clothes in black plastic bags, to be collected by a local charity shop the following day, keeping only a fur wrap and a gown for herself. Then she selected a few of her mother's favorite possessions to give to close friends after the funeral: a leather handbag; some china cups and saucers; a herd of ivory elephants that had belonged . . . she had forgotten who they had belonged to. Some relative, long gone.

Once the clothes and bric-a-brac had been organized, she turned her attention to the mail, sorting the outstanding bills into one pile and the personal correspondence, whether recent or remote, into another. Each letter, however old or difficult to follow, she read carefully. Most she dispatched to the small fire she had lit in the living-room grate. It was soon a cave

of bat-wing ashes; black and veined with burned words.
Once only, a letter found tears in her: a note, written
in her father's gossamer hand, which awakened ago-
nies of regret for the wasted years of antagonism between them. There were photographs among the leaves,
too; most as frozen as Alaska: arid, fruitless territory.
Some, however, catching a true moment between the
poses, were as fresh as yesterday, and a din of voices
spilled from the aged image:

—*Wait! Not yet! I'm not ready!*

—*Daddy! Where's Daddy? We must have Daddy in
this one!*

—*He's tickling me!*

Laughter pealed off these images; their fixed joy
parodied the truth of deterioration and annihilation
whose proof was borne by the empty house.

—*Wait!*

—*Not yet!*

—*Daddy!*

She could hardly bear to look at some of them. She
burned first the ones that hurt the most.

—*Wait!* someone shouted. Herself, perhaps, a child
in the arms of the past. *Wait!*

But the pictures cracked in the heart of the fire,
then browned and burst with blue flame, and the
moment—

—*Wait!*

—the moment went the way of all the moments that
had surrounded the instant that the camera had fixed,
gone away forever like fathers and mothers and, in
time, daughters too.

She retired to bed at three-fifteen A.M., the bulk of her
self-assigned chores done for the day. Her mother
would have applauded her efficiency, she suspected.
How ironic that Miriam, the daughter who had never
been daughterly enough, who had always wanted the
world instead of being content to stay at home, was
now being as meticulous as any parent could have
possibly wished. Here she was, cleaning away a whole
history; consigning the leavings of a life to the fire,

scouring the house more thoroughly than her mother had ever done.

A little after three-thirty, having mentally arranged the business of the following day, she drained the last of the half tumbler of whiskey she'd been sipping all evening and sank, almost immediately, into sleep.

She dreamed nothing. Her mind was clear. As clear as darkness is clear, as emptiness is clear; not even Boyd's face, or his body (she often dreamed of his chest, of the fine pattern of hair on his stomach) crept into her head to pollute the featureless bliss.

It was raining when she awoke. Her first thought was: *Where am I*?

Her second thought was: *Is today the funeral, or tomorrow*?

Her third thought was: *In two days I'll be back with Boyd. The sun will be shining. I'll forget all of this.*

For today, however, there was more unappetizing work ahead. The funeral was not until tomorrow, which was Wednesday. Today the business was mundane: checking the cremation arrangements with Beckett and Dawes, writing notes of thanks for the many letters of condolence she'd received, a dozen other minor duties. In the afternoon she would visit Mrs. Furness, a friend of her mother's who was now too crippled with arthritis to attend the funeral. She would give the old lady that leather handbag, as a keepsake. In the evening it would be again the same, sorry business of sorting through her mother's belongings and organizing their redistribution. There was so much to give to the needy—or the greedy—whichever asked first. She didn't care who took the stuff, as long as the job was finished soon.

About mid-morning, the telephone rang. It was the first noise she'd heard in the house since waking that she hadn't made herself, and it startled her. She lifted the receiver, and a warm word was spoken in her ear: her name.

"Miriam?"

"Yes. Who is this?"

"Oh, love, you sound absolutely washed out. It's Judy, sweetheart; Judy Cusack."

"Judy?"

The very name was a smile.

"Don't you remember?"

"Of course I remember. How lovely to hear your voice."

"I didn't ring any earlier. I thought you'd have so much on your hands. I'm so sorry, pet, about your mother. It must have been a blow. My dad died the year before last. It really knocked me sideways."

Vaguely Miriam could picture Judy's father, a slender, elegant man who'd smiled once in a while and had said very little.

"He'd been very ill. It was a blessing, really. God, I never thought I'd hear myself say that. Funny, isn't it?"

Judy's voice had scarcely changed at all; she frothed with pleasure the way she always had, the body Miriam saw in her mind's eye was still rounded, with a lingering puppy fat. Eighteen years ago they had been the best of friends, soul mates; and for a moment, exchanging pleasantries with that breezy voice, it was as though the time between this conversation and their last had shrunk to hours.

"It's so good to hear your voice," said Miriam.

It *was* good. It was the past speaking, but it was a good past, a sunlit past. She had almost forgotten, in the toil of this autopsy she was busy with, how fine some memories could be.

"I heard from the people next door about your coming home," Judy said, "but I was of two minds whether to call. I know it must be a very difficult time for you. So sad and all."

"Not really," Miriam said.

The plain truth sneaked out without her meaning to say it; but there it was now, said. It *wasn't* a sad time. It was a drudge, it was a limbo, but she wasn't holding a flood of sorrows in abeyance. She saw that now, and her heart lightened with the simplicity of the confession. Judy offered no reproof, only an invitation.

"Are you feeling well enough to come over for a drink?"

"I've still got a lot of sorting to do."

"I promise we won't talk about old times," Judy said. "Not one word. I couldn't bear it; it makes me feel antiquated." She laughed.

Miriam laughed with her. "Yes," she said. "I'd love to come. . . ."

"Good. It's a bind, isn't it, when you're an only child, and it's all your responsibility. Sometimes you really think there's no end to it."

"It's crossed my mind," Miriam replied.

"When it's all over, you'll wonder what the fuss was about," Judy said. "I coped with Dad's funeral, though at the time I thought I was going to fall apart."

"You didn't have to handle it alone, did you?" Miriam asked. "What about . . ." She wanted to name Judy's husband; she recalled her mother writing to her about Judy's late—and if she remembered correctly, scandalous—marriage. But she couldn't remember the groom's name.

"Donald?" Judy prompted her.

"Donald."

"Separated, pet. We've been separated two and a half years."

"Oh, I'm sorry."

"I'm not." The answer came back in a flash. "It's a long story. I'll tell you about it this evening. About seven?"

"Could we make it a little later? I've got so much to do. Is eight all right?"

"Anytime, love, don't rush yourself. I'll expect you when I see you; we'll leave it at that."

"Fine. And thanks for ringing."

"I've been itching to call since I heard you were back. It's not often you get a chance to see old friends, is it?"

A few minutes shy of noon, Miriam faced what she expected to be the most debilitating of her duties. Though she wouldn't confess it to herself, she felt a tremor of disgust as she parked outside the funeral home. There was a dull, stale taste at the back of her throat, and her eyes seemed spoiled with grit. She frankly had no wish to see her mother again, not now that they couldn't talk, and yet when the urbane Mr. Beckett had said to her on the phone, "You will want to view the deceased?" she had replied, "Of course," as though the request had been on the tip of her tongue all along.

And what was there to fear? Veronica Blessed was dead; she'd died peacefully in her sleep. But Miriam found that a phrase, a random phrase that she remembered from school, had crept into the back of her head that morning and she couldn't rid herself of it:

"Everyone dies because they run out of breath."

That thought was there now, as she looked at Mr. Beckett, and the paper lilies and the scuffed corner of his desk. To run out of breath, to choke on a tongue, to suffocate under a blanket. She had known all those fears when she was young, and now they came back to her in Mr. Beckett's office and held her hand. One of them leaned over and whispered maliciously in her ear: Suppose one day you simply forget to breathe? Black face, tongue bitten off.

Was that what made her throat so dry? The thought that Mama, Veronica, Mrs. Blessed, widow of Harold Blessed, now deceased, would be lying on silk with her face as black as the Earl of Hell's riding boots? Vile notion: vile, ridiculous notion.

But they kept coming, these unwelcome ideas, one quick upon the heels of another. Most she could trace back to childhood; absurd, irrelevant images floating up from her past like squid to the sun.

The Levitation Game, a favorite school pastime, came to mind: six girls ranged around a seventh, trying to lift her up with one finger apiece. And the accompanying ceremony:

"She looks *pale*," says the girl at the head.

"She *is* pale."

"She *is* pale."

"She *is* pale."

"She *is* pale."

"She *is* pale," the attendants answer by rote, counterclockwise.

"She looks *ill,*" the high priestess announces.

"She *is* ill."

"She *is* ill."

"She *is* ill."

"She *is* ill."

"She *is* ill," the others reply.

"She looks *dead*—"

She *is*—

There'd been a murder, too, when she was only six, two streets down from where they'd lived. The body had been wedged behind the front door—she'd heard Mrs. Furness tell all to her mother—and it was so softened by putrefaction that when the police forced the door open it had concertinaed into a bundle that proved impossible to unglue. Sitting now beside the scentless lilies, Miriam could smell the day she'd stood, hand in her mother's hand, listening to the women talk of murder. Crime, come to think of it, had been a favorite subject of Mrs. Furness. Had it been through her good offices that Miriam had first learned that her nightmares of the Bogey-Walk had their counterpart in the adult world?

Miriam smiled, thinking of the women casually debating slaughter as they stood in the sun. Mr. Beckett seemed not to notice her smile; or, more likely, was well prepared for any manifestation of grief, however bizarre. Perhaps mourners came in here and threw off all their clothes in their anguish or wet their pants. She looked at him more closely, this young man who had made a profession of bereavement. He was not unattractive, she thought. He was an inch or two shorter than she, but height didn't matter in bed; and moving coffins around would put some muscle on a body, wouldn't it?

Listen to yourself, she thought, pulling herself up short. *What are you contemplating*?

Mr. Beckett plucked at his pale ginger mustache and offered a look of practiced condolence to Miriam. She saw his charm—what meager supply there was— vanish in that one look.

He seemed to be waiting for some cue from her; she wondered what. At last he said:

"Shall we go through to the Chapel of Rest, or shall we discuss the business first?"

Ah, *that* was it. Better to get the farewells over with, she thought. He could wait a while longer for his money. "I'd like to see my mother," she said.

"Of course you would," he replied, nodding as though he'd known all along that she wanted to view the body; as if he were somehow completely conversant with her most intimate workings. She resented his fake familiarity but made no sign of it.

He stood up and ushered her through the glass-paneled door and into a corridor flanked by vases of flowers. They, like the lilies on his desk, were artificial. The scent she could smell was that of floor polish, not blossoms; no bee had hope of succor here, unless there was nectar to be taken from the dead.

Mr. Beckett halted at one of the doors, turned the handle, and ushered Miriam ahead of him. This was it, then: face-to-face at last. *Smile, Mother, Miriam's home.* She entered the room. Two candles burned on a small table against the far wall, and there was a further abundance of artificial flowers, their fake fecundity more distasteful here than ever.

The room was small. Space enough for a coffin, a chair, a table, bearing the candles, and one or two living souls.

"Shall I leave you with your mother?" Mr. Beckett asked.

"No," she said with more urgency and more volume than the tiny room could accommodate. The candles coughed lightly at her indiscretion. More softly she said, "I would prefer you to stay, if you don't mind."

"Of course," Mr. Beckett dutifully replied.

She wondered briefly how many people, at this juncture, chose to keep their vigil unaccompanied. It would be an interesting statistic, she thought, her mind dividing into disinterested observer and frightened participant. How many mourners, faced with the dear dead, asked for company, however anonymous, rather than be left alone with a face they had known a lifetime?

Taking a deep breath, she stepped toward the coffin, and there, snoozing on a sheet of pale cream cloth in this narrow, high-sided bed, was her mother. What a foolish and neglectful place to fall asleep in, she thought; and in your favorite dress. So unlike you, Mother, to be so impractical. Her face had been tastefully rouged, and her hair recently brushed, although not in a style she had favored. Miriam felt no horror at seeing her like this; just a sharp thrill of recognition and the instinct, barely suppressed, to reach into the coffin and shake her mother awake.

Mother, I'm here. It's Miriam.

Wake up.

At the thought of that, Miriam felt her cheeks flush, and hot tears well up in her eyes. The tiny room was abruptly a single sheet of watery light; the candles two bright eyes. "Mama," she said once.

Mr. Beckett, clearly long inured to such spectacles, said nothing, but Miriam was acutely aware of his presence behind her and wished she'd asked him to leave. She took hold of the side of the coffin to steady herself, while the tears dripped off her cheeks and fell into the folds of her mother's dress.

So this was death's house; this was its shape and nature. Its etiquette was perfect. At its visitation there had been no violence; only a profound and changeless calm that denied the need for further show of affection.

Her mother, she realized, didn't require her any longer; it was as simple as that. Her first and final rejection. *Thank you*, said that cold, discrete body, *but I have no further need of you. Thank you for your concern, but you may go.*

She stared at Veronica's well-dressed corpse through a haze of unhappiness, not hoping to wake her mother now, not hoping even to make sense of the sight. Then she said, "Thank you," very quietly. The words were for her mother; but Mr. Beckett, taking Miriam's arm as she turned to go, took it for himself.

"It's no trouble," he replied. "Really."

Miriam blew her nose and tasted the tears. The duty was done. Time now for business. She drank weak tea with Beckett and finalized the financial arrangements, watching for him to smile once, to break his covenant with sympathy. He didn't. The interview was conducted with indecent reverence, and by the time he ushered her out into the cold afternoon, she had grown to despise him.

She drove home without thinking, her mind not blank with the loss but with the exhaustion of having wept. It was not a conscious decision that made her choose the route back to the house that led alongside the quarry. But as she turned into the street that ran past her old playground, she realized that some part of her wanted—perhaps even *needed*—a confrontation with the Bogey-Walk.

She parked the car at the safe end of the quarry, a short walk from the path itself, and got out. The wire gates she'd scrambled through as a child were locked, but a hole had been torn in the wire, as ever. Doubtless the quarry was still a playground. New wire, new gates; but the same games. She couldn't resist ducking through the gap, though her coat snagged in a hook of wire as she did so. Inside, little seemed to have changed. The same chaos of boulders, steps and plateaus, litter, weeds and puddles, lost and broken toys, bicycle parts. She thrust her fists into her coat pockets and ambled through the rubble of childhood, keeping her eyes fixed on her feet, easily finding again the familiar routes between the stones.

She would never get lost here. In the dark—in death, even, as a ghost—she would be certain of her steps. Finally she located the spot she'd always loved the best and, standing in the lee of a great stone, raised her head to look at the cliff across the quarry. From this distance the Walk was barely visible, but she scanned its length meticulously. The quarry face looked less imposing than she'd remembered; less majestic. The intervening years had shown her more perilous heights, more tremendous depths. And yet she still felt her bowels contracting as though an octopus had been sewn up at the crux of her body, and she knew that the child in her, insusceptible to reason, was searching the cliff for a sign, however negligible, of the Walk's haunter. The twitch of a stone-colored limb, perhaps, as it kept its relentless vigil; the flicker of a terrible eye.

But she could see nothing.

Almost ashamed of her fears, she retraced her steps through the canyon of stones, slipped through the gate like an errant child, and returned to the car.

The Bogey-Walk was *safe*. Of course it was safe. It held no horrors, and never had. The sun was valiantly trying to share her exhilaration now, forcing wan and heatless beams through the rain clouds. The wind was at her side, smelling of the river. Grief was a memory.

She would go to the Walk now, she decided, and give herself time to savor each fearless step she took along it, jubilating in her victory over history. She drove around the side of the quarry and slammed the car door with a smile on her face as she climbed the three steps that led off the pavement onto the footpath itself.

The shadow of the brick wall fell across the Walk, of course; and its length was darker than the street behind her. But nothing could sour her confidence. She walked from one end of the weed-clogged corridor to the other without incident, her whole body high with the sheer ease of it. *How could I ever have feared this?* she asked herself as she turned and began the journey to the waiting car.

This time, as she walked, she allowed herself to think back on the specifics of her childhood nightmares. There had been a place—halfway along the Walk and therefore at the greatest distance from help—that had been the high-water mark of her terror. That particular spot—that forbidden few yards that, to the unseeing eye, were no different from every other yard along the Walk—was the place the thing in the quarry would choose to pounce when her last moments came. That was its killing ground, its sacrificial grove, marked, she had fervently believed, with blood of countless other children.

Even as the taste of that memory returned to her, she approached the point. The signs that had marked the place were still to be seen: an arrangement of five discolored bricks; a crack in the cement that had been minuscule eighteen years ago and had grown larger. The spot was as recognizable as ever; but it had lost its potency. It was just another few of a hundred identical yards, and she bypassed the spot without the contentment on her face faltering for more than an instant. She didn't even glance behind her.

The wall of the Bogey-Walk was old. It had been built a decade before Miriam was born, by men who had known their craft indifferently well. Erosion had eaten at the quarry face beneath the teetering brick, unseen by Council inspectors and safety officials from the Department of the Environment; in places the rain-sodden sandstone had crumbled and fallen away. Here and there, the bricks were unsupported across as much as half their breadth. They hung over the abyss of the quarry while rain and wind and gravity ate at the crumbling mortar that kept them united.

Miriam saw none of this. She would have had to have waited a while before she heard the uneasy grinding of the bricks as they leaned out against the air, waiting, aching, begging to fall. As it was, she went away, elated, certain that she'd sloughed off her terrors forever.

That evening she saw Judy.

Judy had never been beautiful; there had always been an excess in her features: her eyes too big, her mouth too broad. Yet now, in her mid-thirties, she was radiant. It was a sexual bloom, certainly, and one that might wither and die prematurely, but the woman who met Miriam at the front door was in her prime.

They talked through the evening about the years they'd been apart—despite their contract not to discuss the past—exchanging tales of their defeats and their successes. Miriam found Judy's company enchanting; she was immediately comfortable with this bright, happy woman. Even the subject of her separation from Donald didn't inhibit her flow.

"It's not *verboten* to talk about old husbands, pet; it's just a bit boring. I mean, he wasn't a bad sort."

"Are you divorcing him?"

"I suppose so; if I have a moment. These things take months, you know. Besides, I'm a Libra; I can never make up my mind what I want." She paused. "Well," she said with a half-secret smile, "that's not altogether true."

"Was he unfaithful?"

"Unfaithful?" She laughed. "That's a word I haven't heard in a long time."

Miriam blushed a little. Was life really so backward in the colonies, where adultery was not yet compulsory?

"He screwed around," said Judy. "That's the simple truth of it. But then, so did I."

She laughed again, and this time Miriam joined in with the laughter, not quite certain of the joke.

"How did you find out?"

"I found out when *he* found out."

"I don't understand."

"It was all so obvious, it sounds like a farce when I tell it; but he found a letter, you see, from someone I'd been with. Nobody particularly important to me—just a casual friend, really. Anyway, he was *triumphant*; I mean, he *really* crowed about it, said he'd had more affairs than I had. Treated it all like some sort of competition—who could cheat the most often and with whom." She paused; the same mischievous smile appeared again. "As it was, when we put our cards on the table, I was doing rather better than he was. That *really* pissed him off."

"So you separated?"

"There didn't seem to be much point in staying together; we didn't have any kids. And there wasn't any love lost between us. There never really had been. The house was in his name, but he let me have it."

"So you won the competition?"

"I suppose I did. But then, I had a hidden advantage."

"What?"

"The other man in my life was a woman," Judy said, "and poor Donald couldn't handle that at all. He more or less threw in the towel as soon as he found out. Told me he realized he'd never understood me and that we were better apart." She looked up at Miriam and only now saw the effect her statement had had. "Oh," she said, "I'm sorry. I just opened my mouth and put my foot in it."

"No," said Miriam, "it's me. I'd never thought of you . . ."

". . . as a Lesbian? Oh, I think I've always known it, right back to school days. Writing love letters to the games mistress."

"We all did that," Miriam reminded her.

"Some of us meant it more seriously than others." Judy smiled.

"And where's Donald now?"

"Oh, somewhere in the Middle East, last I heard. I'd like him to write to me, just to tell me he's well. But he won't. His pride wouldn't let him. It's a pity. We might have been good friends if we hadn't been husband and wife."

That seemed to be all there was to say on the subject; or all Judy wanted to say.

"Shall I go and make some coffee?" she suggested, and went through to the kitchen, leaving Miriam to toy with the cat and her thoughts. Neither were particularly fleet-footed that night.

"I'd like to go to your mum's funeral," Judy called through from the kitchen. "Would you mind?"

"Of course not."

"I didn't know her well, but I used to see her out shopping. She always looked so *smart*."

"She was," Miriam said. Then: "Why don't you come in the lead car with me?"

"I'm not a relative."

"I'd like you to." The cat turned over in its sleep and presented its winter-furred belly to Miriam's comforting fingers. "Please."

"Then thank you. I will."

They spent the remaining hour and a half drinking coffee, and then whiskey, and then more whiskey, and talking about Hong Kong and their parents, and finally about memory. Or rather, about the irrational nature of memory; how their minds had selected such odd details to fix events while neglecting others more apparently significant: the smell in the air when the words of affection were spoken, not the words themselves; the color of a lover's shoes, but not of their eyes.

At last, way after midnight, they parted.

"Come to the house about eleven," Miriam said. "The cars are leaving at about a quarter past."

"Right. I'll see you tomorrow, then."

"Today," Miriam pointed out.

"That's right, today. Take care driving, love, it's a foul night."

The night *was* breezy; the car radio reported gale-force winds in the Irish Sea. She drove home cautiously through the empty streets, the same gusts that buffeted the car raising leaves from the dead and whirling them up into the glare of the headlamps. In Hong Kong, she thought, there would still be plenty of life in the streets this time of night. Here? Just sleep-darkened houses, closed curtains, locked doors. As she drove, she mentally followed her footsteps through the day and the three encounters that had marked it out. With her mother, with Judy, and with the Bogey-Walk. By the time she'd done her thinking, she was home.

Sleep came fitfully through the blustery night, punctuated by dustbin lids whipped off by vicious licks of wind, the rain, and the scratching of sycamore branches against the windows.

The next day was Wednesday, December 1, and the rain had turned to sleet by dawn.

The funeral was not insufferable. It was at best a functional farewell to someone Miriam had once known and now had lost sight of; at worst, its passionless solemnity and well-oiled ritual smacked of frigidity, ending as a conveyor belt took the coffin through a pair of lilac curtains to the furnace and the chimney beyond. Miriam could not help but imagine the interior of the coffin as it shuddered through the theatrical divide of the curtains; could not help but visualize the way her mother's body shook with each tiny jerk of her box toward the incinerator. The thought, though self-inflicted, was all but unbearable. She had to dig her fingernails into the flesh of her palm simply to prevent herself from standing up and demanding a halt to the proceedings: to have the lid prised off the coffin, to fumble in the shroud, and to pluck that blank body up in her arms one more time; lovingly, adoringly thanking her. That moment was the worst; she held herself in check until the curtains closed, and then it was over.

As partings went, it was perfunctory, but it clung, in its plain way, to a measure of dignity.

The wind was biting as they left the tiny red brick chapel of the crematorium, the mourners already dividing to their cars with murmurs of thanks and faint looks of embarrassment. There were flakes of snow in the wind: too large and too wet to amount to much as they flopped to the ground, but rendering the glum surroundings yet more inhospitable. Miriam's teeth ached in her head; and the ache was spreading up her nose to her eyes.

Judy hooked her arm.

"We must get together again, love, before you leave."

Miriam nodded. Leaving was less than twenty-four hours away, and tonight, as a foretaste of liberty, Boyd would ring. He'd promised to do so, and he was sweetly reliable. She knew she'd be able to smell the heat of the street down the telephone wire.

"Tonight . . ." Miriam suggested to Judy. "Come round to the house tonight."

"Are you sure? Isn't it a bit of a trial being there?"

"Not really. Not now."

Not now. Veronica had gone, once and for all. The house was not a home any longer.

"I've still got a lot of cleaning up to do," Miriam said. "I want to hand it over to the agents with all Mother's belongings dealt with. I don't like the thought of strangers going through her stuff."

Judy murmured her agreement.

"I'll help, then," she said. "If you don't think I'll get in the way."

"A working evening?"

"Fine."

"Seven?"

"Seven."

A sudden, vehement gust of wind caught Miriam's breath, dispersing a few lingering mourners to the warmth of their cars. One of her mother's neighbors—Miriam could never remember the woman's name—lost her hat. It blew off and bowled across the Lawn of Remembrance, her pop-eyed husband clumsily pursuing it across the ash-enriched grass.

At the height of the quarry, the wind was even stronger. It came up from the sea and down the river, funneling its fury into a snow-specked fist; then it scoured the city for victims.

The wall of the Bogey-Walk was ideal material. Weak from the flux of years, it needed little bullying to persuade it to surrender. In the late afternoon, a particularly ambitious gust took three or four glass-crowned bricks off the top of the wall and pitched them into the quarry lake. The structure was weakest there, in the middle of its length, and once the wind had started the demolition, gravity lent its elbow to the work.

A young man, cycling home, was just about to reach the middle of the footpath when he heard a roar of capitulation and saw a section of the wall buckle outward in a cloud of mortar fragments. There was a diminishing percussion of bricks against rock as the ruins danced their way down to the foot of the cliff. A gap, fully six feet across, had opened up in the wall, and the wind, triumphant, roared through it, tugging at the exposed edges of the wall and coaxing them to follow. The young man got off his bicycle and wheeled it to the spot, grinning at the spectacle.

It was a long way down, he thought as he stepped toward the breach and cautiously peered over the edge. The wind was at his heels and at the small of his back, curling around him, begging him to step a little farther. He did. The vertigo he felt excited him, and the idiot urge to fling himself over, though resistible, was strong. Leaning over, he was able to see the bottom of the quarry; but the face of the stone directly beneath the hole in the wall was out of sight. A small overhang obscured the place.

The young man leaned farther out, the icy wind hot for him. *Come on*, it said. *Come on, look closer, look deeper.*

Something, not a yard below the yawning gap in the wall, moved. The young man saw, or thought he saw, a form—whose bulk was hidden by the overhang—move. Then, sensing that it was observed, freeze against the cliff wall.

Get on with it, said the wind. *Give in to your curiosity.*

The young man thought better of it. The thrill of the test was souring. He was cold; the fun was over. Home time. He stepped back from the hole and began to wheel his bicycle away, a whistle coming to his lips that was part in celebration of escape and part to keep whatever he felt at his back at bay.

At seven, Miriam was sorting through the last of her mother's jewelry. There was very little of value in the small perfumed boxes, but there were one or two pretty brooches nesting in beds of greying cotton wool that she had decided to take home with her, for remembrance. Boyd had rung a little after six, as he had promised, his voice watery on a bad line, but full of reassurance and affection. Miriam was still high from his conversation. Now the telephone rang again. It was Judy.

"Lovey, I don't think I ought to come over this evening. I'm feeling pretty bad at the moment. I came on at the funeral, and the pains are always bad when it's cold."

"Oh, dear."

"I'd be lousy company, I'm afraid. Sorry to let you down."

"Don't worry; if you're not well . . ."

"Pity is, I might not get to see you again before you go back." She sounded genuinely distressed at the thought.

"Listen," Miriam said, "if I get this work finished before it gets too late, I'll wander round your way. I hate telephone farewells."

"Me too."

"I can't promise."

"Well, if I see you, I see you; we'll leave it at that, eh? If I don't, take care, love, and drop me a line to tell me you got home safely."

By the time she stepped out of the house at nine-fifty, the gale had long since blown itself out, only to be followed by a stillness so profound, it was almost more unnerving than the preceding din. Miriam locked the door and took a step back to look at the front of the house. The next time she set foot here (if, indeed, she ever did), the house would be re-occupied and, no doubt, repainted. She would have no right-of-way here; the pains of remembrance she had experienced in the last few days would themselves be memories.

She walked to the car, keys in hand, but decided on the spur of the moment that she would walk to Judy's house. The gale-cleansed air was invigorating, and she would take the opportunity to wander around the old neighborhood one final time.

She would even take the Bogey-Walk, she thought; she'd be at Judy's in five or ten minutes.

There was a long, deceptive curve in the Walk as it followed the rim of the quarry. From one end, it was not possible to see the other, or even the middle. So Miriam was almost upon the gap in the wall before she saw it. Her confident step faltered. In her lower belly something uncoiled its arms in welcome.

The hole gaped in front of her, vast and inviting. Beyond the edge, where the meager light from the street had no strength to go, the darkness of the quarry was apparently infinite. She could have been standing on the edge of the world; there was neither depth nor distance beyond the lip of the path, just a blackness that hummed with anticipation.

Even as she stared, morsels of cement crumbled into space. She heard them patter away from her; she could even hear their distant splashes.

But now, entranced by her sudden dread, she heard another noise, close by, a noise she had prayed never to hear in the waking world, the grit of nails on the stone face of the quarry, the rush of caustic breath from a creature that had waited oh, so patiently for this moment and was now slowly and purposefully dragging its way up the last few feet of the cliff toward her. And why should it hurry? It knew she was frozen to the spot.

It was coming; there was no help to be had. Its arms were splayed over the stone, and its head, dark with grime and depravity, was almost at the rim of the Walk. Even now, with its victim almost in view, it didn't hasten its steady climb but took its awful time.

The little girl Miriam had been wanted to die now, before it saw her, but the woman she was wanted to see the face of her ageless tormentor. Just to *see,* for the horrid instant before it took her, what the thing was like. After all, it had been here so long, waiting. It had its reasons for such patient malice, surely; maybe the face would show them.

How could she have thought there could ever be escape from this? In sunlight she'd laughed off her fears, but that had been a sham. The sweat of childhood, the night tears (hot, and running straight from the corners of her eyes into her hair), the unspeakable terrors, were here. They had come out of the dark, and she was, at the last, alone. Alone as only children are alone: sealed in with feelings beyond articulation, in private hells of ignorance whose corridors run, unseen, into adulthood.

Now she was crying, loudly, bawling like a ten-year-old, her crumpled face red and shining with tears. Her nose ran, her eyes burned.

In front of her, the Bogey-Walk was weakening, and she felt the irrevocable pull of the dark. One of her steps toward the gap in the wall was matched by another hauling of the flat black belly over the quarry's face. Another step, and now she was a foot from the crumbling edge of the Bogey-Walk, and in a matter of moments it would take her by the hair and split her apart.

She stood by the dizzying edge, and the face of her dread swam up from the bottomless night to look at her. *It was her mother's face.* Horribly bloated to twice or three times its true size, her jaundiced eyelids flickering to reveal whites without irises, as though she were hanging in the last moment between life and death.

Her mouth opened; her lips blackened and stretched to thin lines around a toothless hole, which worked the air uselessly, trying to speak Miriam's name. So even now there was to be no moment of recognition; the thing had cheated her, offering that dead, beloved face in place of its own.

Her mother's mouth chewed on, her rasping tongue trying vainly to shape the three syllables. The beast wanted to summon her, and it knew, with its age-old cunning, which face to use to make the call. Miriam looked down through her tears at the flickering eyes; she could half see the deathbed pillow beneath her mother's head, half smell her last, sour breath.

The name was almost said. Miriam closed her eyes, knowing that when the word was spoken, that would be the end. She was without will. The Bogey had her; this brilliant mimicry was the final, triumphant turn of the screw. It would speak with her mother's voice, and she would go to it.

"*Miriam,*" it said.

The voice was lovelier than she'd anticipated.

"*Miriam.*" It called in her ear, its claws now on her shoulder.

"*Miriam, for God's sake,*" it demanded. "*What are you doing?*"

The voice was familiar, but it was not her mother's voice, nor that of the beast. It was Judy's voice, Judy's hands. They dragged her back from the gap and all but threw her against the opposite wall. She felt the security of cold brick at her back, against the cushion of her palms. The tears cleared a little.

"*What are you doing?*"

Yes, no doubt of it. Judy, plain as day.

"Are you all right, love?"

Behind Judy, the dark was deep, but from it there came only a pattering of stones as the Bogey retreated down the quarry face. Miriam felt Judy's arms around her, tight; more possessive of her life than she had been.

"I didn't mean to give you such a heave," she said, "I just thought you were going to jump."

Miriam shook her head in disbelief. "It hasn't taken me," she said.

"What hasn't, sweetheart?"

She couldn't bring herself to talk in earshot of it. She just wanted to be away from the wall; and the Walk.

"I thought you weren't coming," said Judy, "so I thought—bugger it—I'll go round and see you. It's a good thing I took the shortcut. What in heaven's name possessed you to go peering over the edge like that? It's not safe."

"Can you take me home?"

"Of course, love."

Judy put her arm around her and led her away from the gap in the wall.

Behind them, silence and darkness. The lamp flickered. The mortar crumbled a little more.

They stayed together through the night at the house, and they shared the big bed in Miriam's room innocently, as they had as children. Miriam told the story from beginning to end: the whole history of the Bogey-Walk. Judy took it all in, nodded, smiled, and let it be. At last, in the hour before dawn, the confessions over, they slept.

*   *   *

At that same hour, the ashes of Miriam's mother were cooling, mingled with the ashes of thirteen others who had gone to the incinerator that Wednesday, December 1. In the morning, the remaining bones would be ground up and the dust would be divided into fourteen equal parts, then shoveled scrupulously into fourteen urns bearing the names of the loved ones. Some of the ashes would be scattered; some sealed in the Wall of Remembrance; some would go to the bereaved, as a focus for their grief.

At that same hour, Mr. Beckett dreamed of his father and half woke, sobbing, only to be soothed back to sleep by the girl at his side.

And, at that same hour, the husband of the late Marjorie Elliot took a shortcut along the Bogey-Walk. His feet crunched on the gravel, the only sound in the world at that weary hour before dawn. He had come this way every day of his working life, exhausted from the night shift at the bakery. His fingernails were lined with dough, and under his arm he carried a large white loaf and a bag of six crusty rolls. These he had carried home, fresh each morning, for almost twenty-three years. He still repeated the ritual, though since Marjorie's premature death, most of the bread was uneaten and went to the birds.

Toward the middle of the Bogey-Walk, his steps slowed. There was a fluttering in his belly; a scent in the air had awakened a memory. Was it not his wife's scent? Five yards farther on and the lamp flickered. He looked down at the gap in the wall and from out of the quarry rose his long-mourned Marjorie, her face huge.

It spoke his name once, and without bothering to reply to her call, he stepped off the Walk and was gone.

The loaf he had been carrying was left behind on the gravel.

Loosened from its tissue wrapping, it cooled, slowly forfeiting the warmth of its birth to the night.

THOMAS TESSIER, born 1947 in Waterbury, Connecticut, was the managing director of Britain's Millington Books before he returned to the United States to write full-time. His novels include *The Fates*, *The Nightwalker*, *Shockwaves*, *Phantom*, and *Finishing Touches*. Tessier turns rarely to the short story form, but always, as in "Food," with unforgettable results. His newest novel is *Rapture*.

Thomas Tessier

Food

"It's almost over now," Miss Rowe said, more to herself than to Mr. Whitman. There was a faraway look in her eyes, but her mouth struggled to form a smile and her voice was bright with anticipation. "Don't worry, though. I'll be fine."

Almost over? What did that mean? Mr. Whitman preferred not to think about it. As far as he was concerned, it was just a typical summer Saturday. The August heat had eased a bit, and there was a sweet breeze in the air. Other people would go swimming or shopping or would watch a baseball game. Mr. Whitman and Miss Rowe would do what they usually did on Saturday afternoon. To look at it any other way would be too frightening.

"But you aren't well," he was compelled to say. "I mean, you're experiencing pain now, real pain. I can see it."

"No," she replied without much conviction. "I know what I feel, and it's not pain. Not really." Miss Rowe quivered dismissively, adjusted herself on the mattresses, and tried to change the subject. "What did you bring for me today?"

Mr. Whitman ignored that. "I do think you should let me get a doctor. You ought to be in a hospital, but the least you can do is have a doctor examine you."

"Absolutely not. If you do anything like that, I'll never speak to you again."

Miss Rowe said this not harshly but more as a pout. Unfortunately Mr. Whitman knew it was also the truth.

He was incapable of dealing with her on any terms other than her own. His sense of duty wasn't as strong as his fear of destroying the friendship they shared.

Mr. Whitman crossed the room, picking his way carefully through the debris, and stood for a few moments by the open French doors. He enjoyed more of the breeze there, but the backyard was a distressing sight. The lawn hadn't been mowed in weeks. As if on cue, someone's power mower started up and whined steadily in the distance. The garden at the far end of the yard didn't quite exist. Mr. Whitman had cleared and spaded a patch for carrots and tomato plants, but he had never gotten around to putting them in. The bare black soil sprouted a few weeds instead. But he had been busy, he told himself. Miss Rowe had taken over his life that summer.

"What have you brought?" she asked again.

"Oh, Balzac," Mr. Whitman answered distractedly. He had almost forgotten the book he held in one hand. Every Saturday afternoon he read a story to Miss Rowe. Balzac was one of her favorites, and his. Today he intended to recite "Facino Cane," a tale he practically knew by heart but which never failed to move him deeply.

Miss Rowe's face showed pleasure, but she was unable to speak. At that moment she was eagerly cramming a thick slice of Italian bread into her mouth. The sight was too depressing for Mr. Whitman to bear, so he turned to the volume of Balzac and flipped through its pages. It wasn't just the bread, nor the generous layers of brandy pâté and cream cheese that coated it. Food: that was the problem, the whole wretched problem. Miss Rowe was a compulsive eater. Nearly all of her waking hours were devoted to the consumption of food. She was half his age and, by his conservative estimate, triple his weight.

Their strange relationship had begun six months earlier when Mr. Whitman had moved in and become her neighbor. They were a couple of refugees from the outside world, occupying the two ground-floor apartments in a converted Victorian house on the outskirts of Cairo. Not the Cairo in Egypt, but rather a country village in the central part of eastern Connecticut, where many towns have oddly incongruous names, like Westminster, Brooklyn, and Versailles.

Mr. Whitman had never married, but he had saved and invested his money shrewdly over the years, so that when he reached the age of fifty, he was able to retire from his editorial job in Manhattan and leave the city behind him. He could please himself and do what he wanted, which was to deal in rare books. Mr. Whitman's specialty was crime, true and fictional, though he loved all literature. He had a respectable collection which he kept in the two-room shop he rented in the village. He also had a dozen or so truly valuable books in a safe-deposit box at the bank. Mr. Whitman didn't make much money at this business, in part because he hated to sell any of his books and invariably overpriced them. But money had ceased to be an important factor in his life, and he was happy to spend several hours a day in his shop, surrounded by his collection, listening to public radio on the FM and tending to a very small mail-order trade. He discouraged off-the-street customers by keeping the door locked and the shades drawn. He was in the process of compiling a catalog of his collection, but in a leisurely fashion. More often than not, he would push the lists aside and settle back to lose himself in a book. Mr. Whitman knew he would never be able to read everything he wanted to in one lifetime.

Miss Rowe was something of a mystery to him. She disliked talking about herself, but she dropped occasional hints. Her only relatives were a couple of cousins on the West Coast. However, Miss Rowe had come to Cairo from Boston, where something unspecified had apparently rocked her life about a year ago. An accident, an assault, an emotional trauma? Mr. Whitman had no idea. Whatever it was, Miss Rowe had come to stay in Cairo with enough money to do nothing . . . but eat.

When Mr. Whitman first met her, she still moved around a bit, going out to buy what she wanted or to drive the back roads and take in the countryside. But now it was virtually impossible for her to leave her apartment. These last few months had seen Miss Rowe put on weight at an alarming rate. Clearly she was approaching the six-hundred-pound mark, if she hadn't already passed it. She had arranged for several area food stores to deliver groceries to her, and fresh supplies arrived daily.

Her apartment had been transformed into a center for this remarkable consumption. Furniture was literally pushed out to make room for the essentials. A schoolboy with a perpetually dazed look on his face came around every afternoon to dispose of the piles of trash that Miss Rowe produced, while she spent most of her time reclining on an arrangement of four king-size mattresses, stacked two across two, and an array of pillows. She covered her epic bulk with overlapping sheets so that only her head, shoulders, and arms were visible.

Around her and within easy reach, like a ring of sophisticated equipment in the intensive-care unit of a hospital, waited a microwave oven, a hot plate, three small refrigerators, a toaster, a blender, and a bookshelf that held plenty of paper plates and plastic tumblers, forks, spoons, and knives. Then there were the garbage sacks and the cartons of food.

Mr. Whitman was used to all this because he had become a frequent visitor, as fascinated as he was appalled by Miss Rowe's extraordinary way of life. In the beginning they had argued, often heatedly. He would tell her she simply had to go on a diet and get help—whatever it took to stop her from gorging herself incessantly. But Miss Rowe would have none of that. She was happy and positively cheerful about her habits. Mr. Whitman took to reading to her from articles and books on the subject of bulimia, compulsive eating. But Miss Rowe refuted these expertly, pointing out that she never vomited, never purged herself with laxatives, and never suffered any guilt or depression. In short, she wasn't bulimic.

She just enjoyed eating.

Mr. Whitman persisted, explaining over and over the dangers, the very real threat, to her heart and health. But again Miss Rowe smiled away his warnings. "Your body tells you," she would say calmly while devouring another can of spiced apple rings. "Most people don't pay attention to their bodies, but I do. I really do. When it tells me to eat, I eat. When it says enough, then I'll stop." Her body, it seemed, urged her only, always, to eat.

Mr. Whitman then adopted a different tactic. He told her about his past travels to Europe and Asia, his vacations in Mexico and the Caribbean. He would go on eloquently and at length about the sights he'd seen and the people he'd met. But travel seemed to hold little interest for Miss Rowe, and in desperation he began describing some of the food he had eaten abroad. He didn't like doing this, but he reasoned that if she were sufficiently intrigued, she might want to do some traveling herself to sample foreign cuisine—and then she would have to impose some dietary discipline just to be able to undertake any trip. That also failed, however. Miss Rowe loved food, but indiscriminately. The thought of toad in the hole, coq au vin, Arnold Bennett omelets, prawn vindaloo, Creole crayfish, and five-snake soup aroused no excitement in her. She was perfectly happy to zap in the microwave three or four chicken pot pies fresh from the freezer section of the supermarket and tamp them down with pickled herring, some hot dogs, and a quart of applesauce. Miss Rowe was not averse to good food, but she had no time for extraneous effort.

Although his concern never diminished—on the contrary, it continued to grow—Mr. Whitman did begin to concede the struggle after a month or so. The arguments were pointless, in the sense that they achieved nothing. Miss Rowe's confidence was unbreakable, her appetite supreme. Mr. Whitman could see himself turning into a nag, and that wouldn't do. Besides, by then he liked the girl too much to fight with her. He would still try, with a remark here, a caution there, to get through to her, but he had come to accept her as she was. He hardly realized it, but she had quickly become very dear to him. She was practically the only other person in his life.

The power mower continued to drone down the street, but the breeze had died for the time being. Mr. Whitman sat on the room's only chair and found his place in the book.

" 'I was living at that time in a little street you probably don't know . . .' "

Miss Rowe closed her eyes and listened contentedly. She chewed marshmallows because they were quiet. Books had never interested her, but she loved to hear Mr. Whitman read stories to her. He was very good, seldom stumbling over a word, and he could be dramatic without sounding hammy. No one else had ever read to her, not even when she was a small child, so she had nobody to compare him with, but all the same, she knew he was the best.

" 'I don't know how I have been able to keep untold for so long the story I am about to tell you . . .' "

He lit a cigarette when he finished the Balzac tale. He had made a point of telling Miss Rowe the first time they chatted that he limited himself to ten smokes a day, thinking she might find a way to apply his example to her own situation. But while she saluted his willpower, she did not take up the suggestion. Now they talked about the story and the author, with Mr. Whitman carrying most of the conversation and Miss Rowe saying that "Facino Cane" was beautiful but so sad—and how many cups of coffee did Balzac drink every night? Finally Mr. Whitman was ready to conclude his visit.

"Please come back and see me again this evening," Miss Rowe said when he stood up.

"Sure. I'll look in later," he promised, but then it occurred to him that there was something odd in the way she had spoken. Some extra hint of urgency. "Are you all right?"

"Oh, yes," Miss Rowe replied, but with pro forma assurance. "It's just that I'd like to see you again. This evening."

"Fine. Well." Mr. Whitman started to go.

"Something's happening," she whispered breathlessly, to hold him there a moment longer.

"What is it?" Mr. Whitman asked. Now he was worried.

"I don't know. I just feel . . . different. Like something's changing inside me. But it's not bad," she added hastily. "It feels good, in a funny way."

"You can't judge things like that by yourself," he said sharply. "I really do think you need to see a doctor. It could be your heart. Funny signs often mean there is something very unfunny just around the corner."

"No, *no*." Then Miss Rowe made an effort to restrain herself and went on daintily, "I will not be poked and prodded and tested and otherwise treated like a freak. Next thing you know, I'd be in the *National Enquirer*. As it is, I worry all day and half the night that word will get out through one of the delivery boys and I'll be besieged by reporters, photographers, curiosity seekers, and self-important doctors. I couldn't bear it." She hesitated, then brightened. "Anyway, I told you: I feel good, not ill. In fact, I've never felt better. I'm tingly all over."

Mr. Whitman sighed unhappily. The whole thing would be nonsensical if it weren't fraught with danger. Tingly all over, indeed. He couldn't imagine what that meant in the context of her general health. And the remark that something was happening: What was he supposed to make of that? He knew Miss Rowe had a penchant for the dramatic and was always trying to make something out of the sheer uneventfulness of her daily life. That's all there is to it, he tried to persuade himself.

But she did look somewhat different. Miss Rowe's face had a little more color to it than usual. She appeared to be slightly flushed; her cheeks were pink, whereas they were usually rather sallow because she spent all her time indoors.

Mr. Whitman and Miss Rowe touched each other rarely, and then only when their hands met to exchange something. But now Mr. Whitman had to be decisive. He sat on the edge of the mattresses and placed the back of his hand on her forehead.

"Are you running a temperature?" he asked, to make his intentions quite clear.

"Oh," she said, perhaps a little disappointed. "I don't think so."

"Hmmn." Mr. Whitman marveled silently at the feel of her skin. Miss Rowe's head was not as large as a beach ball but gave the impression that it was. He had expected it to be soft and spongy with so much fat, but it was surprisingly firm. Although there were layers of jowls pleated below the jawline, the forehead was smooth, nearly taut. The texture was silky and supple. Mr. Whitman discovered he was reluctant to take his hand away. "Perhaps just a slight temperature," he announced, though he was not at all certain.

"I think you're imagining it," Miss Rowe said with a girlish smile. "But it's nice that you care. I don't know what I'd do without you."

You'd just keep on eating, Mr. Whitman thought sadly. But he smiled back at her, for he was truly fond of the young woman.

"Take it easy," he advised her. "You know, I wish you would eat more fruits and vegetables and go easier on the junk food." He had delivered this message countless times.

"Oh, but I do," Miss Rowe insisted enthusiastically. "Did I tell you that I made a Waldorf salad this morning? I did, all by myself."

"Well, that's good," Mr. Whitman responded, his face achieving something like a grin. She was so proud of herself for managing such a trivial feat that he didn't tell her a Waldorf salad was not only healthier but a step up in taste.

"I'm surprised more people don't realize just how good a salad can be for breakfast," Miss Rowe went on.

"Yes."

Mr. Whitman left then; otherwise, he would be stuck there for a long and expanding rhapsody on salads, breakfasts, and food in general. He went directly to his shop in town and picked Rufus King's *The*

Lesser Antilles Case and Kirby Williams's *The C.V.C.
Murders* for his Saturday night and Sunday afternoon
reading treats.

Back in his apartment, Mr. Whitman filled a pilsner
glass with cold beer and looked through the few items
of mail he'd found at the shop. Nothing of interest
except a catalog from a dealer in St. Paul. He soon
pushed the catalog aside and lit another cigarette.

Miss Rowe worried him. If something happened to
her, if her heart suddenly gave out, he would be
morally responsible. Now he wondered if he wouldn't
also be legally at risk for failing to bring her to the
attention of some medical authority. He had no idea
what the law said, if anything, about a situation like
this. Would he be liable to a charge of negligence? Or
even negligent homicide?

It didn't seem fair. Miss Rowe was, after all, an
adult, and as such, she was responsible for herself. She
was compulsive but not mentally incompetent. Should
his loyalty be directed to her as a personal friend,
accepting her as she was, or to her health and well-being?
The two should not be mutually exclusive, though in
this case they seemed to be, and Mr. Whitman thought
that sooner or later he would have to discuss the matter
with a physician—or a lawyer. But he would mention
no names, at least until he had received some guid-
ance. It was a matter that demanded clarification.

Later, when the sun was gone but darkness had not
yet settled in completely, Mr. Whitman tapped on
Miss Rowe's door and entered her apartment. There
were no lights on and it was hard to see, but he was
aware of her stirring as the sheets rustled softly. Perhaps she had dozed off for a while.

"Turn on the lamp." Groggy, she struggled to ele-
vate herself against the pillows.

"Am I disturbing you?"

"No, not at all. Come in."

Mr. Whitman switched on the light and took his
seat. Her eyes were puffier than usual, he thought,
her complexion even more flushed than it had been
that afternoon.

"Come closer," she said. He slid the wooden chair nearer to her bed, wedging himself between a refrigerator and the shelves of paper plates. "No, not there. Sit next to me on the bed, please. I'm feeling kind of down."

Mr. Whitman perched himself cautiously on the edge of the mattresses. He was surprised that Miss Rowe didn't suffer blue moods more frequently. It wasn't right that a young woman in her twenties should lead such a solitary, reclusive existence. And no matter how strongly she denied it, the constant eating had to take a psychological toll. Mr. Whitman wondered if her high spirits were finally beginning to weaken.

"You're so good to me." Miss Rowe took his hand, squeezed it, refused to let go. Her grip was warm and strangely inviting. "I wish I could thank you in some way."

"Oh, don't be silly," Mr. Whitman responded with a nervous smile. "The funny thing is, only a few minutes ago I was thinking that I've really been quite negligent about you."

"That's not true. Far from it. You've been just the person I needed. Without you, I don't know if I could have . . . well, you've made all the difference, believe me."

She squeezed his hand again. Odd, Mr. Whitman thought. It was almost as if she were comforting him.

"I must look awful," Miss Rowe went on. "I haven't looked in a mirror in ages. Do I . . . look awful?"

"No, of course not." She wasn't begging a compliment, but Mr. Whitman naturally wanted to answer as positively as he could. "You do look tired, though, and as I've told you before, you need to make some changes in—"

"I *am* changing," she interrupted, looking away from him but also tightening her grip on his hand. "I *am* changing."

"Good. Well, good." Mr. Whitman didn't know what else to say because he didn't understand what she meant. He had the vague feeling that she was trying to edge him closer to something. "Can you tell me—or would you like to tell me—what happened?"

"When?"

"In Boston."

"Oh." She looked at him again and smiled. "Does it make a difference? What would you say if I told you that I killed someone? My family, for instance."

"I wouldn't believe it," he scoffed. The idea was absurd.

"You see? It doesn't make any difference."

"But something did happen," he insisted. "You must tell me, Frances. It'll be good for you to talk about it with a friend you can trust."

They rarely addressed each other by their first names, and Miss Rowe seemed touched. But she merely shrugged and gave him a bewildering smile.

"That's just it," she said quietly. "Nothing happened."

Mr. Whitman found that hard to believe, although there was nothing deceptive or evasive about her manner and tone of voice. On the contrary, they carried the weight of truth.

"I want to talk to someone about you," he told her finally. "I'm sorry if it upsets you, but I have to, and this time I mean to do it."

To his surprise, Miss Rowe didn't object. She nodded slowly as if to say she understood, and she even pulled his hand closer to her. "Not tonight, though," she said. "You won't do anything tonight."

"Well, no," he allowed. It was the weekend, after all, and he probably wouldn't have any luck getting a doctor or a lawyer, even if he tried. "But first thing Monday morning."

"That's all right."

It seemed too easy, and for a few moments Mr. Whitman wasn't sure that he'd actually said what he meant, or that she had grasped it. Not that it really mattered; he knew what he was going to do on Monday, and already he felt better about things.

"Lawrence."

"Hmm?" He had to swallow to clear his throat. "Yes?"

"Would you lie down here next to me on the bed?" Her voice was tiny and distant, painfully vulnerable. "I just need you to be here with me and to hold me for a few minutes."

Mr. Whitman couldn't speak, but he felt an emotional surge that made his body tremble and his cheeks redden. He slipped off his loafers. She must be terribly lonely, he thought. She needs comfort, a little human warmth. He stretched out on the mattress and moved tentatively closer to her enormous bulk. Miss Rowe pulled him closer still, until the length of his body pressed against hers. She handled him easily, like a toy doll, so that he had one arm across the expanse of her middle and his head on her breast. Then she seemed to sigh and to settle, and they stayed that way for some time.

Mr. Whitman was glad that she was under the sheet and he was not. He was paralyzed—caught in a state of diffuse, but undeniable, erotic tension. Perhaps he needed this human warmth, too, and the contact was all the more exciting because it was essentially chaste. He stopped thinking about it and let himself enjoy it, drifting along dreamily, half awake, until it eventually occurred to him that he had been lying in her embrace for quite a while.

The air was cooler. The French doors were still open, and it was dark outside. Miss Rowe's breathing was slightly congested but regular, and her arm fell away from him when Mr. Whitman stirred. She was asleep. He moved carefully, picked up his shoes, turned off the lamp, and went back to his own apartment.

He had another beer and smoked a cigarette. He couldn't sit still. His feelings were alarming, exciting, and above all, mysterious to him. Did he love her? Yes. But not as a lover—although, he had to admit, there was a disturbing new physical element to it now. The feel of her body and her touch lingered on him like a tactile afterglow. He almost believed that if he looked in the bathroom mirror, he would see it on his hand and cheek, a radiance, an aura.

Then a shocking thought came to him. She was

beautiful. Miss Rowe, Frances, the nearly six hundred pounds of her, was truly beautiful. And not in spite of her massive size but because of it. The one thing about her that had frightened and even repelled him now struck him as nothing less than miraculous. Maybe she did suffer from a dangerous compulsion, but wasn't it also a sign of her strength and courage, her quality and character?

Mr. Whitman drank three more bottles of beer and didn't bother to count the cigarettes. His mind raced from one thought to another, uncovering pockets of illumination where there had been only uncertainty before. Yes, he loved her. In all ways. He would take care of her, more devotedly than ever, but without trying to change her. He would keep her alive, healthy, happy; there were ways. The discipline of a love, a better diet; somehow it could all be made to work. In a way, he had to surrender to her for her to surrender to him.

Mr. Whitman glanced at the clock, but he didn't care that it was after eleven. He wanted to see her again, tell her things. And to be with her—for the warmth and peace of her all-inclusive embrace.

At the door of his apartment, he hesitated one last time. Was he making an idiot of himself, a pathetic, middle-aged joke? Was he drunk, deluded, hysterical? No, he decided; and, anyway, he didn't care.

Mr. Whitman listened at her door and heard sounds of movement. He tapped, got no response, and then knocked a little louder. Still nothing but those peculiar noises, muffled and unfamiliar. He turned the handle and went inside. The room was dark, but moonlight through the open French doors provided some faint definition; his eyes began to adjust.

Miss Rowe was writhing on her makeshift bed like a person lost in an increasingly uncomfortable dream. She appeared to be asleep, but Mr. Whitman felt a shiver when he noticed that her eyes were half open, glassy, unseeing. She made sounds that were strangled in her throat. A fever, he thought, or convulsions. Something terrible was happening; of that he was certain. He banged his knee against a refrigerator and crushed a carton of cheese crackers underfoot as he approached the bed, but Miss Rowe gave no sign that she recognized his presence. Her movements were becoming sharper and more violent by the minute, thrashing and jerking.

Mr. Whitman put his hand on her forehead and was startled to find that she was not feverish but unnaturally cold. Her skin was slick with moisture, her hair smeared back on her skull. More than anything, he was frightened by how cold she felt. It was all wrong. But there was something else. The skin itself felt different. It was hard, almost scaly.

Then her head turned again and caught the meager light. Mr. Whitman saw that her eyes had changed. They were closed now, swollen so tightly that it was nearly impossible to make out the thin slits on either side of her nose—itself so broad and flat now that it looked as if it had been pressed, squashed to her face. She continued to toss and squirm but with her arms tight to her body and her legs rigidly straight together, as if she were tied from her head to her feet.

The noises emanating from her grew in intensity and as she shrugged free of the sheet, Mr. Whitman saw that her jowl-ringed, flabby neck was somehow changed. It melded smoothly into her shoulders, as if there were no real neck there at all. And the skin, like that of her face, was so pale, it was almost a brilliant white, shiny and hard.

Mr. Whitman shook with fear, but he could hardly move. He managed to put a hand on her shoulder— the round slope where her shoulder had been—and again he was shocked at how cold she felt. He had to do something, but that thought was nothing more than a disembodied voice in his brain. Miss Rowe escaped the sheet. Naked, he realized dimly, she's naked. But her body had lost its features—breasts, hips, buttocks— and become a long, large, tubular thing. She was not Miss Rowe. She was something more or less than human. The word, Mr. Whitman thought insanely, is *larval*.

She was struggling on the bed, heaving and shrugging her entire body as if she were trying to escape that place. Mr. Whitman clambered across the lower part of the bed as he realized she was trying to move away from him. It seemed that the most important thing was for her to remain where she was and to get expert help. It was the only way she might overcome whatever terrible illness had seized her. But Miss Rowe would not stay still. She squirmed vigorously, rolling and flipping herself, advancing off the edge of the bed. She was so big—for an instant Mr. Whitman was frightened by the sheer, naked size of her as she reared up at him.

I love you, he thought hopelessly. He leapt at her, arms spread wide, his legs pushing with all the strength he could manage. He hoped to embrace her and get through to her, to force her back onto the bed. Their bodies met and froze together, Mr. Whitman clinging to what once had been Miss Rowe.

"Frances," he gasped, dizzy with love and fear. "Frances."

The moment lasted only a second or two, but seemed much longer to Mr. Whitman because it was his last. He thought she recognized him in some way—his warmth; his physical presence, if nothing else. But then whatever forces held her drove Miss Rowe over him with irresistible power, and Mr. Whitman was bent back like a blade of grass as she surged and slid on her way. The appliances around the bed, the cartons of food, and the shelves were all knocked easily aside like hollow stage props. Picking up speed, Miss Rowe slithered out into the night and was gone.

In the morning the delivery boy found the French doors wide open. There was a trail of sticky wetness across the back lawn, a wide, unbroken ribbon that snaked through the grass to the unused garden plot. It looked like a tunnel had been dug there, and then had collapsed in on itself. A huge mound of soil had been turned up, and this dirt had the round, nodal appearance of digested earth.

Of Mr. Whitman, there was not a trace.

M. JOHN HARRISON, born 1945 in Rugby, England, served for eight years as literary editor of *New Worlds* magazine. His novels include *The Centaur Device* and the *Viriconium Sequence* of high fantasy—*The Pastel City, A Storm of Wings,* and *In Viriconium*—while his short fiction has been collected in *The Ice Monkey and Other Stories*. "The Great God Pan," named after the classic Arthur Machen story, showcases Harrison's penchant for horrors of a sublime and chilling subtlety.

M. John Harrison

The Great God Pan

*But is there really something far more horrible
than ever could resolve itself into reality,
and is it that something which terrifies me so?*
—KATHERINE MANSFIELD,
Journals, March 1914

Ann took drugs to manage her epilepsy. They often
made her depressed and difficult to deal with; and
Lucas, who was nervous himself, never knew what to
do. After their divorce he relied increasingly on me as
a go-between. "I don't like the sound of her voice,"
he would tell me. "You try her." The drugs gave her a
screaming, false-sounding laugh that went on and on.
Though he had remained sympathetic over the years,
Lucas was always embarrassed and upset by it. I think
it frightened him. "See if you can get any sense out of
her." It was guilt, I think, that encouraged him to see
me as a steadying influence: not his own guilt so much
as the guilt he felt all three of us shared. "See what
she says."

On this occasion what she said was:

"Look, if you bring on one of my turns, bloody
Lucas Fisher will regret it. What business is it of his
how I feel, anyway?"

I was used to her, so I said carefully, "It was just
that you wouldn't talk to him. He was worried that
something was happening. Is there something wrong,
Ann?" She didn't answer, but I had hardly expected

her to. "If you don't want to see me," I suggested, "couldn't you tell me now?"

I thought she was going to hang up, but in the end there was only a kind of paroxysm of silence. I was phoning her from a call box in the middle of Huddersfield. The shopping precinct outside was full of pale bright sunshine, but windy and cold; sleet was forecast for later in the day. Two or three teenagers went past, talking and laughing. I heard one of them say, "What acid rain's got to do with my career, I don't know. But that's what they asked me: 'What do you know about acid rain?' " When they had gone, I could hear Ann breathing raggedly.

"Hello?" I said.

Suddenly she shouted, "Are you mad? I'm not talking on the phone. Before you know it, the whole thing's public property!"

Sometimes she was more dependent on medication than usual; you knew when, because she tended to use that phrase over and over again. One of the first things I ever heard her say was, "It looks so easy, doesn't it? But before you know it, the bloody thing's just slipped straight out of your hands," as she bent down nervously to pick up the bits of a broken glass. How old were we then? Twenty? Lucas believed she was reflecting in language some experience either of the drugs or the disease itself, but I'm not sure he was right. Another thing she often said was, "I mean, you have to be careful, don't you?" drawing out in a wondering, childlike way both *care* and *don't,* so that you saw immediately it was a mannerism learned in adolescence.

"You must be mad if you think I'm talking on the phone!"

I said quickly, "Okay, then, Ann. I'll come over this evening."

"You might as well come now and get it over with. I don't feel well."

Epilepsy since the age of twelve or thirteen, as regular as clockwork; and then, later, a classic migraine to fill in the gaps, a complication which, rightly or wrongly, she had alway associated with our experiments at Cambridge in the late sixties. She must never get angry or excited. "I reserve my adrenaline," she would explain, looking down at herself with a comical distaste. "It's a physical thing. I can't let it go at the time." Afterward, though, the reservoir would burst, and it would all be released at once by some minor stimulus—a lost shoe, a missed bus, rain—to cause her hallucinations, vomiting, loss of bowel control. "Oh, and then euphoria. It's wonderfully relaxing," she would say bitterly. "Just like sex."

"Okay, Ann, I'll be there soon. Don't worry."

"Piss off. Things are coming to bits here. I can already see the little floating lights."

As soon as she put the receiver down, I telephoned Lucas.

"I'm not doing this again," I said. "Lucas, she isn't well. I thought she was going to have an attack there and then."

"She'll see you, though? The thing is, she just kept putting the phone down on me. She'll see you today?"

"You knew she would."

"Good."

I hung up.

"Lucas, you're a bastard," I told the shopping precinct.

The bus from Huddersfield wound its way for thirty minutes through exhausted mill villages given over to hairdressing, dog breeding, and an undercapitalized tourist trade. I got off the bus at three o'clock in the afternoon. It seemed much later. The church clock was already lit, and a mysterious yellow light was slanting across the window of the nave—someone was inside with only a forty-watt bulb for illumination. Cars went past endlessly as I waited to cross the road, their exhaust steaming in the dark air. For a village it was quite noisy: tires hissing on the wet road, the bang and clink of soft-drink bottles being unloaded from a lorry, some children I couldn't see, chanting one word over and over again. Suddenly, above all this, I heard the pure musical note of a thrush and stepped out into the road.

"You're sure no one got off the bus behind you?"

Ann kept me on the doorstep while she looked anxiously up and down the street, but once I was inside, she seemed glad to have someone to talk to.

"You'd better take your coat off. Sit down. I'll make you some coffee. No, here, just push the cat off the chair. He knows he's not supposed to be there."

It was an old cat, black and white, with dull, dry fur, and when I picked it up, it was just a lot of bones and heat that weighed nothing. I set it down carefully on the carpet, but it jumped back onto my knee again immediately and began to dribble on my pullover. Another, younger animal was crouching on the windowsill, shifting its feet uncomfortably among the little intricate baskets of paper flowers as it stared out into the falling sleet, the empty garden. "Get down off there!" Ann shouted suddenly. It ignored her. She shrugged. "They act as if they own the place." It smelled as if they did. "They were strays," she said. "I don't know why I encouraged them." Then, as though she were still talking about the cats:

"How's Lucas?"

"He's surprisingly well," I said. "You ought to keep in touch with him, you know."

"I know." She smiled briefly. "And how are you? I never see you."

"Not bad. Feeling my age."

"You don't know the half of it yet," she said. She was standing in the kitchen doorway holding a tea towel in one hand and a cup in the other. "None of us do." It was a familiar complaint. When she saw I was too preoccupied to listen, she went and banged things about in the sink. I heard water rushing into the kettle. While it filled up, she said something she knew I wouldn't catch; then, turning off the tap:

"Something's going on in the Pleroma. Something new. I can feel it."

"Ann," I said, "all that was over and done with twenty years ago."

The fact is that even at the time I wasn't at all sure what we *had* done. This will seem odd to you, I suppose; but it was 1968 or 1969, and all I remember now is a June evening drenched with the half-confectionary, half-corrupt smell of hawthorn blossoms. It was so thick, we seemed to swim through it, through that and the hot evening light that poured between the hedgerows like transparent gold. I remember Sprake because you don't forget him. What the four of us did escapes me, as does its significance. There was, undoubtedly, a loss; but whether you described what was lost as "innocence" was very much up to you—anyway, that was how it appeared to me. Lucas and Ann made a lot more of it from the very start. They took it to heart. Afterward—perhaps two or three months afterward, when it was plain that something had gone wrong, when things first started to pull out of shape—it was Ann and Lucas who convinced me to go and talk to Sprake, whom we had promised never to contact again. They wanted to see if what we had done could somehow be reversed or annulled; if what we'd lost could be bought back again.

"I don't think it works that way," I warned them; but I could see they weren't listening.

"He'll have to help us," Lucas said.

"Why did we ever do it?" Ann asked me.

Though he hated the British Museum, Sprake had always lived one way or another in its shadow. I met him at the Tivoli Espresso Bar, where I knew he would be every afternoon. He was wearing a thick, old-fashioned black overcoat—the weather that October was raw and damp—but from the way his wrists stuck out of the sleeves, long and fragile-looking and dirty, covered with sore grazes as though he had been fighting with some small animal, I suspected he wore no shirt or jacket underneath it. For some reason he had bought a copy of the *Church Times*. The top half of his body curled painfully around it; along with his stoop and his grey-stubbled lower jaw, the newspaper gave him the appearance of a disappointed verger. It was folded carefully to display part of a headline, but I never saw him open it.

At the Tivoli in those days, they always had the radio on. Their coffee was watery and, like most espresso, too hot to taste of anything. Sprake and I sat on stools by the window. We rested our elbows on a narrow counter littered with dirty cups and half-eaten sandwiches and watched the pedestrians in Museum Street. After ten minutes, a woman's voice said clearly from behind us:

"The fact is, the children just won't try."

Sprake jumped and glanced round haggardly, as if he expected to have to answer this.

"It's the radio," I reassured him.

He stared at me the way you would stare at someone who was mad, and it was some time before he went on with what he had been saying.

"You knew what you were doing. You got what you wanted, and you weren't tricked in any way."

"No," I admitted tiredly.

My eyes ached, even though I had slept on the journey down, waking—just as the train from Cambridge crawled the last mile into London—to see sheets of newspaper fluttering round the upper floors of an office block like butterflies courting a flower.

"I can see that," I said. "That isn't at issue. But I'd like to be able to reassure them in some way. . . ."

Sprake wasn't listening. It had come on to rain quite hard, driving visitors—mainly Germans and Americans who were touring the Museum—in from the street. They all seemed to be wearing brand-new clothes. The Tivoli filled with steam from the espresso machine, and the air was heavy with the smell of wet coats. People trying to find seats constantly brushed our backs, murmuring, "Excuse me, please. Excuse me." Sprake soon became irritated, though I think their politeness affected him more than the disturbance itself. "Dog muck," he said loudly in a matter-of-fact voice; and then, as a whole family pushed past him one by one,

"Three generations of rabbits." None of them seemed to take offense, though they must have heard him. A drenched-looking woman in a purple coat came in, looked anxiously for an empty seat, and, when she couldn't see one, hurried out again. "Mad bitch!" Sprake called after her. "Get yourself reamed out." He stared challengingly at the other customers.

"I think it would be better if we talked in private," I said. "What about your flat?"

For twenty years he had lived in the same single room above the Atlantis Bookshop. He was reluctant to take me there, I could see, though it was only next door, and I had been there before. At first he tried to pretend it would be difficult to get in. "The shop's closed," he said. "We'd have to use the other door." Then he admitted:

"I can't go back there for an hour or two. I did something last night that means it may not be safe."

He grinned.

"You know the sort of thing I mean," he said.

I couldn't get him to explain further. The cuts on his wrists made me remember how panicky Ann and Lucas had been when I last spoke to them. All at once I was determined to see inside the room.

"If you don't want to go back there for a bit," I suggested, "we could always talk in the Museum."

Researching in the manuscript collection one afternoon a year before, he had turned a page of Jean de Wavrin's *Chroniques d'Angleterre*—that oblique history no complete version of which is known—and come upon a miniature depicting in strange, unreal greens and blues the coronation procession of Richard Coeur de Lion. Part of it had moved; which part, he would never say. "Why, if it is a coronation," he had written almost plaintively to me at the time, "are these four men carrying a coffin? And who is walking there under the awning—with the bishops not with them?" After that he had avoided the building as much as possible, though he could always see its tall iron railings at the end of the street. He had begun, he told me, to doubt the authenticity of some of the items in the medieval collection. In fact, he was frightened of them.

"It would be quieter there," I insisted.

He didn't respond but sat hunched over the *Church Times,* staring into the street with his hands clamped violently together in front of him. I could see him thinking.

"That fucking pile of shit!" he said eventually.

He got to his feet.

"Come on, then. It's probably cleared out by now, anyway."

Rain dripped from the blue-and-gold front of the Atlantis. There was a faded notice, CLOSED FOR COMPLETE REFURBISHMENT. The window display had been taken down, but they had left a few books on a shelf for the look of things. I could make out, through the condensation on the plate glass, de Vries's classic *Dictionary of Symbols & Imagery.* When I pointed it out to Sprake, he only stared at me contemptuously. He fumbled with his key. Inside, the shop smelled of cut timber, new plaster, paint, but this gave way on the stairs to an odor of cooking. Sprake's bed-sitter, which was quite large and on the top floor, had uncurtained sash windows on opposing walls. Nevertheless, it didn't seem well lit.

From one window you could see the sodden facades of Museum Street, bright green deposits on the ledges, stucco scrolls and garlands grey with pigeon dung; out of the other, part of the blackened clock tower of St. George's Bloomsbury, a reproduction of the tomb of Mausoleus lowering up against the racing clouds.

"I once heard that clock strike twenty-one," said Sprake.

"I can believe that," I said, though I didn't. "Do you think I could have some tea?"

He was silent for a minute. Then he laughed.

"I'm not going to help them," he said. "You know that. I wouldn't be allowed to. What you do in the Pleroma is irretrievable."

*   *   *

"All that was over and done with twenty years ago, Ann."

"I know. I know that. But—"

She stopped suddenly, and then went on in a muffled voice, "Will you just come here a minute? Just for a minute?"

The house, like many in the Pennines, had been built right into the side of the valley. A near vertical bank of earth, cut to accommodate it, was held back by a dry-stone revetment twenty or thirty feet high, black with damp even in the middle of July, dusted with lichen and tufted with fern like a cliff. In December, the water streamed down the revetment day after day and, collecting in a stone trough underneath, made a sound like a tap left running in the night. Along the back of the house ran a passage hardly two feet wide, full of broken roof slates and other rubbish. It was a dismal place.

"You're all right," I told Ann, who was staring, puzzled, into the gathering dark, her head on one side and the tea towel held up to her mouth as if she thought she might be sick.

"It knows who we are," she whispered. "Despite the precautions, it always remembers us."

She shuddered, pulled herself away from the window, and began pouring water so clumsily into the coffee filter that I put my arm around her shoulders and said, "Look, you'd better go and sit down before you scald yourself. I'll finish this, and then you can tell me what's the matter."

She hesitated.

"Come on," I said. "All right?"

"All right."

She went into the living room and sat down heavily. One of the cats ran into the kitchen and looked up at me. "Don't give them milk," she called. "They had it this morning."

"How are you feeling?" I asked. "In yourself, I mean?"

"About how you'd expect." She had taken some propranolol, she said, but it never seemed to help much. "It shortens the headaches, I suppose." As a side effect, though, it made her feel so tired. "It slows my heartbeat down. I can feel it slow right down." She watched the steam rising from her coffee cup, first slowly, and then with a rapid, plaiting motion as it was caught by some tiny draft. Eddies form and break to the same rhythm on the surface of a deep, smooth river. A slow coil, a sudden whirl. What was tranquil is revealed as a mass of complications that can be resolved only as motion.

I remembered when I had first met her: she was twenty then, a small, excitable, attractive girl who wore moss-colored jersey dresses to show off her waist and hips. Later, fear coarsened her. With the divorce a few grey streaks appeared in her blond bell of hair, and she chopped it raggedly off and dyed it black. She drew in on herself. Her body broadened into a kind of dogged, muscular heaviness. Even her hands and feet seemed to become bigger.

"You're old before you know it," she would say. "Before you know it." Separated from Lucas, she was easily chafed by her surroundings; moved every six months or so, although never very far, and always to the same sort of dilapidated, drearily furnished cottage, though you suspected that she was looking for precisely the things that made her nervous and ill; and tried to keep down to fifty cigarettes a day.

"Why did Sprake never help us?" she asked me. "You must know."

Sprake fished two cups out of a plastic washing-up bowl and put tea bags in them.

"Don't tell me you're frightened too!" he said. "I expected more from you."

I shook my head. I wasn't sure whether I was afraid or not. I'm not sure today. The tea, when it came, had a distinctly greasy aftertaste, as if somehow he had fried it. I made myself drink half while Sprake watched me cynically.

"You ought to sit down," he said. "You're worn-out." When I refused, he shrugged and went on as if we were still at the Tivoli. "Nobody tricked them, or tried to pretend it would be easy. If you get anything out of an experiment like that, it's by keeping your head and taking your chance. If you try to move cautiously, you may never be allowed to move at all."

He looked thoughtful.

"I've seen what happens to people who lose their nerve."

"I'm sure," I said.

"They were hardly recognizable, some of them."

I put the teacup down.

"I don't want to know," I said.

"I bet you don't."

He smiled to himself.

"Oh, they were still alive," he said softly, "if that's what you're worried about."

"You talked us into this," I reminded him.

"You talked yourselves into it."

Most of the light from the street was absorbed as soon as it entered the room, by the dull green wallpaper and sticky-looking yellow veneer of the furniture. The rest leaked eventually into the litter on the floor, pages of crumpled and partly burned typescript, hair clippings, broken chalks that had been used the night before to draw something on the flaking lino: among this stuff, it died. Though I knew Sprake was playing some sort of game with me, I couldn't see what it was; I couldn't make the effort. In the end, he had to make it for me.

When I said from the door, "You'll get sick of all this mess one day," he only grinned, nodded, and advised me:

"Come back when you know what you want. Get rid of Lucas Fisher, he's an amateur. Bring the girl if you must."

"Fuck off, Sprake."

He let me find my own way back down to the street.

That night I had to tell Lucas, "We aren't going to be hearing from Sprake again."

"Christ," he said, and for a second I thought he was

going to cry. "Ann feels so ill," he whispered. "What did he say?"

"Forget him. He could never have helped us."

"Ann and I are getting married," Lucas said in a rush.

What could I have done? I knew as well as he did that they were doing it only out of a need for comfort. Nothing would be gained by making them admit it. Besides, I was so tired by then, I could hardly stand. Some kind of visual fault, a neon zigzag like a bright little flight of stairs, kept showing up in my left eye. So I congratulated Lucas and, as soon as I could, began thinking about something else.

"Sprake's terrified of the British Museum," I said. "In a way, I sympathize with him."

As a child I had hated it too. All the conversations, every echo of a voice or a footstep or a rustle of clothes, gathered up in its high ceilings in a kind of undifferentiated rumble and sigh—the blurred and melted remains of meaning—which made you feel as if you had been abandoned in a derelict swimming bath. Later, when I was a teenager, it was the vast, shapeless heads in Room 25 that frightened me, the vagueness of the inscriptions. I saw clearly what was there—"Red sandstone head of a king" . . . "Red granite head from a colossal figure of a king"—but what was I looking at? The faceless wooden figure of Ramses emerged perpetually from an alcove near the lavatory door, a Ramses who had to support himself with a stick—split, syphilitic, worm-eaten by his passage through the world, but still condemned to struggle helplessly on.

"We want to go and live up north," Lucas said. "Away from all this."

As the afternoon wore on, Ann became steadily more disturbed. "Listen," she would ask me, "*is* that someone in the passage? You can always tell me the truth." After she had promised several times in a vague way—"I can't send you out without anything to eat. I'll cook us something in a minute, if you'll make some more

THE GREAT GOD PAN • 157

coffee"—I realized she was frightened to go back into
the kitchen. "No matter how much coffee I drink,"
she explained, "my throat is dry. It's all that smoking." She returned often to the theme of age. She had
always hated to feel old. "You comb your hair in the
mornings and it's just another ten years gone, every
loose hair, every bit of dandruff, like a lot of old
snapshots showering down." She shook her head and
said, as if the connection would be quite clear to me:

"We moved around a lot after university. It wasn't
that I couldn't settle, more that I had to leave something behind every so often, as a sort of sacrifice. If I
liked a job I was in, I would always give it up. Poor
old Lucas!"

She laughed.

"Do you ever feel like that?" She made a face. "I
don't suppose you do," she said. "I remember the first
house we lived in, over near Dunford Bridge. It was
huge, and falling apart inside. It was always on the
market until we bought it. Everyone who'd had it
before us had tried some new way of dividing it up to
make it livable. They put in a new staircase or knocked
two rooms together. They'd abandoned parts of it
because they couldn't afford to heat it all. Then they'd
buggered off before anything was finished and left it to
the next one—"

She broke off suddenly.

"I could never keep it tidy," she said.

"Lucas always loved it."

"Does he say that? You don't want to pay too much
attention to him," she warned me. "The garden was
so full of builders' rubbish, we could never grow anything. And the winters!" She shuddered. "Well, you
know what it's like out there. The rooms reeked of
Calor gas; before he'd been there a week, Lucas had
every kind of portable heater you could think of. I
hated the cold, but never as much as he did."

With an amused tenderness she chided him—"Lucas,
Lucas, Lucas"—as if he were in the room there with
us. "How you hated it, and how untidy you were!"

By now it was dark outside, but the younger cat was

still staring out into the greyish, sleety well of the garden, beyond which you could just make out—as a swelling line of shadow with low clouds racing over it—the edge of the moor. Ann kept asking the cat what it could see. "There are children buried all over the moor," she told the cat. Eventually she got up with a sigh and pushed it onto the floor. "That's where cats belong. Cats belong on the floor." Some paper flowers were knocked down; stooping to gather them up, she said, "If there is a God, a real one, He gave up long ago. He isn't so much bitter as apathetic." She winced, held her hands up to her eyes.

"You don't mind if I turn the main light off?" And then: "He's filtered away into everything, so that now there's only this infinitely thin, stretched *thing*, presenting itself in every atom, so tired it can't go on, so haggard you can only feel sorry for it and its mistakes. That's the real God. What we saw is something that's taken its place."

"What did we see, Ann?"

She stared at me.

"You know, I was never sure what Lucas thought he wanted from me." The dull yellow light of a table lamp fell across the left side of her face. She was lighting cigarettes almost constantly, stubbing them out, half smoked, into the nest of old ends that had accumulated in the saucer of her cup. "Can you imagine? In all those years I never knew what he wanted from me."

She seemed to consider this for a moment or two. She looked at me, puzzled, and said, "I don't feel he ever loved me." She buried her face in her hands. I got up, with some idea of comforting her. Without warning, she lurched out of her chair and in a groping, desperately confused manner took a few steps toward me. There, in the middle of the room, she stumbled into a low fretwork table someone had brought back from a visit to Kashmir twenty years before. Two or three paperback books and a vase of anemones went flying. The anemones were blowsy, past their best. She looked down at *The Last of Cheri* and *Mrs. Pal-*

frey at the Claremont, strewn with great blue and red petals like dirty tissue paper; she touched them thoughtfully with her toe. The smell of the fetid flower water made her retch.

"Oh, dear," she murmured. "Whatever shall we do, Lucas?"

"I'm not Lucas," I said gently. "Go and sit down, Ann."

While I was gathering the books and wiping their covers, she must have overcome her fear of the kitchen—or, I thought later, simply forgotten it—because I heard her rummaging about for the dustpan and brush she kept under the sink. By now, I imagined, she could hardly see for the migraine; I called impatiently, "Let me do that, Ann. Be sensible." There was a gasp, a clatter, my name repeated twice. "Ann, are you all right?"

No one answered.

"Hello? Ann?"

I found her by the sink. She had let go of the brush and pan and was twisting a damp floor cloth so tightly in her hands that the muscles of her short forearms stood out like a carpenter's. Water had dribbled out of it and down her skirt.

"Ann?"

She was looking out of the window into the narrow passage where, clearly illuminated by the fluorescent tube in the kitchen ceiling, something big and white hung in the air, turning to and fro like a chrysalis in a privet hedge.

"Christ!" I said.

It wriggled and was still, as though whatever it contained was tired of the effort to get out. After a moment it curled up from its tapered base, seemed to split, welded itself together again. All at once I saw that these movements were actually those of two organisms, two human figures hanging in the air, unsupported, quite naked, writhing and embracing and parting and writhing together again, never presenting the same angle twice, so that now you viewed the man from the back, now the woman, now both of them from one side or the other. When I first saw them, the woman's mouth was fastened on the man's. Her eyes were closed; later she rested her head on his shoulder. Later still, they both turned their attention to Ann. They had very pale skin, with the curious bloom of white chocolate; but that might have been an effect of the light. Sleet blew between us and them in eddies, but never obscured them.

"What are they, Ann?"

"There's no limit to suffering," she said. Her voice was slurred and thick. "They follow me wherever I go."

I found it hard to look away from them.

"Is this why you move so often?" It was all I could think of to say.

"No."

The two figures were locked together in something that—had their eyes been fastened on each other rather than on Ann—might have been described as love. They swung and turned slowly against the black, wet wall like fish in a tank. They were smiling. Ann groaned and began vomiting noisily into the sink. I held her shoulders. "Get them away," she said indistinctly. "Why do they always look at me?" She coughed, wiped her mouth, ran the cold tap. She had begun to shiver, in powerful, disconnected spasms. "Get them away."

Though I knew quite well they were there, it was my mistake that I never believed them to be real. I thought she might calm down if she couldn't see them. But she wouldn't let me turn the light out or close the curtains; and when I tried to encourage her to let go of the edge of the sink and come into the living room with me, she only shook her head and retched miserably. "No, leave me," she said. "I don't want you now." Her body had gone rigid, as awkward as a child's. She was very strong. "Just try to come away, Ann, please." She looked at me helplessly and said, "I've got nothing to wipe my nose with." I pulled at her angrily, and we fell down. My shoulder was on the dustpan, my mouth full of her hair, which smelled of cigarette ashes. I felt her hands move over me.

"Ann! Ann!" I shouted.

I dragged myself from under her—she had begun to groan and vomit again—and, staring back over my shoulder at the smiling creatures in the passage, ran out of the kitchen and out of the house. I could hear myself sobbing with panic—"I'm phoning Lucas, I can't stand this, I'm going to phone Lucas"—as if I were still talking to her. I blundered about the village until I found the telephone box opposite the church.

I remember Sprake—though it seems too well-put to have been him—once saying, "It's no triumph to feel you've given life the slip." We were talking about Lucas Fisher. "You can't live intensely except at the cost of the self. In the end, Lucas's reluctance to give himself wholeheartedly will make him shabby and unreal. He'll end up walking the streets at night staring into lighted shop windows." At the time I thought this harsh. I still believed that with Lucas it was a matter of energy rather than will, of the lows and undependable zones of a cyclic personality rather than any deliberate reservation of powers.

When I told Lucas, "Something's gone badly wrong here," he was silent. After a moment or two I prompted him. "Lucas?"

I thought I heard him say:

"For God's sake, put that down and leave me alone."

"This line must be bad," I said. "You sound a long way off. Is there someone with you?"

He was silent again—"Lucas? Can you hear me?"— and then he asked, "How is Ann? I mean, in herself?"

"Not well," I said. "She's having some sort of attack. You don't know how relieved I am to talk to someone. Lucas, there are two completely hallucinatory figures in that passage outside her kitchen. What they're doing to one another is . . . look, they're a kind of dead white color, and they're smiling at her all the time. It's the most appalling thing—"

He said, "Wait a minute. Do you mean that you can see them too?"

"That's what I'm trying to say. The thing is that I don't know how to help her. Lucas?"

The line had gone dead. I put the receiver down and dialed his number again. The engaged signal went on and on. Afterward I would tell Ann, "Someone else must have called him," but I knew he had simply taken his phone off the hook. I stood there for some time, anyway, shivering in the wind that blustered down off the moor, in the hope that he would change his mind. In the end, I got so cold, I had to give up and go back. Sleet blew into my face all the way through the village. The church clock said half past six, but everything was dark and untenanted. All I could hear was the wind rustling the black plastic bags of rubbish piled around the dustbins.

"Fuck you, Lucas," I whispered. "Fuck you, then."

Ann's house was as silent as the rest. I went into the front garden and pressed my face up to the window, in case I could see into the kitchen through the open living room door; but from that angle, the only thing visible was a wall calendar with a color photograph of a Persian cat: *October*. I couldn't see Ann. I stood in the flower bed and the sleet turned to snow.

The kitchen was filled less with the smell of vomit than a sourness you felt somewhere in the back of your throat. Outside, the passage lay deserted under the bright suicidal wash of fluorescent light. It was hard to imagine anything had happened out there. At the same time, nothing looked comfortable, not the disposition of the old roof slates, or the clumps of fern growing out of the revetment, or even the way the snow was settling in the gaps between the flagstones. I found that I didn't want to turn my back on the window. If I closed my eyes and tried to visualize the white couple, all I could remember was the way they had smiled. A still, cold air seeped in above the sink, and the cats came up to rub against my legs and get underfoot; the taps were still running.

In her confusion Ann had opened all the kitchen cupboards and strewn their contents on the floor. Saucepans, cutlery, and packets of dried food had been

mixed up with a polythene bucket and some yellow
J-cloths; she had upset a bottle of household detergent
among several tins of cat food, some of which had
been half opened, some merely pierced, before she
dropped them or forgot where she had put the opener.
It was hard to see what she had been trying to do. I
picked it all up and put it away. To make them leave
me alone, I fed the cats. Once or twice I heard her
moving about on the floor above.

She was in the bathroom, slumped on the old-
fashioned pink lino by the sink, trying to get her
clothes off. "For God's sake, go away," she said. "I
can do it."

"Oh, Ann."

"Put some disinfectant in the blue bucket, then."

"Who are they, Ann?" I asked.

That was later, when I had gotten her to bed. She
answered:

"Once it starts, you never get free."

I was annoyed.

"Free from what, Ann?"

"You know," she said. "Lucas said you had hallucinations for weeks afterward."

"Lucas had no right to say that!"

This sounded absurd, so I added as lightly as I
could, "It was a long time ago. I'm not sure anymore."

The migraine had left her exhausted, though much
more relaxed. She had washed her hair, and between
us we had found her a fresh nightdress to wear. Sitting
up in the cheerful little bedroom with its cheap ornaments and modern wallpaper, she looked vague and
young; she kept apologizing for the design on her
Continental quilt, some bold diagrammatic flowers in
black and red, the intertwined stems of which she
traced with the index finger of her right hand across a
clean white background. "Do you like this? I don't
really know why I bought it. Things look so bright and
energetic in the shops," she said wistfully, "but as
soon as you get them home, they just seem crude."

The older cat had jumped up onto the bed; whenever Ann spoke, it purred loudly. "He shouldn't be in here, and he knows it." She wouldn't eat or drink, but I had persuaded her to take some more propranolol, and so far she had kept it down.

"Once it starts, you never get free," she repeated. Her finger followed the pattern across the quilt. Inadvertently she touched the cat's dry, greying fur, stared suddenly at her own hand as if it had misled her. "It was some sort of smell that followed you about, Lucas seemed to think."

"Some sort," I agreed.

"You won't get rid of it by ignoring it. We both tried that to begin with. A scent of roses, Lucas said." She laughed and took my hand. "Very romantic! I've no sense of smell—I lost it years ago, luckily."

This reminded her of something else.

"The first time I had a fit," she said, "I kept it from my mother because I saw a vision with it. I was only a child, really. The vision was very clear: a seashore, steep and with no sand, and men and women lying on some rocks in the sunshine like lizards, staring quite blankly at the spray as it exploded up in front of them; huge waves that might have been on a cinema screen for all the notice they took of them."

She narrowed her eyes, puzzled. "You wondered why they had so little common sense."

She tried to push the cat off her bed, but it only bent its body in a rubbery way and avoided her hand. She yawned suddenly.

"At the same time," she went on after a pause, "I could see that some spiders had made their webs between the rocks, just a foot or two above the tide line." Though they trembled and were sometimes filled with spraylike dewdrops so that they glittered in the sun, the webs remained unbroken. She couldn't describe, she said, the sense of anxiety with which this filled her. "So close to all that violence. You wondered why they had so little common sense," she repeated. "The last thing I heard was someone saying,

'On your own, you really can hear voices in the tide. . . .' "

Before she fell asleep, she clutched my hand harder and said:

"I'm so glad you got something out of it. Lucas and I never did. Roses! It was worth it for that."

I thought of us as we had been twenty years before. I spent the night in the living room and awoke quite early in the morning. I didn't know where I was until I walked in a drugged way to the window and saw the street full of snow.

For a long time after that last meeting with Sprake, I had a recurrent dream of him. His hands were clasped tightly across his chest, the left hand holding the wrist of the right, and he was going quickly from room to room of the British Museum. Whenever he came to a corner or a junction of corridors, he stopped abruptly and stared at the wall in front of him for thirty seconds before turning very precisely to face in the right direction before he moved on. He did this with the air of a man who has for some reason taught himself to walk with his eyes closed through a perfectly familiar building; but there was also, in the way he stared at the walls—and particularly in the way he held himself so upright and rigid—a profoundly hierarchal air, an air of premeditation and ritual. His shoes, and the bottoms of his faded corduroy trousers, were soaking wet, just as they had been the morning after the rite, when the four of us had walked back through the damp fields in the bright sunshine. He wore no socks.

In the dream I was always hurrying to catch up with him. I was stopping every so often to write something in a notebook, hoping he wouldn't see me. He strode purposefully through the Museum, from cabinet to cabinet of twelfth-century illuminated manuscripts. Suddenly he stopped, looked back at me, and said:

"There are sperm in this picture. You can see them quite plainly. What are sperm doing in a religious picture?"

He smiled, opened his eyes very wide.

Pointing to the side of his own head with one finger, he began to shout and laugh incoherently.

When he had gone, I saw that he had been examining a New Testament miniature from Queen Melisande's Psalter, depicting "The Women at the Sepulchre." In it an angel was drawing Mary Magdalen's attention to some strange luminous shapes that hovered in the air in front of her. They did, in fact, look something like the spermatozoa that often border the tormented Paris paintings of Edvard Munch.

I would wake up abruptly from this dream, to find that it was morning and that I had been crying.

Ann was still asleep when I left the house, with the expression people have on their faces when they can't believe what they remember about themselves. "On your own, you really can hear voices in the tide, cries for help or attention," she had said. "I started to menstruate the same day. For years I was convinced that my fits began then too."

That was the last time I saw her.

A warm front had moved in from the southwest during the night; the snow had already begun to melt, the Pennine stations looked like leaky downspouts, the moors were locked beneath grey clouds. Two little boys sat opposite me on the train until Stalybridge, holding their Day Rover tickets thoughtfully in their laps. They might have been eight or nine years old. They were dressed in tiny, perfect workman's jackets, tight trousers, Dr. Marten's boots. Close up, their shaven skulls were bluish and vulnerable, perfectly shaped. They looked like acolytes in a Buddhist temple: calm, wide-eyed, compliant. By the time I got to Manchester, a fine rain was falling. It was blowing the full length of Market Street and through the door of the Kardomah Café, where I had arranged to meet Lucas Fisher.

The first thing he said was, "Look at these pies! They aren't plastic, you know, like a modern pie. These are from the plaster era of café pies, the earthenware era. Terra-cotta pies, realistically painted, glazed in places to have exactly the cracks and imperfections any real pie would have! Aren't they wonderful? I'm going to eat one."

I sat down next to him.

"What happened to you last night, Lucas? It was a bloody nightmare."

He looked away. "How *is* Ann?" he asked. I could feel him trembling.

"Fuck off, Lucas."

He smiled over at a toddler in an appalling yellow suit. The child stared back vacantly, upset, knowing full well they were from competing species. A woman near us said, "I hear you're going to your grandma's for dinner on Sunday. Something special, I expect?" Lucas glared at her, as if she had been speaking to him. She added: "If you're going to buy toys this afternoon, remember to look at them where they are, so that no one can accuse you of stealing. Don't take them off the shelf." From somewhere near the kitchens came a noise like a tray of crockery falling down a short flight of stairs; Lucas seemed to hate this. He shuddered.

"Let's get out!" he said. He looked savage and ill. "I feel it as badly as Ann," he said. He accused me: "You never think of that." He looked over at the toddler again. "Spend long enough in places like this and your spirit will heave itself inside out."

"Come on, Lucas, don't be spoiled. I thought you liked the pies here."

All afternoon he walked urgently about the streets, as if he were on his own. I could hardly keep up with him. The city centre was full of wheelchairs, old women slumped in them with impatient, collapsed faces, partially bald, done up in crisp white raincoats. Lucas had turned up the collar of his grey cashmere jacket against the rain but left the jacket itself hanging open, its sleeves rolled untidily back above his bare wrists. He left me breathless. He was forty years old, but he still had the ravenous face of an adolescent. Eventually he stopped and said, "I'm sorry." It was halfway through the afternoon, but the neon signs were on and the lower windows of the office blocks were already lit up. Near Piccadilly Station, an arm of the canal appears suddenly from under the road; he stopped and gazed down at its rain-pocked surface, dim and oily, scattered with lumps of floating Styrofoam like sea gulls in the fading light.

"You often see fires on the bank down there," he said. "They live a whole life down there, people with nowhere else to go. You can hear them singing and shouting on the old towpath."

He looked at me with wonder.

"We aren't much different, are we? We never came to anything, either."

I couldn't think of what to say.

"It's not so much that Sprake encouraged us to ruin something in ourselves," he said, "as that we never got anything in return for it. Have you ever seen Joan of Arc kneel down to pray in the Kardomah Café? And then a small boy comes in leading something that looks like a goat, and it gets on her there and then and fucks her in a ray of sunlight?"

"Look, Lucas," I explained, "I'm never doing this again. I was frightened last night."

"I'm sorry."

"Lucas, you always are."

"It isn't one of my better days today."

"For God's sake, fasten your coat."

"I can't seem to get cold."

He gazed dreamily down at the water—it had darkened into a bottomless, opal-colored trench between the buildings—perhaps seeing goats, fires, people who had nowhere to go. " 'We worked but we were not paid,' " he quoted. Something forced him to ask shyly:

"You haven't heard from Sprake?"

I felt sick with patience. I seemed to be filled up with it.

"I haven't seen Sprake for twenty years, Lucas. You know that. I haven't seen him for twenty years."

"I understand. It's just that I can't bear to think of Ann on her own in a place like that. I wouldn't have mentioned it otherwise. We said we'd always stick together, but—"

"Go home, Lucas. Go home now."

He turned away miserably and walked off. I meant to leave him to that maze of unredeemed streets between Piccadilly and Victoria, the failing pornography and pet shops, the weed-grown car parks that lie in the shadow of the yellowish-tiled hulk of the Arndale Centre. In the end, I couldn't. He had gotten as far as the Tib Street fruit market when a small figure came out of a side street and began to follow him closely along the pavement, imitating his typical walk, head thrust forward, hands in pockets. When he stopped to button his jacket, it stopped too. Its own coat was so long, it trailed in the gutter. I started running to catch up with them, and it paused under a street lamp to stare back at me. In the sodium light I saw that it was neither a child nor a dwarf but something of both, with the eyes and gait of a large monkey. Its eyes were quite blank, stupid and implacable in a pink face. Lucas became aware of it suddenly and jumped with surprise; he ran a few aimless steps, shouting, then dodged around a corner, but it only followed him hurriedly. I thought I heard him pleading, "Why don't you leave me alone?" and in answer came a voice at once tinny and muffled, barely audible but strained, as if it were shouting. Then there was a terrific clatter and I saw some large object like an old zinc dustbin fly out and go rolling about in the middle of the road.

"Lucas!" I called.

When I rounded the corner, the street was full of smashed fruit boxes and crates; rotten vegetables were scattered everywhere; a barrow lay as if it had been thrown along the pavement. There was such a sense of violence and disorder and idiocy that I couldn't express it to myself. But neither Lucas nor his persecutor was there; and though I walked about for an hour afterward, looking into doorways, I saw nobody at all.

A few months later Lucas wrote to tell me that Ann had died.

"A scent of roses," I remembered her saying. "How lucky you were!"

"It was a wonderful summer for roses, anyway," I had answered. "I never knew a year like it." All June, the hedgerows were full of dog roses, with their elusive, fragile odor. I hadn't seen them since I was a boy. The gardens were bursting with Gallicas, great blowsy things whose fragrance was like a drug. "How can we ever say that Sprake had anything to do with that, Ann?"

But I sent roses to her funeral, anyway, though I didn't go myself.

What did we do, Ann and Lucas and I, in the fields of June, such a long time ago?

"It is easy to misinterpret the Great God," writes de Vries. "If He represents the long slow panic in us which never quite surfaces, if He signifies our perception of the animal, the uncontrollable in us, He must also stand for that direct sensual perception of the world that we have lost by ageing—perhaps even by becoming human in the first place."

Shortly after Ann's death, I experienced a sudden, inexplicable resurgence of my sense of smell. Common smells became so distinct and detailed, I felt like a child again, every new impression astonishing and clear, my conscious self not yet the sore lump encysted in my own skull, as clenched and useless as a fist, impossible to modify or evict, as it was later to become. This was not quite what you should call memory; all I recollected in the smell of orange peel or ground coffee or rowan blossom was that I once had been *able* to experience things so powerfully. It was as if, before I could recover one particular impression, I had to rediscover the language of all impressions. But nothing further happened. I was left with an embarrassment, a ghost, a hyperesthesia of middle age. It was cruel and undependable; it made me feel like a fool. I was troubled by it for a year or two, and then it went away.

SECRETS

This is the sound of poisons,
The sickness no one knows ...

—SHRIEKBACK

DAVID MORRELL, born 1943 in Kitchener, Ontario, is a former literature professor at the University of Iowa. He is best known as the author of *First Blood* (which created the character of John Rambo) and the thriller trilogy *The Brotherhood of the Rose, The Fraternity of the Stone*, and *The League of Night and Fog*. But his writing has always been flavored with a taste for the macabre, most evident in his single horror novel, *The Totem*, and occasional short fiction such as the following novelette.

David Morrell

Orange Is for Anguish,
Blue for Insanity

Van Dorn's work was controversial, of course. The scandal his paintings caused among Parisian artists in the late 1800s provided the stuff of legend. Disdaining conventions, thrusting beyond accepted theories, Van Dorn seized upon the essentials of the craft to which he'd devoted his soul. Color, design, and texture. With those principles in mind, he created portraits and land-scapes so different, so innovative, that their subjects seemed merely an excuse for Van Dorn to put paint onto canvas. His brilliant colors, applied in passionate splotches and swirls, often so thick that they projected an eighth of an inch from the canvas in the manner of a bas-relief, so dominated the viewer's perception that the person or scene depicted seemed secondary to technique.

Impressionism, the prevailing avant-garde theory of the late 1800s, imitated the eye's tendency to perceive the edges of peripheral objects as blurs. Van Dorn went one step farther and so emphasized the lack of distinction among objects that they seemed to melt together, to merge into an interconnected, pantheistic universe of color. The branches of a Van Dorn tree became ectoplasmic tentacles, thrusting toward the sky and the grass, just as tentacles from the sky and grass thrust toward the tree, all melding into a radiant swirl. He seemed to address himself not to the illusions of light but to reality itself, or at least to his theory of it. The tree *is* the sky, his technique asserted. The grass is the tree, and the sky the grass. All is one.

Van Dorn's approach proved so unpopular among theorists of his time that he frequently couldn't buy a meal in exchange for a canvas upon which he'd labored for months. His frustration produced a nervous breakdown. His self-mutilation shocked and alienated such onetime friends as Cézanne and Gauguin. He died in squalor and obscurity. Not until the 1920s, thirty years after his death, were his paintings recognized for the genius they displayed. In the 1940s, his soul-tortured character became the subject of a bestselling novel, and in the 1950s a Hollywood spectacular. These days, of course, even the least of his efforts can't be purchased for less than three million dollars.

Ah, art.

It started with Myers and his meeting with Professor Stuyvesant. "He agreed . . . reluctantly."

"I'm surprised he agreed at all," I said. "Stuyvesant hates Postimpressionism and Van Dorn in particular. Why didn't you ask someone easy, like Old Man Bradford?"

"Because Bradford's academic reputation sucks. I can't see writing a dissertation if it won't be published, and a respected dissertation director can make an editor pay attention. Besides, if I can convince Stuyvesant, I can convince anyone."

"Convince him of . . . ?"

"That's what Stuyvesant wanted to know," Myers said.

I remember that moment vividly, the way Myers straightened his lanky body, pushed his glasses close to his eyes, and frowned so hard that his curly red hair scrunched forward on his brow.

"Stuyvesant asked, even disallowing his own disinclination toward Van Dorn—God, the way that pompous asshole talks—why would I want to spend a year of my life writing about an artist who'd been the subject of countless books and articles, whose ramifications had been exhausted? Why not choose an obscure but promising Neo-Expressionist and gamble that *my* reputation would rise with his? Naturally the artist he recommended was one of Stuyvesant's favorites."

"Naturally," I said. "If he named the artist I think he did . . ."

Myers mentioned the name.

I nodded. "Stuyvesant's been collecting him for the past five years. He hopes the resale value of the paintings will buy him a town house in London when he retires. So what did you tell him?"

Myers opened his mouth to answer, then hesitated. With a brooding look, he turned toward a print of Van Dorn's swirling *Cypresses in a Hollow,* which hung beside a ceiling-high bookshelf crammed with Van Dorn biographies, analyses, and bound collections of reproductions. He didn't speak for a moment, as if the sight of the familiar print—its facsimile colors incapable of matching the brilliant tones of the original, its manufacturing process unable to recreate the exquisite texture of raised, swirled layers of paint on canvas—still took his breath away.

"So what did you tell him?" I asked again.

Myers exhaled with a mixture of frustration and admiration. "I said, what the critics wrote about Van Dorn was mostly junk. He agreed, with the implication that the paintings invited no less. I said, even the gifted critics hadn't probed to Van Dorn's essence. They were missing something crucial."

"Which is?"

"Exactly Stuyvesant's next question. You know how he keeps relighting his pipe when he gets impatient. I had to talk fast. I told him I didn't know what I was looking for, but there's something"—Myers gestured toward the print—"something there. Something nobody's noticed. Van Dorn hinted as much in his diary. I don't know what it is, but I'm convinced his paintings hide a secret." Myers glanced at me.

I raised my eyebrows.

"Well, if nobody's noticed," Myers said, "it *must* be a secret, right?"

"But if *you* haven't noticed . . ."

Compelled, Myers turned toward the print again,

his tone filled with wonder. "How do I know it's there? Because when I look at Van Dorn's paintings, I *sense* it. I *feel* it."

I shook my head. "I can imagine what Stuyvesant said to that. The man deals with art as if it's geometry, and there aren't any secrets in—"

"What he said was, if I'm becoming a mystic, I ought to be in the School of Religion, not Art. But if I wanted enough rope to hang myself and strangle my career, he'd give it to me. He liked to believe he had an open mind, he said."

"That's a laugh."

"Believe me, he wasn't joking. He had a fondness for Sherlock Holmes, he said. If I thought I'd found a mystery and could solve it, by all means do so. And at that, he gave me his most condescending smile and said he would mention it at today's faculty meeting."

"So what's the problem? You got what you wanted. He agreed to direct your dissertation. Why do you sound so—?"

"Today there *wasn't* any faculty meeting."

"Oh," I said. "You're fucked."

Myers and I had started graduate school at Iowa together. That had been three years earlier, and we'd formed a strong enough friendship to rent adjacent rooms in an old apartment building near campus. The spinster who owned it had a hobby of doing watercolors—she had no talent, I might add—and rented only to art students so they would give her lessons. In Myers's case, she'd made an exception. He wasn't a painter, as I was. He was an art historian. Most painters work instinctively. They're not skilled at verbalizing what they want to accomplish. But words and not pigment were Myers's specialty. His impromptu lectures had quickly made him the old lady's favorite tenant.

After that day, however, she didn't see much of him. Nor did I. He wasn't at the classes we took together. I assumed he spent most of his time at the library. Late at night, when I noticed a light beneath his door and knocked, I didn't get an answer. I phoned him. Through the wall I heard the persistent, muffled ringing.

One evening I let the phone ring eleven times and was just about to hang up when he answered. He sounded exhausted.

"You're getting to be a stranger," I said.

His voice was puzzled. "Stranger? But I just saw you a couple of days ago."

"You mean, two weeks ago."

"Oh, shit," he said.

"I've got a six-pack. You want to—?"

"Yeah, I'd like that." He sighed. "Come over."

When he opened his door, I don't know what startled me more, the way Myers looked or what he'd done to his apartment.

I'll start with Myers. He'd always been thin, but now he looked gaunt, emaciated. His shirt and jeans were rumpled. His red hair was matted. Behind his glasses, his eyes looked bloodshot. He hadn't shaved. When he closed the door and reached for a beer, his hand shook.

His apartment was filled with, covered with—I'm not sure how to convey the dismaying effect of so much brilliant clutter—Van Dorn prints. On every inch of the walls. The sofa, the chairs, the desk, the TV, the bookshelves. And the drapes, and the ceiling, and, except for a narrow path, the floor. Swirling sunflowers, olive trees, meadows, skies, and streams surrounded me, encompassed me, seemed to reach out for me. At the same time I felt swallowed. Just as the blurred edges of objects within each print seemed to melt into one another, so each print melted into the next. I was speechless amid the chaos of color.

Myers took several deep gulps of beer. Embarrassed by my stunned reaction to the room, he gestured toward the vortex of prints. "I guess you could say I'm immersing myself in my work."

"When did you eat last?"

He looked confused.

"That's what I thought." I walked along the narrow

path among the prints on the floor and picked up the phone. "The pizza's on me." I ordered the largest supreme the nearest Pepi's had to offer. They didn't deliver beer, but I had another six-pack in my fridge, and I had the feeling we'd be needing it.

I set down the phone. "Myers, what the hell are you doing?"

"I told you . . ."

"Immersing yourself? Give me a break. You're cutting classes. You haven't showered in God knows how long. You look like shit. Your deal with Stuyvesant isn't worth destroying your health. Tell him you've changed your mind. Get another, an *easier*, dissertation director."

"Stuyvesant's got nothing to do with this."

"Damnit, what *does* it have to do with? The end of comprehensive exams, the start of dissertation blues?"

Myers gulped the rest of his beer and reached for another can. "No, blue is for insanity."

"*What*?"

"That's the pattern." Myers turned toward the swirling prints. "I studied them chronologically. The more Van Dorn became insane, the more he used blue. And orange is his color of anguish. If you match the paintings with the personal crises described in his biographies, you see a correspondent use of orange."

"Myers, you're the best friend I've got. So forgive me for saying I think you're off the deep end."

He swallowed more beer and shrugged as if to say he didn't expect me to understand.

"Listen," I said. "A personal color code, a connection between emotion and pigment, that's bullshit. I should know. You're the historian, but I'm the painter. I'm telling you, different people react to colors in different ways. Never mind the advertising agencies and their theories that some colors sell products more than others. It all depends on context. It depends on fashion. This year's 'in' color is next year's 'out.' But an honest-to-God great painter uses whatever color will give him the greatest effect. He's interested in creating, not selling."

"Van Dorn could have used a few sales."

"No question. The poor bastard didn't live long enough to come into fashion. But orange is for anguish and blue means insanity? Tell that to Stuyvesant and he'll throw you out of his office."

Myers took off his glasses and rubbed the bridge of his nose. "I feel so . . . maybe you're right."

"There's no maybe about it. I *am* right. You need food, a shower, and sleep. A painting's a combination of color and shape that people either like or they don't. The artist follows his instincts, uses whatever techniques he can master, and does his best. But if there's a secret in Van Dorn's work, it isn't a color code."

Myers finished his second beer and blinked in distress. "You know what I found out yesterday?"

I shook my head.

"The critics who devoted themselves to analyzing Van Dorn . . ."

"What about them?"

"They went insane, the same as he did."

"*What*? No way. I've studied Van Dorn's critics. They're as conventional and boring as Stuyvesant."

"You mean, the mainstream scholars. The safe ones. I'm talking about the truly brilliant ones. The ones who haven't been recognized for their genius, just as Van Dorn wasn't recognized."

"What happened to them?"

"They suffered. The same as Van Dorn."

"They were put in an asylum?"

"Worse than that."

"Myers, don't make me ask."

"The parallels are amazing. They each tried to paint. In Van Dorn's style. And just like Van Dorn, they stabbed out their eyes."

I guess it's obvious by now—Myers was what you might call "high-strung." No negative judgment intended. In fact, his excitability was one of the reasons I liked him. That and his imagination. Hanging around with him was never dull. He loved ideas. Learning was his passion. And he passed his excitement on to me.

The truth is, I needed all the inspiration I could get. I wasn't a bad artist. Not at all. On the other hand, I wasn't a great one, either. As I neared the end of grad school, I'd painfully come to realize that my work never would be more than "interesting." I didn't want to admit it, but I'd probably end up as a commercial artist in an advertising agency.

That night, however, Myers's imagination wasn't inspiring. It was scary. He was always going through phases of enthusiasm. El Greco, Picasso, Pollock. Each had preoccupied him to the point of obsession, only to be abandoned for another favorite and another. When he'd fixated on Van Dorn, I'd assumed it was merely one more infatuation.

But the chaos of Van Dorn prints in his room made clear he'd reached a greater excess of compulsion. I was skeptical about his insistence that there was a secret in Van Dorn's work. After all, great art can't be explained. You can analyze its technique, you can diagram its symmetry, but ultimately there's a mystery words can't communicate. Genius can't be summarized. As far as I could tell, Myers had been using the word *secret* as a synonym for indescribable brilliance.

When I realized he literally meant that Van Dorn had a secret, I was appalled. The distress in his eyes was equally appalling. His references to insanity, not only in Van Dorn but in his critics, made me worry that Myers himself was having a breakdown. Stabbed out their eyes, for Christ's sake?

I stayed up with Myers till five A.M., trying to calm him, to convince him he needed a few days' rest. We finished the six-pack I'd brought, the six-pack in my refrigerator, and another six-pack I bought from an art student down the hall. At dawn, just before Myers dozed off and I staggered back to my room, he murmured that I was right. He needed a break, he said. Tomorrow he'd call his folks. He'd ask if they'd pay his plane fare back to Denver.

Hung over, I didn't wake up till late afternoon. Disgusted that I'd missed my classes, I showered and managed to ignore the taste of last night's pizza. I wasn't surprised when I phoned Myers and got no answer. He probably felt as shitty as I did. But after sunset, when I called again, then knocked on his door, I started to worry. His door was locked, so I went downstairs to get the landlady's key. That's when I saw the note in my mail slot.

> Meant what I said. Need a break. Went home. Will be in touch. Stay cool. Paint well. I love you, pal. Your friend forever,
>
> > Myers

My throat ached. He never came back. I saw him only twice after that. Once in New York, and once in . . .

Let's talk about New York. I finished my graduate project, a series of landscapes that celebrated Iowa's big-sky rolling, dark-soiled, wooded hills. A local patron paid fifty dollars for one of them. I gave three to the university's hospital. The rest are who knows where.

Too much has happened.

As I predicted, the world wasn't waiting for my good-but-not-great efforts. I ended where I belonged, as a commercial artist for a Madison Avenue advertising agency. My beer cans are the best in the business.

I met a smart, attractive woman who worked in the marketing department of a cosmetics firm. One of my agency's clients. Professional conferences led to personal dinners and intimate evenings that lasted all night. I proposed. She agreed.

We'd live in Connecticut, she said. Of course.

When the time was right, we might have children, she said.

Of course.

Myers phoned me at the office. I don't know how he knew where I was. I remember his breathless voice.

"I found it," he said.

"Myers?" I grinned. "Is it really—? *How are you? Where have—?*"

"I'm telling you. I found it!"

"I don't know what you're—"

"Remember? Van Dorn's secret!"

In a rush, I did remember—the excitement Myers could generate, the wonderful, expectant conversations of my youth—the days and especially the nights when ideas and the future beckoned. "Van Dorn? You're still—?"

"Yes! I was right! There *was* a secret!"

"You crazy bastard, I don't care about Van Dorn. But I care about you! Why did you—? I never forgave you for disappearing."

"I had to. Couldn't let you hold me back. Couldn't let you—"

"For your own good!"

"So *you* thought. But I was right!"

"Where *are* you?"

"Exactly where you'd expect me to be."

"For the sake of old friendship, Myers, don't piss me off. *Where are you*?"

"The Metropolitan Museum of Art."

"Will you stay there, Myers? While I catch a cab? I can't wait to see you."

"I can't wait for you to see what *I* see!"

I postponed a deadline, canceled two appointments, and told my fiancée I couldn't meet her for dinner. She sounded miffed. But Myers was all that mattered.

He stood beyond the pillars at the entrance. His face was haggard, but his eyes were stars. I hugged him. "Myers, it's so good to—"

"I want you to see something. Hurry."

He tugged at my coat, rushing.

"But where have you been?"

"I'll tell you later."

We entered the Postimpressionist gallery. Bewildered, I followed Myers and let him anxiously sit me on a bench before Van Dorn's *Fir Trees at Sunrise*.

I'd never seen the original. Prints couldn't compare. After a year of drawing ads for feminine beauty aids, I was devastated. Van Dorn's power brought me close to . . .

Tears?

For my visionless skills.

For the youth I'd abandoned a year before.

"Look!" Myers said. He raised his arm and gestured toward the painting.

I frowned. I looked.

It took time—an hour, two hours—and the coaxing vision of Myers. I concentrated. And then, at last, I saw.

Profound admiration changed to . . .

My heart raced. As Myers traced his hand across the painting one final time, as a guard who had been watching us with increasing wariness stalked forward to stop him from touching the canvas, I felt as if a cloud had dispersed and a lens had focused.

"Jesus," I said.

"You see? The bushes, the trees, the branches?"

"Yes! Oh, God, yes! Why didn't I—?"

"Notice before? Because it doesn't show up in the prints," Myers said. "Only in the originals. And the effect's so deep, you have to study them—"

"Forever."

"It seems that long. But I knew. I was right."

"A secret."

When I was a boy, my father—how I loved him— took me mushroom hunting. We drove from town, climbed a barbed-wire fence, walked through a forest, and reached a slope of dead elms. My father told me to search the top of the slope while he checked the bottom.

An hour later he came back with two large paper sacks filled with mushrooms. I hadn't found even one.

"I guess your spot was lucky," I said.

"But they're all around you," my father said.

"All around me? Where?"

"You didn't look hard enough."

"I crossed this slope five times."

"You searched, but you didn't really see," my father said. He picked up a long stick and pointed it toward the ground. "Focus your eyes toward the end of the stick."

I did . . .

And I've never forgotten the hot excitement that surged through my stomach. The mushrooms appeared as if by magic. They'd been there all along, of course, so perfectly adapted to their surroundings, their color so much like dead leaves, their shape so much like bits of wood and chunks of rock that they'd been invisible to ignorant eyes. But once my vision adjusted, once my mind reevaluated the visual impressions it received, I saw mushrooms everywhere, seemingly thousands of them. I'd been standing on them, walking over them, staring at them, and hadn't realized.

I felt an infinitely greater shock when I saw the tiny faces Myers made me recognize in Van Dorn's *Fir Trees at Sunrise*. Most were smaller than a quarter of an inch, hints and suggestions, dots and curves, blended perfectly with the landscape. They weren't exactly human, though they did have mouths, noses, and eyes. Each mouth was a black, gaping maw, each nose a jagged gash, the eyes dark sinkholes of despair. The twisted faces seemed to be screaming in total agony. I could almost hear their anguished shrieks, their tortured wails. I thought of damnation. Of hell.

As soon as I noticed the faces, they emerged from the swirling texture of the painting in such abundance that the landscape became an illusion, the grotesque faces reality. The fir trees turned into an obscene cluster of writhing arms and pain-racked torsos.

I stepped back in shock an instant before the guard would have pulled me away.

"Don't touch the—" the guard said.

Myers had already rushed to point at another Van Dorn, the original *Cypresses in a Hollow*. I followed, and now that my eyes knew what to look for, I saw small, tortured faces in every branch and rock. The canvas swarmed with them.

"Jesus."

"And this!"

Myers hurried to *Sunflowers at Harvest Time*, and again, as if a lens had changed focus, I no longer saw flowers but anguished faces and twisted limbs. I lurched back, felt a bench against my legs, and sat.

"You were right," I said.

The guard stood nearby, scowling.

"Van Dorn did have a secret," I said. I shook my head in astonishment.

"It explains everything," Myers said. "These agonized faces give his work depth. They're hidden, but we *sense* them. We *feel* the anguish beneath the beauty."

"But why would he—?"

"I don't think he had a choice. His genius drove him insane. It's my guess that this is how he literally saw the world. These faces are the demons he wrestled with. The festering products of his insanity. And they're not just an illustrator's gimmick. Only a genius could have painted them for all the world to see and yet have so perfectly imposed them on the landscape that *no one* would see. Because he took them for granted in a terrible way."

"No one? *You* saw, Myers."

He smiled. "Maybe that means I'm crazy."

"I doubt it, friend." I returned his smile. "It does mean you're persistent. This'll make your reputation."

"But I'm not through yet," Myers said.

I frowned.

"So far all I've got is a fascinating case of optical illusion. Tortured souls writhing beneath, perhaps producing, incomparable beauty. I call them 'secondary images.' In your ad work I guess they'd be called 'subliminal.' But this isn't commercialism. This is a genuine artist who had the brilliance to use his madness as an ingredient in his vision. I need to go deeper."

"What are you taking about?"

"The paintings here don't provide enough examples. I've seen his work in Paris and Rome, in Zurich and London. I've borrowed from my parents to the limits of their patience and my conscience. But I've seen, and I know what I have to do. The anguished faces began in 1889, when Van Dorn left Paris in disgrace. His early paintings were abysmal. He settled in La Verge in the south of France. Six months later his genius suddenly exploded. In a frenzy, he painted. He returned to Paris. He showed his work, but no one appreciated it. He kept painting, kept showing. Still no one appreciated it. He returned to La Verge, reached the peak of his genius, and went totally insane. He had to be committed to an asylum, but not before he stabbed out his eyes. That's my dissertation. I intend to parallel his course. To match his paintings with his biography, to show how the faces increased and became more severe as his madness worsened. I want to dramatize the turmoil in his soul as he imposed his twisted vision on each landscape."

It was typical of Myers to take an excessive attitude and make it even more excessive. Don't misunderstand. His discovery was important. But he didn't know when to stop. I'm not an art historian, but I've read enough to know that what's called "psychological criticism," the attempt to analyze great art as a manifestation of neuroses, is considered off-the-wall, to put it mildly. If Myers handed Stuyvesant a psychological dissertation, the pompous bastard would throw Myers out of his office.

That was one misgiving I had about what Myers planned to do with his discovery. Another troubled me more. *I intend to parallel Van Dorn's course*, he'd said, and after we left the museum and walked through Central Park, I realized how literally Myers meant it.

"I'm going to southern France," he said.

I stared in surprise. "You don't mean—"

"La Verge? That's right. I want to write my dissertation there."

"But—"

"What place could be more appropriate? It's the village where Van Dorn suffered his nervous breakdown and eventually went insane. If it's possible, I'll even rent the same room *he* did."

"Myers, this sounds too far out, even for you."

"But it makes perfect sense. I need to immerse myself. I need atmosphere, a sense of history. So I can put myself in the mood to write." ·

"The last time you immersed yourself, you crammed your room with Van Dorn prints, didn't sleep, didn't eat, didn't bathe. I hope—"

"I admit I got too involved. But last time I didn't know what I was looking for. Now that I've found it, I'm in good shape."

"You look strung out to *me*."

"An optical illusion." Myers grinned.

"Come on, I'll treat you to drinks and dinner."

"Sorry. Can't. I've got a plane to catch."

"You're leaving *tonight*? But I haven't seen you since—"

"You can buy me that dinner when I finish the dissertation."

I never did. I saw him only one more time. Because of the letter he sent two months later. Or asked his nurse to send. She wrote down what he'd said and added an explanation of her own. He'd blinded himself, of course.

> You were right. Shouldn't have gone. But when did I ever take advice? I always knew better, didn't I? Now it's too late. What I showed you that day at the Met—God help me, there's so much more. I found the truth, and now I can't bear it. Don't make my mistake. Don't look ever again, I beg you, at Van Dorn's paintings. The headaches. Can't stand the pain. Need a break. Am going home. Stay cool. Paint well. I love you, pal. Your friend forever,
>
> Myers

In her postscript, the nurse apologized for her English. She sometimes took care of aged Americans on the Riviera, she said, and had to learn the language. But she understood what she heard better than she could speak it or write it, and hoped that what she'd written made sense. It didn't, but that wasn't her fault. Myers had been in great pain, sedated with morphine, not thinking clearly, she said. The miracle was that he'd managed to be coherent at all.

> Your friend was staying at our only hotel. The manager says that he slept little and ate even less. His research was obsessive. He filled his room with reproductions of Van Dorn's work. He tried to duplicate Van Dorn's daily schedule. He demanded paints and canvas, refused all meals, and wouldn't answer his door. Three days ago, a scream woke the manager. The door was blocked. It took three men to break it down. Your friend used the sharp end of a paintbrush to stab out his eyes. The clinic here is excellent. Physically your friend will recover, although he will never see again. But I worry about his mind.

Myers had said he was going home. It had taken a week for the letter to reach me. I assumed his parents would have been informed immediately by phone or telegram. He was probably back in the States by now. I knew his parents lived in Denver, but I didn't know their first names or address, so I took a cab to the New York Public Library, checked the Denver phone book, and went down the list for Myers, using my credit card to call every one of them till I made contact. Not with his parents but with a family friend watching their house. Myers hadn't been flown to the States. His parents had gone to the south of France. I caught the next available plane. Not that it matters, but I was supposed to be married that weekend.

La Verge is thirty kilometers inland from Nice. I hired a driver. The road curved through olive trees and farmland, crested cypress-covered hills, and often skirted cliffs. Passing an orchard, I had the eerie conviction that I'd seen it before. Entering La Verge, my déjà vu strengthened. The village seemed trapped in the nineteenth century. Except for phone poles and power lines, it looked exactly as Van Dorn had painted it. I recognized the narrow, cobbled streets and rustic shops that Van Dorn had made famous. I asked directions. It wasn't hard to find Myers and his parents.

The last time I saw my friend, the undertaker was putting the lid on his coffin. I had trouble sorting out the details, but despite my burning tears, I gradually came to understand that the local clinic was as good as the nurse had assured me in her note. All things being equal, he'd have lived.

But the damage to his mind had been another matter. He'd complained of headaches. He'd also become increasingly distressed. Even morphine hadn't helped. He'd been left alone only for a minute, appearing to be asleep. In that brief interval he'd managed to stagger from his bed, grope across the room, and find a pair of scissors. Yanking off his bandages, he'd jabbed the scissors into an empty eye socket and tried to ream out his brain. He'd collapsed before accomplishing his purpose, but the damage had been sufficient. Death had taken two days.

His parents were pale, incoherent with shock. I somehow controlled my own shock enough to try to comfort them. Despite the blur of those terrible hours, I remember noticing the kind of irrelevance that signals the mind's attempt to reassert normality. Myers's father wore Gucci loafers and an eighteen-karat Rolex watch. In grad school Myers had lived on as strict a budget as I had. I had no idea he came from wealthy parents.

I helped them make arrangements to fly his body back to the States. I went to Nice with them and stayed by their side as they watched the crate that contained his coffin being loaded onto the baggage compartment of the plane. I shook their hands and hugged them. I waited as they sobbed and trudged down the boarding tunnel. An hour later I was back in La Verge.

I returned because of a promise. I wanted to ease his parents' suffering—and my own. Because I'd been his friend. "You've got too much to take care of," I'd said to his parents. "The long trip home. The arrangements for the funeral." My voice had choked. "Let me help. I'll settle things here, pay whatever bills he owes, pack up his clothes and . . ." I took a deep breath. "And his books and whatever else he had and send them home to you. Let me do that. I'd consider it a kindness. Please. I need to do *something*."

True to his ambition, Myers had managed to rent the same room taken by Van Dorn at the village's only hotel. Don't be surprised that it was available. The management used it to promote the hotel. A plaque announced the historic value of the room. The furnishings were the same style as when Van Dorn had stayed there. Tourists, to be sure, had paid to peer in and sniff the residue of genius. But business had been slow this season, and Myers had wealthy parents. For a generous sum, coupled with his typical enthusiasm, he'd convinced the hotel's owner to let him have that room.

I rented a different room—more like a closet—two doors down the hall and, my eyes still burning from tears, went into Van Dorn's musty sanctuary to pack my dear dead friend's possessions. Prints of Van Dorn paintings were everywhere, several splattered with dried blood. Heartsick, I made a stack of them.

That's when I found the diary.

During grad school I'd taken a course in Postimpressionism that emphasized Van Dorn, and I'd read a facsimile edition of his diary. The publisher had photocopied the handwritten pages and bound them, adding an introduction and footnotes. The diary had been cryptic from the start, but as Van Dorn became more feverish about his work, as his nervous breakdown became more severe, his statements deteriorated into riddles. His handwriting—hardly neat, even when he was sane—went quickly out of control and finally turned into almost indecipherable slashes and curves as he rushed to unloose his frantic thoughts.

I sat at a small wooden desk and paged through the diary, recognizing phrases I'd read years before. With each passage my stomach turned colder. Because this diary *wasn't* the published photocopy. Instead, it was a notebook, and though I wanted to believe that Myers had somehow, impossibly, gotten his hands on the original diary, I knew I was fooling myself. The pages in this ledger weren't yellow and brittle with age. The ink hadn't faded till it was brown more than blue. The notebook had been purchased and written in recently. It wasn't Van Dorn's diary. It belonged to *Myers*. The ice in my stomach turned to lava.

Glancing sharply away from the ledger, I saw a shelf beyond the desk and a stack of other notebooks. Apprehensive, I grabbed them and in a fearful rush flipped through them. My stomach threatened to erupt. Each notebook was the same, the words identical.

My hands shook as I looked again to the shelf, found the facsimile edition of the original, and compared it with the notebooks. I moaned, imagining Myers at this desk, his expression intense and insane as he reproduced the diary word for word, slash for slash, curve for curve. Eight times.

Myers had indeed immersed himself, straining to put himself into Van Dorn's disintegrating frame of mind. And in the end he'd succeeded. The weapon Van Dorn had used to stab out his eyes had been the sharp end of a paintbrush. In the mental hospital, Van Dorn had finished the job by skewering his brain with a pair of scissors. Like Myers. Or vice versa. When Myers had finally broken, had he and Van Dorn been horribly indistinguishable?

I pressed my hands to my face. Whimpers squeezed from my convulsing throat. It seemed forever before I stopped sobbing. My consciousness strained to control my anguish. ("Orange is for anguish," Myers had said.) Rationality fought to subdue my distress. ("The critics who devoted themselves to analyzing Van Dorn," Myers had said. "The ones who haven't been recognized for their genius, just as Van Dorn wasn't recognized. They suffered . . . And just like Van Dorn, they stabbed out their eyes.") Had they done it with a paintbrush? I wondered. Were the parallels that exact? And in the end, had they, too, used scissors to skewer their brains?

I scowled at the prints I'd been stacking. Many still

surrounded me—on the walls, the floor, the bed, the windows, even the ceiling. A swirl of colors. A vortex of brilliance.

Or at least I once had thought of them as brilliant. But now, with the insight Myers had given me, with the vision I'd gained in the Metropolitan Museum, I saw behind the sun-drenched cypresses and hayfields, the orchards and meadows, toward their secret dark- ness, toward the minuscule, twisted arms and gaping mouths, the black dots of tortured eyes, the blue knots of writhing bodies. ("Blue is for insanity," Myers had said.)

All it took was a slight shift of perception, and there *weren't* any orchards and hayfields, only a terrifying gestalt of souls in hell. Van Dorn had indeed invented a new stage of Impressionism. He'd impressed upon the splendor of God's creation the teeming images of his own disgust. His paintings didn't glorify. They abhorred. Everywhere Van Dorn had looked, he'd seen his own private nightmare. Blue was for insanity, indeed, and if you fixated on Van Dorn's insanity long enough, you, too, became insane. ("Don't look ever again, I beg you, at Van Dorn's paintings," Myers had said in his letter.) In the last stages of his breakdown, had Myers somehow become lucid enough to try to warn me? ("Can't stand the headaches. Need a break. Am going home.") In a way I'd never suspected, he'd indeed gone home.

Another startling thought occurred to me. ("The critics who devoted themselves to analyzing Van Dorn. They each tried to paint in Van Dorn's style," Myers had said a year ago.) As if attracted by a magnet, my gaze swung across the welter of prints and focused on the corner across from me, where two canvas originals leaned against the wall. I shivered, stood, and halt- ingly approached them.

They'd been painted by an amateur. Myers was an art *historian,* after all. The colors were clumsily ap- plied, especially the splotches of orange and blue. The cypresses were crude. At their bases, the rocks looked like cartoons. The sky needed texture. But I knew what the black dots among them were meant to suggest. I understood the purpose of the tiny blue gashes. The miniature, anguished faces and twisted limbs were implied, even if Myers had lacked the talent to depict them. He'd contracted Van Dorn's madness. All that had remained were the terminal stages.

I sighed from the pit of my soul. As the village's church bell rang, I prayed that my friend had found peace.

It was dark when I left the hotel. I needed to walk, to escape the greater darkness of that room, to feel at liberty, to think. But my footsteps and inquiries led me down a narrow cobbled street toward the village's clinic, where Myers had finished what he'd started in Van Dorn's room. I asked at the desk and five minutes later introduced myself to an attractive, dark-haired, thirtyish woman.

The nurse's English was more than adequate. She said her name was Clarisse.

"You took care of my friend," I said. "You sent me the letter he dictated and added a note of your own."

She nodded. "He worried me. He was so distressed."

The fluorescent lights in the vestibule hummed. We sat on a bench.

"I'm trying to understand why he killed himself," I said. "I think I know, but I'd like your opinion."

Her eyes, a bright, intelligent hazel, suddenly were guarded. "He stayed too long in his room. He studied too much." She shook her head and stared toward the floor. "The mind can be a trap. It can be a torture."

"But he was excited when he came here?"

"Yes."

"Despite his studies, he behaved as if he'd come on vacation?"

"Very much."

"Then what made him change? My friend was unusual, I agree. What we call high-strung. But he *enjoyed* doing research. He might have looked sick from too much work, but he thrived on learning. His body was nothing, but his mind was brilliant. What tipped the balance, Clarisse?"

"Tipped the—?"

"Made him depressed instead of excited. What did he learn that made him—?"

She stood and looked at her watch. "Forgive me. I stopped work twenty minutes ago. I'm expected at a friend's."

My voice hardened. "Of course. I wouldn't want to keep you."

Outside the clinic, beneath the light at its entrance, I stared at my own watch, surprised to see that it was almost eleven-thirty. Fatigue made my knees ache. The trauma of the day had taken away my appetite, but I knew I should try to eat, and after walking back to the hotel's dining room, I ordered a chicken sandwich and a glass of Chablis. I meant to eat in my room but never got that far. Van Dorn's room and the diary beckoned.

The sandwich and wine went untasted. Sitting at the desk, surrounded by the swirling colors and hidden horrors of Van Dorn prints, I opened a notebook and tried to understand.

A knock at the door made me turn.

Again I glanced at my watch, astonished to find that hours had passed like minutes. It was almost two A.M.

The knock was repeated, gentle but insistent. The manager?

"Come in," I said in French. "The door isn't locked."

The knob turned. The door swung open.

Clarisse stepped in. Instead of her nurse's uniform, she now wore sneakers, jeans, and a sweater whose tight-fitting yellow accentuated the hazel in her eyes.

"I apologize," she said in English. "I must have seemed rude at the clinic."

"Not at all. You had an appointment. I was keeping you."

She shrugged self-consciously. "I sometimes leave the clinic so late, I don't have a chance to see my friend."

"I understand perfectly."

She drew a hand through her lush, long hair. "My friend got tired. As I walked home, passing the hotel, I saw a light up here. On the chance it might be you . . ."

I nodded, waiting.

I had the sense she'd been avoiding it, but now she turned toward the room. Toward where I'd found the dried blood on the prints. "The doctor and I came as fast as we could when the manager phoned us that afternoon." She stared at the prints. "How could so much beauty cause so much pain?"

"Beauty?" I glanced toward the tiny, gaping mouths.

"You mustn't stay here. Don't make the mistake your friend did."

"Mistake?"

"You've had a long journey. You've suffered a shock. You need to rest. You'll wear yourself out as your friend did."

"I was just looking through some things of his. I'll be packing them to send them back to America."

"Do it quickly. You mustn't torture yourself by thinking about what happened here. It isn't good to surround yourself with the things that disturbed your friend. Don't intensify your grief."

"Surround myself? My friend would have said 'immerse.' "

"You look exhausted. Come." She held out her hand. "I'll take you to your room. Sleep will ease your pain. If you need some pills to help you . . ."

"Thanks. But a sedative won't be necessary."

She continued to offer her hand. I took it and went to the hallway.

For a moment I stared back toward the prints and the horror within the beauty. I said a silent prayer for Myers, shut off the lights, and locked the door.

We went down the hall. In my room, I sat on the bed.

"Sleep long and well," she said.

"I hope."

"You have my sympathy." She kissed my cheek.

I touched her shoulder. Her lips shifted toward my own. She leaned against me.

We sank toward the bed. In silence, we made love.
Sleep came like her kisses, softly smothering.
But in my nightmares there were tiny, gaping mouths.

Sunlight glowed through my window. With aching eyes
I looked at my watch. Half past ten. My head hurt.
Clarisse had left a note on my bureau.

> Last night was sympathy. To share and ease
> your grief. Do what you intended. Pack your
> friend's belongings. Send them to America.
> Go with them. Don't make your friend's mis-
> take. Don't, as you said *he* said, "immerse"
> yourself. Don't let beauty give you pain.

I meant to leave. I truly believe that. I phoned the
front desk and asked the concierge to send up some
boxes. After I showered and shaved, I went to Myers's
room, where I finished stacking the prints. I made
another stack of books and another of clothes. I packed
everything into the boxes and looked around to make
sure I hadn't forgotten anything.

The two canvases that Myers had painted still leaned
against a corner. I decided not to take them. No one
needed to be reminded of the delusions that had overcome him.

All that remained was to seal the boxes, to address
and mail them. But as I started to close the flap on a
box, I saw the notebooks inside.

So much suffering, I thought. So much waste.

Once more I leafed through a notebook. Various
passages caught my eye. Van Dorn's discouragement
about his failed career. His reasons for leaving Paris to
come to La Verge—the stifling, backbiting artists' community, the snobbish critics and their sneering responses
to his early efforts. *Need to free myself of convention.
Need to void myself of aesthete politics, to shit it out of
me. To find what's never been painted. To feel instead
of being told what to feel. To see instead of imitating what
others have seen.*

I knew from the biographies how impoverished Van

Dorn's ambition had made him. In Paris he'd literally eaten slops thrown into alleys behind restaurants. He'd been able to afford his quest to La Verge only because a successful but very conventional (and now ridiculed) painter friend had loaned him a small sum of money. Eager to conserve his endowment, Van Dorn had walked all the way from Paris to the south of France.

In those days, you have to remember, the Riviera was an unfashionable area of hills, rocks, farms, and villages. Limping into La Verge, Van Dorn must have been a pathetic sight. He'd chosen this provincial town precisely because it *was* unconventional, because it offered mundane scenes so in contrast with the salons of Paris that no other artist would dare to paint them.

Need to create what's never been imagined, he'd written. For six despairing months he tried and failed. He finally self-doubted, then suddenly reversed himself and, in a year of unbelievably brilliant productivity, gave the world thirty-eight masterpieces. At the time, of course, he couldn't trade any canvas for a meal. But the world knows better now.

He must have painted in a frenzy. His sudden-found energy must have been enormous. To me, a would-be artist with technical facility but only conventional eyes, he achieved the ultimate. Despite his suffering, I envied him. When I compared my maudlin, Wyeth-like depictions of Iowa landscapes to Van Dorn's trendsetting genius, I despaired. The task awaiting me back in the States was to imitate beer cans and cigarettes for magazine ads.

I continued flipping through the notebook, tracing the course of Van Dorn's despair and epiphany. His victory had a price, to be sure. Insanity. Self-blinding. Suicide. But I had to wonder if perhaps, as he died, he'd have chosen to reverse his life if he'd been able. He must have known how remarkable, how truly astonishing, his work had become.

Or perhaps he didn't. The last canvas he'd painted before stabbing his eyes had been of himself. A lean-faced, brooding man with short, thinning hair, sunken features, pallid skin, and a scraggly beard. The famous portrait reminded me of how I always thought Christ would have looked just before he was crucified. All that was missing was the crown of thorns. But Van Dorn had a different crown of thorns. Not around but *within* him. Disguised among his scraggly beard and sunken features, the tiny, gaping mouths and writhing bodies told it all. His suddenly acquired vision had stung him too much.

As I read the notebook, again distressed by Myers's effort to reproduce Van Dorn's agonized words and handwriting exactly, I reached the section where Van Dorn described his epiphany: *La Verge! I walked! I saw! I feel! Canvas! Paint! Creation and damnation!*

After that cryptic passage, the notebook—and Van Dorn's diary—became totally incoherent. Except for the persistent refrain of severe and increasing headaches.

I was waiting outside the clinic when Clarisse arrived to start her shift at three o'clock. The sun was brilliant, glinting off her eyes. She wore a burgundy skirt and a turquoise blouse. Mentally I stroked their cottony texture.

When she saw me, her footsteps faltered. Forcing a smile, she approached.

"You came to say good-bye?" She sounded hopeful.

"No. To ask you some questions."

Her smile disintegrated. "I mustn't be late for work."

"This'll take just a minute. My French vocabulary needs improvement. I didn't bring a dictionary. The name of this village. La Verge. What does it mean?"

She hunched her shoulders as if to say the question was unimportant. "It's not very colorful. The literal translation is 'the stick.' "

"That's all?"

She reacted to my frown. "There are rough equivalents. 'The branch.' 'The switch.' A willow, for example, that a father might use to discipline a child."

"And it doesn't mean anything else?"

"Indirectly. The synonyms keep getting farther from the literal sense. A wand, perhaps. Or a rod. The kind of forked stick that people who claim they can find water hold ahead of them when they walk across a field. The stick is supposed to bend down if there's water."

"We call it a divining rod. My father once told me he'd seen a man who could actually make one work. I always suspected the man just tilted the stick with his hands. Do you suppose this village got its name because long ago someone found water here with a divining rod?"

"Why would anyone have bothered when these hills have so many streams and springs? What makes you interested in the name?"

"Something I read in Van Dorn's diary. The village's name excited him for some reason."

"But *anything* could have excited him. He was insane."

"Eccentric. But he didn't become insane until after that passage in his diary."

"You mean, his *symptoms* didn't show themselves until after that. You're not a psychiatrist."

I had to agree.

"Again, I'm afraid I'll seem rude. I really must go to work." She hesitated. "Last night . . ."

"Was exactly what you described in the note. A gesture of sympathy. An attempt to ease my grief. You didn't mean it to be the start of anything."

"Please do what I asked. Please leave. Don't destroy yourself like the others."

"*Others*?"

"Like your friend."

"No, you said, 'others.' " My words were rushed. "Clarisse, tell me."

She glanced up, squinting as if she'd been cornered. "After your friend stabbed out his eyes, I heard talk around the village. Older people. It could be merely gossip that became exaggerated with the passage of time."

"What did they say?"

She squinted harder. "Twenty years ago a man came here to do research on Van Dorn. He stayed three months and had a breakdown."

"He stabbed out his eyes?"

"Rumors drifted back that he blinded himself in a mental hospital in England. Ten years before, another man came. He jabbed scissors through an eye, all the way into his brain."

I stared, unable to control the spasms that racked my shoulder blades. "What the hell is going on?"

I asked around the village. No one would talk to me. At the hotel the manager told me he'd decided to stop renting Van Dorn's room. I had to remove Myers's belongings at once.

"But I can still stay in *my* room?"

"If that's what you wish. I don't recommend it, but even France is still a free country."

I paid the bill, went upstairs, moved the packed boxes from Van Dorn's room to mine, and turned in surprise as the phone rang.

The call was from my fiancée.

When was I coming home?

I didn't know.

What about the wedding this weekend?

The wedding would have to be postponed.

I winced as she slammed down the phone.

I sat on the bed and couldn't help recalling the last time I'd sat there, with Clarisse standing over me, just before we'd made love. I was throwing away the life I'd tried to build.

For a moment I came close to calling back my fiancée, but a different sort of compulsion made me scowl toward the boxes, toward Van Dorn's diary. In the note Clarisse had added to Myers's letter, she'd said that his research had become so obsessive that he'd tried to recreate Van Dorn's daily habits. Again it occurred to me—at the end, had Myers and Van Dorn become indistinguishable? Was the secret to what had happened to Myers hidden in the diary, just as the suffering faces were hidden in Van Dorn's paintings? I grabbed one of the ledgers. Scanning the pages, I looked for references to Van Dorn's daily routine. And so it began.

*   *   *

I've said that except for telephone poles and electrical lines, La Verge seemed caught in the previous century. Not only was the hotel still in existence, but so were Van Dorn's favorite tavern, and the bakery where he'd bought his morning croissant. A small restaurant he favored remained in business. On the edge of the village, a trout stream where he sometimes sat with a mid-afternoon glass of wine still bubbled along, though pollution had long since killed the trout. I went to all of them, in the order and at the time he recorded in his diary.

After a week—breakfast at eight, lunch at two, a glass of wine at the trout stream, a stroll to the countryside, then back to the room—I knew the diary so well, I didn't need to refer to it. Mornings had been Van Dorn's time to paint. The light was best then, he'd written. And evenings were a time for remembering and sketching.

It finally came to me that I wouldn't be following the schedule exactly if I didn't paint and sketch when Van Dorn had done so. I bought a notepad, canvas, pigments, a palette, whatever I needed, and, for the first time since leaving grad school, I tried to *create*. I used local scenes that Van Dorn had favored and produced what you'd expect: uninspired versions of Van Dorn's paintings. With no discoveries, no understanding of what had ultimately undermined Myers's sanity, tedium set in. My finances were almost gone. I prepared to give up.

Except . . .

I had the disturbing sense that I'd missed something. A part of Van Dorn's routine that wasn't explicit in the diary. Or something about the locales themselves that I hadn't noticed, though I'd been painting them in Van Dorn's spirit, if not with his talent.

Clarisse found me sipping wine on the sunlit bank of the no longer trout-filled stream. I felt her shadow and turned toward her silhouette against the sun.

I hadn't seen her for two weeks, since our uneasy

conversation outside the clinic. Even with the sun in my eyes, she looked more beautiful than I remembered.

"When was the last time you changed your clothes?" she asked.

A year ago I'd said the same to Myers.

"You need a shave. You've been drinking too much. You look awful."

I sipped my wine and shrugged. "Well, you know what the drunk said about his bloodshot eyes. You think they look bad to you? You should see them from *my* side."

"At least you can joke."

"I'm beginning to think that *I'm* the joke."

"You're definitely not a joke." She sat beside me. "You're becoming your friend. Why don't you leave?"

"I'm tempted."

"Good." She touched my hand.

"Clarisse?"

"Yes?"

"Answer some questions one more time?"

She studied me. "Why?"

"Because if I get the right answers, I might leave." She nodded slowly.

Back in town, in my room, I showed her the stack of prints. I almost told her about the faces they contained, but her brooding features stopped me. She thought I was disturbed enough as it was.

"When I walk in the afternoons, I go to the settings Van Dorn chose for his paintings." I sorted through the prints. "This orchard. This farm. This pond. This cliff. And so on."

"Yes, I recognize these places. I've seen them all."

"I hoped if I saw them, maybe I'd understand what happened to my friend. You told me he went to them as well. Each of them is within a five-mile radius of the village. Many are close together. It wasn't difficult to find each site. Except for one."

She didn't ask the obvious question. Instead, she tensely rubbed her arm.

When I'd taken the boxes from Van Dorn's room,

I'd also removed the two paintings Myers had attempted. Now I pulled them from where I'd tucked them under the bed.

"My friend did these. It's obvious he wasn't an artist. But as crude as they are, you can see they both depict the same area."

I slid a Van Dorn print from the bottom of the stack.

"*This* area," I said. "A grove of cypresses in a hollow, surrounded by rocks. It's the only site I haven't been able to find. I've asked the villagers. They claim they don't know where it is. Do *you* know, Clarisse? Can you tell me? It must have some significance if my friend was fixated on it enough to try to paint it *twice*."

Clarisse scratched a fingernail across her wrist. "I'm sorry."

"What?"

"I can't help you."

"Can't or won't? Do you mean you don't know where to find it, or you know but you won't tell me?"

"I said I can't help."

"What's wrong with this village, Clarisse? What's everybody trying to hide?"

"I've done my best." She shook her head, stood, and walked to the door. She glanced back sadly. "Sometimes it's better to leave well enough alone. Sometimes there are reasons for secrets."

I watched her go down the hall. "Clarisse . . ."

She turned and spoke a single word: "North." She was crying. "God help you," she added. "I'll pray for your soul." Then she disappeared down the stairs.

For the first time I felt afraid.

Five minutes later I left the hotel. In my walks to the sites of Van Dorn's paintings, I'd always chosen the easiest routes—east, west, and south. Whenever I'd asked about the distant, tree-lined hills to the north, the villagers had told me there was nothing of interest there, nothing at all to do with Van Dorn. What about cypresses in a hollow? I'd asked. There weren't any cypresses in those hills, only olive trees, they'd answered. But now I knew.

La Verge was in the southern end of an oblong valley, squeezed by cliffs to the east and west. To reach the northern hills, I'd have to walk twenty miles at least.

I rented a car. Leaving a dust cloud, I pressed my foot on the accelerator and stared toward the rapidly enlarging hills. The trees I'd seen from the village were indeed olive trees. But the lead-colored rocks among them were the same as in Van Dorn's painting. I skidded along the road, veering up through the hills. Near the top I found a narrow space to park and rushed from the car. But which direction to take? On impulse, I chose left and hurried among the rocks and trees.

My decision seems less arbitrary now. Something about the slopes to the left was more dramatic, more aesthetically compelling. A greater wildness in the landscape. A sense of depth, of substance.

My instincts urged me forward. I'd reached the hills at quarter after five. Time compressed eerily. At once, my watch showed ten past seven. The sun blazed, crimson, over the bluffs. I kept searching, letting the grotesque landscape guide me. The ridges and ravines were like a maze, every turn of which either blocked or gave access, controlling my direction. I rounded a crag, scurried down a slope of thorns, ignored the rips in my shirt and the blood streaming from my hands, and stopped on the precipice of a hollow. Cypresses, not olive trees, filled the basin. Boulders jutted among them and formed a grotto.

The basin was steep. I skirted its brambles, ignoring their scalding sting. Boulders led me down. I stifled my misgivings, frantic to reach the bottom.

This hollow, this basin of cypresses and boulders, this thorn-rimmed funnel, was the image not only of Van Dorn's painting but of the canvases Myers had attempted. But why had this place so affected them?

The answer came as quickly as the question. I heard before I saw, though hearing doesn't accurately describe my sensation. The sound was so faint and high-pitched, it was almost beyond the range of detection. At first I thought I was near a hornet's nest. I sensed a subtle vibration in the otherwise still air of the hollow. I felt an itch behind my eardrums, a tingle on my skin. The sound was actually many sounds, each identical, merging, like the collective buzz of a swarm of insects. But this was high-pitched. Not a buzz but more like a distant chorus of shrieks and wails.

Frowning, I took another step toward the cypresses. The tingle on my skin intensified. The itch behind my eardrums became so irritating, I raised my hands to the sides of my head. I came close enough to see within the trees, and what I noticed with terrible clarity made me panic. Gasping, I stumbled back. But not in time. What shot from the trees was too small and fast for me to identify.

It struck my right eye. The pain was excruciating, as if the white-hot tip of a needle had pierced my retina and lanced my brain. I clamped my right hand across that eye and screamed.

I continued stumbling back, agony spurring my panic. But the sharp, hot pain intensified, surging through my skull. My knees bent. My consciousness dimmed. I fell against the slope.

It was after midnight when I managed to drive back to the village. Though my eye no longer burned, my panic was more extreme. Still dizzy from having passed out, I tried to keep control when I entered the clinic and asked where Clarisse lived. She'd invited me to visit, I claimed. A sleepy attendant frowned but told me. I drove desperately toward her cottage, five blocks away.

Lights were on. I knocked. She didn't answer. I pounded harder, faster. At last I saw a shadow. When the door swung open, I lurched into the living room. I barely noticed the negligee Clarisse clutched around her, or the open door to her bedroom, where a startled woman sat up in bed, held a sheet to her breasts, and stood quickly to shut the bedroom door.

"What the hell do you think you're doing?" Clarisse yelled. "I didn't invite you in! I didn't—!"

I managed the strength to talk: "I don't have time to explain. I'm terrified. I need your help."

She clutched her negligee tighter.

"I've been stung. I think I've caught a disease. Help me stop whatever's inside me. Antibiotics. An antidote. Anything you can think of. Maybe it's a virus, maybe a fungus. Maybe it acts like bacteria."

"*What happened?*"

"I told you, no time. I'd have asked for help at the clinic, but they wouldn't have understood. They'd have thought I'd had a breakdown, the same as Myers. You've got to take me there. You've got to make sure I'm injected with as much of any and every drug that might possibly kill this thing."

"I'll dress as fast as I can."

As we rushed to the clinic, I described what had happened. She phoned the doctor the moment we arrived. While we waited, she disinfected my eye and gave me something for my rapidly developing headache. The doctor showed up, his sleepy features becoming alert when he saw how distressed I was. True to my prediction, he reacted as if I'd had a breakdown. I shouted at him to humor me and saturate me with antibiotics. Clarisse made sure it wasn't just a sedative he gave me. He used every compatible combination. If I thought it would have worked, I'd have swallowed Drāno.

What I'd seen within the cypresses were tiny, gaping mouths and minuscule, writhing bodies, as small and camouflaged as those in Van Dorn's paintings. I know now that Van Dorn wasn't imposing his insane vision on reality. He wasn't an Impressionist. At least not in his *Cypresses in a Hollow.* I'm convinced that this painting was his first after his brain became infected. He was literally depicting what he'd seen on one of his walks. Later, as the infection progressed, he saw the gaping mouths and writhing bodies like an overlay on everything else he looked at. In that sense, too, he wasn't an Impressionist. To him, the gaping mouths and writhing bodies *were* in all those later scenes. To the limit of his infected brain, he painted what to him *was* reality. His art was representational.

I know, believe me. Because the drugs didn't work. My brain is as diseased as Van Dorn's . . . or Myers's. I've tried to understand why they didn't panic when they were stung, why they didn't rush to a hospital to make a doctor understand what had happened. My conclusion is that Van Dorn had been so desperate for a vision to enliven his paintings that he gladly endured the suffering. And Myers had been so desperate to understand Van Dorn that when stung, he'd willingly taken the risk to identify even more with his subject until, too late, he'd realized his mistake.

Orange is for anguish, blue for insanity. How true. Whatever infects my brain has affected my color sense. More and more, orange and blue overpower the other colors I know are there. I have no choice. I see little else. My paintngs are *rife* with orange and blue.

My paintings. Because I've solved another mystery. It always puzzled me how Van Dorn could have suddenly been seized by such energetic genius that he painted thirty-eight masterpieces in one year. I know the answer now. What's in my head, the gaping mouths and writhing bodies, the orange of anguish and the blue of insanity, cause such pressure, such headaches that I've tried everything to subdue them, to get them out. I went from codeine to Demerol to morphine. Each helped for a time but not enough. Then I learned what Van Dorn understood and Myers attempted. Painting the disease somehow gets it out of you. For a time. And then you paint harder, faster. Anything to relieve the pain. But Myers wasn't an artist. The disease had no release and reached its terminal stage in weeks instead of Van Dorn's year.

But *I'm* an artist—or used to hope I was. I had skill without a vision. Now, God help me, I've got a vision. At first I painted the cypresses and their secret. I accomplished what you'd expect. An imitation of Van

Dorn's original. But I refuse to suffer pointlessly. I vividly recall the portraits of Midwestern landscapes I produced in grad school. The dark-earthed Iowa landscape. The attempt to make an observer feel the fecundity of the soil. At the time the results were ersatz Wyeth. But not anymore. The twenty paintings I've so far stored away aren't versions of Van Dorn, either. They're my own creations. Unique. A combination of the disease and my experience. Aided by powerful memory, I paint the river that flows through Iowa City. Blue. I paint the cornfields that cram the big-sky rolling country outside of town. Orange. I paint my innocence. My youth. With my ultimate discovery hidden within them. Ugliness lurks within the beauty. Horror festers in my brain.

Clarisse at last told me about the local legend. When La Verge was founded, she said, a meteor streaked from the sky. It lit the night. It burst upon the hills north of here. Flames erupted. Trees were consumed. The hour was late. Few villagers saw it. The site of the impact was too far away for those few witnesses to rush that night to see the crater. In the morning the smoke had dispersed. The embers had died. Though the witnesses tried to find the meteor, the lack of the roads that now exist hampered their search through the tangled hills to the point of discouragement. A few among the few witnesses persisted. The few of the few of the few who had accomplished their quest staggered back to the village, babbling about headaches and tiny, gaping mouths. Using sticks, they scraped disturbing images in the dirt and eventually stabbed out their eyes. Over the centuries, legend has it, similar self-mutilations occurred whenever someone returned from seeking the crater in those hills. The unknown had power then. The hills acquired the negative force of taboo. No villager, then or now, intruded on what came to be called the place where God's wand touched the earth. A poetic description of a blazing meteor's impact. La Verge.

I don't conclude the obvious: that the meteor carried spores that multiplied in the crater, which became a hollow eventually filled with cypresses. No—to me, the meteor was a cause but not an effect. I saw a pit among the cypresses, and from the pit, tiny mouths and writhing bodies resembling insects—how they wailed!—spewed. They clung to the leaves of the cypresses, flailed in anguish as they fell back, and instantly were replaced by other spewing, anguished souls.

Yes. Souls. For the meteor, I insist, was just the cause. The effect was the opening of hell. The tiny, wailing mouths are the damned. As *I* am damned. Desperate to survive, to escape from the ultimate prison we call hell, a frantic sinner lunged. He caught my eye and stabbed my brain, the gateway to my soul. My soul. It festers. I paint to remove the pus.

I talk. That helps somehow. Clarisse writes it down while her female lover rubs my shoulders.

My paintings are brilliant. I'll be recognized, as I'd always dreamed. As a genius, of course.

At such a cost.

The headaches grow worse. The orange is more brilliant. The blue more disturbing.

I try my best. I urge myself to be stronger than Myers, whose endurance lasted only weeks. Van Dorn persisted for a year. Maybe genius is strength.

My brain swells. How it threatens to split my skull. The gaping mouths blossom.

The headaches! I tell myself to be strong. Another day. Another rush to complete another painting.

The sharp end of my paintbrush invites. Anything to lance my seething mental boil, to jab my eyes for the ecstasy of relief. But I have to endure.

On a table near my left hand, the scissors wait.

But not today. Or tomorrow.

I'll outlast Van Dorn.

Peter Straub

The Juniper Tree

It is a school yard in my Midwest of empty lots, waving green and brilliant with tiger lilies, of ugly new "ranch" houses set down in rows in glistening clay, of treeless avenues cooking in the sun. Our school yard is black asphalt—on June days, patches of the asphalt loosen and stick like gum to the soles of our high-top basketball shoes.

Most of the playground is black empty space from which heat radiates up like the wavery images on the screen of a faulty television set. Tall wire mesh surrounds it. A new boy named Paul is standing beside me.

Though it is now nearly the final month of the semester, Paul came to us, carroty-haired, pale-eyed, too shy to ask even the whereabouts of the lavatory, only six weeks ago. The lessons baffle him, and his Southern accent is a fatal error of style. The popular students broadcast in hushed, giggling whispers the terrible news that Paul "talks like a nigger." Their voices are *almost* awed—they are conscious of the enormity of what they are saying, of the enormity of its consequences.

Paul is wearing a brilliant red shirt too heavy, too enveloping, for the weather. He and I stand in the shade at the rear of the school, before the cream-colored brick wall in which is placed at eye level a newly broken window of pebbly green glass reinforced with strands of copper wire. At our feet is a little scatter of green, edible-looking pebbles. The pebbles dig into the soles of our shoes, too hard to shatter against the softer asphalt. Paul is singing to me in his slow, lilting voice that he will never have friends in this school. I put my foot down on one of the green candy pebbles and feel it push up, hard as a bullet, against my foot. "Children are so cruel," Paul casually sings. I think of sliding the pebble of broken glass across my throat, slicing myself wide open to let death in.

Paul did not return to school in the fall. His father, who had beaten a man to death down in Mississippi, had been arrested while leaving a movie theater near my house named the Orpheum-Oriental. Paul's father had taken his family to see an Esther Williams movie costarring Fernando Lamas, and when they came out, their mouths raw from salty popcorn, the baby's hands sticky with spilled Coca-Cola, the police were waiting for them. They were Mississippi people, and I think of Paul now, seated at a desk on a floor of an office building in Jackson filled with men like him at desks: his tie perfectly knotted, a good shine on his cordovan shoes, a necessary but unconscious restraint in the set of his mouth.

In those days I used to spend whole days in the Orpheum-Oriental.

I was seven. I held within me the idea of a disappearance like Paul's, of never having to be seen again. Of being an absence, a shadow, a place where something no longer visible used to be.

Before I met that young-old man whose name was "Frank" or "Stan" or "Jimmy," when I sat in the rapture of education before the movies at the Orpheum-Oriental, I watched Alan Ladd and Richard Widmark and Glenn Ford and Dane Clark. *Chicago Deadline.* Martin and Lewis, tangled up in the same parachute in *At War With the Army.* William Boyd and Roy Rogers. Openmouthed, I drank down movies about spies and criminals, wanting the passionate and shadowy ones to fulfill themselves, to gorge themselves on what they needed.

The feverish gaze of Richard Widmark, the anger of Alan Ladd, Berry Kroeger's sneaky eyes, girlish and watchful—vivid, total elegance.

When I was seven, my father walked into the bathroom and saw me looking at my face in the mirror. He slapped me, not with his whole strength, but hard, raging instantly. "What do you think you're looking at?" His hand cocked and ready. "What do you think you see?"

"Nothing," I said.

"Nothing is right."

A carpenter, he worked furiously, already defeated, and never had enough money—as if, permanently beyond reach, some quantity of money existed that would have satisfied him. In the morning he went to the job site hardened like cement into anger he barely knew he had. Sometimes he brought men from the taverns home with him at night. They carried transparent bottles of Miller High Life in paper bags and set them down on the table with a bang that said: Men are here! My mother, who had returned from her secretary's job a few hours earlier, fed my brothers and me, washed the dishes, and put the three of us to bed while the men shouted and laughed in the kitchen.

He was considered an excellent carpenter. He worked slowly, patiently; and I see now that he spent whatever love he had in the rented garage that was his workshop. In his spare time he listened to baseball games on the radio. He had professional, but not personal, vanity, and he thought that a face like mine should not be examined.

Because I saw "Jimmy" in the mirror, I thought my father, too, had seen him.

One Saturday my mother took the twins and me on the ferry across Lake Michigan to Saginaw—the point of the journey was the journey, and at Saginaw the boat docked for twenty minutes before wallowing back out into the lake and returning. With us were women like my mother, her friends, freed by the weekend from their jobs, some of them accompanied by men like my father, with their felt hats and baggy weekend trousers flaring over their weekend shoes. The women wore blood-bright lipstick that printed itself onto their cigarettes and smeared across their front teeth. They laughed a great deal and repeated the words that had made them laugh. "Hot dog," "slippin' 'n' slidin'," "opera singer." Thirty minutes after departure, the men disappeared into the enclosed deck bar; the women, my mother among them, arranged deck chairs into a long oval tied together by laughter, attention, gossip. They waved their cigarettes in the air. My brothers raced around the deck, their shirts flapping, their hair glued to their skulls with sweat—when they squabbled, my mother ordered them into empty deck chairs. I sat on the deck, leaning against the railings, quiet. If someone had asked me: What do you want to do this afternoon, what do you want to do for the rest of your life? I would have said, I want to stay right here, I want to stay here forever.

After a while I stood up and left the women. I went across the deck and stepped through a hatch into the bar. Dark, deeply grained imitation wood covered the walls. The odors of beer and cigarettes and the sound of men's voices filled the enclosed space. About twenty men stood at the bar, talking and gesturing with half-filled glasses. Then one man broke away from the others with a flash of dirty blond hair. I saw his shoulders move, and my scalp tingled and my stomach froze and I thought: Jimmy. "Jimmy." But he turned all the way around, dipping his shoulders in some ecstasy of beer and male company, and I saw that he was a stranger, not "Jimmy," after all.

*   *   *

I was thinking: Someday when I am free, when I am out of this body and in some city whose name I do not even know now, I will remember this from beginning to end and then I will be free of it.

The women floated over the empty lake, laughing out clouds of cigarette smoke, the men, too, as boisterous as the children on the sticky asphalt playground with its small green spray of glass like candy.

*   *   *

In those days I knew I was set apart from the rest of my family, an island between my parents and the twins. Those pairs that bracketed me slept in double beds in adjacent rooms at the back of the ground floor of the duplex owned by the blind man who lived above us. My bed, a cot coveted by the twins, stood in their room. An invisible line of great authority divided my territory and possessions from theirs.

*   *   *

This is what happened in the morning in our half of the duplex. My mother got up first—we heard her showering, heard drawers closing, the sounds of bowls and milk being set out on the table. The smell of bacon frying for my father, who banged on the door and called out my brothers' names. "Don't you make me come in there, now!" The noisy, puppyish turmoil of my brothers getting out of bed. All three of us scramble into the bathroom as soon as my father leaves it. The bathroom was steamy, heavy with the odor of shit and the more piercing, almost palpable smell of shaving—lather and amputated whiskers. We all pee into the toilet at the same time. My mother frets and frets, pulling the twins into their clothes so that she can take them down the street to Mrs. Candee, who is given a five-dollar bill every week for taking care of them. I am supposed to be running back and forth on the playground in Summer Play School, supervised by two teenage girls who live a block away from us. (I went to Play School only twice.) After I dress myself in clean underwear and socks and put on my everyday shirt and pants, I come into the kitchen while my father finishes his breakfast. He is eating strips of bacon and golden-brown pieces of toast shiny with butter. A cigarette smolders in the ashtray before him. Everybody else has already left the house. My father and I can hear the blind man banging on the piano in his living room. I sit down before a bowl of cereal. My father looks at me, looks away. Angry at the blind man for banging at the piano this early in the morning, he is sweating already. His cheeks and forehead shine like the golden toast. My father glances at me, knowing he can postpone this no longer, and reaches wearily into his pocket and drops two quarters on the table. The high-school girls charge twenty-five cents a day, and the other quarter is for my lunch. "Don't lose that money," he says as I take the coins. My father dumps coffee into his mouth, puts the cup and his plate into the crowded sink, looks at me again, pats his pockets for his keys, and says, "Close the door behind you." I tell him that I will close the door. He picks up his grey toolbox and his black lunch pail, claps his hat on his head, and goes out, banging his toolbox against the door frame. It leaves a broad grey mark like a smear left by the passing of some angry creature's hide.

Then I am alone in the house. I go back to the bedroom, close the door and push a chair beneath the knob, and read *Blackhawk* and *Henry* and *Captain Marvel* comic books until at last it is time to go to the theater.

While I read, everything in the house seems alive and dangerous. I can hear the telephone in the hall rattling on its hook, the radio clicking as it tries to turn itself on and talk to me. The dishes stir and rattle in the sink. At these times all objects, even the heavy chairs and sofa, become their true selves, violent as the fire that fills the sky I cannot see, and races through the secret ways and passages beneath the streets. At these times other people vanish like smoke.

When I pull the chair away from the door, the house immediately goes quiet, like a wild animal feigning sleep. Everything inside and out slips cunningly back into place, the fires bank, men and women reappear on the sidewalks. I must open the door and I do. I walk swiftly through the kitchen and the living room to the front door, knowing that if I look too carefully at any one thing, I will wake it up again. My mouth is so dry, my tongue feels fat. "I'm leaving," I say to no one. Everything in the house hears me.

*   *   *

The quarter goes through the slot at the bottom of the window, the ticket leaps from its slot. For a long time, before "Jimmy," I thought that unless you kept your stub unfolded and safe in a shirt pocket, the usher could rush down the aisle in the middle of the movie, seize you, and throw you out. So into the pocket it goes, and I slip through the big doors into the cool, cross the lobby and pass through a swinging door with a porthole window.

Most of the regular daytime patrons of the Orpheum-Oriental sit in the same seats every day—I am one of those who comes here every day. A small, talkative gathering of bums sits far to the right of the theater, in the rows beneath the sconces fastened like bronze torches to the walls. The bums choose these seats so that they can examine their bits of paper, their "documents," and show them to each other during the movie. Always on their minds is the possibility that they might have lost one of these documents, and they frequently consult the tattered envelopes in which they are kept.

I take the end seat, left side of the central block of seats, just before the broad horizontal middle aisle. There I can stretch out. At other times I sit in the middle of the last row, or the first; sometimes when the balcony is open I go up and sit in its first row. From the first row of the balcony, seeing a movie is like being a bird and flying down into the movie from above. To be alone in the theater is delicious. The curtains hang heavy, red, anticipatory; the mock torches glow on the walls. Swirls of gilt wind through the red paint. On days when I sit near a wall, I reach out toward the red, which seems warm and soft, and find my fingers resting on a chill dampness. The carpet of the Orpheum-Oriental must once have been a bottom-lessly rich brown; now it is a dark non-color, mottled with the pink and grey smears, like melted Band-Aids, of chewing gum. From about a third of the seats dirty grey wool foams from slashes in the worn plush.

On an ideal day I sit through a cartoon, a travel-ogue, a sequence of previews, a movie, another car-toon, and another movie before anyone else enters the theater. This whole cycle is as satisfying as a meal. On other mornings, old women in odd hats and young women wearing scarves over their rollers, a few teen-age couples, are scattered throughout the theater when I come in. None of these people ever pays attention to anything but the screen and, in the case of the teen-agers, each other.

Once, a man in his early twenties, hair like a haystack, sat up in the wide middle aisle when I took my seat. He groaned. Rusty-looking dried blood was spattered over his chin and his dirty white shirt. He groaned again and then got to his hands and knees. The carpet beneath him was spotted with what looked like a thou-sand red dots. The young man stumbled to his feet and began reeling up the aisle. A bright, depthless pane of sunlight surrounded him before he vanished into it.

At the beginning of July, I told my mother that the high-school girls had increased the hours of the Play School because I wanted to be sure of seeing both features twice before I had to go home. After that I could learn the rhythms of the theater itself, which did not impress themselves upon me all at once but re-vealed themselves gradually, so that by the middle of the first week, I knew when the bums would begin to move toward the seats beneath the sconces—they usu-ally arrived on Tuesdays and Fridays shortly after eleven o'clock, when the liquor store down the block opened up to provide them with the pints and half-pints that nourished them. By the end of the second week, I knew when the ushers left the interior of the theater to sit on padded benches in the lobby and light up their Luckies and Chesterfields, when the old men and women would begin to appear. By the end of the third week, I felt like the merest part of a great, orderly machine. Before the beginning of the second showing of *Beautiful Hawaii* or *Curiosities Down Under*, I went out to the counter and with my second quarter purchased a box of popcorn or a packet of Good 'N Plenty candy.

In a movie theater nothing is random except the customers and hitches in the machine. Filmstrips break and lights fail; the projectionist gets drunk or falls asleep; and the screen presents a blank yellow face to the stamping, whistling audience. These inconsistencies are summer squalls, forgotten as soon as they have ended.

The occasion for the lights, the projectionist, the boxes of popcorn and packets of candy, the movies, enlarged when seen over and over. The truth gradually came to me that this deepening and widening out, this enlarging, was why movies were shown over and over all day long. The machine revealed itself most surely in the exact, limpid repetitions of the actors' words and gestures as they moved through the story. When Alan Ladd asked "Blackie Franchot," the dying gangster, "Who did it, Blackie?" his voice widened like a river, grew *sandier* with an almost unconcealed tenderness I had to learn to hear—the voice within the speaking voice.

*   *   *

Chicago Deadline was the exploration by a newspaper reporter named "Ed Adams" (Alan Ladd) of the tragedy of a mysterious young woman, "Rosita Jandreau," who had died alone of tuberculosis in a shabby hotel room. The reporter soon learns that she had many names, many identities. She had been in love with an architect, a gangster, a crippled professor, a boxer, a millionaire, and had given a different facet of her being to each of them. Far too predictably, the adult me complains, the obsessed "Ed" falls in love with "Rosita." When I was seven, little was predictable—I had not yet seen *Laura*—and I saw a man driven by the need to understand, which became identical to the need to protect. "Rosita Jandreau" was the embodiment of memory, which was mystery.

Through the sequences of her identities, the various selves shown to brother, boxer, millionaire, gangster, all the others, her memory kept her whole. I saw, twice a day, for two weeks, before and during "Jimmy," the machine deep within the machine. Love and memory were the same. Both love and memory accommodated us to death. (I did not understand this, but I saw it.) The reporter, Alan Ladd, with his dirty blond hair, his perfect jawline, and brilliant, wounded smile, gave her life by making her memory his own.

"I think you're the only one who ever understood her," Arthur Kennedy—"Rosita's" brother—tells Alan Ladd.

Most of the world demands the kick of sensation, most of the world must gather and spend money, hunt for easier and more temporary forms of love, must feed itself, sell newspapers, destroy the enemy's plots with plots of its own. . . .

"I don't know what you want," "Ed Adams" says to the editor of *The Journal*. "You got two murders . . ."

*   *   *

". . . and a mystery woman," I say along with him. His voice is tough and detached, the voice of a wounded man acting. The man beside me laughs. Unlike his normal voice, his laughter is breathless and high-pitched. It is the second showing today of *Chicago Deadline*, early afternoon—after the next showing of *At War With the Army* I will have to walk up the aisle and out of the theater. It will be twenty minutes to five, and the sun will still burn high over the cream-colored buildings across wide, empty Sherman Boulevard.

I met the man, or he met me, at the candy counter. He was at first only a tall presence, blond, dressed in dark clothing. I cared nothing for him, he did not matter. He was vague even when he spoke. "Good popcorn." I looked up at him—narrow blue eyes, bad teeth smiling at me. Stubble on his face. I looked away and the uniformed man behind the counter handed me popcorn. "Good for you, I mean. Good stuff in popcorn—comes right out of the ground. Grows on big plants tall as I am, just like other corn. You know that?"

When I said nothing, he laughed and spoke to the man behind the counter. "*He* didn't know that—the kid thought popcorn grew inside poppers." The counterman turned away. "You come here a lot?" the man asked me.

I put a few kernels of popcorn in my mouth and turned toward him. He was showing me his bad teeth.

"You do," he said. "You come here a lot."

I nodded.

"Every day?"

I nodded again.

"And we tell little fibs at home about what we've been doing all day, don't we?" he asked, and pursed his lips and raised his eyes like a comic butler in a movie. Then his mood shifted and everything about him became serious. He was looking at me, but he did not see me. "You got a favorite actor? I got a favorite actor. Alan Ladd."

And I saw—both saw and understood—that he thought he looked like Alan Ladd. He did, too, at least a little bit. When I saw the resemblance, he seemed like a different person, more glamorous. Glamour surrounded him, as though he were acting, impersonating a shabby young man with stained, irregular teeth.

"The name's Frank," he said, and stuck out his hand. "Shake?"

I took his hand.

"Real good popcorn," he said, and stuck his hand into the box. "Want to hear a secret?"

A secret.

"I was born twice. The first time, I died. It was on an Army base. Everybody *told* me I should have joined the Navy, and everybody was right. So I just had myself get born somewhere else. Hey—the Army's not for everybody, you know?" He grinned down at me. "Now I told you my secret. Let's go in—I'll sit with you. Everybody needs company, and I like you. You look like a good kid."

He followed me back to my seat and sat down beside me. When I quoted the lines along with the actors, he laughed.

Then he said—

Then he leaned toward me and said—

He leaned toward me, breathing sour wine over me, and took—

No.

"I was just kidding out there," he said. "Frank ain't my real name. Well, it was my name. Before. See? Frank *used* to be my name for a while. But now my good friends call me Stan. I like that. Stanley the Steamer. Big Stan. Stan the Man. See? It works real good."

*   *   *

You'll never be a carpenter, he told me. You'll never be anything like that—because you got that look. *I* used to have that look, okay? So I know. I know about you just by looking at you.

He said he had been a clerk at Sears; after that he had worked as the custodian for a couple of apartment buildings owned by a guy who used to be a friend of his but was no longer. Then he had been the janitor at the high school where my grade school sent its graduates. "Good old booze got me fired, story of my life," he said. "Tight-ass bitches caught me drinking down in the basement, in a room I used there, and threw me out without a fare-thee-well. Hey, that was my *room*. My *place*. The best things in the world can do the worst things to you; you'll find that out someday. And when you go to that school, I hope you'll remember what they done to me there."

These days he was resting. He hung around, he went to the movies.

He said: You got something special in you. Guys like me, we're funny, we can tell.

We sat together through the second feature, Dean Martin and Jerry Lewis, comfortable and laughing. "Those guys are bigger bums than us," he said. I thought of Paul backed up against the school in his enveloping red shirt, imprisoned within his inability to be like anyone around him.

You coming back tomorrow? If I get here, I'll check around for you.

Hey. Trust me. I know who you are.

You know that little thing you pee with? Leaning sideways and whispering into my ear. That's the best thing a man's got. Trust me.

*　　*　　*

The big providential park near our house, two streets past the Orpheum-Oriental, is separated into three different areas. Nearest the wide iron gates on Sherman Boulevard through which we enter was a wading pool divided by a low green hedge, so rubbery it seemed artificial, from a playground with a climbing frame, swings, and a row of seesaws. When I was a child of two and three, I splashed in the warm pool and clung to the chains of the swings, making myself go higher and higher, terror and joy and grim duty so woven together that no one could pull them apart.

Beyond the children's pool and playground was the

zoo. My mother walked my brothers and me to the playground and wading pool and sat smoking on a bench while we played; both of my parents took us into the zoo. An elephant extended his trunk to my father's palm and delicately lipped peanuts toward his maw. The giraffe stretched toward the constantly diminishing supply of leaves, ever fewer and higher, above his cage. The lions drowsed on amputated branches and paced behind the bars, staring out not at what was there but at the long, grassy plains imprinted on their memories. I knew the lions had the power not to see us, to look straight through us to Africa. But when they saw you instead of Africa, they looked right into your bones, they saw the blood traveling through your body. The lions were golden brown, patient, green-eyed. They recognized me and could read thoughts. The lions neither liked nor disliked me, they did not miss me during their long weekdays, but they took me into the circle of known beings.

("You shouldn't have looked at me like that," June Havoc ("Leona") tells "Ed Adams." She does not mean it, not at all.)

Past the zoo and across a narrow park road down which khaki-clothed park attendants pushed barrows heavy with flowers stood a wide, unexpected lawn bordered with flower beds and tall elms—open space hidden like a secret between the caged animals and the elm trees. Only my father brought me to this section of the park. Here he tried to make a baseball player of me.

"Get the bat off your shoulders," he says. "For God's sake, will you try to hit the ball, anyhow?"

When I fail once again to swing at his slow, perfect pitch, he spins around, raises his arm, and theatrically asks everyone in sight, "Whose kid is this, anyway? Can you answer me that?"

He has never asked me about the Play School I am supposed to be attending, and I have never told him about the Orpheum-Oriental—I will never come any closer to talking to him than now, for "Stan," "Stanley the Steamer," has told me things that cannot be true, that must be inventions and fables, part of the world of children wandering lost in the forest, of talking cats and silver boots filled with blood. In this world, dismembered children buried beneath juniper trees can rise and speak, made whole once again. Fables boil with underground explosions and hidden fires, and for this reason, memory rejects them, thrusts them out of its sight, and they must be repeated over and over. I cannot remember "Stan's" face—cannot even be sure I remember what he said. Dean Martin and Jerry Lewis are bums like us. I am certain of only one thing: Tomorrow I am again going to see my newest, scariest, most interesting friend.

"When I was your age," my father says, "I had my heart set on playing pro ball when I grew up. And you're too damned scared or lazy to even take the bat off your shoulder. Kee-rist! I can't stand looking at you anymore."

He turns around and begins to move quickly toward the narrow park road and the zoo, going home, and I run after him. I retrieve the softball when he tosses it into the bushes.

"What the hell do you think you're going to do when you grow up?" my father asks, his eyes still fixed ahead of him. "I wonder what you think life is all *about*. I wouldn't give you a job, I wouldn't trust you around carpenter tools, I wouldn't trust you to blow your nose right—to tell you the truth, I wonder if the hospital mixed up the goddamn babies."

I follow him, dragging the bat with one hand, in the other cradling the softball in the pouch of my mitt.

At dinner my mother asks if Summer Play School is fun, and I say yes. I have already taken from my father's dresser drawer what "Stan" asked me to get for him, and it burns in my pocket as if it were alight.

I want to ask: Is it actually true and not a story? Does the worst thing always have to be the true thing? Of course, I cannot ask this. My father does not know about worst things—he sees what he wants to see, or he tries so hard, he thinks he does see it.

"I guess he'll hit a long ball someday. The boy just needs more work on his swing." He tries to smile at me, a boy who will someday learn to hit a long ball. The knife is upended in his fist—he is about to smear a pat of butter on his steak. He does not see me at all. My father is not a lion, he cannot make the switch to seeing what is really there in front of him.

Late at night Alan Ladd knelt beside my bed. He was wearing a neat grey suit, and his breath smelled like cloves. "You okay, son?" I nodded. "I just wanted to tell you that I like seeing you out there every day. That means a lot to me."

"Do you remember what I was telling you about?"

And I knew: It was true. He had said those things, and he would repeat them like a fairy tale, and the world was going to change because it would be seen through changed eyes. I felt sick—trapped in the theater as if in a cage.

"You think about what I told you?"

"Sure," I said.

"That's good. Hey, you know what? I feel like changing seats. You want to change seats too?"

"Where to?"

He tilted his head back, and I knew he wanted to move to the last row. "Come on. I want to show you something."

We changed seats.

For a long time we sat watching the movie from the last row, nearly alone in the theater. Just after eleven, three of the bums filed in and proceeded to their customary seats on the other side of the theater—a rumpled greybeard I had seen many times before; a fat man with a stubby, squashed face, also familiar; and one of the shaggy, wild-looking young men who hung around the bums until they became indistinguishable from them. They began passing a flat brown bottle back and forth. After a second I remembered the young man—I had surprised him awake one morning, passed out and spattered with blood, in the middle aisle.

Then I wondered if "Stan" was not the young man I had surprised that morning; they looked as alike as twins, though I knew they were not.

"Want a sip?" "Stan" said, showing me his own pint bottle. "Do you good."

Bravely, feeling privileged and adult, I took the bottle of Thunderbird and raised it to my mouth. I wanted to like it, to share the pleasure of it with "Stan," but it tasted horrible, like garbage, and the little bit I swallowed burned all the way down my throat.

I made a face, and he said, "This stuff's really not so bad. Only one thing in the world can make you feel better than this stuff."

He placed his hand on my thigh and squeezed. "I'm giving you a head start, you know. Just because I liked you the first time I saw you." He leaned over and stared at me. "You believe me? You believe the things I tell you?"

I said I guessed so.

"I got proof. I'll show you it's true. Want to see my proof?"

When I said nothing, "Stan" leaned closer to me, inundating me with the stench of Thunderbird. "You know that little thing you pee with? Remember how I told you how it gets real big when you're about thirteen? Remember I told you about how incredible that feels? Well, you have to trust Stan now, because Stan's going to trust you." He put his face right beside my ear. "Then I'll tell you another secret."

He lifted his hand from my thigh and closed it around mine and pulled my hand down onto his crotch. "Feel anything?"

I nodded, but I could not have described what I felt any more than the blind men could describe the elephant.

"Stan" smiled tightly and tugged at his zipper in a way even I could tell was nervous. He reached inside his pants, fumbled, and pulled out a thick, pale club that looked like nothing human. I was so frightened I thought I would throw up, and I looked back up at the screen. Invisible chains held me to my seat.

"See? Now you understand me."

Then he noticed that I was not looking at him. "Kid. Look. I said, look. It's not going to hurt you."

I could not look down at him. I saw nothing.

"Come on. Touch it, see what it feels like."

I shook my head.

"Let me tell you something. I like you a lot. I think the two of us are friends. This thing we're doing, it's unusual to you because this is the first time, but people do this all the time. Your mommy and daddy do it all the time, but they just don't tell you about it. We're pals, aren't we?"

I nodded dumbly. On the screen, Berry Kroeger was telling Alan Ladd, "Drop it, forget it, she's poison."

"Well, this is what friends do when they really like each other, like your mommy and daddy. Look at this thing, will you? Come on."

Did my mommy and daddy like each other? He squeezed my shoulder, and I looked.

Now the thing had folded up into itself and was drooping sideways against the fabric of his trousers. Almost as soon as I looked, it twitched and began to push itself out like the slide of a trombone.

"There," he said. "He likes you, you got him going. Tell me you like him too."

Terror would not let me speak. My brains had turned to powder.

"I know what—let's call him Jimmy. We'll say his name is Jimmy. Now that you've been introduced, say hi to Jimmy."

"Hi, Jimmy," I said, and, despite my terror, could not keep myself from giggling.

"Now go on, touch him."

I slowly extended my hand and put the tips of my fingers on "Jimmy."

"Pet him. Jimmy wants you to pet him."

I tapped my fingertips against "Jimmy" two or three times, and he twitched up another few degrees, as rigid as a surfboard.

"Slide your fingers up and down on him."

If I run, I thought, he'll catch me and kill me. If I don't do what he says, he'll kill me.

I rubbed my fingertips back and forth, moving the thin skin over the veins.

"Can't you imagine Jimmy going in a woman? Now you can see what you'll be like when you're a man. Keep on, but hold him with your whole hand. And give me what I asked you for."

I immediately took my hand from "Jimmy" and pulled my father's clean white handkerchief from my back pocket.

He took the handkerchief with his left hand and with his right guided mine back to "Jimmy." "You're doing really great," he whispered.

In my hand "Jimmy" felt warm and slightly gummy. I could not join my fingers around its width. My head was buzzing. "Is Jimmy your secret?" I was able to say.

"My secret comes later."

"Can I stop now?"

"I'll cut you into little pieces if you do," he said, and when I froze, he stroked my hair and whispered, "Hey, can't you tell when a guy's kidding around? I'm really happy with you right now. You're the best kid in the world. You'd want this, too, if you knew how good it felt."

After what seemed an endless time, while Alan Ladd was climbing out of a taxicab, "Stan" abruptly arched his back, grimaced, and whispered, "Look!" His entire body jerked, and too startled to let go, I held "Jimmy" and watched thick, ivory-colored milk spurt and drool almost unendingly onto the handkerchief. An odor utterly foreign but as familiar as the toilet or the lakeshore rose from the thick milk. "Stan" sighed, folded the handkerchief, and pushed the softening "Jimmy" back into his trousers. He leaned over and kissed the top of my head. I think I nearly fainted. I felt lightly, pointlessly dead. I could still feel him pulsing in my palm and fingers.

When it was time for me to go home, he told me his secret—his own real name was Jimmy, not Stan. He had been saving his real name until he knew he could trust me.

"Tomorrow," he said, touching my cheek with his fingers. "We'll see each other again tomorrow. But you don't have anything to worry about. I trust you enough to give you my real name. You trusted me not to hurt you, and I didn't. We have to trust each other not to say anything about this, or both you and me'll be in a lot of trouble."

"I won't say anything," I said.

I love you.

I love you, yes I do.

Now *we're* a secret, he said, folding the handkerchief into quarters and putting it back in my pocket. A lot of love has to be secret. Especially when a boy and a man are getting to know each other and learning how to make each other happy and be good, loving friends— not many people can understand that, so the friendship has to be protected. When you walk out of here, he said, you have to forget that this happened. Otherwise people will try to hurt us both.

Afterward I remembered only the confusion of *Chicago Deadline,* how the story had abruptly surged forward, skipping over whole characters and entire scenes, how for long stretches the actors had moved their lips without speaking. I could see Alan Ladd stepping out of the taxicab, looking straight through the screen into my eyes, knowing me.

My mother said that I looked pale, and my father said that I didn't get enough exercise. The twins looked up from their plates, then went back to spooning macaroni and cheese into their mouths. "Were you ever in Chicago?" I asked my father, who asked what was it to me. "Did you ever meet a movie actor?" I asked, and he said, "This kid must have a fever." The twins giggled.

Alan Ladd and Donna Reed came into my bedroom together late that night, moving with brisk, cool theatricality, and kneeled down beside my cot. They smiled at me. Their voices were very soothing. I saw you missed a few things today, Alan said. Nothing to worry about. I'll take care of you. I know, I said; I'm your number-one fan.

Then the door cracked open, and my mother put her head inside the room. Alan and Donna smiled and stood up to let her pass between them and the cot. I missed them the second they stepped back. "Still awake?" I nodded. "Are you feeling all right, honey?" I nodded again, afraid that Alan and Donna would leave if she stayed too long. "I have a surprise for you," she said. "The Saturday after this, I'm taking you and the twins all the way across Lake Michigan on the ferry. There's a whole bunch of us. It'll be a lot of fun." Good, that's nice, I'll like that.

*   *   *

"I thought about you all last night and all this morning."

When I came into the lobby, he was leaning forward on one of the padded benches where the ushers sat and smoked, his elbows on his knees and his chin in his hand, watching the door. The metal tip of a flat bottle protruded from his side pocket. Beside him was a package rolled up in brown paper. He winked at me, jerked his head toward the door into the theater, stood up, and went inside in an elaborate charade of not being with me. I knew he would be just inside the door, sitting in the middle of the last row, waiting for me. I gave my ticket to the bored usher, who tore it in half and handed over the stub. I knew exactly what had happened yesterday, just as if I had never forgotten any of it, and my insides began shaking. All the colors of the lobby, the red and the shabby gilt, seemed much brighter than I remembered them. I could smell the popcorn in the case and the oily butter heating in the machine. My legs moved me over a mile of sizzling brown carpet and past the candy counter.

Jimmy's hair gleamed in the empty, darkening theater. When I took the seat next to him, he ruffled my hair and grinned down and said he had been thinking about me all night and all morning. The package in brown paper was a sandwich he'd brought for my lunch—a kid had to eat more than popcorn.

The lights went all the way down as the series of curtains opened over the screen. Loud music, beginning in the middle of a note, suddenly jumped from the speakers, and the Tom and Jerry cartoon "Bull Dozing" began. When I leaned back, Jimmy put his arm around me. I felt sweaty and cold at the same time, and my insides were still shaking. I suddenly realized that part of me was glad to be in this place, and I shocked myself with the knowledge that all morning I had been looking forward to this moment as much as I had been dreading it.

"You want your sandwich now? It's liver sausage, because that's my personal favorite." I said no thanks, I'd wait until the first movie was over. Okay, he said, just as long as you eat it. Then he said, look at me. His face was right above mine, and he looked like Alan Ladd's twin brother. You have to know something, he said. You're the best kid I ever met. Ever. The man squeezed me up against his chest and into a dizzying funk of sweat and dirt and wine, along with a trace (imagined?) of that other, more animal odor that had come from him yesterday. Then he released me.

*   *   *

You want me to play with your little "Jimmy" today?
No.
Too small, anyhow, he said with a laugh. He was in
perfect good humor.
Bet you wish it was the same size as mine.
That wish terrified me, and I shook my head.
Today we're just going to watch the movies together, he said. I'm not greedy.
Except for when one of the ushers came up the
aisle, we sat like that all day, his arm around my
shoulders, the back of my neck resting in the hollow of
his elbow. When the credits for *At War With the Army*
rolled up the screen, I felt as though I had fallen
asleep and missed everything. I couldn't believe that it
was time to go home. Jimmy tightened his arm around
me and in a voice full of amusement said *Touch me.* I
looked up into his face. Go on, he said, I want you to
do that little thing for me. I prodded his fly with my
index finger. "Jimmy" wobbled under the pressure of
my fingers, seeming as long as my arm, and for a
second of absolute wretchedness I saw the other children running up and down the school playground behind the girls from the next block.
"Go on," he said.

*   *   *

Trust me, he said, investing "Jimmy" with an identity
more concentrated, more focused, than his own.
"Jimmy" wanted "to talk," "to speak his piece," "was
hungry," "was dying for a kiss." All these words meant
the same thing. *Trust me:* I trust you, so you must
trust me. Have I ever hurt you? No. Didn't I give you
a sandwich? Yes. Don't I love you? You know I won't
tell your parents what you do—as long as you keep
coming here, I won't tell your parents anything because I won't *have* to, see? And you love me, too,
don't you?
There. You see how much I love you?

*   *   *

I dreamed that I lived underground in a wooden room. I dreamed that my parents roamed the upper world, calling out my name and weeping because the animals had captured and eaten me. I dreamed that I was buried beneath a juniper tree, and the cut-off pieces of my body called out to each other and wept because they were separate. I dreamed that I ran down a dark forest path toward my parents, and when I finally reached the small clearing where they sat before a bright fire, my mother was Donna and Alan was my father. I dreamed that I could remember everything that was happening to me, every second of it, and that when the teacher called on me in class, when my mother came into my room at night, when the policeman went past me as I walked down Sherman Boulevard, I had to spill it out. But when I tried to speak, I could not remember what it was that I remembered, *only that there was something to remember,* and so I walked again and again toward my beautiful parents in the clearing, repeating myself like a fable, like the jokes of the women on the ferry.

Don't I love you? Don't I show you, can't you tell, that I love you? *Yes.* Don't you, can't you, love me too?

He stares at me as I stare at the movie. He could see me, the way I could see him, with his eyes closed. He has me memorized. He has stroked my hair, my face, my body into his memory, stroke after stroke, stealing me from myself. Eventually he took me in his mouth and his mouth memorized me, too, and I knew he wanted me to place my hands on that dirty blond head resting so hugely in my lap, but I could not touch his head.

I thought: I have already forgotten this, I want to die, I am dead already, only death can make this not have happened.

When you grow up, I bet you'll be in the movies and I'll be your number-one fan.

*   *   *

By the weekend, those days at the Orpheum-Oriental
seemed to have been spent under water; or underground. The spiny anteater, the lyrebird, the kanga-
roo, the Tasmanian devil, the nun bat, and the frilled
lizard were creatures found only in Australia. Australia was the world's smallest continent, its largest
island. It was cut off from the Earth's great landmasses.
Beautiful girls with blond hair strutted across Australian beaches, and Australian Christmases were hot and
sunbaked—everybody went outside and waved at the
camera, exchanging presents from lawn chairs. The
middle of Australia, its heart and gut, was a desert.
Australian boys excelled at sports. Tom Cat loved
Jerry Mouse, though he plotted again and again to
murder him, and Jerry Mouse loved Tom Cat, though
to save his life he had to run so fast he burned a track
through the carpet. Jimmy loved me and he would be
gone someday, and then I would miss him a lot.
Wouldn't I? *Say you'll miss me.*

I'll—

"I'll miss—

I think I'd go crazy without you.

When you're all grown-up, will you remember me?

Each time I walked back out past the usher, tearing in
half the tickets of the people just entering, handing
them the stubs, every time I pushed open the door and
walked out onto the heat-filled sidewalk of Sherman
Boulevard and saw the sun on the buildings across the
street, I lost my hold on what had happened inside the
darkness of the theater. I didn't know what I wanted.
I had two murders and a . . . My right hand felt as
though I had been holding a smaller child's sticky
hand very tightly between my palm and fingers. If I
lived in Australia, I would have blond hair like Alan
Ladd and run forever across tan beaches on Christmas
Day.

*   *   *

I walked through high school in my sleep, reading novels, daydreaming in classes I did not like but earning spuriously good grades; in the middle of my senior year Brown University gave me a full scholarship. Two years later I amazed and disappointed all my old teachers and my parents and my parents' friends by dropping out of school shortly before I would have failed all my courses but English and history, in which I was getting A's. I was certain that no one could teach anyone else how to write. I knew exactly what I was going to do, and all I would miss of college was the social life.

For five years I lived inexpensively in Providence, supporting myself by stacking books in the school library and by petty thievery. I wrote when I was not working or listening to the local bands; then I destroyed what I had written and wrote it again. In this way I saw myself to the end of a novel, like walking through a park one way and then walking backward and forward through the same park, over and over, until every nick on every swing, every tawny hair on every lion's hide, had been witnessed and made to gleam or allowed to sink back into the importunate field of details from which it had been lifted. When this novel was rejected by the publisher to whom I sent it, I moved to New York City and began another novel while I rewrote the first all over again at night. During this period an almost impersonal happiness, like the happiness of a stranger, lay beneath everything I did. I wrapped parcels of books at the Strand Bookstore. For a short time, no more than a few months, I lived on Shredded Wheat and peanut butter. When my first book was accepted, I moved from a single room on the Lower East Side into another, larger single room, a "studio apartment," on Ninth Avenue in Chelsea, where I continue to live. My apartment is just large enough for my wooden desk, a convertible couch, two large crowded bookshelves, a shelf of stereo equipment, and dozens of cardboard boxes of records. In this apartment everything has its place and is in it.

My parents have never been to this enclosed, tidy space, though I speak to my father on the phone every two or three months. In the past ten years I have returned to the city where I grew up only once, to visit my mother in the hospital after her stroke. During the four days I stayed in my father's house I slept in my old room, my father upstairs. After the blind man's death my father bought the duplex—on my first night home he told me that we were both successes. Now, when we speak on the telephone, he tells me of the fortunes of the local baseball and basketball teams and respectfully inquires about my progress on "the new book." I think: This is not my father, he is not the same man.

My old cot disappeared long ago, and late at night I lay on the twins' double bed. Like the house as a whole, like everything in my old neighborhood, the bedroom was larger than I remembered it. I brushed the wallpaper with my fingers, then looked up to the ceiling. The image of two men tangled up in the ropes of the same parachute, comically berating each other as they fell, came to me, and I wondered if the image had a place in the novel I was writing, or if it was a gift from the as yet unseen novel that would follow it. I could hear the floor creak as my father paced upstairs in the blind man's former territory. My inner weather changed, and I began brooding about Mei-Mei Levitt, whom fifteen years earlier at Brown I had known as Mei-Mei Cheung.

Divorced, an editor at a paperback firm, she had called to congratulate me after my second novel was favorably reviewed in the *Times,* and on this slim but well-intentioned foundation we began to construct a long and troubled love affair. Back in the surroundings of my childhood, I felt profoundly uneasy, having spent the day beside my mother's hospital bed without knowing if she understood or even recognized me, and I thought of Mei-Mei with sudden longing. I wanted her in my arms, and I yearned for my purposeful, orderly, dreaming adult life in New York. I wanted to call Mei-Mei, but it was past midnight in the Midwest, an hour later in New York, and Mei-Mei, no owl, would have gone to bed hours earlier. Then I remembered my mother lying stricken in the narrow hospital bed, and suffered a spasm of guilt for thinking about my lover. For a deluded moment I imagined that it was my duty to move back into the house and see if I could bring my mother back to life while I did what I could for my retired father. At that moment I remembered, as I often did, an orange-haired boy enveloped in a red wool shirt. Sweat poured from my forehead, my chest.

Then a terrifying thing happened to me. I tried to get out of bed to go to the bathroom and found that I could not move. My arms and legs were cast in cement; they were lifeless and *would not move*. I thought that I was having a stroke, like my mother. I could not even cry out—my throat, too, was paralyzed. I strained to push myself up off the narrow bed and smelled that someone very near, someone just out of sight or around a corner, was making popcorn and heating butter. Another wave of sweat gouted out of my inert body, turning the sheet and the pillowcase slick and cold.

I saw—as if I were writing it—my seven-year-old self hesitating before the entrance of a theater a few blocks from this house. Hot, flat, yellow sunlight fell over everything, cooking the life from the wide boulevard. I saw myself turn away, felt my stomach churn with the smoke of underground fires, saw myself begin to run. Vomit backed up in my throat. My arms and legs convulsed, and I fell out of bed and managed to crawl out of the room and down the hall to throw up in the toilet behind the closed door of the bathroom.

*　　*　　*

My age, as I write these words, is forty-three. I have written five novels over a period of nearly twenty years, "only" five, each of them more difficult, harder to write than the one before. To maintain this hobbled pace of a novel every four years, I must sit at my desk at least six hours every day; I must consume hundreds of boxes of typing paper, scores of yellow legal pads, forests of pencils, miles of black ribbon. It is a fierce, voracious activity. Every sentence must be tested three or four ways, made to clear fences like a horse. The purpose of every sentence is to be an arrow into the secret center of the book. To find my way into the secret center I must hold the entire book, every detail and rhythm, in my memory. This comprehensive act of memory is the most crucial task of my life.

My books get flattering reviews, which usually seem to describe other, more linear novels, and they win occasional awards—I am one of those writers whose advances are funded by the torrents of money spun off by best-sellers. Lately I have had the impression that the general perception of me, to the extent that such a thing exists, is that of a hermetic painter inscribing hundreds of tiny, grotesque, fantastical details over every inch of a large canvas. (My books are unfashionably long.) I teach writing at various colleges, give occasional lectures, am modestly enriched by grants. This is enough, more than enough. Now and then I am both dismayed and amused to discover that a young writer I have met at a PEN reception or a workshop regards my life with envy. Envy misses the point completely.

"If you were going to give me one piece of advice," a young woman at a conference asked me, "I mean, *real* advice, not just the obvious stuff about keeping on writing, what would it be? What would you tell me to do?"

I won't tell you, but I'll write it out, I said, and picked up one of the conference flyers and printed a few words on its back. Don't read this until you are out of the room, I said, and watched while she folded the flyer into her bag.

What I had printed on the back of the flyer was:
GO TO A LOT OF MOVIES.

On the Sunday after the ferry trip I could not hit a
single ball in the park. My eyes kept closing, and as
soon as my eyelids came down, visions started up like
movie-quick, automatic dreams. My arms seemed too
heavy to lift. After I had trudged home behind my
dispirited father, I collapsed on the sofa and slept
straight through to dinner. In a dream a spacious box
confined me, and I drew colored pictures of elm trees,
the sun, wide fields, mountains, and rivers on its walls.
At dinner loud noises, never scarce around the twins,
made me jump. That kid's not right, I swear to you,
my father said. When my mother asked if I wanted to
go to Play School on Monday, my stomach closed up
like a fist. I have to, I said, I'm really fine. I have to
go. Sentences rolled from my mouth, meaning nothing, or meaning the wrong thing. For a moment of
confusion I thought that I really was going to the
playground, and saw black asphalt, deep as a field,
where a few children, diminished by perspective, clus-
tered at the far end. I went to bed right after dinner.
My mother pulled down the shades, turned off the
light, and finally left me alone. From above came the
sound, like a beast's approximation of music, of random notes struck on a piano. I knew only that I was
scared, not why. The next day I had to go to a certain
place, but I could not think where until my fingers
recalled the velvety plush of the end seat on the middle aisle. Then black-and-white images, full of inten-
tional menace, came to me from the previews I had
seen for two weeks—*The Hitchhiker,* starring Edmund
O'Brien. The spiny anteater and nun bat were animals
found only in Australia.

I longed for Alan Ladd, "Ed Adams," to walk into
the room with his reporter's notebook and pencil, and
knew that I had *something to remember* without knowing what it was.

After a long time the twins cascaded into the bedroom, undressed, put on pajamas, brushed their teeth. The front door slammed—my father had gone out to the taverns. In the kitchen, my mother ironed shirts and talked to herself in a familiar, rancorous voice. The twins went to sleep. I heard my mother put away the ironing board and walk down the hall to the living room.

I saw "Ed Adams" calmly walking up and down on the sidewalk outside our house, as handsome as a god in his neat grey suit. "Ed" went all the way to the end of the block, put a cigarette in his mouth, and leaned into a sudden, round flare of brightness before exhaling smoke and walking away. I knew I had fallen asleep only when the front door slammed for the second time that night and woke me up.

*   *   *

In the morning my father struck his fist against the bedroom door and the twins jumped out of bed and began yelling around the bedroom, instantly filled with energy. As in a cartoon, into the bedroom drifted tendrils of the odor of frying bacon. My brothers jostled toward the bathroom. Water rushed into the sink and the toilet bowl, and my mother hurried in, her face tightened down over her cigarette, and began yanking the twins into their clothes. "You made your decision," she said to me, "now I hope you're going to make it to the playground on time." Doors opened, doors slammed shut. My father shouted from the kitchen, and I got out of bed. Eventually I sat down before the bowl of cereal. My father smoked and did not meet my eyes. The cereal tasted of dead leaves. "You look the way that asshole upstairs plays piano," my father said. He dropped quarters on the table and told me not to lose that money.

After he left, I locked myself in the bedroom. The piano dully resounded overhead like a sound track. I heard the cups and dishes rattle in the sink, the furniture moving by itself, looking for something to hunt down and kill. *Love me, love me,* the radio called from beside a family of brown-and-white porcelain spaniels. I heard some light, whispery thing, a lamp or a magazine, begin to slide around the living room. *I am imagining all this,* I said to myself, and tried to concentrate on a *Blackhawk* comic book. The pictures jigged and melted in their panels. *Love me,* Blackhawk cried out from the cockpit of his fighter as he swooped down to exterminate a nest of yellow, slant-eyed villains. Outside, fire raged beneath the streets, trying to pull the world apart. When I dropped the comic book and closed my eyes, the noises ceased and I could hear the hovering stillness of perfect attention. Even Blackhawk, belted into his airplane within the comic book, was listening to what I was doing.

*   *   *

In thick, hazy sunlight I went down Sherman Boulevard toward the Orpheum-Oriental. Around me the world was motionless, frozen like a frame in a comic strip. After a time I noticed that the cars on the boulevard and the few people on the sidewalk had not actually frozen into place but instead were moving with great slowness. I could see men's legs advancing within their trousers, the knee coming forward to strike the crease, the cuff slowly lifting off the shoe, the shoe drifting up like Tom Cat's paw when he crept toward Jerry Mouse. The warm, patched skin of Sherman Boulevard. . . . I thought of walking along Sherman Boulevard forever, moving past the nearly immobile cars and people, past the theater, past the liquor store, through the gates, and past the wading pool and swings, past the elephants and lions reaching out to be fed, past the secret park where my father flailed in a rage of disappointment, past the elms and out the opposite gate, past the big houses on the opposite side of the park, past picture windows and past lawns with bikes and plastic pools, past slanting driveways and basketball hoops, past men getting out of cars, past playgrounds where children raced back and forth on a surface shining black. Then past fields and crowded markets, past high yellow tractors with mud dried like old wool inside the enormous hubs, past wagons piled high with hay, past deep woods where lost children followed trails of bread crumbs to a gingerbread door, past other cities where nobody would see me because nobody knew my name, past everything, past everybody.

At the Orpheum-Oriental, I stopped still. My mouth was dry and my eyes would not focus. Everything around me, so quiet and still a moment earlier, jumped into life as soon as I stopped walking. Horns blared, cars roared down the boulevard. Beneath these sounds I heard the pounding of great machines, and the fires gobbling up oxygen beneath the street. As if I had eaten them from the air, fire and smoke poured into my stomach. Flame slipped up my throat and sealed the back of my mouth. In my mind I saw myself taking the first quarter from my pocket, exchanging it for a ticket, pushing through the door, and moving into the cool air. I saw myself holding out the ticket to be torn in half, going over an endless brown carpet toward the inner door. From the last row of seats on the other side of the inner door, inside the shadowy but not yet dark theater, a shapeless monster whose wet black mouth said *Love me, love me* stretched yearning arms toward me. Shock froze my shoes to the sidewalk, then shoved me firmly in the small of the back, and I was running down the block, unable to scream because I had to clamp my lips against the smoke and fire trying to explode from my mouth.

The rest of that afternoon remains vague. I wandered through the streets, not in the clean, hollow way I had imagined but almost blindly, hot and uncertain. I remember the taste of fire in my mouth and the loudness of my heart. After a time I found myself before the elephant enclosure in the zoo. A newspaper reporter in a neat grey suit passed through the space before me, and I followed him, knowing that he carried a notebook in his pocket, that he had been beaten by gangsters, that he could locate the speaking secret that hid beneath the disconnected and dismembered pieces of the world. He would fire his pistol on an empty chamber and trick evil "Solly Wellman," Berry Kroeger, with his girlish, watchful eyes. And when "Solly Wellman" came gloating out of the shadows, the reporter would shoot him dead.

Dead.

Donna Reed smiled down from an upstairs window: Has there ever been a smile like that? Ever? I was in Chicago, and behind a closed door "Blackie Franchot" bled onto a brown carpet. "Solly Wellman," something like "Solly Wellman," called and called to me from the decorated grave where he lay like a secret. The man in the grey suit finally carried his notebook and his gun through a front door, and I saw that I was only a few blocks from home.

Paul leans against the wire fence surrounding the playground, looking out, looking backward. Alan Ladd brushes off "Leona" (June Havoc), for she has no history that matters and exists only in the world of work and pleasure, of cigarettes and cocktail bars. Beneath this world is another, and "Leona's" life is a blind, strenuous denial of that other world.

My mother held her hand to my forehead and declared that I not only had a fever but had been building up to it all week. I was not to go to the playground the next day; I had to spend the day lying down on Mrs. Candee's couch. When she lifted the telephone to call one of the high-school girls, I said not to bother, other kids were gone all the time, and she put down the receiver.

* * *

I lay on Mrs. Candee's couch staring up at the ceiling of her darkened living room. The twins squabbled outside, and maternal, slow-witted Mrs. Candee brought me orange juice. The twins ran toward the sandbox, and Mrs. Candee groaned as she let herself fall into a wobbly lawn chair. The morning newspaper folded beneath the lawn chair said that *The Hitchhiker* and *Double Cross* had begun playing at the Orpheum-Oriental. *Chicago Deadline* had done its work and traveled on. It had broken the world in half and sealed the monster deep within. Nobody but me knew this. Up and down the block, sprinklers whirred, whipping loops of water onto the dry lawns. Men driving slowly up and down the street hung their elbows out of their windows. For a moment free of regret and nearly without emotion of any kind, I understood that I belonged utterly to myself. Like everything else, I had been torn asunder and glued back together with shock, vomit, and orange juice. The knowledge sifted into me that I was all alone. "Stan," "Jimmy," whatever his name was, would never come back to the theater. He would be afraid that I had told my parents and the police about him. I knew that I had killed him by forgetting him, and then I forgot him again.

The next day I went back to the theater and went through the inner door and saw row after row of empty seats falling toward the curtained screen. I was all alone. The size and grandeur of the theater surprised me. I went down the long, descending aisle and took the last seat, left side, on the broad middle aisle. The next row seemed nearly a playground's distance away. The lights dimmed and the curtains rippled slowly away from the screen. Anticipatory music filled the air, and the first letters appeared on the screen.

What I am, what I do, why I do it. I am simultaneously a man in his early forties, that treacherous time, and a boy of seven before whose bravery I shall forever fall short. I live underground in a wooden room and patiently, in joyful concentration, decorate the walls. Before me, half unseen, hangs a large and appallingly complicated vision I must explore and memorize, must witness again and again in order to locate its hidden center. Around me, everything is in its proper place. My typewriter sits on the sturdy table. Beside the typewriter a cigarette smolders, raising a grey stream of smoke. A record revolves on the turntable, and my small apartment is dense with music. ("Bird of Prey Blues," with Coleman Hawkins, Buck Clayton, and Hank Jones.) Beyond my walls and windows is a world toward which I reach with outstretched arms and an ambitious and divided heart. As if "Bird of Prey Blues" has evoked them, the voices of sentences to be written this afternoon, tomorrow, or next month stir and whisper, beginning to speak, and I lean over the typewriter toward them, getting as close as I can.

SPINNING
TALES

*We Poets in our youth begin in gladness;
But thereof come in the end despondency
and madness.*

—WILLIAM WORDSWORTH

CHARLES L. GRANT, born 1942 in Newark, New Jersey, is the leading modern exponent of the atmospheric tale of terror. As an anthologist he has produced a remarkable twenty volumes of short fiction, including the critically acclaimed *Shadows* series. As a writer he has published fourteen horror novels (including the *Oxrun Station* series and *The Pet*) and five fiction collections (including *Tales from the Nightside* and *The Orchard*). His new novel is *For Fear of the Night*.

Charles L. Grant

Spinning Tales
with the Dead

The stream was no more than a dozen feet across: clear, fast, silver-slashed and smooth where rocks from its shallows pushed the surface toward the sun. Weeds draped over the banks, spiders skated side to side, and in deeper pools there were slim and nervous fish that scattered to the center when a pebble dropped in or a spider skated too slow. The trees and branches were high, the underbrush thin, and daylight was almost as bright as if the stream had passed through a meadow.

And there was shade.

Beneath a fat and wrinkled sycamore whose roots broke through the ground and were coated with moss, there was shade as cool as an early autumn evening, and Jerry Downe never failed to bring his old denim jacket, even on the hottest of the worst days of July. Or his floppy-brimmed cap with the lures pinned through the shapeless crown; or the paperback books in the knapsack, for when the fishing was slow.

In the old days, before he knew the agony of being a teenager in a world that wanted him to grow up before his time, he brought lemonade, or cola from the corner store, or a bottle of root beer his father had made in the cellar.

In his twenties it was beer, or a small earthen jug of Rooney's milky dandelion wine.

Now, when he had a difficult time remembering just how old he was, though he was sure it wasn't old, he brought whatever he had in the refrigerator, whatever was left at the end of the week when he couldn't stand to stay home anymore, in the living room, with the television screen blank and the radio dead and the neighbors on the prowl for people to visit. Pausing on the pavement to point at his house and whisper behind their hands. Sliding by at night in their slow-moving cars. Running up to the porch to ring the door bell and running away, pale faces red with laughter once they'd crossed the street.

Every day, in the beginning.

Proving courage and strength.

Once a week after a while.

Proving nothing at all but that memories die hard when the dying was even harder.

Halloween was the best time now, and moonless December nights when the wind lurked in the hedge and snow was thin and fresh on the ground, and the police had better things to do than to chase them away.

How old was he? he wondered; it didn't matter. The sun was out and warm.

It was long past noon, and he checked the bamboo pole for the fifth time in as many minutes, convincing himself it was still secure in its place between two large rocks that had been there since the first day he'd come, with Rooney, whose father had been a farrier until the farms around were sold to people who built houses and supermarkets and roads that followed the paths the cows took home to the barn.

He opened a beer, took a drink, and looked at the fingers curled around the can—long, short-nailed, knuckles slightly swollen. Veins heavy and wide. Just a hint of a tremble.

"Rooney," he said, "this is getting to be a pain in the ass, you know."

On the far side, between two cages of white birch, in a shower of mint light, a shadow stirred and came forward, fly rod hooked loosely over its shoulder, battered creel dangling from one shoulder.

"Wasn't my idea," Rooney said, grumbling. "You

were the one who talked me out here in the first place. Soon as you stop coming, so will I. Never did like it, anyway. I never knew worms could bleed."

Jerry sighed, drank again, and set the can on a space flattened by years of using it for a table. "They don't bleed, how many times do I have to tell you?"

Rooney worked at a tangle in his reel. "They got stuff coming out of them, that's blood enough for me."

Jerry raised an eyebrow, gave a groan to himself, and looked down at the boy sitting beside him. A small boy, not much more than nine or ten. Red-headed, freckled, wearing brand-new jeans and a shirt that was too snug for the warmth of the sun. He was staring into the water, humming to himself and rocking his head back and forth. Jerry touched the red hair lightly, and the boy squirmed as if touched by the exploring of a spider.

Leaves gossiped overhead when a breeze darted through.

The line from the bamboo pole was pulled downstream by the rush of the current.

The sky was a darkening blue in puzzle pieces through the foliage, and Jerry hunched his shoulders, relaxed them, reached out and tested the pole's shoring again. He refused to believe that one day it wouldn't pull loose at the yank of a bite; he refused to believe that one day he'd come here alone, without the boy, without Rooney, or without the woman coming toward him over there, daintily picking her way through the low brush and cattails on the other side of the water.

Her hair was dark, her complexion a mottled tan. The dress she wore was made more for walking down a street at Easter than walking through the woods in a summer when all the flies seemed determined to settle on his face and remind him that soon they'd be feeding there as well. She didn't complain. She never looked up. She stopped at the first cage and looked through it to Rooney, who looked back without a nod or even a wink of recognition.

Jerry waited to see if anything would be said.

It never was.

There was always a first time.

A cloud cut off a slice of the sun, and shadows sprang from their burrows to hide her face, make Rooney vanish and return as the cloud moved on, leaving behind a cool Jerry couldn't seem to shake no matter how hard he blew on his hands, no matter how often he told himself this time would be the last, this time would end it and he'd be alone with the stream.

The boy shifted himself to sit closer to the water, down the short slope of the grassy bank that seemed forever poised on the edge of collapse. He wiped his nose with a sleeve. He picked up a pebble and tossed it into a pool at Rooney's feet, paying no attention to the look the bald man gave him, or to the smile from the woman whose lips were wide and red.

"Eph," the how-old man said, quietly and sternly.

The boy looked over his shoulder, no life in his eyes, and looked back and threw another pebble into the pool, at Rooney's feet.

Jerry had thought from the second his son had been born that it was a crime to name a kid Ephraim in this day and age. His friends at school were nice enough, he supposed, but he knew they wondered. Ephraim. What kind of name was that for a kid who only wanted to grow up and knock the hell out of baseballs?

It wasn't his idea.

And the woman wasn't talking.

Never had.

"Damn trees," Rooney muttered, tugging at his line, which was trapped in the crook of an overhanging branch.

"This isn't the place for one of those," Jerry told him. Had been telling him for thirty years, probably more.

"Gotta use it," the old man said. "It was a gift."

"I didn't give it to you to use here, you old jackass," Jerry snapped. "It was for—"

For the boat they were going to have, the one they

were going to sail along the East Coast, sailing up rivers along the way, seeing new towns, new friends, new kinds of fish they could bring home to show their families; for the times they would have when retirement forced them out but before age forced them into caves where they'd be displayed like stuffed animals in museums; for the pictures they'd show their families when they returned from their travels, Rooney on a dock, grinning with a fifty-pound something or other hanging at his side.

The woman found herself a dry place on the bank, hiked her skirt a little, and sat. She was whistling. She was working her shoes and stockings off so her feet would feel the cold shock of the water.

Jerry willed her to go away.

She looked up and smiled.

"You know, Eph," he said, looking away and down and touching the boy's hair again, "once upon a time I decided I was going to be president of the United States."

Eph didn't look around, but he knew the boy was listening.

"That's right. I decided to chuck it all—the security of a good job, the love of a good woman, friends, and family—and spend my millions becoming head of this country so I could straighten it all out before it fell into disrepair. I ran a good race too. Took more states than the papers said I would, and some they said I wouldn't win on a cold day in hell." He pulled in the line hand over hand, clucked at the empty hook, and delicately wound and stabbed a new worm around it. "Trouble was, of course, Cody took more than I did. At least he took the ones with the most electoral votes. That's what counts, you know. It don't matter how many people vote for you; if the other guy has the electoral votes, you're a footnote in the next history book unless you're stupid enough to try again."

"Dad," the boy said, still not looking around, "you never ran for president."

"Sure I did."

"Against William Cody?"

"Right."

"He never did, either."

"Then who did all those people vote for, Sitting Bull?"

The boy shook a little, and Jerry grinned. The first laugh of the day, and the day was nearly done. For a while he'd thought he'd lost the knack.

He leaned back against the sycamore and took the pole in his hands, feeling the smoothness of it, the limber strength, the memories that stained it dark brown here and there. He ran a palm along it as far as he could reach, not caring that he might be disturbing the fish trying to get at the worm; it was the feel of fishing that counted, not the fish that were caught. Like it was the feel of loving that counted, not the woman who was loved.

So he had thought when he was younger.

So he had believed until the day he'd met Pru and lost all his sense and regained all his feeling.

Now there, he thought, is another dumb name. Prudence. Who names their girl-child Prudence anymore? Not since the Pilgrims, for god's sake. Not until his Pru walked into his life without even bothering to knock. And when he glanced at his son, he couldn't help a sigh for the red hair and the freckles—none of it belonged to his wife, all of it was his, right down to the stub of a nose and the long, piano-playing fingers.

"Goddamn," Rooney said, yanking at another tangle, this one halfway up the rod.

"Watch your mouth," Jerry said softly.

"Go to hell," Rooney answered, yanked again, swore again when the line parted, and he was forced into his creel for another lure.

The woman looked sideways up the stream and shook her head. Then she turned until she was facing the sun and tilted her head back, closed her eyes, pursed her lips, still whistling.

Jerry nearly dropped the pole.

He could still see it—the thin line of white along the slope of her throat.

The spray of dried blood along the slopes of her breasts.

"You know, Eph," he said, "this is the kind of day I used to take the ship out of dry dock and take off after whales."

Ephraim tossed another pebble. "You never did."

"Of course I did. You ought to know, you were there."

The boy plucked at the grass beside him. "I was?"

"First mate."

A twitch on the cheek Jerry could see.

Another cloud, wider and darker and more kind to the twilight that lifted from the woodland floor and made the stream at once brighter and deeper.

"Moby Dick," Ephraim said in the brief darkening. "You had a peg leg then, right?"

"Absolutely. You used to carve notches on it for every whale we caught."

"We never did get the big white one, though, Dad."

"Nope. Never did. No one ever does, Eph. That goddamned fish is bigger than any ten ships put together, and a hundred times as tough. I have to admit, though, you were the best harpooner a captain could ever wish for."

The boy punched a fist into a palm. "Got him right between the eyes too," he said. "Should have had the creep. But he sneezed."

Jerry sat forward. "He sneezed?"

"Don't you remember? There you were, up in the crow's nest screaming like an old woman, and I put that harpoon right between his eyes, and you kept shouting we should tie down the line more, and that whale got so sick of you yelling and spitting and waving your arms, he got allergic. So he sneezed. And *pop*! That damned harpoon came right out and I lost it." He shook his head sadly. "Best harpoon a man ever had."

"Goddamn liar," Rooney said.

"Watch it," Jerry warned him. "This isn't lying, this is tale-telling."

Rooney rolled his eyes and gave up trying to tie a new hook and lure onto his line. He threw the rod down, sat down, and pulled a bottle from the creel. The drink was long, and some of it spilled over his chin where a piece of bone flared when the sun came out again.

The woman was still sunning herself.

The boy was back to tossing pebbles into the stream.

Jerry stared at the length of bamboo in his hand and told himself it was all right; he wasn't exactly as young as he used to be, but he wasn't so old that he was going crazy. A look at the beer can and the two others lying empty beside it. And he wasn't drunk. Not on three beers over the course of a few hours.

He coughed loudly, then shifted.

He said, "Eph, I ever tell you about the time I decided I ought to chuck it all and run for president of the United States?"

"You just did, Dad," the boy said flatly.

He nodded. Right. So he had.

The woman kicked the water lightly, silver flashing from her toes, glittering, tiny rainbows in the air before the breeze took them away. Then, with a glance at Jerry, she reached behind her and began to work on the buttons that ranged along her spine. Her chest was thrust out, her feet were still kicking, and he emptied the can of beer because his throat was abruptly dry.

Rooney was watching.

The boy was watching a dragonfly hover over the stream, swinging with the direction of the breeze, wings like paddles. From his hip pocket he pulled a penknife and thumbnailed out its longest blade, which he stabbed into the dirt each time the dragonfly turned around.

The sound was quiet—a faraway club striking something slowly growing soft.

The woman's hands were spread over her chest,

holding up the front of her dress. Looking at him. Smiling. Looking at Rooney and grinning.

Rooney scratched his hairless scalp as though he were trying to make up his mind about something.

Don't do it, Jerry thought; for chrissakes, Rooney, don't do it.

"I used to be in show business, you know, Eph," he said, jamming the pole back into place. "They called it vaudeville in my day. A whole bunch of different acts. Singers, dancers, guys with trained dogs and pigeons, magicians, comedians, women who thought they could do opera, stuff like that. I was a tap dancer, you know. I had this act where I put a board between two chairs and held a pig in my arms. I would tap from the floor to the board, hold the pig over my head, and sing 'Old MacDonald.' "

The boy stabbed harder.

"Did I tell you I was blindfolded? I was blindfolded. And I had one leg tied up behind me. Like Long John Silver. I even wore a pirate's hat. You know, the kind with the three corners and a big feather sticking out of it."

Sunlight.

Clouds.

Rooney pushing back the memory of his hair, a monstrous red thicket that made women's fingers itch and men's insides crawl away in shame for the thinning that made them comb their hair sideways.

Sunlight.

The woman slowly lowering her dress.

Ephraim's hand, rising, falling, the blade cutting the ground.

Clouds.

Slides flicking on and off a screen in a cavernous room where every breath was an echo, and every echo was a scream.

Jerry closed his eyes against it, as he did every time it happened, knowing that when he opened them again, the flickering would happen so fast, he would get dizzy. He would feel faint. He would lay down on the ground and wait for the hush of the stream to calm him, the setting of the sun to banish the others, the cry of the first night bird to bring him to his feet and send him home again.

To the neighbors.

To the whispering.

And he thought: Damnit, I'm getting too old for this crap.

He held up a hand, his eyes opened, and there was only the cloud that rolled across the sun, rolling shadows and a wind over the surface of the stream, into his face. He flinched as if slapped, but he didn't look away.

"Rooney," he said, "you're a bastard."

Rooney was indistinct, a shadow in shadow, little more than the glow of his eyes hovering above the ground like a pair of dragonflies, watching.

The woman lowered her hands even more, and the tops of her breasts were exposed to the twilight.

Jerry didn't look away. Not from the memory of them when they were soft and warm in his hands, not from the sight of them now, gleaming red.

"And you," he said, "are a bitch."

"Dad," the boy said, not looking out, staring at the trench he had stabbed into the earth. "Dad."

She leaned over, folded nearly in half, the top of the dress now an apron in her lap as she batted at the water, spraying it high, spraying it wide, her mouth open in silent laughter. The cool sound of the water, the distant sound of her voice, and she leaned back for a moment to brush the hair from her cheek, her fingers white enough to be bone.

"Dad."

Jerry forced himself to look away, forced himself to pull the line in, hand over shaking hand. The worm was gone. He put on another, and the point of the hook pricked the fat of his thumb, and the woman stared at the glint of blood from the far side of the stream, her eyes slightly wider, her lips wider still, and the tongue that lurked inside like the coil of a serpent.

"Damn," he muttered, sucking at the tiny wound.

"You have to be careful," the boy said, still stabbing.

"I know," he answered, finishing the job and tossing the line in again. "Reminds me of the time—"

"About Mom?" the boy asked.

Rooney, shadow and light, laughed.

"No. I wasn't going to say that."

"She's so pretty," Ephraim whispered, the knife poised for another strike. "I wish I had hair like that. I wish I had a best friend I could go fishing with."

"Hey," Jerry said, reaching for the boy's shoulder. "Hey, aren't I your best friend?"

Ephraim shook his head. "It's not the same." He looked downstream. "She's so pretty. So . . . pretty."

Rooney stepped into the sunlight and stepped back again, the bottle empty in his hand, his shirt in rags, his boots gone.

"There was a time, you know," Jerry said quickly, "when I decided that being a cowboy wasn't the greatest life in the world. I mean, I couldn't stand the damned cows, and them Injuns were all the time—"

The boy sighed and wiped the knife clean on his knee.

"—bothering the herds and the hands, and I'll tell you, boy, it wasn't worth it, it really wasn't worth it until I decided to take the bit between my teeth. It was just before the trouble at Wounded Knee. You ever hear of Wounded Knee, son? A terrible thing, and I decided that if I was ever going to get my friend, the chief, out of there alive—"

"Dad, please."

"Shut up, kid," said Rooney, sinking to the ground, hands wrapped around his knees that gleamed white bone in the light-and-shadow sun.

"—I'd have to round up some of my buddies. They thought, you see, that Frank knew where Jesse really lived, that he wasn't really dead. They were right. But aside from Frank, I was the only one who knew the truth."

Perspiration on his brow.

The woman sitting up, gleaming red, gleaming hate.
"Dad?"

"So I rode out of Abilene one morning at dawn,
and I started east for Missouri. Terrible in those days,
you know. God, a man couldn't hardly find himself—"

The knife rose, and Jerry watched it; the knife lowered a little at a time, and Jerry watched it; the knife
sliced the air between them, snake-fast and hissing.

"I loved her," he said at last.

"So did I, Dad."

Rooney nodded, bald scalp dotted with shadows
that crawled, one bare foot tapping on the ground,
one hand languidly waving, but the flies didn't leave.

"I don't think so."

Jerry touched the bamboo pole.

The woman rubbed her hands over her stomach and
smeared the red to pink.

The boy looked over at Rooney and ran a hand
through his tousled hair, stared at his reflection in the
blade, and finally, for the first time, rose to his feet
and stretched.

"Eph," Jerry said, voice old, bones old, bamboo
rod cracking, splitting in half with age.

Sunlight.

Cloud.

Rooney was gone; Rooney was laughing.

"You know," the boy said, looking at the water, "I
remember a time when we had the elephants in the
backyard. Four of them, right? And the tiger. The
lion, too, I think. I used to feed them my cousins
every Sunday, and every Monday the poor things would
throw my cousins up. You used to get so mad, it was
funny. I mean, your face would go all funny, like you
couldn't decide whether you were going to eat me or
cut my throat."

"Ephraim!"

The boy shrugged.

The woman fastened her dress at the back, hiked up
her skirts, and waded into the stream. Mouth turned
in a smile, face aimed at the sky, one eye closed, the
other eye missing.

"Then there was the time," the boy said, leaning far over the bank to watch the fish follow the shadow of another cloud, "we went over to China and started digging, because you wanted to be the first man in the world to come up in Oklahoma. We had such fights, do you remember? I said it wasn't Oklahoma at all, it was South Dakota, and you got so mad at me because I wouldn't listen to you that you put me in a rice paddy and tried to run me over with a water buffalo. When that didn't work, you tried to run me over with a plow."

"Ephraim, damnit!"

The boy shrugged.

Jerry shut his eyes, clenched his teeth, clenched his fists, felt the beer grow warm and heavy in his stomach.

"You don't do it right," he said quietly.

"Sure I do."

The woman moved downstream, in and out of black-rimmed sunlight. She didn't look around. She didn't wave good-bye. She didn't stop or miss a step when the wind attacked her from behind and tattered the rotted dress.

"No," Jerry said. "Tales aren't grotesque, they aren't cruel. And they always have a little nut of truth somewhere deep inside them. You ought to know that by now. Damn, you've heard enough of them. You ought to know."

The boy looked over his shoulder. "I know."

Jerry looked at the ground.

Sunlight died.

Clouds and twilight, dusk and wind.

The bamboo pole and the empty cans of beer, and Jerry rubbed a hand too hard over his face, pressed too hard into his eyes, giving him a headache that made him wince, that made him groan.

One of these days, he thought, I'm not going to come back. One of these days, I'm going to stay home. I'm going to stay in bed late, I'm going to eat crap for breakfast, I'm going to stop exercising, I'm going to stay up until dawn, I'm going to starve myself to death and by Christ, nobody in this goddamn world's going to stop me.

"Dad," the boy said, "you'd better get going. It's getting late."

Jerry waited deliberately, then took his time getting his things together. And when he was done, pole over his shoulder, hat low over his eyes, he stepped across the sycamore's roots and stood beside his son.

"The thing is," he said, "it's a matter of belief. You take the tale, and for the time you're telling it, you've got to believe it, or it won't be anything more than a dumb and stupid lie."

The boy giggled.

Moonlight in darts of silver following the stream.

The boy got the hiccups and laughed and held his stomach until Jerry threw the pole down and grabbed him, lifted him by the shoulders, and felt his face begin to twist into the mask he had worn before the house filled with dust.

"Shut up," he said hoarsely.

Ephraim only laughed the harder.

"Shut up," he screamed, "or I'll kill you!"

The boy licked his lips once, looked once at each hand holding him off the ground, and said, "No. I bet you don't."

Jerry dropped him, grabbed the pole, and started to leave the clearing. When he reached the path that would take him home, the anger left him just as abruptly as it had come, and he turned around.

"I didn't do it, you know," he said plainly, not begging, waving his free hand toward the places where Rooney and the woman had been watching.

The boy glanced up and down the stream as if looking for someone to come on them in a canoe, then flipped the knife in the air. Caught it. Sheathed it. Face hidden, colors gone, a silhouette of a ghost with moonlight for a mirror.

"The thing is, Dad," he said, "like you said, you gotta have belief, you know what I mean? If you believe we're gonna do this forever, then we will. If you believe we're never going to grow older, then we won't. If you believe you didn't do it, then you didn't."

"But I didn't," he insisted.

Moonlight.

Clouds.

And the boy smiled and said, "I know."

THOMAS LIGOTTI, born 1953 in Detroit, Michigan, is one of the bright new talents of contemporary horror fiction. His short stories have been published in several of horror's "little" magazines (including *Grue, Nyctalops,* and *Fantasy Tales*) and recently were collected in *Songs of a Dead Dreamer.* Like the antagonist of "Alice's Last Adventure," Ligotti is indeed "a conjurer of stylish nightmares."

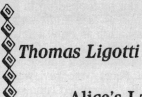

Thomas Ligotti

Alice's Last Adventure

> *"Preston, stop laughing. They ate the whole backyard. They ate your mother's favorite flowers! It's not funny, Preston."*
> *"Aaaaa ha-ha-ha-ha-ha. Aaaaa ha-ha-ha-ha-ha."*
> —Preston and the *Starving Shadows*

A long time ago, Preston Penn made up his mind to ignore the passing years and to join the ranks of those who remain forever in a kind of half-world between childhood and adolescence. He would not give up the bold satisfaction of eating insects (crispy flies and crunchy beetles are his favorites), nor that peculiar drunkenness of a child's brain, induplicable once grown-up sobriety has set perniciously in. The result was that Preston successfully negotiated several decades without ever coming within hailing distance of puberty; he lived unchanged throughout many a perverse adventure in the forties and fifties and even into the sixties. He lived long after I ceased writing about him.

Did he have a prototype? I should say so. One doesn't just *invent* a character like Preston using only the pitiful powers of imagination. He was very much a concoction of reality, later adapted for my popular series of children's books. Preston's status in both reality and imagination has always had a great fascination for me. In the past year, however, this issue has especially demanded my attention, not without some personal annoyance and even anxiety. Then again, perhaps, I'm just getting senile.

My age is no secret, since it can be looked up in a number of literary reference sources (see *Children's Authors of Today*) whose information is only a few years off—I won't tell you in which direction. Over two decades ago, when the last Preston book appeared (*Preston and the Upside-Down Face*), one reviewer rather snootily referred to me as the " 'Grande Damned' of a particular sort of children's literature." What *sort* you can imagine if you don't otherwise know, if you didn't grow up—or not grow up, as it were—reading Preston's adventures with the Dead Mask, the Starving Shadows, or the Lonely Mirror.

Even as a little girl, I knew I wanted to be an author; and I also knew just the kinds of things I would write. Let someone else give the preadolescents their literary introductions to life and love, guiding them through those volatile years when *anything* might go wrong, and landing them safely on the shores of incipient maturity. That was never my destiny. I would write about my adventures with Preston—my real-life childhood playmate, as everybody knew. Preston would then initiate others into the mysteries of an upsidedown, inside-out, sinistral, always faintly askew (if not entirely reversed) universe. A true avatar of topsyturveydom, Preston gave himself body and soul to the search—in common places such as pools of rainwater, tarnished ornaments, November afternoons—for zones of fractured numinosity, usually with the purpose of fracturing in turn the bizarre icons of his foul and bloated twin, the adult world. He became a conjurer of stylish nightmares, and what he could do with mirrors gave the grown-ups fits and sleepless nights. No dilettante of the extraordinary, but its embodiment. Such is the spiritual biography of Preston Penn.

But I suppose it was my father, as much as Preston's original, who inspired the stories I've written. To put it briefly, Father had the blood of a child coursing through his big adult body, nourishing the oversophisticated brain of Foxborough College's associate professor of philosophy. Typical of his character was a love for the books of Lewis Carroll, and thus the genesis of my name, if not my subsequent career. (My mother told me that while she was pregnant, Father *willed* me into a little Alice.) Father thought of Carroll not merely as a clever storyteller but more as an inhumanly jaded aesthete of the imagination, no doubt projecting some of his own private values onto poor Mr. Dodgson. To him the author of the Alice books was, I think, a personal symbol of power, the strange ideal of an unstrictured mind manipulating reality to its whim and gaining a kind of objective force through the minds of others.

It was very important that I share these books, and many other things, in the same spirit. "See, honey," he would say while rereading *Through the Looking Glass* to me, "see how smart little Alice right away notices that the room on the other side of the mirror is not as 'tidy' as the one she just came from. Not as *tidy*," he repeated with professorial emphasis but chuckling like a child, a strange little laugh that I inherited from him. "Not tidy. We know what *that* means, don't we?" I would look up at him and nod with all the solemnity that my six, seven, eight years could muster.

And I did know what *that* meant. I felt intimations of a thousand discrete and misshapen marvels: of things going wrong in curious ways, of the edge of the world where an endless ribbon of road continued into space by itself, of a universe handed over to new gods. Father would gaze at my round little face, squinting his eyes as if I were giving off light. "Moon face," he called me. When I got older, my features became more angular, an involuntary betrayal of my father's conception of his little Alice, among all the other betrayals once I'd broken the barrier of maturity. I suppose it was a blessing that he did not live to see me grow up and change, saved from disappointment by a sudden explosion in his brain while he was giving a lecture at the college.

But perhaps he would have perceived, as I did not for many years, that my "change" was illusory, that I

merely picked up the conventional gestures of an aging
soul (nervous breakdown, divorce, remarriage, alco-
holism, widowhood, stoic tolerance of a second-rate
reality) without destroying the Alice he loved. She was
always kept very much alive, though relegated to the
role of an author for children. *Obviously* she endured,
because it was she who wrote all those books about
her soul mate Preston, even if she has not written one
for many years now. Not too many, I hope. Oh, those
years, those years.

So much for the past.

At present I would like to deal with just a single
year, the one ending today—about an hour from now,
judging by the clock that five minutes ago chimed
eleven P.M. from the shadows on the other side of this
study. During the past three hundred and sixty-five
days I have noticed, sometimes just barely, an accu-
mulation of peculiar episodes in my life. A lack of
tidiness, you might say. (As a result, I've been drinking heavily again; and loneliness is getting to me in
ways it never did in the past. Ah, the past.)

Some of these episodes are so elusive and insubstan-
tial that it would be impossible to talk about them
sensibly, except perhaps in the moods they leave behind like fingerprints, and which I've learned to read
like divinatory signs. My task will be much easier if I
confine myself to recounting but a few of the inci-
dents, thereby giving them a certain form and structure I so badly need just now. A tidying up, so to
speak.

I should start by identifying tonight as that sacred
eve that Preston always devotedly observed, celebrat-
ing it most intensely in *Preston and the Ghost of the
Gourd.* (At least there should be a few minutes remaining of this immovable feast, according to the clock
ticking at my back; though from the look of things, the
hands seem stuck on the time I reported a couple of
paragraphs ago. Perhaps I misjudged it before.)

For the past several years I've made an appearance
at the local suburban library on this night to give a
reading from one of my books as the main event of an

annual Halloween fest. Tonight I managed to show up once again for the reading, even if I hesitate to say everything went *as usual*. Last year, however, I did not make it at all to the costume party. This brings me to what I *think* is the first in a year-long series of disruptions unknown to a biography previously marked by nothing more than episodes of conventional chaos. My apologies for taking two steps backward before one step forward. As an old hand at storytelling, I realize this is always a risky approach when bidding for a reader's attention. But here goes.

Around this time last year I attended the funeral of someone from my past, long past. This was none other than that sprite of special genius whose exploits served as the *prima materia* for my Preston Penn books. The gesture was one of pure nostalgia, for I hadn't actually seen this person since my twelfth birthday party. It was soon afterward that my father died, and my mother and I moved out of our house in North Sable, Mass. (see *Childhood Homes of Children's Authors* for a photo of the old two-story frame job), heading for the big city and away from sad reminders. A local teacher who knew of my work, and its beginnings in North S, sent me a newspaper clipping from the *Sable Sentinel*, which reported the demise of my former playmate and even mentioned his secondhand literary fame.

I arrived in town very quietly and was immediately overwhelmed by the lack of change in the place, as if it had existed all those years in a state of suspended animation and had been only recently reanimated for my benefit. It almost seemed that I might run into my old neighbors, schoolmates, and even Mr. So and So, who ran the ice-cream shop, which I was surprised to see still in operation. On the other side of the window, a big man with a walrus mustache was digging ice cream from large cardboard cylinders, while two chubby kids pressed their bellies against the counter. The man hadn't changed in the least over the years. He looked up and saw me staring into the shop, and there really seemed to be a twinkle of recognition in his puffy eyes. But that was impossible. He never could have perceived behind my ancient mask the child's face he once knew, even if he had been Mr. So and So and not his look-alike (son? grandson?). Two complete strangers gawking at each other through a window smeared with the sticky handprints of sloppy patrons. The scene depressed me more than I can say.

Unfortunately, an even more depressing reunion waited a few steps down the street. G. V. Ness and Sons, Funeral Directors. For all the years I'd lived in North Sable, this was only my second visit ("Good-bye, Daddy") to that cold Colonial building. But such places always seem familiar: that perfectly vacant, neutral atmosphere common to all funeral homes, the same in my hometown as in the suburb outside New York ("Good riddance, Hubby") where I'm now secluded.

I strolled into the proper room unnoticed, another anonymous mourner who was a bit shy about approaching the casket. Although I drew a couple of small-town stares, the elderly, elegant author from New York did not stand out as much as she thought she would. But with or without distinction, it remained my intention to introduce myself to the widow as a childhood friend of her deceased husband. This intention, however, was shot all to hell by two oxlike men who rose from their seats on either side of the grieving lady and approached me. For some reason I panicked.

"You must be Dad's Cousin Winnie from Boston. The family's heard so much about you over the years," they said.

I smiled widely and gulped deeply, which must have looked like a nod of affirmation to them. In any case, they led me over to "Mom" and introduced me under my inadvertent pseudonym to the red-eyed, half-delirious old woman. (Why, I wonder, did I allow this goof to go on?)

"Nice to finally meet you, and thank you for the lovely card you sent," she said, sniffing loudly and working on her eyes with a grotesquely soiled handkerchief. "I'm Elsie."

Elsie Chester, I thought immediately, though I wasn't

entirely sure that this was the same person who was rumored to have sold kisses and other things to the boys at North Sable Elementary. So he had married *her*, whaddaya know? Possibly they *had* to get married, I speculated cattily. At least one of her sons looked old enough to have been the consequence of teenage impatience. Oh, well. So much for Preston's vow to wed no one less than the Queen of Nightmares.

But even greater disappointments awaited my notice. After chatting emptily with the widow for a few more moments, I excused myself to pay my respects at the coffinside of the deceased. Until then I'd deliberately averted my gaze from that flower-crazed area at the front of the room, where a shiny, pearl-grey casket held its occupant in much the same position as the "Traveling Tomb" racer he'd once constructed. The whole stale ritual reminded me of those corpse-viewing sessions to which children in the nineteenth century were subjected in order to acquaint them with their own mortality. At my age this was unnecessary, so allow me to skip quickly over this scene with a few tragic and inevitable words. . . .

Bald and blemished, that was unconsciously expected. *Totally* unfamiliar, that wasn't. The mosquito-faced child I once knew had had his features smushed and spread by the years—bloated, not with death but with having overfed himself at the turgid banquet of life, lethargically pushing away from the table just prior to explosion. A portrait of lazy indulgence. Defunct. Used up. The eternal adult. (But perhaps in death, I consoled myself, a truer self was even now ripping off the false face of the thing before me. This must be so, for the idea of an afterworld populated with a preponderance of old, withered souls is too hideous to contemplate.)

After paying homage to the remains of a memory, I slipped out of that room with a stealth my Preston would have been proud of. I'd left behind an envelope with a modest contribution to the widow's fund. I had half a mind to send a batch of gaping black orchids to the funeral home with a note signed by Laetitia Simpson, Preston's dwarfish girlfriend. But this was something that the other Alice would have done. The one who wrote those strange books.

As for me, I got into my car and drove out of town to a nice big Holiday Inn near the interstate, where I found a nice suite—spoils of a successful literary career—and a bar. And as it turned out, this overnight layover must take us down another side road (or back road, if you like) of my narrative. Please stand by.

A late-afternoon crowd had settled into the motel's barroom, relieving me of the necessity of drinking in total solitude, which at the time I was quite prepared to do. After a couple of Scotches on the rocks, I noticed a young man looking my way from the other side of that greenish room. At least he appeared young, extremely so, from a distance. But as I walked over to sit at his table, with a boldness I've never attributed to alcohol, he seemed to gain a few years with every step I took. He was now only relatively young—from an old dowager's point of view, that is. His name was Hank De Vere, and he worked for a distributor of gardening tools and other such products, in Maine. But let's not pretend to care about the details. Later we had dinner together, after which I invited him to my suite.

It was the next morning, by the way, that inaugurated that year-long succession of experiences which I'm methodically trying to sort out with a few select examples. Half step forward coming up: pawn to king three.

I awoke in the darkness peculiar to motel bedrooms, abnormally heavy curtains masking the morning light. Immediately it became apparent that I was alone. My new acquaintance seemed to have a more developed sense of tact and timing than I had given him credit for. At least I thought so at first. But then I looked through the open doorway into the other room, where I could see a convex mirror in an artificial wood frame on the wall.

The bulging eye of the mirror reflected almost the entire next room, in varying degrees of convexed distortion; and I noticed someone moving around in there. In the mirror, that is. A tiny, misshapen figure seemed to be gyring about, leaping almost, in a way that should have been audible to me. But it wasn't.

I called out a name I barely remembered from the night before. There came no answer from the next room, but the movement in the mirror stopped, and the tiny figure (whatever it was) disappeared. Very cautiously I got up from the bed, robed myself, and peeked around the corner of the doorway like a curious child on Christmas morning. A strange combination of relief and confusion arose in me when I saw that there was no one else in the suite.

I approached the mirror, perhaps to search its surface for the fly that might have caused the illusion. My memory is a little vague on this point, since at the time I was a bit hung over. But I can recall with spectacular vividness what I finally saw after gazing into the mirror for a few moments. Suddenly the sphered glass before me became clouded with a mysterious fog, from the depths of which appeared the waxy face of a corpse. It was the visage of that old cadaver I'd seen at the funeral home, now with eyes open and staring reproachfully into mine. . . .

Of course I really saw nothing of the kind. I did not even imagine it, except just now. But somehow this imaginary manifestation seems more fitting and conclusive than what I actually found in the mirror, which was only my old and haggard face . . . a corpselike countenance if ever there was one.

But there was another conclusion, let's say *encore*, to this episode with the mirror. A short while later I was checking out of the motel, and as the desk clerk was fiddling with my bill, I happened to look out of a nearby window, beyond which two children were romping on the lawn in front of the motel: an arm-swinging, leaping mime show. After a few seconds the kids caught me watching them. They stopped and stared back at me, standing perfectly still, side by side . . . then suddenly they were running away. The room took a little spin that only I seemed to notice, while others went calmly about their business. Possibly this experience can be attributed to my failure to employ the usual post-debauch remedies that morning. The old nerves were somewhat shot, and my stomach was giving me no peace. Still I was—and am—in pretty good shape for my years, and I drove back to New York without further incident.

That was a year ago. (Get ready for one giant step forward: the old queen is now in play.)

In the succeeding months I noted a number of similar happenings, though they occurred with varying degrees of clarity. Most of them approached the fleeting nature of déjà-vu phenomena. A few could almost be pegged as self-manufactured, while others lacked a definite source. I might see a phrase or the fragment of an image that would make my heart flip over (not a healthy thing at my age), while my mind searched for some oblique correspondence that triggered this powerful sense of repetition and half familiarity: the sound of a delayed echo with indirect origins. I delved into dreams, unconscious perceptions, and the distortions of memory, but all that remained was a chain of occurrences with links as weak as smoke rings.

And today, one year later, this tenuous haunting has regained the clarity of the first incident at the motel. Specifically I refer to a pair of episodes that have caused me to become a little insecure about my psychic balance and to attempt to confirm my lucidity by writing it all out. Organization is what's needed. Thus:

Episode One. Place: The Bathroom. Time: A Little After Eight A.M., the Last Day of October.

The water was running for my morning bath, cascading into the tub a bit noisily for my sensitive ears. The night before, I suffered from an advanced case of insomnia, which even extra doses of my beloved Guardsman's Reserve Stock did not help. I was very glad to see a sunny autumn morning come and rescue me. My bathroom mirror, however, would not let me forget the sleepless night I'd spent, and I combed and creamed myself without noticeable improvement. Sandal was with me, lying atop the toilet tank and scrutinizing the waters of the bowl below. She was actually staring very hard and deliberately at something. I'd never seen a cat stare at its own reflection and have always been under the impression that they cannot see reflected images of themselves. (Lucky them!) But this one saw something. "What is it, Sandal?" I asked with the patronizing voice of a pet owner. Her tail had a life of its own; she stood up and hissed, then yowled in that horribly demonic falsetto of threatened felines. Finally she dashed out of the bathroom, relinquishing her ground for the first time in all my memory of her.

I had been loitering at the other side of the room, a groggy bystander to an unexpected scene. With a large plastic hairbrush gripped in my left hand, I investigated. I gazed down into the same waters, and though at first they seemed clear enough, something soon appeared from within that porcelain burrow. . . . It had dozens of legs and looked all backward and inside out, but what was most disgusting about the thing was that it had a tiny human head, one like a baby's except all blue and shriveled.

This latter part, of course, is an exaggeration; or rather, it's an alarm without a fire. It helps if I can tack a neat storybook finish onto these episodes, because what seem to be their real conclusions just leave me hanging. You can't have stories end that way and still expect to hold your reader's esteem. Some genius once said that literature was invented the first time a certain boy cried "Wolf!" and there was none. I suppose this is what I'm doing now. Crying wolf. Not that it's my intention to make a fiction out of what is real. (Much too real, judging by my recent overdrinking and resultant late-night vomiting sessions.) But stories, even very nasty ones, are traditionally considered more satisfying than reality—which, as we all know, is a grossly overrated affair. So don't worry about my cries of wolf. Even if it turns out that I'm making *everything* up, at least what you have left can be enjoyed as a story—no small value to my mind. It's just a different story, that's all: one about *another* old-lady author of children's yarns, which, incidentally, has nothing to do with the "truth" one way or the other.

So: Yes, I was in the bathroom, staring into the toilet bowl. The truth is that there was nothing in there, except nice, disinfected water of a bluish tint. The water was still, like a miniature lake, and cruelly reflected a miniature face. That's all I really saw, my hysterical kitty notwithstanding. I gazed at my wrinkled self in the magic pool for a few moments longer and then cocked the handle to flush it away. (You were right, Father, it doesn't pay to get old and ugly.)

I spent the rest of the morning lying around the baggy old suburban home my second husband left me when he died some years ago. An old war movie on television helped me pass the time. (And vain lady that I am, what I remember most about the war is the shortage of silk and other luxury items, like the quicksilver needed to make a mirror of superior reflective powers.)

In the afternoon I began preparing myself for the reading I was to give at the library, the preparation being mostly alcoholic. I've never looked forward to this annual ordeal and only put up with it out of a sense of duty, vanity, and other less comprehensible motives. Maybe this is why I welcomed the excuse to skip it last year. And I wanted to skip it this year, too, if only I could have come up with a reason satisfactory to the others involved—and, more importantly, to myself. Wouldn't want to disappoint the children, would I? Of course not, though heaven only knows why. Children have made me nervous ever since I stopped being one of them. Perhaps this is why I never had any of my own—adopted any, that is—for the doctors told me long ago that I'm as fertile as the seas of the moon.

The other Alice is the one who's really comfortable with kids and kiddish things. How else could she have written *Preston and the Laughing This* or *Preston and the Twitching That*? So when it comes time to do this reading every year, I try to put *her* onstage as much as possible, something that's becoming more difficult with the passing years. Oddly enough, it's my grown-up's weakness for booze that allows me to do this most effectively. Each drink I had this afternoon peeled away a few more winters, and soon I was ready to confront the most brattish child without fear. Which leads me to introduce:

Episode Two. Place: The Car in the Driveway. Time: A Radiant Twilight.

With a selection of Preston stories on the seat beside me (I was still undecided on which to read, hoping for inspiration), I was off to do my duty at the library. A routine adjustment of the rearview mirror straightened the slack-mouthed angle it had somehow assumed since I'd last driven the car. The image I saw in the mirror was also routine. Across the street and staring into my car by way of the rear window was the odious and infinitely old Mr. Thompson. (Worse than E Nesbit's U. W. Ugli, let me assure you.)

He seemed to appear out of nowhere, for I hadn't seen him when I was getting into the car. But there he was now, ogling the back of my head. This was quite normal for the lecherous old boy, and I didn't think anything of it. While I was adjusting the mirror, however, a strange little trick took place. I must have hit the switch that changes the position of the mirror for night driving, flipping it back and forth very quickly like the snap of a camera. So what I saw for an instant was a nighttime, negative version of Mr. Thompson as he stood there with his hands deep in his trouser pockets. What a horrendous idea. The unappealingly lubricious Thompson on this side of reality is bad enough without *anti*-Thompsons running around and harassing me for dates. Thank goodness there's only one of everybody, I thought. (But then again, perhaps the other Mr. T would be *completely* inverted, and thus no longer a threat to aged but well-preserved women.) I didn't pull out of the driveway until I saw Thompson move on down the sidewalk, which he did after a few moments, leaving me to stare at my own shriveled eye sockets in the rearview mirror.

The sun was going down in a pumpkin-colored blaze when I arrived at the little one-story library. Some costumed kids were hanging around outside: a were-wolf, a black cat with a long curling tail, and what looked like an Elvis Presley, or at least some teen idol of a bygone age. And coming up the walk were two identical Tinkerbells, who I later found out were Tracy and Trina Martin. I had forgotten about twins. So much for the comforting notion that there's only one of everybody.

I was actually feeling quite confident, even as I entered the library and suddenly found myself confronted with a huddling mass of youngsters. But then the spell was broken maliciously when some anonymous smart aleck called out from the crowd, saying: "Hey, lookit the mask *she's* wearing." After that I propelled myself down several glossy linoleum hallways in search of a friendly adult face. (Someone should give that wisecracker a copy of *Struwwelpeter*; let him see what happens to his kind of kid.)

Finally I passed the open door of a tidy little room where a group of ladies and the head librarian, Mr. Grosz, were sipping coffee. Mr. Grosz said how nice it was to see me again and introduced me to the moms who were helping out with the party.

"My William's read all your books," said a Mrs. Harley, as if she were relating a fact to which she was completely indifferent. "I can't keep him away from them."

I didn't know whether or not to thank her for this comment, and ended up replying with a dignified and slightly liquorish smile. Mr. Grosz offered me some coffee and I declined: bad for the stomach. Then he wickedly suggested that, as it was getting quite dark outside, the time seemed right for the festivities to begin. My reading was to inaugurate the evening's fun, a good spooky story "to get everyone in the mood." First, though, I needed to get myself in the mood, and discreetly retired to a nearby ladies' room where I could refortify my fluttering nerves. Mr. Grosz, in one of the strangest and most embarrassing social gestures I've ever witnessed, offered to wait right outside the lavatory until I finished.

"I'm quite ready now, Mr. Grosz," I said, glaring down at the little man from atop an unelderly pair of high heels. He cleared his throat, and I almost thought he was going to extend a crooked arm for me to take. But instead, he merely stretched it out, indicated the way to an old woman who might not see as well as she once did.

He led me back down the hallway toward the children's section of the library, where I assumed my reading would take place as it always had in the past. However, we walked right by this area, which was dark and ominously empty, and proceeded down a flight of stairs leading to the library's basement. "Our *new* facility," bragged Mr. Grosz. "Converted one of the storage rooms into a small auditorium of sorts." Down at the end of the hallway, two large green doors faced each other on opposite walls. "Which one will it be tonight?" asked Mr. Grosz while staring at my left hand. *"Preston and the Starving Shadows,"* I answered, showing him the book I was holding. He smiled and confided that it was one of his favorites. Then he opened the door to the library's *new* facility.

Over fifty kids were sitting (quietly!) in their seats. At the front of the long, narrow room, a big witch was outlining the party activities for the night; and when she saw Mr. Grosz and me enter, she began telling the children about a "special treat for us all," meaning that the half-crocked lady author was about to give her half-cocked oration. Walking a very straight line to the front, I took the platform and thanked everyone for that nice applause—most of it, in fact, coming from the sweaty hands of Mr. Grosz. On the platform was a lamp-bearing podium decorated with wizened cornstalks. I fixed my book in place before me, disguising my apprehension with a little stage patter about the story everyone was going to hear. When I invoked the name of Preston Penn, a few kids actually cheered, or at least one did. Just as I was ready to begin reading, however, the lights went out, which was rather unexpected. And for the first time I noticed that facing each other on opposite sides of the room were two rows of jack-o'-lanterns, shining bright orange and yellow in the darkness. They all had identical faces—triangular eyes and noses, wailing *O's* for mouths—and could have been mirror reflections of themselves. (As a child, I was convinced that pumpkins naturally grew this way, complete with facial features and phosphorescent insides.) Furthermore, they seemed to be suspended in space, the darkness concealing their means of support. As the blackness prevented my seeing the faces of the children, these jack-o'-lanterns became my audience.

But as I read, the real audience asserted itself with giggles, whispers, and some rather ingenious noises made with the folding wooden chairs they were sitting in. At one point, toward the end of the reading, there came a low moan from somewhere in the back, and it sounded as if someone had fallen out of his seat. "It's all right," I heard an adult voice call out. The door at the back opened, allowing a moment of brightness to break the spooky spell, and some shadows exited. When the lights came on at the end of the story, one of the seats toward the back was missing its occupant.

"Okay, kids," said the big witch after some minor applause for Preston, "everyone move their chairs back to the wall and make room for the games and stuff."

The games and stuff had the room in a low-grade uproar. Masked and costumed children ruled the night, indulging their appetite for movement, sweet things to eat and drink, and noise. I stood at the periphery of the commotion and chatted with Mr. Grosz.

"What exactly was the disturbance all about?" I asked him.

He took a sip from a plastic cup of cider and smacked his lips offensively. "Oh, nothing, really. You see that child there with the black-cat outfit? She seemed to have fainted. Not entirely, of course. Once we got her outside, she was all right. She was wearing her kitty mask all through your reading, and I think the poor thing hyperventilated or something like that. Complained that she saw something horrible in her mask and was very frightened for a while. At any rate, you can see she's fine now, and she's even wearing her mask again. Amazing how children can put things right out of their minds and recover so quickly."

I agreed that it was amazing, and then asked precisely what it was the child thought she saw in her mask. I couldn't help being reminded of another cat earlier in the day who also saw something that gave her a fright.

"She couldn't really explain it," replied Mr. Grosz. "You know how it is with children. Yes, I daresay you *do* know how it is with them, considering you've spent your life exploring the subject."

I took credit for knowing how it is with children, knowing instead that Mr. Grosz was really talking about someone else, about *her*. Not to overdo this quaint notion of the split between my professional and my private personae, but at the time I was already quite self-conscious about the matter. While I was reading the Preston book to the kids, I had had the uncanny experience of having almost no recognition of my own words. Of course, this is rather a cliché with writers, and it has happened to me many times throughout my long career. But never so completely. They were the words of a mind (I stop just short of writing *soul*) entirely alien to me. This much I would like to note in passing, never to be mentioned again.

"I do hope," I said to Mr. Grosz, "that it wasn't the story that scared the child. I have enough angry parents on my hands as it is."

"Oh, I'm sure it wasn't. Not that it wasn't a good scary children's story. I didn't mean to imply that, of course. But you know, it's that time of year. Imaginary things are supposed to seem more real. Like your Preston. He was always a big one for Halloween, am I right?"

I said he was quite right and hoped he would not pursue the subject. The reality of fictional characters was not at all what I wanted to talk about just then. I tried to laugh it away. And you know, Father, for a moment it was exactly like your own laugh, and not my usual hereditary impersonation of it.

Much to everyone's regret, I did not stay very long at the party. The reading had largely sobered me up, and my tolerance level was running quite low. Yes, Mr. Grosz, I promise to do it again next year; anything you say, just let me get back to my car and my bar.

The drive home through the suburban streets was something of an ordeal, made hazardous by pedestrian trick-or-treaters. The costumes did me no good. (The same ghost was everywhere.) The masks did me no good. And those Prestonian shadows fluttering against two-story facades (why did I have to choose *that* book?) certainly did me no good at all. This was not my place anymore. Not my style. Dr. Guardsman, administer your medicine in tall glasses . . . but please not looking-ones.

And now I'm safe at home with one of the tallest of those glasses resting full and faithful on my desk as I write. A lamp with a shade of Tiffany glass (circa 1922) casts its amiable glow on the many pages I've filled over the past few hours. (Although the hands of the clock seem locked in the same *V* position as when I started writing.) The lamplight shines upon the window directly in front of my desk, allowing me to see a rather flattering reflection of myself in the black mirror of the glass. The house is soundless, and I'm a rich, retired authoress-widow.

Is there still a problem? I'm really not sure.

I remind you that I've been drinking steadily since early this afternoon. I remind you that I'm old and no stranger to the mysteries of senile neuroticism. I remind you that some part of me has written a series of children's books whose hero is a disciple of the bizarre. I remind you of what night this is and to what zone the imagination can fly on this particular eve.

(But we can discount this last one, owing to my status as an elderly cynic and disbeliever.) I need not, however, remind you that this world is stranger than we know, or at least mine seems to be, especially this past year. And I now notice that it's *very* strange—and, once again, untidy.

Exhibit One. Outside my window is a late-October moon hanging in the blackness. Now, I have to confess that I'm not up on lunar phases ("loony faces," as Preston might say), but there seems to have been a switch since I last peeked out the window—the thing looks reversed. Where it used to be concaving to the right, it's now con*vex*ing in that direction, last quarter changed to first quarter, or something of that nature. But I doubt Nature has anything to do with it; more likely the explanation lies with Memory. And there's really not much troubling me about the moon, which, even if reversed, would still look as neat as a storybook illustration. The trouble is with everything else below, or at least what I can see of the suburbanscape in the darkness. Like writing that can only be read in a mirror, the shapes outside my window—trees, houses, but thank goodness, no people—now look awkward and wrong.

Exhibit Two. To the earlier list of reasons for my diminished competence, I would like to add an upcoming alcohol withdrawal. The last sip I took out of that glass on my desk tasted indescribably strange, strange to the point where I doubt I'll be having any more. I almost wrote, and now have, that the booze tasted inside out. Of course, there are certain diseases with the power to turn the flavor of one's favorite drink into that of a hellbroth. So perhaps I've fallen victim to such a malady. But I remind you that I've never been physically ill a day in my life.

Exhibit Three (the last). My reflection in the window before me. Perhaps something unusual in the melt of the glass. My face. The surrounding shadows seem to be overlapping it a little at a time, like bugs attracted to something sweet. But the only thing sweet about Alice is her blood, highly sugared over the years from her drinking habit. So what is it, then? Shadows of senility? Or those starving things I read about earlier this evening come back for a repeat performance, another in a year-long series of echoes? But whenever that happens, it's always the reflection, the warped or imaginary image first . . . and then the real-life echo. Since when does reading a story constitute an incantation calling up its imagery before the body's eyes and not the mind's?

Something's backward here. Backward into a corner: *checkmate*.

Now, perhaps this seems like merely another cry of wolf, the most elaborate one so far. I can't actually say that it isn't. I can't say that what I'm hearing right now isn't some Halloween trick of my besotted brain.

The laughing out in the hallway, I mean. That childish chuckling. Even when I concentrate, I'm still not able to tell if the sound is inside or outside my head. It's like looking at one of those toy pictures that yield two distinct scenes when tilted this way or that, but, at a certain angle, form only a merging blur of them both. Nonetheless, the laughing is there, somewhere. And the voice is extremely familiar. Of course, it is. No, it isn't. Yes, it is, it is!

Aaaaa ha-ha-ha-ha-ha.

Ex. 4 (the shadows again). They're all over my face in the window. Stripping away, as in the story. But there's nothing under that old mask; no child's face there, Preston. It *is* you, isn't it? I've never heard your laughter, except in my imagination, but that's exactly how I imagined it sounds. Or has my imagination given you, too, a hand-me-down, inherited laugh?

My only fear is that it isn't you but some impostor. The moon, the clock, the drink, the window. This is all very much your style, only it's not being done in fun, is it? It's *not funny*. Too horrible for me, Preston, or whoever you are. And who is it? Who could be doing this to a harmless old lady? Too horrible. The shadows in the window. No, not my face.

I can t   see anymore   I   can t see
Help me
Father

RAMSEY CAMPBELL, born 1946 in Liverpool, England, is one of the most widely published horror writers on either side of the Atlantic, with some twelve novels, two hundred short stories, seven fiction collections, and four anthologies to his credit. His most recent books are the story collections *Scared Stiff* and *Dark Feasts,* and the novels *The Hungry Moon* and *The Influence.* The following manuscript arrived in an envelope bearing his return address.

Ramsey Campbell

Next Time You'll Know Me

Not this time, oh, no. You don't think I'd be taken in like that now, do you? This time I don't care whose name you use, not now I can tell what it is. I only wish I'd listened to my mother sooner. "Always stay one step ahead of the rest," she used to say. "Don't let them get the better of you."

Now you'll pretend you don't know anything about my mother, but you and me know better, don't we? Shall I tell everyone about her so you can say it's the first time you've heard? I <u>will</u> tell about her, so everyone knows. She deserves that at least. She was the one who helped me be a writer.

Oh, but I'm not a writer, am I? I can't be, I haven't had any stories published. That's what you'd like everyone to think. You and me know whose names were on my stories, and maybe my mother did finally. I don't believe she could have been taken in by the likes of you. She was the finest person I ever knew, and she had the best mind.

That's why my father left us, because she made him feel inferior. I never knew him but she told me so. She taught me how to live my life: "Always live as if the most important thing that ever happened to you is just about to happen," she'd advise, and she would always be cleaning our flat at the top of the house with all her bracelets on when I came home from the printer's. She'd have laid the table so the mats covered the holes she'd mended in the tablecloth, and she'd put on her tiara before she ladled out the rice with her wooden spoon she'd carved herself. We always had rice because she said we ought to remember the starving peoples and not eat meat that had taken the food out of their mouths. And then we'd just sit quietly and not need to talk because she always knew what I was going to tell her. She always knew what my father was going to say too, that was what he couldn't stand. "My dear, he never had an original thought in his head," she used to affirm. She was one step ahead of everyone, except for just one thing: she never knew what my stories would be about until I told her.

Now you'll pretend you don't see how that matters, or maybe you really haven't the intelligence, so I'll tell you again: my mother, who was always a step ahead of everyone because they didn't know how to think for themselves, didn't know what my ideas for stories were until I told her. She said so. "That's your best idea yet," she would always applaud. She used to make me tell her a story at bedtime before she would tell me one. Sometimes I'd lie watching my night-light floating away and be thinking of ways to make the story better until I fell asleep. I never remembered the ways in the morning, and I never wondered where they went. But you and me know, don't we? I just wish I'd been able to follow them sooner. And believe me, you'll wish that too.

When I left school I went to work for Mr. Twist, the only printer in town. I thought I'd enjoy it because I thought it had to do with books. I didn't mind at first when he didn't hardly speak to me because I got to be as good as my mother at knowing what he was going to say. Then I realized it was because he thought I wasn't as good as he was the day he told me off for correcting the grammar and spelling on the poster for tours of the old mines. "You're the apprentice here and don't you forget it," he proclaimed with a red face. "Don't you go trying to be cleverer than the customer. He gets what he asks for, not what you think he wants. Who do you think you are?" he queried.

He was asking, so I told him. "I'm a writer," I stated.

"And I'm the Oxford University Press."

I laughed because I thought he meant me to. "No, you aren't," I contradicted.

"That's right," he stressed, and stuck his red face up against mine. "I'm a second-rate printer in a third-rate town and you're no better than me. Don't play at being a writer with me. I'm old enough to know a writer when I see one."

All I wanted was to tell my mother when I got home, but of course she already knew. "You're a writer, Oscar, and don't let anyone tell you different," she warned. "Just try a bit harder to finish your stories. You ought to have been top of your class in English. I expect the teacher was just jealous."

So I finished some stories to read to her. She was losing her sight by then, and I read her library books every night, but she used to say she'd rather have my stories than any of them. "You ought to get them published," she counselled. "Show people what real stories are like."

So I tried to find out how to. I joined a writers' circle because I thought they could and would help. Only most of them weren't published and tried to put me off trying by telling me that publishing was full of cliques and all about knowing the right people. And when that didn't work they tried to make me stop believing in myself by having a competition for the three best short stories and none of mine got anywhere. The judges had all been published and they said my ideas weren't new and the way I told them wasn't the way you were supposed to tell stories. "Take no notice of them," my mother countermanded. "They're the clique, they want to keep you out. You're too original for them. I'll give you the money to send your work to publishers and just you wait and see, they'll buy it and we can move somewhere you'll be appreciated." And I was just going to when you and Mrs. Mander destroyed her faith in me.

Of course you don't know Mrs. Mander either, do you? I don't suppose you do. She lived downstairs and I never liked her and I don't believe my mother did, only she was sorry for her because she lived on her own. She used to wear old slippers that left bits on the carpet after my mother had spent half the day cleaning up even though she couldn't see hardly, and she kept picking up ornaments to look at and putting them down somewhere else. I always thought she meant to steal them when she'd got my mother confused about where they were. She came up when I wasn't there to read books to my mother, and now you can guess what she did.

Oh, I'll tell, don't worry, I want everyone to know. It was the day they told Mr. Twist not to print any more posters about the old mines because the tours hadn't gone well and they'd stopped them, and I was looking forward to telling my mother that the grammar and spelling had put people off, but Mrs. Mander was there with a pile of paperbacks you could see other people's fingermarks on that she'd bought in the market. As soon as I came in she got up. "You'll be wanting to talk to the boy," she deduced, and went out with some of her books.

She always called me "the boy," which was another reason why I didn't like her. I was going to talk about Mr. Twist, but then I saw how sad my mother looked. "I'm disappointed in you, Oscar," she rebuked.

She'd never said that before, never. I felt as if I was someone else. "Why?" I inquired.

"Because you led me to believe your ideas were original and every one of them are in these books."

She showed me where Mrs. Mander had marked pages for her with bits of newspaper, and by the time I'd finished reading I had a headache from all the small print and fingermarks, I was almost as blind as she was. All the books were the number one bestseller and soon to be major films, but I'd never read a word of them before, and yet they were all _my_ stories. You know they were. And my mother ought to have, but for the first time ever she didn't believe me.

That's the first thing you're going to pay for.

I had to take some aspirins and go to bed and lie there until it was dark and I couldn't see the small print dancing any more. Then my headache went away and I knew what must have happened. It was being one step ahead, I knew what stories were going to be about before people wrote them, except they were _my_ stories and I had to be quick enough to write them first and get them published. So I went to tell my mother who was still awake because I'd heard her crying, though she tried to make me think it was just her eyes hurting. I told her what I knew and she looked sadder. "It's a good idea for a story," she dismissed as if she didn't even want me to write any more.

So I had to prove the true facts to her. I went back to the writers' circle and asked what to do about stolen ideas. They didn't seem to believe me, and all they said was that I should go and ask the writers to pay me some of their royalties. So I looked the writers of the books up in the _Authors and Writers Who's Who,_ and most of them lived in England because Mrs. Mander liked English

books. None of the writers' circle were listed, so
that shows it's all a clique.

I couldn't wait until the weekend and I could
tell the writers they were my ideas they'd used,
but then I realized I'd have to leave my mother
for the first time I ever had and keep the money
from my Friday pay packet to pay for the train.
She hadn't hardly been speaking to me since
Mrs. Mander and her books, she'd just kept looking as if she was waiting for me to say I was
sorry, and when I told her where I was going she
looked twice as sad. "That's going too far, Oscar," she asserted, but she didn't mean to London, she meant I was trying to trick her again
when I hadn't really even once. Then on Friday
evening when I was going she entreated, "Please
don't go, Oscar. I believe you," but I knew she was
only pretending that to stop me. I felt as if I was
growing out of her and the further I went the
more it hurt, but I had to go.

I had to stand all the way on the train because
of the football, and I'd have been sick with all
the being thrown back and forth except I couldn't
hardly breathe. Then I had to go in the tube to
Hampstead. The sun had gone down at last, but
it was just as hot down there. But being hot
meant I could wait outside the writer's house all
night when I found it and I could see he'd gone
to bed.

I lay down on what they call the heath for a
while and I must have fallen asleep, because
when I woke up in the morning I felt like I had
toothache all over and there was another car
outside the big white writer's house. When I could
walk I went and rang the bell, and when I couldn't
hear it I banged on the door with my fists to show
I didn't care it was so tall.

A man who looked furious opened the door, but
he was too young to be the writer, and anyway
I wouldn't have cared if he had been since he'd

made my mother lose her faith in me. "What do you want?" he interrogated.

"I'm a writer and I want to talk to him about his book," I announced.

He was going to shut the door in my face, but just then the writer clamoured, "Who is it?" and his son yelled back, "He says he's a writer."

"Let him in, then, for God's sake. If I can let you in, I might as well let in the rest of the world. You and I have said all we have to say to each other."

His son tried to shut the door but I wriggled past him and down the big hall to the room where the writer was. I could see he was a famous writer because he could drink whisky at breakfast time and smoke a pipe before getting dressed. He gave me a look that made his face lopsided and I could see he really meant it for his son. "You're not here for a handout as well, are you?" he demanded.

"If that means wanting some of your money I am," I sued.

He wiped his hand over his face and shook his head with a grin. "Well, that's honest, I can't deny that. See if you can make a better case for yourself than he's been doing."

His son kept trying to interrupt me and then started punching his thighs as if he wanted to punch me while I told the writer how I'd had his idea first and the story I'd made it into. Then the writer was quiet until he acclaimed, "It took me a quarter of a million words and you did it in five minutes."

His son jumped up and stood in the middle. "You're just depressed, Dad. You know you often get like this. All he did was tell you an anecdote built around your book. He probably hasn't even the discipline to write it down."

I caught the writer's eye and I could see he thought his son was worried about whatever money he'd asked for, so I winked at him.

"Get out of the way," he directed, and shoved his son with his foot. "Who the devil are you to tell us about discipline? Keep a job for a year and maybe I'll listen to you. And you've the gall to tell us about writing," he enunciated and looked at me. "You and I know better, whatever your name is. Ideas are in the air for whoever grabs them first and gets lucky with them. Nobody owns an idea."

He went over to his desk as if the house was a ship. "I was about to write a cheque when you appeared, and I'm glad I can do so with some justice," he relished. "Who do I make it out to?"

"Dad," his son bleated. "Dad, listen to me." But both of us writers ignored him, and I told his father to make the cheque out to my mother. He started pleading with his father as I put it in my pocket and ran after me to say his father had only been trying to teach him a lesson and he'd give it back for me. But he didn't touch me because he must have seen I'd have burst his eyes if he'd tried to steal my mother's cheque.

I didn't want her to apologize for doubting me, I just wanted her to be pleased, but she wasn't that when I gave her the cheque. First she thought I'd bought it in a joke shop and then she started thinking the joke was on me because the writer would stop the cheque. She had me believing it had been too easy and meaning to go back to make him write another, but when I got round her to pay it into her account where she kept her little savings, the bank said it had been honoured. Then she was frightened because she'd never seen five hundred pounds before. "He must have taken pity on you," she fathomed. "Don't try any more, Oscar. I believe you now."

I knew she didn't and I had to carry on until she did, and now there was money involved, I knew who to go to, the solicitor who'd got her the

divorce. He didn't believe me until I told him
about the cheque and then he was interested. He
told me to write down all my ideas I didn't think
anyone had used yet for him to keep in a safe at
the bank, though Mr. Twist tried to put me off
writing in my lunch hour, and then he said
we'd have to wait and see if the ideas got written
after I'd already written them. That wasn't
soon enough for me and I went off again at the
weekends.

You'd been putting your heads together about
me though, hadn't you? The writer in the Isle
of Man would only talk to me through a gate-
post. He wouldn't let me in. The one in Norfolk
lived on a barge where I could hear men sobbing.
He wouldn't even talk to me. And the one in
Scotland pretended she had no money and I
should go to America where the money was. I
wasn't sure if I believed her but I couldn't hurt
a woman, not then. Maybe that's why you chose
her to trick me. She'll be even sorrier than the
rest of you.

So I went to America instead of the seaside with
my mother. I told her I was going to sell publishers my stories but she tried to stop me. She
didn't think I could be published any more. "If
you go away now you may never see me again,"
she predicted, but I thought that was like saying
the other time she believed me and I kept on at
her until she gave me the money. Mrs. Mander
promised to look after her, seeing as she wouldn't
go away without me. I only wanted the money
for her and to make her believe me.

I got off at New York and went to Long Island.
That's where the number one best seller who
stole my best idea lives. Maybe he didn't know he
was stealing it, but if I didn't know I'd stolen a
million pounds I'd still be sent to prison and he
stole more than that from me, all of you did. He
had a big long house and a private beach with an

electric fence all around, and it was so hot all
the way there that when I tried to talk to the
phone at the gate all I could do was cough. The
sand was getting in my eyes and making my
cough worse when two men came up behind me
and carried me through the fence.

They didn't stop until they were in the house
and threw me in a chair where I had to rub my
eyes to see, so the writer must have thought I was
crying when he came in naked from the beach.
"Relax, maybe we won't have to hurt you," he
prognosticated as if he was my friend. "You're
another reporter looking for dirt, right? Just take
a minute to get yourself together and say your
piece."

So I told him about my idea he'd used and tried
to ignore the men standing behind me until he
nodded at them and they each took hold of one of
my ears just lightly, as if I'd be able to stand
up if I wanted to. "Nothing my friends here like
better than a tug-of-war," the writer heralded,
then he leaned at me. "But you know what we
don't like? Bums who try to earn money with
cheap tricks."

I was going to lean at him but I couldn't move
my head after all. My ears felt as if they'd been
set on fire but suddenly I knew I could show him
it wasn't a trick, because all at once it was like
what my mother did, not just knowing what someone was going to say but knowing which idea
of mine he was going to steal next, one I hadn't
even written down. "I can tell you what the book
you're going to write is about," I prefaced, and I
did.

He stared at me and then he nodded. But the
men mustn't have understood at first, because
I thought they were tearing my head in half before they let me go. "I don't know who you are
or what you want," the writer gainsaid to me, "but
you'd better hope I never hear of you again. Be-

cause if you manage to get into print ahead of me
I'll sue you down to your last suit of clothes, and
believe me I can do it. And then my friends here,"
he nuncupated, "will come visit you and per-
form a little surgery on your hands, absolutely free
and with my compliments."

They marched me out and onto a lonely stretch
of path where I couldn't see the house or the
bus stop. They dragged me over the gravel for a
while, then they dusted me off and waited with
me until the bus came. There was a curve where
you could see the house, and when I looked
back off the bus I saw the writer talking to
them and they jumped into a car. They followed
me all the way to New York and either the writer
had sent them to find out how I'd known what
he was thinking or to get rid of me straight
away.

But they couldn't keep up with the bus in the
traffic. I got off into a crowd and wished I could
go back to England, only they must have known
that's where I'd go and be watching the airport
if they'd read any books. So I hid in New York until my holiday was over. If I'd gone to any more
writers they might have given me away. I didn't
go out except to post a letter to my mother every
day.

When I got to the airport I hid at the bookstall
and pretended to be choosing books until the
plane was ready. That's how I found out what
you'd done to me. I leafed through the best sell-
ers and found all my ideas that were locked in the
safe. The date on all the books was the year before I'd locked my ideas up. You nearly tricked me
like you tricked everyone until I realized the
whole clique of you'd put your heads together, publishers and writers, and changed the dates on
the books.

I bought them all and couldn't wait to show
them to the solicitor. I was sure he'd help me

prove they'd been written after I'd written them
first. I thought about all the things I could buy
my mother all the way home on the plane and
the train and the bus. But when I got home my
mother wasn't there and there was dust on the
furniture and my letters to her on the door-
mat, and when I went to Mrs. Mander she told
me my mother was dead.

You killed her. You made me go to America and
leave her alone, and she fell downstairs and
broke her neck when Mrs. Mander was at the
market. They couldn't even get in touch with me
to tell me to go to the hospital because you were
making me hide in New York. I'd forgive you for
stealing my millions before I'd forgive you for taking away my mother. I was so upset I said all
this to the newspaper and they published some
of it before I realized that now the Long Island
men would know who I was and where to find
me.

So I've been hiding ever since and I'm glad, because it gave me time to learn what I can do,
more than my mother could. Maybe her soul's in
me helping, she couldn't just have gone away.
Now I can tell who's going to steal one of my ideas
and which one and when. Otherwise, how do you
think I knew this story was being written? I've
had time to think it all out down here and I
know what to do to make sure I'm published when
I think it's safe. Kill the thieves before they steal
from me, that's what, and don't think I won't enjoy it too.

That's my warning to you thieves in case it
makes you think twice about stealing. But I don't
believe it will. You think you can get away with
it but you'll see, the way Mrs. Mander didn't get
away with not looking after my mother. Because
the morning of the day I hid down here I went
to say good-bye to Mrs. Mander. I told her what I
thought of her and when she tried to push me

out of her room I shut the door on her mouth and then on her head and then on her neck, and leaned on it. Good-bye, Mrs. Mander.

And as for the rest of you who're reading this, don't go thinking you're cleverer than me either. Maybe you think you've guessed where I'm hiding, but if you do I'll know. And I'll come and see you first, before you tell anyone. I mean it. If you think you know, start praying. Pray you're wrong.

BY REASON
OF DARKNESS

[A] shadow darker than the shadow of
the night ... the heart of a conquering
darkness.

—JOSEPH CONRAD

WHITLEY STRIEBER, born 1945 in San Antonio, Texas, is best-known to readers of horror fiction for *The Wolfen* and *The Hunger*. With *War Day* and *Nature's End,* both written with James Kunetka, he turned from traditional supernatural themes to those of apocalyptic science fiction. His most recent book, *Communion: A True Story,* is a disturbing account of Strieber's experiences with apparent nonhuman visitants. The following story, he tells me, is the first fiction that he has written since publicizing those close encounters.

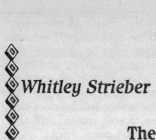

Whitley Strieber

The Pool

That night, I woke up before I had stopped dreaming. I seemed to be running through a forest, dark and so wound with paths that it might as well have been pathless. At the same time I knew that I was lying flat on my bed. As I struggled to consciousness, it felt as if the entire top of my head were open and some sort of wind roaring through the exposed core of my brain. I heard a voice scream out, "I'm being caught inside a body," and then I was fully awake.

I lay there feeling sick and drained, and the thought came to me that our notion of the spirit world may be only partly right: there may be such a world, but the spirits that inhabit it are no longer those of mankind.

I wondered then if there might not have been a war in the other world, and if our mothers and fathers had been displaced. What if bandits have mounted the ramparts of the dead? Would this, then, account for the hunger that many of us now have for death?

That we have such a hunger cannot be denied. Look at the eagerness with which we manufacture engines of destruction. Or take the matter of the environment: the atmosphere is dying; this is more than abundantly clear. And yet we are eager to listen to those who tell us to wait. What compels them to lie, or the rest of us to listen, except a hunger for extinction?

But this story is not about general extinction. It is not even about my own extinction, although I must admit that I hope as much as the next man for death.

It is about a little boy and a black, black pool.

That very word, *pool,* is at the center of my story. Pool. I won't bother you with the etymology; I am not a pedant. But pool. Pool: silver days of summer, the tweak of chlorine in the air, clear splashes and high voices, water voices. Pool, pool, pool: at night another place, singing, yes—but a low, slow song. Now the approach of the frog, smelling water from across the teeming lawn. The frog leaps, a soft splash, and the frog swims in the limitless cool and deep. Pool.

But there are no shallows in our pool, and frogs can't survive in deep water. For a frog the pool is a place of torture and death. So the water sang sweetly while we slept, dreaming our dreams. After hours and hours of blank struggle, the frog died, deep in the embrace of that which it had loved.

The pool is so quiet, so dark. I woke up that night, disturbed, perhaps, by the setting of the moon or the scream of a cicada being torn apart by a bat. An absolute terror enveloped me. My heart thundered. I lay rigid in our bed, sick with woe.

Then I heard, very faintly, a shuffle of water. It came from the deck. From the pool. At first I thought it was another frog—not worth my attention until morning.

Then there was another splash, this one more articulate. I sat up. Could somebody be swimming there in the middle of the night, maybe some kids from town? I got up, slipped on my house shoes, and tucked my little .22 pistol into the pocket of my robe. As an afterthought I grabbed the flashlight.

I went downstairs and moved across the living room toward the door that leads out to the deck. I opened that door as softly as I could and stepped out into the starry night. The air was twinkling with lightning bugs. The heavens were rich with stars. Before me spread the black surface of the pool. It was not still. I saw no dark frog struggling; instead, there was a subtle confusion of ripples.

Then I saw, in the starlight, a pale body beneath the water. I was stunned at this small flesh. Only the three of us lived here, and surely my son was asleep in his bed.

My son of the blond laughter, my brilliant little boy. "Dad, if space is nothing and the universe has an end, then what's on the other side? What's the other side of nothing?"—"Dad, we don't see reality. We see shadows. Reality is too bright for our eyes."—"Dad, I'm glad you-all had me. I love to be alive, so I can think."

I hurled the flashlight to one side, the gun to the other, and leapt into the water. Immediately the pool closed around me, bubbles churning. I came to the surface, swimming madly toward that white shadow.

Then I had him, I felt him in my arms, my boy, and I dragged him to the surface.

He is not a swimmer. He doesn't like the water. He always uses his life vest in the pool. Always. I slogged out of the water with his limp, cool body in my arms and laid him gently on the decking. My mind rushed with lifesaving maneuvers. He was so little, so frail; I could only try mouth-to-mouth resuscitation. I bent down, covered his mouth with mine, and held his nose.

When I blew, he at once coughed and gasped. Then he squirmed away, gagging and belching.

Like some kind of dream creature, he was standing up, my son, naked in the night. His eyes bore down upon me, dark as the pool itself. Then in a low, harsh voice unlike any I had ever heard from him, he said, "Get out of here. Go back to bed."

"Eddie?"

"You heard me!" He stomped his foot and I saw his tiny penis bob with the impact. His fists were clenched, his arms hanging straight down beside him. Again his voice was low and menacing. "Daddy, get—out—of—here."

"Ed, put on your life jacket. I'll go if you put on your life jacket and zip it up."

As I talked, I resolved that I would not move an

inch until he did it. Not an inch. If you are a parent, you can easily imagine how I felt. I loved my child with desperate fervor. I was abandoned to him, frankly. And this was not only because of the wonder of his mind and the supple beauty of his form; it was simply because he was a human child.

Before he was born, I did not know how I would feel about him. Then he came forth and the nurse laid him in my arms, and at once and forever I belonged to that child.

My mind turned and twisted in confusion as I stood staring at him. How could it be that a nine-year-old boy would go swimming alone in the middle of the night—especially one who so disliked and distrusted the water? Why was he here, what was he doing? I wanted him to live.

"We'll swim first thing in the morning," I said. "It won't be long."

He was backing away from me so slowly that I did not realize at first that he had come to the edge of the deck, where the balustrade separates it from the woods. With a swift, cocked movement he crossed the balustrade. The barrier was now between us, the woods behind him.

These are magnificent woods, deep and huge and complicated. Eighty acres of them belong to me; they abut another fifty thousand acres that are owned by the Palisades Water Control District. There are thousands of hundred-foot-plus trees in the woods; they haven't been logged in over a century.

Sometimes at night there are sounds of movement there, great and quick, and the rangers say that there is an enormous and cunning old bear.

"Ed, come on back. I'll cuddle you. I'll rub your forehead."

"We have to die. We're needed. If we don't kill ourselves, they'll kill us with the weather. The battle is waiting."

My mind did not really grasp what he said. It seemed like gibberish, and I told him so.

"You're old; your mind is covered with scales. Mine isn't. I can hear the call."

I pleaded with him to come in. "You've seen too many horror films this summer. You're upset. You've had a bad dream. Please."

Could a nine-year-old somehow get drugs? What if my son had taken LSD?

"It's okay, Dad, I just want to swim a bit longer. I want a little more time in the water. I'm hot."

"If you want to get in the water, why did you go into the woods?"

"You might not let me swim in the pool. So I'll go to the lake."

I was terrified by that statement. The lake is a weedy slough damned by snakes and mosquitoes, its shores full of quicksand pockets. It is also deep, and in its solemn fathoms there are rocks and springs and sucking caves. No fish live there, and its banks at night are silent.

I could imagine him speeding through the woods, slipping between the trees and through the runs of brush, his sweet, pale body far faster than I could ever be. Even if I ran my hardest, he would have easily fifteen or twenty minutes at the lake before I arrived. That would be time enough to die.

By the simple act of crossing the fence, my son had maneuvered me into a hopeless position. I backed up. "No, Eddie, I'll let you use the pool."

Warily he returned from across the fence. He moved toward the water, and as he did, I got a clear glimpse of his face. His expression was so rich with terror—he was in a kind of ecstasy—that my impulse was to reach out and hug him to me and take him into the safety of the house.

I realized then that we were out on the extreme edge. My son had gone beyond what we know as human experience. He was entering another world, and the gates of that world were in the water of the night pool.

I babbled. "Come on inside. I'll make cocoa. I'll fix pancakes. I'll fry bacon."

He moved into the pool like a girl, his body undulant and lazy. The water barely sloshed as he struck out. His head ducked. I could see his arms and legs working frantically.

Then he went still, and his head disappeared. I could see him dropping into the blackness. It was as if my fascination had overcome all my stronger instincts. I felt hypnotized, welded to the spot, even when I saw a single, huge bubble choke to the surface.

At that moment the first morning bird started to sing. It was a warbler, and its voice was so perfectly sharp and clear that it cut my bonds as surely as a knife. Once again I jumped into the water.

But this time my son returned to the surface of his own accord. He choked and churned the water with his arms and did not resist my rescue.

But when we were out of the water, he cursed me with his slight boy's voice. "Damn you, Daddy, you broke my concentration. Learning to swim is hard."

"Learning to swim" was a more appropriate euphemism for suicide than I possibly could have known.

We went inside together. I wrapped him in his white terry-cloth robe and held him. It feels so good to hold your child. There is nothing in this world to compare with it. As I hugged him and felt his leaf-thin body and his beating heart, I watched, through the door, that gleaming pool. There was still a slight movement. And then there was a splash: another frog had begun the intricate struggle that led to death.

My boy started to squirm. I had to command my arms to release their hold on him. But I did release him. "I think I'd like a little brandy," he said. And then I knew why the cognac seemed to be going slightly faster than it should.

I hesitated but a moment, then poured us both snifters. His was very small, mine very large. As I sipped, I watched my son drink, jerking back at the sharpness of the fumes. "I always put it in a regular glass. I don't like the way it smells."

"How long have you been coming down here in the night and drinking brandy?"

"Are you sure you want to know?"

His voice was too even. It sounded dangerous. I nodded, though. Behind me the refrigerator clicked on, filling the shadowy kitchen with its low, drumming roar.

"I started coming down to be alone when I was about four. I usually sit and think for an hour or two, then I have a little, tiny bit of brandy and I go to bed."

A bolt went through me. I felt awful. I had been such a blind fool; all of his life I had been failing him.

"I'm not like you. I love you, but I'm not like you. Your mind has an end. It's got a door, and the door is closed. I was born without a door. When I turn my attention to my own thoughts, it's different from the way it is with you. You go inside something to think. I go outside. Your mind is a nice, neat room. Mine is like the sky."

The room seemed horribly cold, the hum of the refrigerator almost enslaving. My little boy leaned against the kitchen counter in his fluffy robe, contemplating the contents of his glass. And I no longer saw him as my little boy. It was as if he had already died. I grew dizzy, I heard the howl of angels, I struggled to one of the dinette chairs and sank down.

"Dad, will you rub my head? I'd like to go to bed and have you rub my head."

I went into his room with him, and he took off his robe and tossed it on the spare bed, then put on his pajamas. They were in a heap on the floor. I sat on this bedside through thousands of story times, through the sicknesses and the sweats of childhood. Here we read *The Winter Noisy Book* easily two hundred times, taking turns making the sounds, *hisss* for the snow, *cr-r-ack* for the ice, *wooo-hooo* for the lonely foghorn out in the bay. And here we read *Huckleberry Finn* and *Wee Willie Winkie* and "A child awakens and goes

out, and whatever first that child sees, that thing
be becomes," and "trailing clouds of glory do we
come . . ."

Shades of the prison-house begin to close upon the
growing boy.

He lay suddenly innocent beside me, sticks beneath
a night-warm sheet. The only thing that said he was
conscious was the gleam of his Donald Duck night-
light in his eyes. My mind began to weave a normal
hour around the black, surreal wound of the pool. In a
moment we had returned to our familiar roles of wise
lord and gaping disciple.

The clock in the front hall tolled four, and a whip-
poorwill sang through the last of the night. I rubbed
his cool forehead and was glad when the dawn wind
rose and fluttered his curtains. My fear for him was
too great to allow me to leave. I sat sentinel at his
bedside.

When he was born, they put him in my arms. The
nurse said, "Go ahead, you can hold him."

"I might drop him," I said.

When he was seven, he said, "You were afraid you
would drop me when I was born."

He was on the volleyball team at school, and he
played with utter abandon. But his voice was not
that of a competitor, not really; I could hear it
when he shouted. In his cries there was an edge of
design.

Once he said, "God needs us as bad as we need
God. If we die, God will grieve forever. We are God's
dream."

Jenny and I must have been terribly imperceptive
parents not to have seen the relationship between that
statement and the pool. But we did not see it. Instead,
we luxuriated in self-congratulation: "He's so brilliant
and yet he's so happy"—"Thank God we have respect
for his genius. We aren't afraid of it." Two strutting
baboons we were, before the quiet, waiting waters of
the pool.

Morning came suddenly, all bright and rioting with

birds. When I drove him off to day camp, he chattered amiably about his part in the play, to be shown to the parents at the end of the week. "I wanted to play the Raven, but I ended up being Poe. Do you think I look like Poe? I don't look a thing like Poe. If I look like any poet, it's Robert Browning. At least, from the front. I've noticed Swinburne in the profile."

He was a perfectly fine-looking boy. Swinburne was so weak-chinned and pop-eyed that the British Army refused to let him join for fear of how absurd he would look in their beloved uniform.

"You'll be a great Poe."

"Janet Caddoe is the Raven. My Raven."

On the way home I could think of nothing but a thorough and complete search of his room. I was beside myself. To hell with our rules of family privacy; I had to intervene. My little boy, my brilliant little star, was drowning; and if he died, I resolved then and there that I would follow him.

I dashed along in our worn Celica, my mouth dry with terror. I remembered the pool, how still and dark it was, and that pale, lithe body gleaming beneath the surface. You could see stars in the water.

For some reason it did not occur to me to tell Jenny what had happened. I guess that I wanted to cling a little longer to the illusion that all was well, and silence would help me do it.

When I pulled into our driveway, I could hear the bell on St. Peter's Church tolling the hour of ten, its deep clang mingling with the striking of our clock. The dryer blew gently into the driveway, filling the air with a faint perfume of clean clothes. Jenny was sitting on the deck reading the paper. Her usual mug of coffee was at hand. She waved easily, her welcoming voice echoing across the dew-bright lawn.

I wanted to cry. But instead, I went to Eddie's room. What a stupid man I am: I was looking for drugs. My mind reviewed the children he knew. Sullen, thieving Sean. Maybe. Sweet Hillary. Never. Paul, sophisticated beyond his years. Of course. There's the worm in the woodpile.

I did not find drugs, nor paraphernalia, nor anything even remotely connected with such matters. Instead, I found a little homemade radio. At least, I thought it was a radio. It was nothing but a few resistors strung together on a piece of perforated board. They were switched to a lithium battery. I knew it must be a radio because of the crystal.

When I flipped the lamp switch that had been dropped into the circuit, I had an odd experience. A sort of light flashed between my eyes. I decided that it must be the tension.

Afterward I felt that somebody was looking at me. I pleaded sick, stayed away from the office.

I lay in bed staring at the ceiling, wondering what in the world was wrong with my boy.

Jenny picked him up, thank God. While she was gone, I slept, and when I slept, I dreamed of a grey desert. Beyond it waited a red kingdom wreathed in clouds. As I looked at those clouds there came to me an ache of nostalgia. I could hear people singing, as if in fields, marching off to the war, and there stole into my mind an immense sadness.

I woke up suddenly and was stunned to find that it was long past midnight. I could smell the pool. I hungered to swim, to dive down into the waters, to sink away into the silence.

It was as if I were compelled by some hypnosis to get up and throw off my pajamas and go swimming.

But when I got to the pool, I saw that I was too late.

The police, when they came, brought bustle and light; but no light could affect Jenny, who was so broken by the death of her only child that she grieves even now. She will lean her head against the edge of her chair and stare off into space for hours.

I cannot tell her of the voices I hear singing, nor

of the glowing light of the kingdom, nor of the faces that look up at me from the pool's water, of the boy who stole our hearts, and all that army that stands behind him, of the waiting and the dead.

JACK CADY, born 1932 in Columbus, Ohio, teaches writing at Pacific Lutheran University in Tacoma, Washington. His award-winning short stories have been collected in *Tattoo* and *The Burning,* while his novels include *The Well, The Jonah Watch, McDowell's Ghost, Singleton,* and *The Man Who Could Make Things Vanish.* The following short novel is haunted not only by the ghosts of Korea and Vietnam, but by the specter of Cady's spiritual ancestor, Joseph Conrad.

Jack Cady

By Reason of Darkness

Teach us what we shall say unto him; for we cannot order our speech by reason of darkness.

—JOB 37:19

Now the corpses are decayed, not into dust, but have become one with the fertile and well-watered soil of the valleys. The open sun illuminates the forests, and it pries into those dark places where moss softens the tread of men and beasts. Even the skeletons (one supposes) have become soil, although no doubt a polished white fragment is occasionally washed from the hills; the bone glowing spectral and jewellike in a setting of thick foliage. Villages are rebuilt. Rice paddies are tended. If ghosts walk that wet land—and ghosts always have—perhaps we who did so much killing there are still remembered. The living try to forget.

We came in landing craft and airplanes and helicopters, and we breathed the hot screams of war. We left, as if blown by a cold exhalation. A sigh, a murmur from the congregated dead.

You ask which war? It makes no difference. They are all the same. Only the terrain differs. Every few years there is an improvement in weapons. There is never an improvement in illusions.

When I received the phone call from Bjorn North, I was amazed to find I still had illusions. North lived in a small town on the Strait of Juan de Fuca in Washington State. He fished some of the time, drank most of the time; and when the fishing was bad, he ran drugs in a small way.

"I called the Blackbird," he said. "Blackbird is coming. I want you both here."

"The Blackbird is insane," I said. "He isn't just Asiatic, the way we may be. The Bird is genuinely insane."

There is a reason for the Blackbird's insanity, and we both knew it.

"This is more than a reunion," I said into the phone. "What do you want?"

"I have to make a judgment call," North said, "and only you and Blackbird will understand it." North's voice cracked, whispered, lingered over syllables like a man hesitating as he fumbled in a foreign language. I could imagine him hunched inside a phone booth overlooking a harbor where clusters of masts stood shrouded in evening fog. It is a dark wet land in which he lived. North was as tall as I am, but without the balding head and hook nose. His long legs would swell the seams of his pants at the shanks. His narrow chest would seem dubbed onto the body of a wrestler, and above it would ride his equally narrow and Scandinavian face; like a new moon with whitish-blond hair.

"Are you drinking?"

When he was drinking, he had a bad habit of laughing—a white face turning red, a red mouth grotesque. Obscenity often amused him.

"Not enough," he said. "If you mean, am I sober, the answer is that I'm afraid to get drunk." The phone connection carried an echo, one muddled and faint.

"Stay sober. Stay dry for two days. It will take me that long to get there." I paused. North was not fundamentally a liar, although there had probably never been such a thing as a completely truthful sailor.

"What are you afraid of?" I asked.

His voice was a guarded whisper, like a man dredging a secret from a deep well: "I'm afraid there is no safe place to die."

*   *   *

War is normal. If it were not, we would stop having so many of them. One problem with war is that the men who fight are generally voiceless. Even if they find their voices, no one listens. No one can *afford* to listen. When the war is over, the men who survive put on civilian clothes and disappear into the crowd. Occasionally one of them camps alongside a freeway with a rifle, or he tosses his girlfriend from a seven-story window, or he bunkers up and dies in a firefight with the police. Newspapers report the event. People shake their heads and say, "My, my," and "Good God." They are surprised, but the real surprise is not that a few do it but that thousands do not.

A war produces corpses, but it does not bury them. At least, it doesn't bury them deep. I suspected that North's corpses were coming back to greet him, for we all have a string of spirits trailing at our back. They are like the anchoring tail of an enormous kite. If you handle them with respect, they only whisper a little bit sometimes, and the trail behind you is faded and vague. Handle them wrong—as North, perhaps, was finding out—and the spirits turn from mist to the dark smoke of napalm.

"Are you dying?" I had asked him.

"Not right away," North said. "At least if I can help it."

"I will not help you kill yourself. I'm no longer tuned to it, even to help a friend."

He was shocked. Not because of what he heard but because I had spotted a weakness he had tried to conceal.

"I want to live," he said. "If I need killing, I'll ask the Blackbird."

It was then that I discovered I still had illusions. A friend was in need. Maybe it was possible to help.

"Sit tight," I told him. "Forty-eight hours."

It was August, a droning time in my San Francisco law office. The place could run without me for a week. My secretary is a private person. She asked only essential questions. Miss Molly is a forty-five-year-old spinster in a day when spinsters are supposed to be extinct. She did not mean for it to be that way. Jews have close-knit families. I know, because I come from one. Miss Molly's mother died young. She was the youngest daughter. Her career was first housekeeper, now nurse, to her aged father.

"The Blackbird," she said. "It sounds like bad television."

"That's how it sounds," I told her. "The smart Jew lawyer, the Nordic fisherman, and the King Kong Negro. But for once you're wrong. The Bird is small. He even looks like a bird."

Albert Bird is so black that he seems pure African. He could kill Miss Molly while he was shaking her hand. She would be dead before the smile of greeting left her face. But he is not a highly trained killer. The Blackbird simply has a talent.

"This is real," she said as she packed a folder of legal work in my briefcase. "Just in case things get unreal."

The odds on my killing again seemed long. Not impossible. When I returned from war, it was to discover that when men hate their lives or cannot come to terms with them, they must fight against killing those who are familiar or loved. It took a long time to learn. My wife divorced me; largely, I think, because she feared the forces she sensed lying behind my tenderness. At any rate, wives are in danger—and secretaries. When the men do not understand what drives them, the wives and secretaries are in awful danger. Miss Molly is as rare as a dinosaur. It would be a crime to throw the last dinosaur from this thirty-story building.

Sometimes the men kill each other, too, and for those same reasons of love. But more of that later.

"I believe," she said as I packed a pistol in the briefcase, "I'm supposed to remind you to save the last round for yourself." She was not being sarcastic, exactly. She was not being humorous, because she was not smiling. She is small, dark-haired, unsmiling. A cynic but not bitter.

I like her for her toughness. Miss Molly does not ask for sympathy and does not give it in matters short of a death in the family. She knows what sort of monster she works beside. Maybe she thinks of *me* as the last dinosaur.

The route from San Francisco wound past the outskirts of Chinatown. Many-colored banners displayed the breeze. Tourists. Shops selling imitation jade, bamboo, rice paper, tea, carp. All of it a facade, or maybe not. Opium. Sweatshops. Money. Smuggling of every commodity, especially illegal immigrant Chinese. We fight war after war in the Orient. The Orient always wins. It absorbs, takes us over; we disappear into its enormous yawn.

Bad television? The Blackbird's insanity makes him unable to lie. It makes him consult with horses, pigs, dogs, finches; long conversations. He hears their voices. Insanity causes his celibacy. He fears children; or rather, he fears fathering them. Were a daughter or granddaughter to climb on his knee and ask what he did in the war, the Blackbird would say: "I killed little girls just like you. They got in the way."

But to Molly it can only seem like bad television. She does not know the Bird, although she knows some of the rest of us. The rest of us do not suffer the Blackbird's affliction. The rest of us know how to lie.

If my daughter asked what I did in the war, the answer would be: "I sat in the CIC on a destroyer, eating doughnuts, and fired rockets." I would not tell her those rockets were fired at quadrants on a grid; a list of quadrants chosen by a computer programmed to the probability of enemy movements. I would not tell her it was impossible to know what was in each quadrant—an enemy camp, a marketplace, a convent, a grade school. I would say nothing about those days in the jungle with North and the Blackbird.

*　　*　　*

San Francisco to Seattle is a hard day's drive if you take the freeway. I took the coast route, which is interminably slow; a two-day drive. It was a matter of self-protection, a matter of preparation. The mind is not always so strong and exact as we like to believe. I was driving toward some dark hysteria, perhaps toward a dying friend. The very land toward which the car pointed is a land of mist, of darkness; a land of sullen seas and black forests. A land of Chinese ghosts, Indian ghosts, and white fear. Rain covers those forests. Moss grows as carpets on the trunks of trees. Dark stone beaches are whipped by wind, by surf, by the pressing tides that lap at the land like an enormous beast—a cat, perhaps—or something not so agile. Something ancient, geologic; a beast blinking only once while a century passes.

Above San Francisco, in late August, the California hills were burned. The coast was decorated. Enameled road signs, camper trucks, sports cars. Pretty girls wore skimpy clothing, and on the beaches they sometimes wore no clothing at all. Children were like skinny flashes of light, or like small anchors beneath bird and dragon kites pushed by the coastal breeze. They were momentarily like spirits; and there is something particularly horrible in the idea of ghosts walking at high noon and chewing hot dogs. Gulls squawked, glided, flapped, gathered popcorn, bread crusts. The coast was a spectrum of life and movement.

Beaches appear one way when you are standing on them thinking of baseball and sex and sunshine. They carry a different tone when you stand on a steel deck and approach from seaward.

Just below Mendocino, color began to drain from the beaches and return to the land. The coastal fog rolled across the town, across inlets and roads. It lay like a chill thought that comprehended the glistening hoods of cars, the tall windmills of Mendocino, then distilled as raindrops in the corners of windowsills. It coated plastic menus outside restaurants, and it dimmed streetlights to luminous discs in the late afternoon.

The fog seemed a well-tailored recollection for a man on a journey toward the dead.

The Blackbird wears a watch on each wrist. One is a Mickey Mouse watch; a black mouse wearing white gloves, a mouse trapped in timeless semaphore as it measures seconds and days and years. On his other wrist, the Blackbird wears a watch made for combat. It is precise and nearly indestructible. He began wearing the watches to cover the scars on his wrists where he cut them after he killed the sympathizer Corporal Kim. These days the Blackbird wears the watches for other reasons.

North and the Blackbird went ashore in the bright white of dawn. Our harebrained executive officer had detailed them to the beach with cases of canned peaches, boxes of phosphorus grenades, three cases of ice-cream mix, forty canned hams, tins of Dutch cheese, foil packets containing catsup and honey, sixteen bottles of whiskey, twenty cases of beer, boxes of laxative, fifty pounds of apples, sixteen gallons of grey enamel, four reams of U.S. Navy stationery, an enormous cooking pot, twenty pairs of arctic boots, a hand-operated adding machine, a huge world globe on an elaborately carved mahogany stand, a case of ten-gauge shotgun shells, eight dozen assorted brassieres (no one ever figured how these had ended up in the supply room of a destroyer), cartons of menthol cigarettes, cases of aspirin, a bamboo bird cage, twenty gross of carpenter's pencils . . . and I do not recall the rest. The Blackbird still has the original manifest. He claims that it now hangs in a frame on his bedroom wall.

In war, no one knows why anyone else does anything. The most astounding and incoherent things occur with slim reason. Maybe the exec was trying to be helpful to a brother officer in the Army. Maybe he was paying off a gambling debt. Maybe the supply officer was trying to dump inventory he did not want or could not account for. At any rate, the cargo was destined for an Army command area twenty miles into the interior.

North and the Blackbird got hold of a truck, loaded the stuff after reserving the whiskey for trading purposes, and headed inland while drinking beer. It was their initial encounter with the jungle. At first they drove twenty miles an hour. The dirt tracks, which passed for a road, wound beneath dripping, sweetly rotten-smelling leaves. The sun was blocked by enormous trees. The road became more and more narrow. They suspected they had gotten the wrong directions, that they were on a road leading to nowhere. A narrow ribbon of light ran above the road. Ten miles into the interior, the tracks began to dwindle away. They feared they would no longer be able to go forward, and there was no space to turn around. They were inching ahead in low gear. The Blackbird recalls that he worried he might not stand the silence and the claustrophobic grasp of the jungle.

They were captured by the U.S. Marines. The whole affair seemed a burlesque, a mouse show, a convocation orchestrated and spoken by clowns.

The Marines were desperate men, but men strangely efficient and polite. They were not fools. That was proven because they were still alive. They were combat-ridden. Their faces were gaunt, burned with sun. Blackened with soot. The Blackbird at first had trouble discovering which of them were white. Their faces seemed to exist only for the purpose of raising crops of hair; all of them had beards that were chopped short by knives. Beards and mustaches existed only as circling frames for teeth. The men spoke between their teeth or in whispers.

North remembered their seriousness and efficiency. He recalled that he had the choice of giving up the load and not dying, or giving up the load after he died. He felt vaguely violated. After all, the stolen whiskey was his by right. Now it was being taken from him.

Imagine them there: North, a Bosun Mate, and the Blackbird, a Storekeeper. Two sailors accustomed to seeing death fall from the air, shells exploding on distant shores; death painting the slickness of blood across steel. Imagine them standing among crazed men in a mist-laden jungle where death poked its snout through foliage, where blood became only a dark and soaking comment in the soil.

The Marines once had been a full company. Now they amounted to a platoon, although they had native sympathizers with them. One sympathizer was little more than a boy. His nearly unpronounceable name had been distorted to Sidney, then to Sidrey. Sidrey was a tiny fellow. When he stood beside the Blackbird, even the Blackbird seemed a full-size man.

The Marines unloaded the truck. What they did not want, they stacked to one side. North figured that he and Blackbird would be left with the catsup and the grey paint and the arctic boots. Until the last moment, neither North nor Blackbird had the least intimation that before the affair was over, they would walk three hundred miles through jungle as they carried canned peaches and the rifles of dead men.

The Blackbird vividly remembers the enemy attack. He remembers it in slow motion. He recalls watching the boy's face. Actually he was watching Sidrey's mouth. The Blackbird was having trouble understanding the sympathizer's version of English. Blackbird watched the lips moving, listened carefully, was aware in a vague way of a growing stack of canned goods beside the skinny road.

Then the boy's face disappeared. A bullet entered the back of the skull and exploded. The Blackbird found himself carefully listening for a voice to continue from that faceless skull. He saw the inner bone of the skull. He was vaguely aware that his own face was covered with soft matter and liquid. To this day he swears that he stood there for two minutes listening for jumbled language to come pouring from the skull of a standing corpse. He did not, of course. It was a matter of a second, perhaps—no more. The sympathizer Corporal Kim dived forward and knocked the Blackbird to the road. They both rolled behind a small fortress of canned peaches. Up until that point, the Blackbird had not heard a single unusual sound. Once on the ground, he heard gunfire. An enemy patrol lay in ambush.

The history of war contains thousands of futile and desperate battles fought over inconceivably stupid objectives. This battle in the jungle was as desperate as any battle ever waged, and it was between men who were mad for ham and cheese and peaches. When the firefight was over, not one carton had been hit. The Blackbird swears he was safer behind that narrow stack of canned goods than at any other time in his life.

What caused the attack? The question haunted North and the Blackbird. Why would a single squad on patrol—even owning the element of surprise—take such a desperate chance? That squad attacked a platoon of veterans in the game of killing.

The attackers were not starving. North saw whitish fat peeled away from a gut wound opened by a fragmentation grenade. The enemy belly pulsed, digesting, as the man died.

The Marines were not starving; the enemy was not starving; and yet somehow—and North could never even speak of this—somehow the root of the battle was an enormous hunger.

These Marines carried no esprit de corps. Such foolishness is good enough in bars and on drill fields, not so good in a jungle. Instead, they carried a rough honesty. They regarded North and the Blackbird as supercargo, as men of inexperience who would shortly die. Until the time when they would be killed, the two sailors could serve as carriers. The Marines did not actually press the Blackbird and North into service. They simply pointed out that the truck radiator sported a bullet hole. They encouraged the Blackbird and North to discuss the matter. The two men did this as the Marines buried the boy, Sidrey, in a shallow grave. The Bird and North could walk ten miles along a road that might sprout an enemy patrol, or they could walk with a platoon of killers while carrying goods. North recalled being furious about the choice. After all, they were supposed to be in a secured zone. They had been so certain of their safety that they left their helmets in the barge when they came ashore. They were nearly weaponless. North carried an antiquated .45 automatic.

The Blackbird, who was raised on the streets of Philadelphia, did not waste his time in anger. He foraged among the enemy dead for helmets and rifles. Then he made one of those obscure, but somehow significant, gestures for which he would become notorious. The Blackbird stood the huge globe in the middle of the road. It rested on its gorgeously carved mahogany stand. The narrow band of sunlight above the road highlighted the reliefs of the globe. Sunlight and shadow. Colored continents, nations, and seas.

The Blackbird put his white hat on the globe. North recalled his last sight of that road as the platoon faded into the jungle. A fresh grave lay beneath dripping branches; and above it, a world globe wearing a sailor's white hat stood in silent benediction.

No one from our ship saw them for months. I was the one who found them. By that time, it was too late.

I can't explain the exact difference between memory and recollection. Memory is something a person consciously tries for, while recollection more or less comes unbidden. But with recollection, it seems that you chew a little longer; maybe work harder at understanding what pushed it into your mind. It is like analyzing a dream. I thought of the problem as I drove toward Bjorn North and his demons, and as the narrow California road turned into a narrow Oregon road.

I spent the night in a gloomy beach motel on the Oregon coast. It was one of those places where the walls are in need of washing, but where antiseptic light floods the toilet seat and gives the illusion that foul diseases are being flooded away. A narrow paper strip across the seat brags of sanitation.

Another problem with war is that men in combat assume patterns that make the civilized world ridiculous. When, for example, the main disease is bullets, no one going to a whorehouse worries about using prophylactics. Then the men return to a sanitary world where tobacco and alcohol and drugs are supposed to be supplanted by antiseptics and good manners. One never meets good manners in battle, although one occasionally meets compassion. Men find it hard to make the switch from mortar fire to sanitary toilets.

In the jungle you are always surrounded. So is the enemy. There is no clear demarcation. It is a deadly game of hide-and-seek where the enemy will never appear before your guns. The enemy will be to one side or at your back. Day after day, week after week; surrounded. Black men and white men develop cautious patterns of insanity. As do Orientals.

The encirclement continues when the war is over. Then the sanitary people—the ones who started the war in the first place—insist you join their illusions. "Work hard. Get ahead. Don't kill anybody. Find some way to look at children and not imagine burned flesh, empty eye sockets."

The antiseptic people insist that you be nice to the waiter who stiffs you for a dollar. They ask that you think kindly of the politicians who even now plan a war to kill your sons.

"Because," they say, "we are all in this together, my friend. Think kindly thoughts and love us."

I fight back by wielding the law. It makes a little sense to be a lawyer. Not much else does. I'm a good lawyer because I've fired rockets, because I've spent two months in the jungle.

The Marines in that platoon were outlaws. In military terms, those Marines were operating with independence. Their commander, back at Group, could never be certain of what they would do. They were roving, honed, horribly efficient. Their mission was to protect the perimeter of that large Army camp.

In practical terms, they walked and killed. They were phantoms fading through the jungle, phantoms turning to the sudden heat of amazing flame when they encountered resistance. They were survivors because they killed on the basis of probability. If an old native had the bad luck to see them as they crossed a road, the old native was shot. Maybe he would have said nothing about their location. The Marines stayed alive because they always tilted probability in their favor. They were statistical killers, more easily and intimately understandable than computers that fire rockets.

The Blackbird and North were immersed in that destructive element. If the Marines first regarded them as supercargo, Blackbird and North did not. They understood that if they were to survive, they would have to learn fast. The Blackbird learned right away.

By the time I found those Marines, the Blackbird and North had seen a variety of things, done a variety of things more.

It happened this way—one more part of the madness.

Our destroyer ran out of rockets. Incredible. No one had paid attention to my inventory reports. The ship mounted two banks of pom-poms that would depress only far enough to take the top off a mountain at a four-mile range. We mounted some old heat-seeking missiles, which any attack pilot old enough to shave could avoid by dropping a few flares. We had plenty of depth charges, although the enemy had no submarines. In other words, the ship was defenseless. There was lots of maple syrup in the pantry, jugs of whiskey in the captain's quarters, but by God, there were no more rockets. The ship withdrew, hunting for a tender, a mother ship.

Before it withdrew, that same idiot executive officer put me on the beach.

"You caused this," he said. "You made us run out of rockets. No rockets, no gunnery officer." He was a man with Yankee eyes, and cheeks like marinated beef steeped in booze and tropical sun. A great leader of men. A great navigator; with slumped shoulders and a great belly and a great butt. He was the only naval officer in history who had ever crashed into a dock while pulling away from it.

"File charges," I told him.

He knew, and I knew, that if he could get me killed, there would never be an inquiry. No one would ever ask why a destroyer had steamed away from an action because it was defenseless.

"Bring them sailors back," he said, "and the captain will be happy." He was pleased. "If you don't come back, the exec will be happier."

I went ashore, and I was afraid.

Rumors were coming back to the ship: of two sailors crazier than most Marines. Each of the men had shown up once at that large Army base. They came in a captured truck. They drew supplies for that outlaw platoon.

The white sailor was a jolt of savage fear. He arrived unaccompanied, and he wore rotten-smelling scalp locks stitched to his shirt. He eventually went on an alcoholic binge and tore a whorehouse to pieces after bedding every woman in the place. That, of course, was not unusual. The unusual event happened before the drinking began.

The white sailor had become Asiatic, but worse than most. Usually men just mumble through convenient Oriental customs, or played at being Oriental. This sailor was sardonic. His laughter was cruel; his large teeth and flushed face were like a caricatured troll before a carnival fun house. Before he began drinking, he sat beside a Buddhist monk for three hours, sitting in what seemed complete and reverent silence. Then he stood, bowed, and shot the unsurprised and undismayed monk in the face with a .45 pistol. He left town through crowded streets and at high speed. He was indifferent to screams and thumps and raglike, rolling bodies.

It was not, the rumors admitted, that the white sailor did unheard-of things. It was simply, the rumors said, that when other men did such things, they usually had some excuse, no matter how flimsy. This sailor, whose name was North, was like an animal snarling above a carcass. He seemed pressed by fear that there would be a shortage of bodies, of women, of whiskey; a shortage, in fact, of omnipotent illusions that galloped through the corridors of a mind gone wild.

But it was the black sailor who gave pause to even the most seasoned men. The black sailor arrived later, driving the same truck, but accompanied by the sympathizer Corporal Kim. The two men were efficient. They were quiet while drinking, unremarkable while bedding, and they drove carefully through crowded streets.

Where the white sailor sported scalp locks sewn to his shirt, the black sailor simply wore black feathers in his hair. The feathers were intermingled, stitched and braided, so the man's head was a-ruffle with black. He looked like a surprised crow.

The black sailor left live grenades with unbent pins as calling cards. The things were harmless enough, so long as no fool pulled the pin. When he left a bar, a grenade lay on the table. When he left the depot, a grenade lay on the supply sergeant's desk. He left grenades on the beds of women. The black sailor was pleasant, even courteous; and both he and the sympathizer Corporal Kim seemed to think of the grenades not as tips for service, but as party favors. There was an abstract gaiety about the men that seemed to define the war as a cotillion, or a clambake. They were great friends.

I had the bad luck to find them on the day the war heated up, the day the enemy mounted a counteroffensive. An Army truck dropped me, and supplies, at a rendezvous point.

There was a clash of helicopters above the jungle; a whip, whip, whip of rotors thumping like pulse. Along the roads, a frightened native population streamed ahead of the enemy, while overhead, the helicopters hosed the jungle with rockets and gunfire. The sounds seemed gratuitous. The flames were real. The fire sprays everywhere, along roads, or absorbed in the dripping silence of the jungle. Occasionally a rocket hits the top of an enormous tree. When that happens, there is a small tear in what seems the impenetrable umbrella of the jungle.

North saved my life, and not only once. I was confused, vulnerable, in the shocking push-and-shove of forces exploding around us. North was not particularly pleased to see me. "What the hell are *you* doing here," he said—I was, after all, an officer, but we hailed from the same ship. That called on some loyalty that still lay curled and embryonic in North's notions of righteousness.

There was also this: He knew that sooner or later a court-martial was likely. It was obvious that the Marines were not holding the sailors hostage. North may have protected me because I was a lawyer. He kept me alive as counsel for his defense.

For the next two months, North and the Blackbird were never far from my side. We saw, and did, a variety of things. "As sweet as hell and hallelujah," the Bird would say of those things. North remained silent. He stopped taking scalps.

The two months were spent in retreat, circling, counterattack, retreat, and more circling. Somewhere, sitting in the stateroom of an aircraft carrier, a few admirals and generals may have known the overall situation. They probably drank together and called each other by first names: Pete, Tom, Bob. They spoke of strategy and women. We spoke only of tactics, and we called each other by any vulgarity that was convenient.

Toward the end of the second month, there was hope that we would leave the jungle. The military situation steadied. It much resembled what it had been when North and the Blackbird first entered that narrow road. There were no clear lines of defense and offense. We and the enemy were once more surrounding each other. The area was declared secure. The deadly game of hide-and-seek resumed.

At the time there seemed a second reason for hope. At the time.

Looking back on it—as I looked back on it during the final leg of the drive up the Washington coast—that second hopeful reason was at the root of any horror that dwelt in the dark forests of North's mind. It was a horror that lay ancient in my own mind; a horror darker than the wet fir forests of Washington, darker than the tumbling black waters of the Strait of Juan de Fuca.

The second hopeful reason was this: Our ship returned to its station with a fresh bellyful of rockets. The rockets fell in the jungle and made men fearful; but mostly the rockets wrecked a little foliage, changed the smells from rotting vegetation to the sharp scent of high explosive. Once we saw them fall on a village; saw mud rising in fire; mud changed to dust, then to flame. At the time, all I could really understand was that the computers still functioned.

And then—and may all the gods there are, if there are any, protect us—one day the rockets fell in a graveyard.

There were plenty of fresh graves in every graveyard of that country. The native population continued to practice its ceremonies. A part of their ritual was to erect small fences around each grave. The fences were called "spirit fences." Most of them were white. Most of them were made of plain wood. The small fences contained the spirits of the dead and kept away the other, hungry spirits that flew across the world howling and weeping in their relentless and hopelessly eternal quests.

Our ship's rockets took care of the spirit fences. Graves were upturned, corpses tumbled skyward in geysers of flame. The spirits were released.

To North it was a thunderous joke. Lightning and thunder. The absurdity tickled his fancy. He laughed like a demented inquisitor. North's Protestant God was one of the Scandinavian versions, a God consorting with Valkyries. He thought it one more fine offense against one more pagan religion. He was red-faced as he laughed, although his eyebrows were strangely white, as white as his sun-bleached hair. Recall that North had already murdered one Buddhist Monk.

To the sympathizer Corporal Kim, the affair with the graveyard was another matter. All through the two-month ordeal Kim and the Blackbird had retained

their insane gaiety. They shared food. They fought
well and trekked well. They worked together like fingers on the same hand. They sent the enemy to heaven
or hell with impartial joy. Kim's eyes were wide and
seemed almost round. He had a small mouth. When
he laughed, his mouth and eyes were like three flat
circles of mirth across his flat face.

After the business of the graveyard, Kim became
morose. His eyes were heavy-lidded, and they looked
toward North with an occasional flat stare. Kim no
longer laughed. North laughed in defiance, but he
kept his holster flap unbuckled. He was careful about
the direction in which he pointed his back.

Why did Kim take the rockets so seriously? Was it
North's laughter? At the time none of us knew. Perhaps those spirit fences had been Kim's symbolic bun-
ker against reality. The fences might have had the
same illusory protection as, say, the two-inch steel
plate behind which we hid on the destroyer. Neither
fence nor steel plate is at all effective if viewed sanely.
The problem is that no one was sane.

Kim and the Blackbird became even closer. They
often sat in silence. What Kim confided to Blackbird
was unknown, because the Blackbird did not discuss
it.

The final, killing act arrived on the heels of a miracle. It was a mindless miracle, true—a part of the
great absurdity of battle—but a miracle that even the
Old Testament Joshua would have praised.

We were caught in high grass in the middle of fields.
We were crossing those fields just after dawn. We
knew the enemy was not even close. Then we were
blinded by the rising sun.

"It's a sellout." Those were North's first words when
the gunfire began, when everyone was hitting the deck.
North yelled the words before he was fully stretched
on the ground with his weapon pointed. Off to the
left, a man screamed. An enemy voice yelled and
laughed. North's face was as white as his eyebrows.

North was right. This was not an error in command.
The platoon was sold. Euchred. Somebody had been

consorting with the enemy. We were jammed. Pinned. Enfiladed. We were the same as dead men.

Automatic weapons opened up from under the cover of tall grass—only grass—on our left flank. Machine guns opened up from an area of jungle that curved across fields and toward the left side of our line. A narrow neck of trees jutted on our right, and from them machine guns began spouting. The gunfire was solid. It was actually mowing the grass.

Dead men. We could attempt to retreat two hundred yards across flat grassland, or we could lie pinned until the enemy brought up mortars. The machine guns searched the grass, whipped the grass. The air seemed full of flying seeds, pollen, stem heads. The weapons were working by sectors, in much the way our ship's computers worked by sectors. Our problem was that these sectors were small, and there were not many of them. North and I wiggled forward, holding grenades, trying to get in throwing distance. Stupid. Every time we moved, the grass moved. A machine gun hosed above us.

The sun lay like a carpet on the grass. I remember lying with the lip of my helmet pressed against the ground, and I was suddenly smelling soil. It was almost like I could hear movement in the soil, of insects, bacteria, growing roots.

Then the clang and bang of mortars began. Another man screamed, and for a few minutes he continued screaming. I recall thinking silly thoughts about the law. This is a divorce, I thought. A matter of community property.

And then the miracle arrived on the heavy sound of engines.

The sky was clouded with transport planes. Shadows of planes were whipping over us like shadows at a light show. It seemed that every plane owned by every air force in the world had decided to converge over those fields. There must have been enough planes that a man could step from wing to wing, walking across the sky. In less than two minutes, men—and corpses—began falling around us.

Somewhere, at some Army headquarters, a general had looked at a map and seen an area of fields in a zone marked "secured." He ordered a low-level jump for parachute troops, a training exercise. Two thousand men dropped in about fifteen minutes; two thousand dropped into fields enfiladed by machine guns.

A corpse collapsed beside us. The morning was windless. The chute billowed, then fell to cover the grass like a comforting thought. The dead eyes still held more excitement than surprise. There was very little left of the thing from the chest down. The aircraft engines continued pulsing, pulsing.

A living parachutist dropped on the other side of us, rolling on his back, releasing the chute and screaming. He was yelling, "Ted, Ted," and then he was yelling, "Medic, medic." He tried to crawl over us in a desperate attempt to reach the dead man.

"Teddums is deadums," North told him, and giggled. North was hysterical with relief. Color returned to his face. The planes thumped and droned, the shadows flickered. "Lock and load, my man," North said. "Ready on the right, ready on the left, ready on the firing line. . . ." North's hysteria clanged like mortars. He clung to the ground and listened to the cacophony of machine-gun fire, the surprised screams, the curses. It was a shooting gallery, but the enemy could not shoot them all, It was just a matter of time. North lay flat. He began screaming vulgarities, and jokes, at the enemy. The planes droned on.

"There is nothing you can do," I told the parachutist, "except to save yourself. Let the men who land behind the guns take care of it." He was a young Alaskan Indian. The physical type is easy to spot. The dark, fleshy face dropped its grief and took on fear. The boy hugged the ground. He did not even ready his weapon.

At most, it took an hour. Grenades exploded. The machine-gun fire gradually dwindled. Before the last gun was silenced, we heard the thumping of helicopters. They were arriving to bring men back from a successful jump. Instead, they began a long and busy

day carrying wounded and the dead. An incident of
war. The general who ordered the action was later
commended for taking out the last pockets of resistance in the area. Another incident of war.

We rose from that tall grass like resurrected men.
Like men discarding the shrouds of their graves to
stand confused and blinking in sunlight. Like men
released to wander once more the streets of some
unholy city.

Kim and the Blackbird stood. Faced each other
across the sunlit grass. Kim was calm, but the Blackbird was shaking. Kim smiled without fear at his black
face. Kim's smile was not apologetic. The Blackbird
murmured, whispered. Kim shrugged. His weapon was
resting at his side. With his free hand he pointed a
finger at his chest, searching with the finger; the exact
location. Nodded. The Blackbird whispered, "No."
Kim smiled, insisted.

The Blackbird shot Kim precisely, exactly where the
finger had pointed. It was over in less than ten seconds.

We had all once more hit the deck.

"He ought to pay attention where he points that
thing," North complained. "He could mess around
and actually *kill* somebody." North's voice was whining with disbelief.

I said an incredibly stupid thing: "What are friends
for."

We were all shocked. Kim had asked an awful thing
of the Blackbird. Yet it was easy to understand. Kim
knew it was all over for him. Half of the remnants of
that platoon had already figured that Kim was the
betrayer. They had thought through our movements of
the past few days, recognized that only a scout—Kim—
could have made contact with the enemy. Kim no
doubt figured it better to die quickly and with dignity
than to die in the way those Marines would have killed
him.

Why had Kim betrayed us? The Blackbird knew,
but he was not talking. The whole affair was small and
private. When the men from that platoon once more
stood, viewing Kim's body in the grass, a few para-

chutists were looking our way. Then they shrugged and went about their business. One more Oriental face, one more execution: it was routine. What was not routine is that the Blackbird was passing from the insanity of battle into the permanent insanity that would hold him like a bone in a wild dog's teeth.

The Blackbird lay beside Kim all that day. Sometimes he embraced the body, but mostly he lay beside Kim as two lovers might lie beside each other in a field. It was strangely sexual, although nothing of that sort had gone on between those men. At the same time it was as wise as a living beast lying hopelessly beside a dead mate. The Blackbird held long conversations that day. He spoke to Kim, and—at least in the Blackbird's mind—Kim answered. Sometimes the two of them argued, although we only heard Blackbird's side of the matter. If anyone approached them, the Blackbird raised his weapon. After the first few minutes everyone left him alone.

The Blackbird nearly died because he was left alone. As evening came, and as the helicopters began switching on landing lights in order to find the beaten surface of the fields, it was time for us to leave. The remaining Marines were being evacuated. I arranged to take my sailors back to the ship. North and I went to persuade the Blackbird. It was time to leave.

He was nearly dead when we got to him. He sat astraddle Kim's body. The Blackbird had cut his wrists with a great deal of care. The cuts were just deep enough to give a steady, but not gushing, flow of blood. The Blackbird was dripping the blood into the chest wound of the corpse, as though trying to resurrect Kim. He must have been at it for a quite a while. The Blackbird was so weak from loss of blood that he could not struggle. He stared at us dumbly as we stopped the blood and yelled for a medic.

Blackbird was airlifted out. He was sent to a hospital, then to a detention center while his wrists healed. He was discharged for mental disability said to exist prior to his enlistment. No pension. No disability payments. The military, which views routine destruction as a rational process, stands aghast when the subject is suicide.

For some years I received strange postcards from the Blackbird. Sometimes the only message was the drawing of a black face, a black feather. Sometimes he drew flowers or cactus. The postcards came from Reno, Salt Lake, Pocatello; well, the postcards came from all over the West. Once he wrote that he was teaching horses how to fight cowboys. His messages were scrawled in crayon.

And that is the history, except for a little tidying up.

I represented North at his court-martial. He received a month's restriction to the ship, a one-half forfeiture of pay for that month. I was transferred to a small boat basin. A reprimand went with me. My fitness reports stated that I was totally inept at logistics. The reports did admit that I knew how to fire rockets. Tidying up. In the years that followed, I saw North once, on a visit he made to San Francisco. I kept in touch with the Blackbird by mail. Some vague thought of friendship or of penance—something—kept me writing to him.

I figured that sooner or later he would need a lawyer.

It was raining lightly when I passed Portland and out of Oregon, then entered the Far Northwest. The State of Washington seemed intent on showing its most somber tones. The highways were beaten and slick. Dark fir forests were cut here and there with a fainter darkness of alder and madrona. The coast road ran past beaches. It took a long loop into dripping forests as it bypassed an Indian reservation.

It is a rare day, even in summer, when that coast does not get rain. Seals and seabirds appeared like spirits from the coastal mist. Huge rocks stood like ancient tombstones, water-worn testimonials to the twenty thousand years of human life and death that have muttered through this rain. An eternity of rain stained the roofs of cabins, and moss covered the cedar shingles of cabins like thick watch caps. The cabins were shrouded. The land was shrouded.

In the small town the Chinese owner of a sagging and weather-worn restaurant gave me directions to North's house. The Oriental face, here, in a place wetter than the Everglades, was a small shock but not a surprise. Chinese have been on this coast for more than a century; as have Japanese and Taiwanese. The Orientals arrived as bond slaves. They were excellent workers. Enslaved Indians were not.

In late afternoon, and beneath dark and raining skies, North's house was a small beacon in the darkness of the surrounding forest. Every light in the place was glowing. The potholed lane to the house was overhung with branches. Water filled the ditches and in one place crossed the lane. I parked beside an old pickup that was connected to a new horse trailer. Painted on the door of the truck was a cartoon head of a surprised bird. The truck's body was a patched-together shack. It looked like a tent made of shingles; but knowing the Blackbird, was certain it did not leak.

I stepped from the car. There was movement at the edge of the forest.

A deep memory of movement in the jungle automatically pushed me down. I knelt beside the car, onto my knees in wet soil. The pistol was packed in my luggage. Defenseless. Then, remembering where I was, silently cursing the forest and myself, I stood back up.

There were sounds coming from the edge of the forest. A small dark figure stood beside a bulk that moved, stopped, moved. The darkness of the forest was intense, but not intense enough to cover the solid blackness of those two figures. Then a miniature spot of white, like fluorescence, darted between the two figures. It moved like a hand.

"This is no fit place," the Blackbird said. "We'll be out of here in a couple of days."

He stepped from the background of the forest, leading a large black horse with white stockings. The horse was giant, but it moved light-footed and gracefully. It looked stern. Wary. "Stay away from this horse," the Blackbird said conversationally, "he's a meat-eater."

I watched as the Blackbird loaded the horse back into the trailer, then rubbed it down. It looked likely that the horse would be more comfortable than any of us. There was enough room in that dry trailer for two horses.

The Blackbird's right hand was white, like a hand dipped in flour. He was wet. Water soaked his Western hat and his jeans jacket. Water had glistened on the dark hide of the horse. In the growing darkness, the only thing finally visible was that skeletal hand.

"You brought a horse," I said, speaking into the darkness. "All the way from Montana?"

"I got nothing against Montana," the Blackbird said easily. "It's just that nobody else can handle this 'un." He gestured back to the horse. "I'm saving Montana some trouble." He closed the rear of the trailer.

"I'll be along directly," he said to the horse. He turned. "You never know how much they understand," he said. "I always tell him how long it'll be."

He took off his hat. His hair was a thick braid. Feathers were interwoven in the braid; black feathers, crow, raven. The two watches looked oversize on the narrow wrists. He knocked water from the hat. The white hand was not all white. The tattooing traced along the skeletal structure. Some unknown tattoo artist was a genius. The bones seemed to lie above the surface of the hand, the flesh under the bones. The watch built for combat was a thick, low-glowing lump above the whiteness. His left hand was not as dark as the rest of him. Later on, I would see that it was tattooed the color of Kim's face.

"I'd rather be seeing you in San Francisco," the Blackbird said, "but since it's here, I'm glad anyway." The Blackbird does not lie, and so he was glad.

"Sure," I said. "San Francisco. But since we're here . . ."

"C'mon to the truck. We won't be going in there for a while." He motioned toward North's house, then walked toward the truck.

It was no bad thing to sit in the cab of that truck. Smells of oil and harness and horse dung had soaked the worn seat covers. One windshield was cracked. The gearshift knob was a carved blackbird.

"Why not?" I asked, and pointed toward North's house. I looked through the rain-running windshields at the rain-covered forest. The truck cab was dry.

"The doctor figures North is going to die," Blackbird said, and he said it like a joke. "The preacher figures North is going to hell. North is sorta resisting."

"Drinking?"

"I doubt I'd want to do it sober, myself." Blackbird chuckled. "Or maybe I would. If a man gets too crocked, he'd lose all interest. You can see how that would go."

"Drinking now?"

The Blackbird laughed. "He's sitting in there with a fifth and that blamed old .45. He's all set to shoot something. Best if it isn't us."

"Himself. Shoot himself?"

"Nope," Blackbird said. "North never did amount to much, and he sure don't amount to *that* much." The white hand rested on the gearshift. "I've heard of folks having ghosts," he said, "but I never knew a man to have a whole kyoodle of 'em."

"I told him to stay sober," I said. Then I felt like a man confessed to prudishness.

"He *was* sober when I got here. Minute I got here, he felt real safe." The Blackbird laughed, almost giddily. "Safe," he said, chuckling.

"I don't know a thing about horses," I said.

"I don't know a thing about anything else," Blackbird said. "I *think* I know things. I *think* I know just *heaps*. But all I can guarantee is horses."

And then, suddenly, we were both laughing. We were hysterical with the laughter. Laughed in each other's faces. We ho-ho'ed and hee-hee'd, like schoolgirls at a slumber party. We giggled, chortled, yelped with laughter. I mentioned that there was a man in that house, a man who had saved both our lives at one time or another, a dying man. That made us laugh even harder. The Blackbird slapped his knees, slapped mine. We went yuk, yuk, and whoo, whoo. We banged with our fists on the dashboard. Tears came from the laughter. I hugged the Blackbird, as if the Bird were a solid post to which I could cling and not fall into a faint from the laughter.

"Maybe it's the rain," the Blackbird said with a chuckle. "Maybe you got to either laugh or hit somebody." He wiped tears. "Fool," he said. "Our boy figures that Buddhist monk he shot is coming for him. Figures the Buddhist is bringing all his relations."

I sat giggling into the darkness and rain. Maybe death was coming to North, but not in the form of a Buddhist monk. A monk would be indifferent to all that.

"Those people have a lot of relatives," I said; and I tried to say it soberly but still had to swallow a chuckle. "North needn't worry about the Buddhist, just the next of kin."

Blackbird rolled down the window. He stared toward North's house. "He'll pass out directly."

"Something that isn't funny . . ." I said. "This is the first time we've been together when there was no combat." It was a little surprising to think that.

The Blackbird straightened, poked a finger at the rain. "You been living too soft," he muttered, suddenly serious. "Don't let down."

North was a big man. It took a lot of whiskey to put him away. When night came on and the forest turned black, the Blackbird drove me, truck and horse, into town. We parked between logging trucks and ate dinner in a weather-worn hotel. We spoke together like brothers. People around us glanced at the Blackbird's hand and continued chewing: salmon, steak, potatoes. Loggers burped, yawned, scratched their armpits. An Indian waitress and a Chinese waiter made silent crossing patterns around the tables. Along the bar some awfully young drunks, and a few awfully old ones, muttered to each other or gambled on punchboards. The people were indifferent to the Blackbird's hand, and to the feathers in his braided hair. I thought better of the people, if not the place. This is still the frontier, I told myself; or something very much like it.

The Blackbird had a story. He had drifted through both the plains and the mountainous West. He made his living from trading out of his truck ("I got a masterpiece inventory. I got tack and shotgun shells and gimcracks . . . got car parts and rope and mostly legal stuff"). And he made his living by befriending horses no one else could handle ("I got a *way* with them") and working an occasional rodeo ("With never no more than a busted collarbone—not bad for a boy from Philadelphia"). He won races at county fairs, riding that giant horse. Because he won races, he won bets.

"I been nosing around," the Blackbird said. "After North commenced nursing that bottle, I exercised the horse. There's a trail back of North's house. Leads up into the jungle . . ." He grinned at his mistake. "Leads up into the forest."

The Blackbird chewed steak and looked like a man sitting on a thunderous joke. "The fool," he said about North. "His guilts have brought that boy back to the one place he shouldn't ever be. There's two graveyards up there. Indian and Chinese. I don't care for either one of 'em. But that Indian one is special."

The Indian graveyard was filled with elaborately carved cedar rails fashioned to imitate enormous beds. The rails surrounded the Indian graves. The dead were buried in symbolic beds.

"In pretty good shape," the Blackbird said, "considering the rain. Looks like a sort of weird furniture store. Got slugs and moss and spiders. The beds are all decorated with them. Got these great big snails and white worms." He chewed, slurped at coffee, and the feathers in his braided hair gleamed in the fluorescent light of the restaurant. "It all seems pretty honest when you see it that way," he said. "All them slugs and things. I got this kind of calm feeling, like death is okay. Don't like that feeling. We all know *that* ain't right."

"It might not be a bad feeling," I told him. "Sooner

or later it all comes to that. Might feel all right if you could think of dying as a calm feeling."

The Blackbird looked at me in a way that said he worried about me. "You been living way too easy," he said. "And you haven't seen that other graveyard." The Blackbird mopped gravy with a piece of bread. He looked around the room, looked at the Chinese waiter, then looked through the windows into the night. He checked the time on the combat watch. "Let's go see if there's anything left of our boy."

North was passed out and snoring in a chair when we entered the house. A wood fire lay dying in a fireplace. When we switched off some of the lights, the fire became the focus of the room, a comment of darkened coal and ash. Outside, the dripping forest was painted with darkness, a wall of darkness.

I had not seen North in a long time. Beneath the remaining lights his face was red, his hair white; and breath gargled from his throat in sobbing snores. He was dressed in work clothes, booted, wearing a fisherman's coat. In his hand, which lay in his lap, the .45 automatic was dark and oiled. Except for the sleep and the stink of booze, North was a man dressed and armed for action. A man ready to rush into the night. What was he intending to do? Shoot a ghost?

Blackbird fed up the fire. "There's a couple of rooms upstairs," he said. "Take one. I'm going to sleep with the horse." He began searching the house, looking in closets. I stood watching North. The Blackbird was gone for several minutes, rummaging through the kitchen and the upstairs rooms. He returned carrying an old .30-.30 carbine and three kitchen knives. "I'll keep these beside me," he said. "That way, if North berserks, the worst he can do is smack you with a broom."

"He's that far gone?" I was ready to go back to the hotel and take a room.

Blackbird picked up the nearly empty fifth. "I figure you got time for a night's sleep," he said. "I make him to wake up come noon tomorrow." He walked to North. "Or maybe never."

The Blackbird reached toward North, took the .45 from his hand. He stood above North, a small black figure befeathered but contemplative. He seemed to be musing over the effects of history and combat and booze. Blackbird ejected the magazine from the .45, but he did not work the slide. Maybe there was a bullet in the pistol's chamber, maybe not. It all depended on how good North was at soldiering. You do not arm your weapon before you need it.

The Blackbird cocked the piece. He placed the barrel beneath North's chin, pointed at the throat. Smiled. Giggled. Laughed. Lowered the gun and turned to me.

"See this, here?" He indicated North. "We came all this way to help *'is man."

"What are you doing?" I said. "Cut the clowning."

"I'm a·gambler," the Blackbird said. He watched North's flushed face, listened to the breath snorting from North's mouth. "I owe this man a debt, and he owes me. Let's leave North's ghosts to settle us up." The Blackbird did not look insane. He was standing easily, mildly humorous, resigned to some imagined fate that I could not divine.

"It sorts out like this," the Blackbird said. "If there's a shell in this chamber, then North is gone. He's got no more problems. I'll have taken care of him and paid my debt." He looked at me. "You understand that?"

"North doesn't want to die," I said.

"Who does? He doesn't want to live in hell, either. But death or hell are all the choices this boy's got."

Flames were beginning to lick the new wood in the fireplace. The flames were tentative, searching for the easiest area of combustion. In my mind lay an old darkness, cut with flames. "What do you mean?" I said desperately. "What do you mean, let the ghosts decide?" I was stalling for time.

The Blackbird's face gradually woke into a slow smile. Maybe a smile cannot be called historic, but this was a smile filled with memories. "I'm gonna talk here for a minute about Kim," the Blackbird said. "Kim was a man."

North snored. The new fire crackled. Night seemed to press against the windows.

"You know why Kim contacted the enemy?" Blackbird asked. "You ever think about why Kim called down fire?"

"I've thought about it. They weren't good thoughts. So I stopped thinking."

The Blackbird gestured to the dark windows, to the black night. "That's our hearts," he said in a general way. "Our hearts were flat as those windows."

"We were little more than kids. We were in combat."

"*We* were the enemy," the Blackbird said. "We enemized everything: the dead, and the children, and all them others." He looked down at North. "And with never a lick of respect."

The light was growing as fire stood brilliantly in the new logs. Shadows flickered on the wall like spirits. In my mind, deep from the darkness of my mind, figures began to walk. Then the figures began to fall, clutching guts or grabbing at faces that were alight with flames. "Don't," I whispered. "Don't do this." And I meant: Don't make me recall. Just shoot North and get this over. But don't make me recall.

"We were looking at the face of something powerful'," the Blackbird said. "Something mighty old. We didn't even know it."

"Shoot him," I whispered. "Don't talk." I stood shocked, desperate, a willing conspirator in murder; a man betraying a friend. Echoes of rockets seemed to fill the room.

"These ghosts," the Blackbird said easily, "are hungry. They are the spirits of hunger. Kim knew. They'll never feel no peace. Ever. This here"—and he laid the pistol beside North's head—"this here is a blessing for this man. The worst it does, maybe, is send him to his preacher's hell."

The words caused me to gain some self-control. After all, the Blackbird was insane. I was being per-

suaded by insanity. "We've already been there," I
said. "Only one hell to a customer."

"Those ghosts are always lonesome. Always hungry.
They are hungry for food and booze and sex. They are
hungry for some kind of god somewhere. Hungry for
sleep and pretty things, and hungry for stars and being
warm." The Blackbird's voice was an incantation. "Hungry for sunlight and kinfolk and laughing with friends.
They are starving for all those things and blowing
across the world forever, howling and hungry." He
turned to me. "They scream a lot. They just wail and
wail. Kim said so." He looked at North. "And they
are hungry for this man. They will make him one of
them, and they will still be hungry."

"Shoot," I said. The fire crackled. When rockets
fall into the jungle, flame spreads. Mostly, though, it
goes straight up, a steeple of fire pointing diabolic
praise to heaven.

"Shoot," I whispered.

The Blackbird looked at me curiously. The black
weapon glowed dull in the spectral white hand. Blackbird looked around the room, held the pistol to North's
temple, paused. "It'll make a mess," he said, "and
this would make a nice little house for somebody. Best
if we just mess up the chair." He moved the pistol to
North's chest, felt for the exact spot, and the hammer
went click against an empty chamber.

The Blackbird stood looking at North. "Pretty good
soldiering," he said. He threw the .45 on North's lap.
"I've got the magazine," he said to me. "Things'll be
safe around here."

He walked to the door, turned back, looked at
North. The Blackbird checked the time on one watch,
then checked the time on the other. He looked more
serious than he had when he pulled the trigger. "You
got to understand about time," he said, and he sounded
like a teacher leveling with a favorite student. "There's
all the time there is, all the time."

I was confused.

"There's the time when North is a ghost," he said,
"and there's a time when he isn't. Only mystery about

the whole thing was whether he was actually gonna be a ghost." The Blackbird showed me the watches. "There's the time when you weren't a lawyer and the time when you are. There's the time when you weren't born and the time when you're dead. All them times are scampering. Right now. Like the mouse on this watch."

He opened the door, turned back, looked at North. "You shouldn't've laughed," he said to North's sleeping figure. "Everybody did bad things, but you were the man that laughed."

Blackbird stepped into the night. I crossed the room, watching through the window. In the darkness, nothing could be seen but that spectral hand; and it was soon swallowed in darkness. I turned back to North, the man who still snored because he was good at soldiering. I had not expected him to be that good.

"Whatever happens," I said, "remember that the Blackbird tried to help." The thought came that sometimes it is no bad thing to be insane.

The rain stopped sometime during the night. I slept the sleep of combat; it does not allow the luxury of dreams. A part of the mind pays attention for each whisper, each footfall. I was surprised to awake refreshed, but with an accompanying depression. I had been a willing coconspirator to murder. The murder had not happened, but that made no difference. In a dawn of blown clouds my complicity seemed a gauge of madness. I had once again discovered that when you live beside madness, you become mad.

Thick clouds blew before a freshening wind, and the forest turned from black to the sullen darkness of a stormy day. I made coffee, sat in the kitchen, slurped the coffee, and watched through the window. North had rolled from the chair. Now he snored as he lay at full length on the carpet.

No one—except Blackbird, and maybe North—could understand the gift the Blackbird had offered. In a sane world it was an insane gift. All the nicey-nice people would lift hands in horror, would cover their eyes. The sanitary people would insist that North go to a hospital, be needled and probed and sliced and oxygenated; preserved through a sort of medical embalming against whatever was killing him. The nicey-nice people, so busy at *not* dying that they are too busy to live, would insist that North's ghosts were an aberration of psychology.

Kim knew the ghosts were real. North seemed to know it. That was enough to justify, and give praise to, the Blackbird's action. Because insanity causes its own reality. If the ghosts were real to North—and they were clearly more real than most people's sense of their gods—then the ghosts were real.

The Blackbird appeared on horseback. The figures emerged in the lane. They were figures of black on black. It was hard to understand how a man from the slums of Philadelphia could gain complete wisdom of horses. Yet Blackbird looked knitted, not sculptured. He was of a single piece with that horse—a painting, art, or this: he looked somehow like the dreams of men. The primitive energy, and the unconscious power of that man on that horse, made him look the way all of us have *wished* we could look when we were young.

When he broke into a brief run, the horse stretched like a wave. It was agile and godlike. I wondered how the Blackbird could even get someone to bet against him when he raced such a horse. He rode to the house. He tied the horse to a post that held up a sagging porch. I expected him to enter the house. Instead, he leaned against the post and spoke to the horse. He seemed to be having a conversation. A flicker of memory spread painful fingers in my mind, a memory of the Blackbird lying beside Kim's corpse, conversing.

After an hour, several things happened at once. I called my office. A strange voice answered. Miss Molly was not at work, the voice said. The voice claimed it belonged to some temporary helper service. I felt slight indignation.

Miss Molly, the voice said, was tending her father, who was ill.

"Are you a person?" I asked. "I'm not talking to a computer?"

The voice gave a name. Cynthia Seymour or Lydia Claymore. Something. Then, in sanitary tones, the voice said *Mrs.* Claymore or Seymour.

"Not *Mrs.* Computer?" It was not a sarcastic question.

The voice sniffed.

"This is the boss," I recall muttering. "Take messages until Molly returns. Do nothing else. Don't even open mail."

The voice advised me that temporary helper people were skillfully trained.

Behind me, North began to thrash around. Then he began to moan. The Blackbird had finished speaking to the horse. He drifted into the kitchen and headed for the coffeepot.

"Open mail if you must," I told the voice. "Flush the toilet when necessary. But don't *do* anything. Make no decisions." I hung up with an uneasy feeling. Reality and unreality kept shifting in my mind.

North handled his hangover with a good deal of skill. He bumbled into the kitchen, poured coffee and fruit juice and water and beer. He sipped the coffee, gulped from the glasses, and his pale Scandinavian face was a portrait that would frighten a coroner. The face seemed washed by rain. Death was painted in the eyes. The cheeks sagged with death, and death smoothed his already smooth forehead. His hands trembled. The coffee cup clicked against his teeth. When he smiled—and, incredibly, he did smile—the smile was like a flicker of vanishing life swallowed in the death mask of that face.

"Couple more beers," he said, "and this mess will get straight." He looked at me like a man judging a car he might buy, like a man about to kick tires, a man thinking of a deal. "Thanks for making the trip." His voice was half humorous, deprecating, and hung over. "You drove right into hell's half acre."

"You're gonna throw up," the Blackbird said. "Can't mix that much juice with that much beer."

"That's why I'm doing it. Cleans the system." North seemed to be trying to ignore the Blackbird. He seemed nearly apologetic.

"It's your throw-up," the Blackbird said. "Just point it where it don't get controversial."

The Blackbird reached in his shirt pocket. He threw the loaded .45 magazine on the table. "Next time, mind your manners," he said.

"It got that bad?" North slugged juice, slugged beer.

We three ex-warriors sat around the kitchen table that was covered with green oilcloth. The .45 magazine lay on the table. The Blackbird flicked it hard with an index finger. The magazine spun, pointed toward North. "Spin the bottle," the Blackbird said. "You're one down." Blackbird spun the magazine again. "You're one down," he told me. He looked at North.

"We can't be having any lies around here," he said. "I tried to shoot you last night." The Blackbird's face is proportioned to the rest of him, which means it is small. The forehead bulges slightly, but the lips are thin. The voice coming from those lips was conversational.

North looked at me, then at Blackbird. His water-smooth face was dull and unsurprised. Light from the kitchen window glowed softly on the bullet that pressed against the top lip of the magazine.

"You must not have tried very hard," North said. "Not sure what I think about you fouling up." He placed pale hands on the table, pushed himself into a standing position. "This juice is doing its good work. I'll be right back." He headed for the bathroom.

North was never a stupid man. Although cunning, he had no great reputation for lying. He was dying. His face was a shroud behind which countless and awful emotions must have already fought. It seemed to me that he was handling matters pretty well.

Outside, the horse stomped, seemed to be sighing to itself.

"They know," the Blackbird said about the horse. "That one has wanted no part of this since we got here."

The room actually became darker when North returned. Clouds blew in layers. Up there in a gusty firmament, clouds were painting the forest with darkness.

"It'll breeze like this. Come mid-afternoon, it will commence to blow. Then we'll get a couple days of broken clouds." North took his seat at the table. Sipped beer. "The Blackbird hates this place," he said to me, and he spoke as if Blackbird was not sitting beside him. "It's home," he said. "I fished these waters since I was a kid. A man ought to be allowed to die at home."

The horse made snuffling noises. Then it gave a low whinny. Blackbird stood. "You'd be better off doing it in St. Louis," he said. He walked to the door. "His dander is up," he said about the horse. "I've got to level that poor fella out, or he'll drag the house down." He stepped outside.

"What is the problem?" I asked North. "You said over the phone that you needed a safe place to die."

"Spirit fences," North said. "It's a long story."

It was not a particularly long story. In the last century Chinese moved in and caused a graveyard. They did not mean to do it, but they had no idea that they were enlisted as bond slaves to work at processing lime. The work was cruel. Their death rate was appalling. They were buried in that graveyard, and with little hope that their bones would ever be returned to China.

"Folks around here," North said, "never paid it any mind. That graveyard sat there for seventy years. The fences would decay, and somebody would fix them. Folks pretty much mind their own business. The Chinese stay to themselves and do Chinese things. Blackbird says I shouldn't've come home, but Chinese never had any power around here before."

Outside in the narrow clearing, the Blackbird was exercising the horse. Blackbird had the horse on a long tether. The horse was galloping or trotting—or whatever horses do—in a wide circle. The black animal seemed to blend in, then flash from, the black spaces of the forest. The white stockings moved brilliantly, as accurate as the Blackbird's hands.

North still looked pale. But now he was no longer in resigned control. His hands were shaking again. "I never did anything to those people," he said. "I never tore up those graves."

Two decades before, when North and Blackbird and I were in the jungle, Satanic cults in San Francisco began paying a hundred dollars apiece for human skulls.

"Nobody around here did it," North said. "Maybe some people from Oregon. Maybe some San Francisco people."

"So the fences are down again." Feelings of fire, of rocketry, lay in my mind. Beyond the windows, the black horse trotted like a circus horse. Insanity seemed the only normal way of looking at things. I envied the Blackbird.

"It isn't just the fences," North said. "The grave robbers didn't even backfill. Bones exposed. It's all covered with fir needles now, but the graves are holes. Water standing in some." North looked absolutely indignant. "I had nothing to do with it. I wasn't even *around* here at the time."

He looked at me, and then there was supplication in the look. There was also cunning. "I killed a monk," he said. "That guy is coming for me. I hear them up there whispering and squalling. They wail. They do it around the house at night." North was trying to speak matter-of-factly, but his voice trembled, and so did his hands.

"That monk did not have to die," I said. "He was proving a point. You saw monks over there. Sometimes they sat in the paths of tanks. You saw the tanks move into a higher gear. That monk was protesting."

Beyond the windows, the black horse circled, circled, as though it were the second hand on an enormous watch.

"I was the guy who let him do it." North popped open another can of beer, looked at it. "You don't get the d.t.'s until you *stop* drinking," he explained. "It ain't d.t.'s. It's real voices, or at least I think so. And that's why I asked you guys here," he said. "The Blackbird is insane. You are sane. I need some other ways of seeing this, because my judgment is gone."

The man looked pitiful. He was for every intent and purpose dead. The dark skies beyond the window were a frame for a face that was already ghostly. I wished I could get him so drunk the alcohol would kill him. The thought came and left.

"The spirits start wailing at sunset," North said. "At least *I* can hear them. If you, and if Blackbird, *both* hear them, then God help me." He tried to shrug, then drank instead. "My only other chance is to take my boat into deep water and drown." He tapped a pale finger on the oilcloth. "Be a shame," he said. "There's a couple of young fellows around here could use that boat." The look of cunning did not leave his face. North made me feel that he was running a confidence game.

"Don't be so sure that I am sane." It was the only honest reply. "I was all right before I got here." Then I thought of something. "Why didn't the grave robbers tear up the Indian graveyard?"

"When you see it, you'll *feel* why," North said.

The Indian graveyard explained itself better than North, or even Blackbird, could explain. We passed it as we ascended to the Chinese graveyard. But that happened later on, toward sunset.

North drank more beer, forced down some food, and slept. Blackbird did minor work on his truck. When he opened the door of the shacklike truck body, the first thing visible was a row of rifles. "Make a lot of money swapping guns and stuff," Blackbird said.

When I approached the horse, it struck forward with a front hoof. The strike was sharp, deft; the hoof smacked the ground like a hammer.

"He won't make friends," the Blackbird told me. "Don't get stupid and walk behind him."

I had never looked *carefully* at a horse before. This animal showed me nothing about horses, only something about itself. It was as precise as a hawk. It carried the energy and power that can focus so quickly in huge animals. I imagined this horse fighting a grizzly and could see no end to such a fight; at least, no ending that would not leave both beasts dead. This horse was as frightening as elemental force—strong winds or storms, gale force, volcanic.

"He don't much get along with other horses, either." The Blackbird was cleaning spark plugs. Grease from the engine stained his hands. The white hand floated above the engine, deft in the shadowed compartment. "He's not even much of a ladies' man."

Then movement began in the forest. At least, it seemed that movement was going on in there. I no longer trusted my sanity.

"I expect it's Indian ghost stuff," the Blackbird said. "Goes on all the time in Montana. Don't give it a nevermind." Blackbird worked with his back to the forest. He was actually humming as he tightened spark plugs.

Movement in the jungle is almost always felt, not seen. When you watch for it, you may be sure you will not see it. Movement in the jungle is picked up sometimes at the edge of vision. More often, it is picked up by a feeling in the belly, or a chill that starts in the spine. Twice during the afternoon I nearly hit the deck, expecting the rake of gunfire.

The Blackbird finished with the spark plugs. He crawled beneath the truck. "I told you not to let down," he said, "but, man, you are starting to fly. Don't get too high." His voice echoed, and the wind that North had predicted was beginning as a light breeze. "It pays to pay attention," Blackbird said, "but not to that forest."

Memories and compulsions were congregating. For years I had discarded thoughts, reasoned out my position on bad memories. Now I pulled my pistol from the luggage, a little peashooter .38 of the kind favored by judges and attorneys. There are a lot of these snub-noses all through the law business. We pretend they don't exist. But then, we try divorces and assaults and sanity hearings; and we pretend that human emotions are objective—that, for the purpose of law, emotions do not exist. We thus own .38s.

A part of my mind knew it was gripped by old madness, but the madness had its own genius. It kept picking up movement in the forest.

"If it *is* Chinese," the Blackbird said, "I doubt they're after you. If you get too wired, you'll get all wore out." His voice echoed from beneath the truck. He was talking to himself. "Ought to get another ten thousand miles from this clutch . . . old truck . . . don't owe me nothing."

In mid-afternoon, the wind picked up and blew steadily. The forest came alive. Fir tops and cedar tops moved a hundred feet above our heads. Spatters of rain colored them. The Blackbird finished fooling with the truck. North stepped from his house. He was booted, dressed in work clothes, and wore an old down jacket.

"This is August," the Blackbird said. "Don't it ever, *ever* get warm around here?"

"Happens sometimes," North said. "But not so often you come to expect it." He looked at me, at the way I was dressed. "Pretty dandy outfit," he said. "There's old coats and stuff hanging in the pantry." Then he looked at the forest. The treetops still moved. Lower, in the darkness, the movement now seemed random; like nearly invisible targets popping up and down at a shooting gallery. "Go away," he said to the forest. His voice was trembling. "You see that," he said to the Blackbird. "Tell me you don't see that."

Blackbird leaned against his truck. On the door of the truck, the picture of the surprised bird seemed suddenly amusing. I could imagine a time when Blackbird had painted the picture, could imagine him chuckling as he laughed at himself.

"I'm with a bunch of crazies," Blackbird said. "You guys are spooked. The horse is spooked. You crazies have gone and gotten the forest spooked. Of course I see it. Why not?"

"I won't swear that I see it," I told North, "but if I *do* see it, then it's been going on for quite a while."

"How can a man be dying when he don't even feel hurt?" North said. "I walk as good as ever. Got no pain in the gut." He seemed trying to convince himself that the whole business was a charade. He pulled the .45 from a jacket pocket and worked the slide. He placed the pistol to his face and looked down the barrel.

"Hello, old friend," he said to the pistol, "you want to take another ride?"

"Hard to shoot yourself in the nose with a .45" the Blackbird said conversationally. "You about have to tape down that rear safety."

"I got flexible hands," North said. He spun, crouched, and let off a shot into the forest. The boom of the heavy pistol engulfed the clearing, was swallowed in the forest. North let off another shot. The forest stood dark, unmoved but moving.

The horse stomped. Whinnied. It tugged hard at reins tied to the porch. The porch roof shook.

"You do that again," the Blackbird said, "and you don't need to worry about no Chinese." He moved across the clearing, birdlike, a flicker of dark light. He stood by the horse's head, talking to the horse.

"You might be better off drowning," I said to North. "All three of us have lost our senses."

North looked at the forest. "It will be sunset in an hour. Might as well get it over with." He shucked the magazine, then shucked the shell in the chamber. He was stalling, intentionally wasting time. I clucked and cautioned, while Blackbird complained. North went to the house, insisted that we eat. He protested that we must hurry and then held back.

When we finally entered the forest, North led. I followed. The Blackbird walked at the rear. He led the horse.

North complained bitterly about the horse. The Blackbird told him that the horse was spooked, that it was North's fault; and that if North could not handle it, the Blackbird would fix matters so that North *could* handle it. We carried waterproof flashlights, and the Blackbird carried a small duffel. The horse carried a pack. By the time we returned, the forest would be wrapped in night.

The gradually rising trail was wide. With care, two men might walk it side by side. "It narrows after the Indian graveyard," North said.

No description could really prepare me for that place. It was scattered across the face of the hill. Trees were thinned. Large grandfather trees rose into the wind and blowing mist. The color was red, russet, from cedar that towered into the decaying daylight. Red, like the fur of a wet fox or the soft auburn of decaying maple leaves.

The graveyard was a grove in which tangles of salal and vine maple crisscrossed in flowing patterns. Wind moved through the leaves, although this deep in the forest, the wind was shattered and inconstant. High in the tops of the trees, the wind was steady, and it was blowing a gale.

Headstones leaned or had fallen flat. The bedlike structures—some of them ornate—glistened with the rusty color of red cedar. It was not like a furniture store at all. The enormous beds were at many angles and distances. They were not in rows, although where families were buried, some were in clusters. Cedar and fir boughs lay as fresh decorations across the enormous beds. It seemed that the storm was ornamenting the graveyard as it tugged branches from trees and dropped them into the forest.

"You feel it?" The Blackbird was talking to me, or to the horse.

"A dead man could feel it," I whispered.

Power lay calmly across the graveyard. The power was so evident, so serene, that even if my mind were not in a frenzy, I would still feel the power. In fact, as the power became omnipotent, my frenzy faded. Tranquillity. Calm. Peace. Nothing foul could enter here.

North was becoming nervous. I could not understand why.

"It's a trick," he said, and seemed to be speaking to the forest. "A man dies here and you send ravens, don't you? Don't you?" He stopped, looked back at me and Blackbird.

"Don't be fooled," he said. "I know Indians, know their ways. They control ravens and crows, and they get fancy on revenge." His face was pale in the gathering dark, a white moon of a face rising against the red background of the graveyard. "You feel it waiting there? Feel it waiting? They control owls and rats and anything that bites."

"What did you ever do to Indians?"

The Blackbird was actually grinning. The white hand rested on the horse's neck as we stopped. The white hand gestured, seemed to float toward the graveyard. "Indians don't care about you. Listen to how quiet it is. Just *hear* how much they don't care about you."

"People experimented," North said. "Back in the old days. These Indians have got cousins laid out here and up above. There's Chinese Indians, but no Indian Chinese, because"—and he breathed in sobbing snorts, fear-ridden, and finally yelling—"because there wasn't no Chinese *women*." To North the matter was strangely important. It was easy to see just how far his fear and his fantasies had carried him.

"I know lots about Indians." The Blackbird tried to answer seriously, tried not to giggle. "These people are tending their own fences. You're just one more crazy white man. Don't mean nothin' to them." Blackbird dropped his hand, urged the horse forward. "Get along," he said to me and North, "or I'll let go of these reins."

The graveyard was a quiet presence at our backs as we climbed. I followed North, knowing now that he was insane with his fear; a gulf of fear, a chasm. I followed him and waited for him to stumble, to fall, to plead to some Scandinavian god. To pray for storms or the sanctuary of crosses, of angel's wings. A prayer in stained glass, a prayer for burial inside a church.

The trail narrowed. Low-sweeping fir and maple branches brushed the horse's flanks. The strip of sky above the trail was red and distant, a narrow band above a land of wind and growing darkness. North stumbled forward. Movement began in the forest.

I paused, looked back down the trail. The Indian graveyard was obscured by trees and encroaching darkness.

"You see that?" North whispered. "You *see* it?"

"I see it," I said, and I was whispering as well. The movement was as deft as the flicker of bat wings. It was a movement of pale shadows. It appeared and disappeared right on the edge of vision. If the Blackbird's white hand was magic—if it could suddenly appear and disappear in all of the places where eyes were not looking—then that would describe the shadows.

"Whoa up," Blackbird said.

The horse was not shying, but it was focused. It looked the way a horse must look just before a race. The animal was huge. A great, dark bulk filling the narrow trail. Its breath was heavy, the sound like a promise of power layering the darkness and the red gloom of the trail. If the horse decided to break, the Blackbird would be flung like a wadded piece of carbon paper. North and I probably could not dive from the trail quickly enough. We would be trampled.

"No talk," the Blackbird said. "I have to get this poor fellow to that clearing. Quick and quiet. You people know what to do. You been in the jungle."

The word hung like a sudden fury in my mind. *Jungle.* My pattern of movement changed. Which is to say, I accepted the sanity of an old madness. In combat there is no sanity, only useful ways of being insane. Insanity is the only way to survive, and insanity forces its own patterns of movement.

We went rapidly up that trail, and our feet were silent. Our feet knew where to place themselves. Our feet did not kick branches, pebbles. They did not skid on wet soil. Jungle. Combat.

We entered the Chinese graveyard more silently than whispers. Light drained from the forest, like a riptide between rocks. The sun must already have been on the horizon.

There was no peace there. Only violation. In this graveyard there was a state of war.

Pale remnants of spirit fences rose crazily on broken angles above the forest debris. Graves stood nearly erect on the steep hillside, as if the dead had been buried on deliberately uncomfortable angles. The excavated graves were like empty faces, stripped bones. The hill was so steep, one imagined that dead men had stood in congregations. It was a huge graveyard, a lot larger than the Indian graveyard. The Chinese had been in these parts for a hundred years, more or less, and the Indians for twenty thousand; and yet this was a graveyard that seemed as large as the antiquity of all suffering.

"That's why the skulls survived, why they were worth digging," I murmured. "The hillside graves drain. That's a mostly dry hillside in the middle of a rain forest."

Some of the more favored graves were situated along breaks in the hill. When they were interred, the corpses had lain flat. Now stagnant water stood in those torn graves. In the decay—of light and the putridity of stagnant water and debris—total darkness would seem a blessing.

"No matter your fear," I whispered to North. "Nothing makes it right for you to have brought us here. Man, of all places on earth, this is the place where you should *not* be."

Spirit fences are not huge. Many are no taller than the ornamental fences gardeners place around their flowers. The power of the fence is the power of symbol; and here, the symbols were a chaos of killed voices. The symbols denoted the death of delicacy, of faith, of love, trust, respect, honor, memory. Some of the fences had been intricately carved. I directed my flashlight here, there. A fragment lay almost at my feet (was I standing on a grave?) and the fragment—four or five inches of paint-flaked and faded scrap wood—carried such finite and patient carving that it represented years of skill and hours of work.

Enough natural light remained that the flashlight beam was diffused. But I clung to the flashlight. In this place, it was more precious than fire, weapons, food. In this place, it meant survival. A way to get out.

"Pretty quick now," North whispered. His voice trembled. "I pray to God that I hear those voices just because of the d.t.'s—or just from being crazy. Maybe you guys won't hear them." His voice sounded as if he were trying to be sincere but was making a bad job of it.

Blackbird stood silent. He was memorizing the terrain.

There were no trees in the graveyard, except for a few old snags. The wind blew over the lip of the surrounding forest. It poured against the hillside, churned among the violated graves.

The chaos of a battlefield comes not from corpses but from disarray. Trees are broken—bodies are broken as well—but it is the shattered vegetation and the shattered works of men that make the chaos. I once saw explosions in a train carrying passengers and produce. I saw broken leaves of vegetables, the red pulp of tomatoes washing ruptured steel; and newspapers rising from a club car carried like spirits on the wind. The papers rose and circled and circled in a flume of fire.

"Folks say I'm crazy," the Blackbird murmured to the horse. The horse stood silent, nearly calm after the ascent. I had the sudden belief that the horse was listening to Blackbird's explanation and that the horse understood. "Maybe I am," the Blackbird said, "but I ain't crazy now. We get to a place like this and the Bird knows the territory."

North's hand caressed the useless .45. "It's starting."

Only a memory of light remained. The forest was as black as the Blackbird's skin and, like the Blackbird, alive. The wind was a voice, and it pressed high above our heads as if it swept all light toward caverns at the end of the world.

The movement was no longer on the edge of vision. It was no longer entirely in the forest. We watched the movement become a fragmented wave, reaching almost timidly across the graveyard; a wave of white, exhausting itself like surf. The whiteness was not exactly like flickers of light. It seemed, almost, like the absence of darkness. At the same time, it became light when it touched the broken point of a spirit fence, the hollow face of a grave. In my imagination—in the acceptance of a mind that was now in combat—it seemed that there was movement among the graves.

The darkness was complete. North stood beside me, and all that could be seen of him was a smudge of paleness: white face, white hair. The Blackbird stood ten paces away. All I could see was his white hand raised and resting on the neck of the now invisible horse. I heard breathing—my own, the horse's, the Blackbird's—and the panting breath of North.

When the voices began, they were not so alarming as the wind. It was impossible to say when they began. They were faint. The mind accepted that they had been there all along. The voices were like the babel of a public market, or like the disjointed buzz and bustle of a crowded street. As they increased in volume, the imagination sought to place a face behind each voice, and the imagination was quelled. So many faces would fill the forest, obscure even the wind, the sky. Faces. Oriental faces.

"Aw, Kim," the Blackbird said. "No, man. Aw, no."

The Blackbird's voice trembled but not with fear. His voice was alive with grief.

"Aw, my God," he said. "They are blind. They are dead, and they are blind."

His voice sounded as if he were screaming inside, but when he spoke to North, it was in a low mutter. "I should kill you and let them have you," he said. "There's things a man ought not to know. You just made me know one of those things."

The voices grew louder.

"I can't stand to hear it," the Blackbird said, and he was talking to Kim. "Man, don't do this."

"I reckon he can't help it," North said. There was something peculiar, something cruel, in North's voice.

It was a voice of fear; but more, it was the voice of combat. The babel changed. At first it was impossible to say how the voices were modulating. It was only possible to recoil from the sounds of awful sorrow. The voices were intertwined, yet individually were as distinct as each thread of a spiderweb. The voices were like a tapestry of sound; and each thread was dyed in the colors of sorrow. Sound was white, thin red like watered blood. The cries knit in the shroud of darkness.

How can an insane man go crazy, I thought, and the voices began to wail. The wails spoke of every hunger that has ever tormented the human heart.

Hunger for booze and food and sex. Hunger for some kind of god somewhere. Hunger for sleep, and pretty things, and hunger for stars and being warm. Hunger for sunlight, and kinfolk, and laughing with friends . . .

"If you're talking to Kim," North said to the Blackbird, "then tell him I want to make a deal."

"It isn't Kim," the Blackbird said in a low voice that carried all the horror of a scream. "It's what Kim *was*, when he was killing. The rest of him . . . all the rest of him's been *eaten*—" The Blackbird choked off his words. His white hand disappeared into darkness. Sounds of the zipper on his duffel bag, the muffled sounds of steel bumping steel; these said that the Blackbird was armed.

"Lawyer man," Blackbird said, "you better find yourself a ditch somewhere."

I paused. Beside me, North hesitated, then moved. He grabbed at my arm, just as I moved in the opposite direction. I pulled away from him, hit the deck, and rolled.

The pitch of the wailing rose and blanketed the night. Flashes of luminescence were rushing from the interior of the forest. The graveyard was filled with dancing and erratic points of light. It was like being stunned, the brain crashing about in darts and lasers of light. I rolled downhill. There was no cover. A small mound of earth stopped my movement. A grave, perhaps. Most likely it was a rain-beaten pile of soil, a mound between graves. It had been piled by the grave robbers.

"Try it out, baby," the Blackbird said to North. "Let's see how good you really are." The Blackbird chuckled. "You conniving fool. Thought to trick the Bird. Up here in the dark with that swatty old .45. How'd you come to such a mess?"

Blackbird's voice seemed here, there, moving in the darkness. The horse was also moving, but only its breath was audible. It moved silent-footed, the way war-horses had been trained back in the nineteenth century. When the Blackbird stopped speaking, I had the feeling that he was himself a spirit. He could be standing three feet from me and I would not know.

"Turn on your light," North said. "I can't figure what you're talking about." His voice was full of his lie. I searched for him in the darkness. Was it illusion? Madness? I could see the points of light, but they did not illuminate. North and the Blackbird were invisible.

"You turn on *your* light." The Blackbird chuckled. He was very close. Within eight or ten paces. There was a slight rustle as he moved away.

"Try not to get dead, lawyer man." The Blackbird's voice diminished as he moved away. "You die around this here mess and you get stripped. What will be left is what's holding that pistol."

The .38 was in my hand. The old patterns were automatic. I had armed myself even while rolling for cover.

"Ought we take him now?" the Blackbird asked. "Or ought we sweat him that least little bit?" Blackbird was not speaking to me but to the horse.

"You got this wrong." North's voice came from a different position. He was uphill and to the left.

I was not confused about where to point my weapon, only confused about why it pointed at North. Then realization came among the scattering points of light.

Gods of Thunder. Valkyries. Cathedrals. Burial in the church. The sacrificial lamb. *Sacrifice.*

"Brought us up here to kill us," Blackbird said to

the horse. "Thought he could trade two for one, maybe. Trade off his friends." The Blackbird's voice became cruel. "Kim," he said, "shut down your light show. Let it be blacker than black, and tell your boys to wash up. It's suppertime."

The whiteness faded. The wails faded. Only the voice of the wind sang high above the totality of darkness.

"Using my left hand to toss this," the Blackbird said, and he was either talking to the horse or to Kim. "Using the brown hand, the Asiatic hand to fling this here."

His voice was covered by the huge thump of an explosion in the forest. Heat from the grenade flew red into the wet fir needles. The thump vibrated across the graveyard, and the explosion was as red as a furnace. Branches were seared, torn, and thrown. The smell of the explosive shoved across the graveyard like a tide.

"A bag of grenades is a nice thing," the Blackbird said. "Have a lot of fun with a bag of grenades."

"Put the gun down," I said to North, and was moving even while I spoke. "If it's a mistake, then put the gun down." I rolled sideways, then inched downhill toward the forest.

Another grenade exploded. Blackbird was not throwing them into the graveyard. The explosion thumped in the forest. "I got a little H.E. here," the Blackbird said. "Wanna try some plastic?"

It was a waiting game. The night was like the depths of a cave. High overhead, the wind seemed to be moving mountains of darkness toward the graveyard. Deep. Impenetrable. The wind was an enormous carrion crow, a raven; spreading wings of darkness.

When the plastic explosive flashed, it was sharp, white, brilliant. Blackbird had attached the plastic to the trunk of a large fir. The graveyard appeared as in a flash photograph, lighted to show North crouched a hundred feet up the hill and among the graves— Blackbird invisible, the horse invisible—somewhere in the forest.

I chanced a shot with that pathetic little .38. North wheeled and emptied the magazine in my direction. We were both stunned by the light, our ears cracking with the slap of the explosion. Before North's last round crashed beside me, shattering an already broken spirit fence, the rush of the blasted fir was like an exclamation. The tree thumped, bounced, thumped again.

North had lost none of his ability with that pistol. In the hands of most men, a .45 is not particularly dangerous, not at a hundred feet—it's like throwing huge stones—but North was good. His fire was not erratic. It was called "searching fire," and it was statistical. He carefully placed the rounds to cover the area where he last saw me. There was the unmistakable sound of the pistol's slide. North had loaded another magazine.

"Best to quit playin' around," Blackbird drawled to the horse. "That lawyer's gonna get his fool self killed."

I rolled farther. Backed up. Edged toward the forest.

"Keep it shut," the Blackbird whispered to me. He was within a few feet and astride the horse. His whisper was covered by the wind. "Let one off in two minutes. Wait two minutes. Do it again." He passed me two grenades. "Got to keep him outta the forest," he whispered.

If North got into the forest, he need only wait for our flashlights as we tried to leave the graveyard, or wait for daylight to ambush us.

"Got a little timer down there," the Blackbird said. "It all comes together in six minutes." He disappeared into the darkness. The horse was moving fast among the graves. Even that silent-moving horse could not avoid some sound on that steep slope.

A cruel and wonderful joy accompanied those grenades. They nestled in my hands like children. They were more beloved than any woman. The beautiful weight of the things; heavy as sexual urgency, promissory as good books, good whiskey. *My God*, I thought, *this* is what I am: *this*. No madness was so great that it could obscure the beauty of *this*—these sane and perfectly sculptured grenades.

I loved the Blackbird. I loved him like I have never loved a woman. He was my comrade, my friend. He trusted me. Our lives were in each other's hands.

I arched the first grenade back into the forest. It bounced from a tree, exploded in a small gully, a culvert, a stagnant pool, a hidden grave; something. Water and steam rose into the trees like a puff from the breath of hell. North's pistol exploded. One round. The muzzle flash was above me, and now to the right. North was firing across the hill, at some sound of the climbing horse.

The bullet clacked as it hit the saddle or stirrup or pack. The horse screamed, and the scream rose in the wind like the voice of a frightened child. The horse sobbed. Quieted. It was breathing in huge, sucking breaths.

"Aw, man," the Blackbird said, "now I'm gonna have to kill you twice." He was moving fast, and away from the horse. "You better shoot," he yelled, "because the Bird is gonna hurt you."

The Blackbird was intentionally drawing fire. It made no sense, unless he was trying to keep North on the hill. Maybe the Bird was trying to draw North's fire away from the horse. North emptied the magazine into the darkness, toward the Blackbird's voice.

I fired once, just above and behind the pistol flash.

"Dead," the Blackbird said. "North is deadums."

There was the sound of North loading another magazine. I could not believe that I had missed him. My combat sense said that I had *not* missed. I waited for the heavy breathing of a wounded man. I waited for his desperate fire.

Nothing.

Maybe he was only nicked, was moving quickly for the forest. I searched, found a clod of wet soil, and threw it to the right. Silence. Darkness. Wind. When I threw the second grenade, it flashed among shrubbery to the right and at the edge of the forest.

North fired two rounds of random fire. In throwing to the left, then to the right, I had allowed him to bracket me. North was good—nobody could deny that he was good—and he was apparently unwounded. He was as wired on combat as any of us. His fire was random but his instincts were tuned. The bullets slapped within two or three feet of me. He was using a lot of ammunition. He must have come prepared to fight a war.

The second grenade was expended. Two minutes remained.

Silence. Darkness. Wind. The wails of the spirits were abated, hushed; yet the presence—or maybe the awful memory of Kim's bloody chest, the awful memory of the Blackbird dripping his own blood into the wound—hovered above the graveyard; and the silence was momentous with subdued sighs, sobs, weeping.

Oh, he was crazy. Oh, that Blackbird was *crazy.* I loved how truly crazy he was, because when the timer went off, the darkness became a shattered parenthesis for light.

No sane man would be carrying grenades and fireworks. Grenades, maybe. Fireworks, no. Blackbird, both.

I hit the deck as strings of firecrackers began to rattle like small-arms fire. The wind dipped around them. The stink of black powder spread before the twinkling explosions. The wind layered it across the graves. The explosions looked like blasts from a congregation of rifles. There was a long, rapid fuse burning down there. It was a hot glow running a thin line of red through the darkness. Firecrackers popped around a nearly intact spirit fence that stood like skeletal legs. On the ornately carved pickets of the fence, two pinwheels began twirling like a cartoon automobile hell-bent for nowhere. The pinwheels threw gay little twinkles of red; a comedy, a mouse show. Mickey.

The fuse ran. A skyrocket rose, arced, pointed into the graveyard.

"Hit him," the Blackbird yelled. "Hit him, hit him, hit him."

I twisted toward North. The rocket splatted, threw fire in sprays, threw red sparkles, white strokes across the graveyard. North was moving from a crouch. I snapped off a shot as he hit and rolled.

"No," I muttered, "not that. Not even you . . ." I was screaming at North. "You are better off in hell than doing what you've done."

North had dug into the cover of an excavated grave. A macabre foxhole.

Behind me, the rattle died away, and the colors fell as the pinwheels sputtered and died. I took careful aim at the half-hidden figure of North. Fired. Two shots remained in the .38.

Red bloomed a hundred feet above North. In the returning darkness, the fire seemed at first like a spot-light through stained-glass windows. Then it became ordinary, like a flicker of residual napalm. A common railroad flare cast red light through the broken spirit fences. The Blackbird had set those fireworks as a diversion, in order to light that single flare. He waited somewhere behind the flare. Invisible. The flare put the lower part of the graveyard in silhouette.

North fired. Fired again. The horse emerged from darkness, and its flank was slick as it limped down the hill.

"Hit him," the Blackbird said. "Hit him, hit him. Keep him pinned."

North fired. The muzzle blast was concealed, the explosion muffled. It sounded as if he had deliberately fired into the soil of the grave.

Hit him. Keep him pinned. I aimed. Fired. North screamed. His pistol exploded again, firing into the grave.

The horse stumbled, and now timid flickers of light began to appear at the edge of the forest. The horse nearly fell into an excavated grave. Blood flowed on the flank, was black in the red light. Too much blood. The horse staggered directly toward North. In silhou-ette, it seemed as dark and huge as the apocalypse, and it closed on North at an awkward pace—blood, foam. The mouth dripped white.

In red silhouette, a white hand and a boot seemed riding directly on the horse's back. The Blackbird was playing Indian tricks. He rode toward North, and he hung on the far side of the horse.

North fired. He began to scream—and I have heard screams, and know them, and know their caliber—and something terrible was happening to North. His pistol sounded as if it had exploded. Soil packed the barrel. Soil plugging the barrel as he fired into the grave.

How many times has this happened? I thought, and scrambled toward North with the pistol pointed. *How many times has the air been full of smoke and cordite and screams? And how much red is there in the world, of fire, of blood; how many times checking the corpses —or shooting them—to be certain they are comfortably dead?*

The horse closed slowly on the screaming North. Blackbird slid to the ground, holding the reins. The eyes of the horse were wide and red in the light of the flare, and the horse carried its wound as it might carry saddlebags filled with lead. It tried to rear, stumbled; the great body nearly falling. It raised a front hoof, white-stockinged, and kicked futilely at North's head. It gasped. Shuddered. It lowered its head, took North's right forearm in its mouth. Lifted. I heard the bone break.

"Let it be," Blackbird said to the horse. He pulled the reins, pulled the horse backward. "Sweet baby, let it be."

From the forest, like exhausting waves of surf, points of light scattered across the graveyard. The wind caused whispers as it blew around the spirit fences.

North was a big man. He took a lot of killing.

He was as tenacious as the wind above the forest. He half raised on his left arm, screamed; and his legs moved as he tried to push himself from the plundered grave. I leaned down, trying to turn him over. He was trying to help me. He pushed with his left hand, with his legs. I pulled, trying to turn him and find the wounds, but he was stuck in the face of an empty grave. His madness made it impossible for him to move.

No wound was visible. Only a right arm bent at a

wrong angle, a little blood where bone poked through the flesh. Rainwater in the grave was stagnant, smelled putrid, was stained with mud; but not with fresh blood.

In the light of the flare, in the howl of wind, the dancing points of light winked like distant small-arms fire. Red and white. A red-and-white surf seemed blown into the graveyard on the voice of a red-and-white wind.

"How did you know?" I asked the Blackbird. He had shrugged off his jacket, taken off his chambray shirt.

"Gimme your shirt," the Blackbird said. "Forget that thing." He gestured at the screaming North.

I shucked my jacket, my shirt; handed him the shirt.

"Nicked an artery," the Blackbird said. His voice was hollow with grief. "Got to stop it or it'll pump open a big hole."

He tore my shirt into strips. "How did I know?" he grunted. "Kim told me. Of course, Kim coulda been lying." The Blackbird was putting a compress bandage on the horse. "Got to get this fellow to that Indian graveyard before he falls." His voice was low, his black torso visible only beneath flickers of red. "I can't let him die in this place. Man, he was so light and fast. They'd take that away."

In the red-and-white light, Blackbird's face was a small sculpture of grief. He worked rapidly. "Gonna lose him. I'd give my half interest in hell for a sewing needle and some catgut." He turned toward North, and North's screams were choking. North's throat must be stripped raw with the screams—and suddenly, with a rush of fear for my own soul, I realized that I had not really been hearing those screams. They were so common.

"That light show was too real," the Blackbird said. "Maybe this piece of trash"—and he pointed at North—"made it real. Or maybe it really *is* real. That .45 was meant for us. If North had seen all this before, he knew there wasn't enough bullets in the world."

Blackbird looked at North, at the open mouth that sent scream after scream across the graveyard. They

were routine screams—common and ordinary screams—
screams that in combat were less interesting than involuntary curses or the wail of the wind over the lip of
the jungle.

"I'll make you a deal," the Blackbird said to North.
His voice was neutral, neither cruel nor kindly. "You
don't deserve it, but I'll make you a deal. You are the
man who knows how to laugh. So laugh. If you laugh,
I'll pull you out of that hole."

Horror lay somewhere in my mind. It was red like
the flare, as steady as the hand of the wind. It was
wide and large back there somewhere, but in the front
of my mind was cold pleasure.

North's white face—mud-stained, stained by history,
by combat—seemed to flatten as he clenched down on
a scream. His face stared from a shallow grave that,
for him, was as deep as an abandoned quarry. His face
concentrated on what it had to do. The left hand
brushed at soil on the grave's edge. North's teeth were
clenched, then opened. His mouth was a black hollow
in the red light. He smiled—lips white and thin and
ghastly, a thin-lined and awful smile—then chuckled
like oily pebbles rattled in a tin can. He forced a
laugh, a laugh at history, combat; at us. At himself.
The sound was thin, nearly weeping.

"Aw, man," the Blackbird said, "that ain't no kind
of laugh." He gently nudged the horse, the white hand
like the guiding hand of a father. He fumbled for his
flashlight. "But you got tons of time to practice," he
said. "Assuming they leave you anything to laugh
with . . ."

The small spot of Blackbird's flashlight was like a
lightning bug intent on following a line. Blackbird
found the trail. His light disappeared downhill. For a
short while there was the heavy breathing, the near
stumbles, of the dying horse; and these were more
important than the low, returning screams. North's
left hand brushed and clawed on the edge of the
grave. Blackbird disappeared toward the Indian graveyard.

*   *   *

I don't know why I stayed behind. Maybe it was the simple combat dictum of "Don't let a dead man kill you": the rule that says a man who is even a little bit alive can still react. Maybe I stayed because of owing: a man who had saved my life in other days now lay victim of his own betrayal. Worse, I may have stayed because my own death lay somewhere in the future, and I was afraid of those "mighty old and powerful" forces the Blackbird had talked about.

"There's all the time there is, all the time," the Blackbird had said.

Maybe I stayed simply because time was scampering, like the white-gloved mouse hands on a watch.

North was a portrait in red and white. My flashlight glowed on his staring eyes. Wind reached for the flare, turned its tip into a tiny furnace. The flare cast criss-crossed shadows as it illuminated the chaos of torn graves and broken spirit fences. North's white face, his white hair, were grotesqueries painted in red light. Breath panted shallowly in his mouth. He was no longer able to scream. The broken arm had to be causing enormous pain, but he was engrossed with something greater than pain. The panting face, pale eyebrows knitted in concentration, held not horror; but something worse. The face held the knowledge of horror that was about to arrive.

The wind assumed its proper place and proportion. It began to carry the sounds of distant wails. The wails were thin, and they approached behind the advancing flickers of white. Whiteness lay at the top of the grave-yard, as concentrated as a snowstorm. It reached down the hill, obscuring emptied graves, flicking like spar-kles from the carved tips of spirit fences. The white seemed like an artist's field, like gessoed canvas on which could be painted the color of screams.

"No man deserves this," I said to North. "Not even you. I would help you if I could."

Perhaps he heard. I would like to believe he heard; that even as his ghastly immortality descended, there was at least one voice that recognized him as having once been human.

The wails rose, and now they were demonic. These were the wails of hunger, the wails of the blind; the weeping of hollow faces that once had worn eyes. No Gothic cathedral bearing the most awful gargoyles could stand uninvaded by the weeping that now advanced in the tumbling surf of white.

North suffered a last burst of energy. His feet pounded, kicked. He raised on his right elbow, the broken arm askew. He pushed with his left hand. The grave held him firm. The first tongues of whiteness lay at the grave's edge. The wails began to clamor, began to assume hollow and nearly skull-like faces. The first pinpoint of light touched North.

He did not scream. I did. His face was startled. His eyes were wide circles of disbelief. A man sunk in the knowledge of horror, in the knowledge that he would be stripped of everything but hunger; and he was still startled. In the days and months during which the horror had approached—hours of sobriety and hours of drunkenness—nothing had prepared him for this.

The points of light were feeding, but not on his body.

I watched and, at first, thought the weeping in my soul was for North, for myself, for the Blackbird. North's face went from one shock of revelation to another. As the carpet of white wrapped around him, wailing, wailing, wailing, each shock took him deeper into the horror of loss. No death—by napalm or crucifixion or Inquisition—was so terrible as this immortality of hunger.

My weeping increased, from heart to eyes. Sorrow like a field of white filled my mind, body, heart.

Then there was a tug. It was like being nipped by a flea or an ant or an earwig. Fear unlike any I have ever known swelled around me, because the nip was not on the flesh. It was as if a memory had been bitten, some memory of pleasure; sunlight falling through leaves, or shadows and light across the face of a lover. Gone. I backed away. Looked down at North.

So this is how it was with him. His memories of beauty stripped away. The many times his eyes had looked to sea, or looked into rolling banks of Puget Sound mist. Stripped. The calm majesty of the surrounding forest, even the memory of the eternal rain. Stripped.

His face seemed collapsed, already removed from all humanity, yet his mouth still sucked air. His lips were white. Death was due in moments.

There was another tug. Horror was trying to move my legs, trying to make me dash crazily into the red-lined darkness; perhaps to trip and fall into a grave.

Another memory gone. The memory of my daughter as an infant, laughing, creeping across the floor. Then the memory of street music tinkling above the heads of crowds in a market.

North's body was dead. His jaw hung loose, and his eyes seemed like frozen discs that stared over the white waves of hell; a white horizon. The slack lips, the jutting tongue, remained motionless; but deep from what little remained of his spirit, his voice issued. It was a wail. Thin at first. Ascending. Louder. The corpse was wailing North's blindness, his hunger; and the wail was a creature of white, a pinpoint, then a needle, of white.

Whiteness was beginning to spread. Flickers danced around me. The wail from North's mouth rose newborn toward the sky, searching, hunting, in pursuit.

I fled then. Running, but a cautious run behind the strong beam of the flashlight. Broken fences leaned, open graves were dark mouths. I fled the redness and the whiteness, following the flashlight beam into the safety of utter night. Behind me, the white points of light ascended above the despoiled graves like the robes of some ancient sorcerer. As I entered the forest trail, the graveyard was a concatenation of wails. Spirits were ravishing the already ravished graves.

The Indian graveyard lay as black as the Blackbird's skin. It lay as strong as the Blackbird's resolve. On this more level ground, trickles of water moved, and wet fir needles gave back pressure of moisture beneath my feet.

I called to the Blackbird as I entered the Indian graveyard. Behind me, in the narrow river of sky above the trail, clouds of whiteness seemed washed here and there by the wind.

The Blackbird did not answer at first. I nearly switched off the flashlight. It made me a target. When the Blackbird did answer, it was in a subdued voice. I made my way toward him, around the quiet graves enclosed by the oversize beds. He sounded sane. I was not; and for moments it seemed that the boiling white clouds behind me were clouds of insanity.

The Blackbird knelt beside the dark shape of the dead horse. Blood pooled on the carpet of fir needles. A large white slug was at the edge of the pool. Blackbird picked it up, looked at it, threw it into the darkness. There was grief in his voice, but for me the blood and the carcass of the horse were comforts. In the middle of madness, at least the bullets had been real.

"Dead," the Blackbird said. I did not know whether he spoke of North or of the horse.

"Finished." My voice sounded the way voices sound after combat. Men ask questions, assure each other that the perimeter is secured.

"Took it pretty hard, did he?"

"It was bad," I said. "Worse than he deserved."

"Naw, it wasn't," the Blackbird said. "I hope he's trussed like a stuffed pig over a fire pit."

"He would have settled for that," I said, "because it was worse."

"Well, well," the Blackbird said. "That is an elegant thing to say."

"You weren't there."

"Nope," the Blackbird said, "but I heard the ruckus."

I turned off the flashlight to save the batteries. No cave was ever darker than that forest. In the darkness, the power of the graveyard was serene. A question came. Why such unbreachable power here, when up the hill was only despoliation and fury?

"What kind of hell do Indians have?" I was probably speaking to the Blackbird. Maybe to the graveyard.

"Depends on the Indians," the Blackbird said. "Booze, mostly. Little tuberculosis. Bad dreams."

"You know what I mean."

"Mostly they try not to think about it," the Blackbird said.

The aftermath of combat is always the same. The talk is short. There is no space for tears. What is a man supposed to do? Scream? Screaming doesn't work, because in combat you've already tried it. Sometimes the men scream in their sleep.

"Knew a fellow one time"—the Blackbird chuckled, and he did not sound so sane, after all—"had to bury his horse. So he dug a hole." The Blackbird was not laughing at his story. Maybe he was laughing at himself, at his memories. "Only, after he got the hole dug, the horse had stiffened up. Legs stuck out of the hole." The chuckle was not exactly a chuckle, and it was not exactly a sob. I had heard the sound before, but not for many years.

No power in the world could have made me turn on my flashlight. Blackbird was dealing with grief. Blackbird could kill me so quickly that I would not suspect I was being killed.

"So he went to the butcher shop," the Blackbird said, "and he borrowed a meat saw. Cut the legs off. Tossed 'em in the grave. Horse fit just fine."

We sat in darkness. Friends. Men who seemed in the business of saving each other's lives. Men who owed; at least that was true if the lives they owned still held enough memories not tinged in fire.

"I'll help you dig," I said. "Help fold the legs before he stiffens."

"I'd be obliged," the Blackbird said. "We'll go get shovels come day. Have to hurry. Whoever finds North is gonna yell 'cop' for forty miles."

I thought of law, of darkness, of history.

Memories of a wet land. Memories of screams. Parachutes. Oriental faces. Polished fragments of bone washing from the hills. The Buddha's smile.

I would have to throw the .38 into a river.

I thought of Miss Molly and hoped her father was well. Then I hoped he was dead. Then I discovered that I did not like Miss Molly: thoughts disarrayed: all of the nicey-nice people: and I trusted no one but the Blackbird, because the Bird could play the game but he did not order up the game—or purchase it—or applaud it.

"You like being insane?" I asked the Bird.

"I don't *like* it," he said. "But I *sure* don't like the other."

"Me too." I giggled. "You've got the sanity of insanity. I've got the law."

"I know a lot about Indians," the Blackbird said, "and *everything* about horses."

We folded the horse's legs, and we sat on wet fir needles and leaned our backs against the folded legs as rigor mortis set in. We sat safely in darkness, untouched even by the wind that battered the coast and hills and forest.

For us, the darkness was not a curse. We sat waiting for the first touch of morning in the tops of the trees; and sitting, waiting—for the rest of that night, at least—we were safe from the shattering lights of a white and wailing world.

About the Author

DOUGLAS E. WINTER has been hailed as "the conscience of horror and dark fantasy." His fiction, interviews, and criticism have appeared in magazines as diverse as *Gallery, Harper's Bazaar, Saturday Review,* and *Twilight Zone,* and in such major metropolitan newspapers as the *Washington Post,* the *Philadelphia Inquirer,* and the *Cleveland Plain-Dealer.* His books include the definitive biography and literary study *Stephen King: The Art of Darkness,* available in a Signet paperback edition, and a history of modern horror fiction, *Faces of Fear.* He is a partner in the internationally based law firm of Bryan, Cave, McPheeters & McRoberts.